"If you hold to my teaching, you are really my disciples. Then you will know the truth, and the truth will set you free."

~ The Gospel of John 8:31-32 ~

CHAPTER ONE

"I sink in the miry depths, where there is no foothold. I have come into the deep waters, the floods engulf me." ~ Psalm 69:2

Sirens blared in the distance. Peter Sheridan peered through the branches as he hunkered down in the dark alley. The silver moon, full and bright, shone over the treetops on Gold Hill and Peter cursed the clear, summer night. Headlights flashed across his hiding place and, despite the warm air, a chill gripped his skin.

His heart raced as he thought about his next move. He looked through the foliage, desperate to find a better hiding place, and noticed an old abandoned and decrepit building just beyond the alley. Creeping out of his hiding place, Peter slunk across the narrow path and kept to the shadows until he reached the back wall of the old building.

Moss and weeds grew all around the dilapidated structure. An ancient chain-link fence, rusted and broken, vainly guarded the perimeter. He gripped the metal fence and his hands came away covered in amber-brown dust. He sighed and rolled his eyes in frustration as he wiped the grime onto his pant leg. Step by step, Peter crept along the exterior until he happened upon a cement stairwell that descended into the building's basement. He was cautious as he peered into the blackness, listening for the sound of any wild animals. This was just the hole that some cougar or bear would love.

Peter didn't worry too much about running into another person. Darrington had been abandoned for decades, with only a remnant of farmers and loggers remaining, and, of course, the education center. The moon provided some light as it reflected off the snow covered spire of Whitehorse Mountain. He slowly stepped into the darkness and walked down the broken stairs. Fractured cement crumbled beneath his weight which sounded like a miniature avalanche to his ears.

His hands trembled as he tried to quell the sense of panic and slow his racing heart. Cobwebs and dust filled his senses and clung to his clothing. With one hand in front of his face to fend off the grasping webs, he felt along the cold, rough wall until his hands touched metal. A door! Peter pressed his face close to the door, hoping to catch the glimpse of a handle, when a flash of blue and red raced past. He stopped, choked back his breath and waited.

The squad car sped through the alley behind him, rumbling across the gravel as it kicked up dust and debris in its wake. *They're getting close*, he thought. *Too close for comfort.* He turned his attention back to the door. It was a double door, hinged on the inside with no handle, nothing more than a simple fire exit. However, it was slightly ajar at the top. With patience he ran his fingers along the top seam until he could get a grip on it. With a quick tug, the door snapped open, groaning and creaking with every inch.

Anxious because of the noise, he quickly slipped into the building and felt the handle on the other side of the door. As gently as possible, Peter closed the door to make it look like no one had entered. He stopped to listen... nothing. With a sigh, he leaned against the interior wall and tried to get a look at his surroundings.

Moonlight streamed in from several broken windows on his right. The air was damp, musty and carried the scent of mold. In the pale light he could see some tables, broken and cast aside, along with a scattering of chairs. The room was large with several smaller rooms on his left. A hall led away from him and he could make out the faint silhouette of a kitchen in the distance.

Much of the sheetrock had crumbled from the walls leaving a maze of debris he was forced to navigate. As his eyes adjusted to the dim light that filtered in like streams of silver ribbons, he walked down the hall carefully stepping over and around the scattered remains of the walls. Then a light flashed on his left. Peter fell to the ground and looked up through the broken window of a small room. Again a flash of light penetrated the darkness from outside. *Someone's outside with a flashlight!*

Peter's thoughts raced, fearful that the patrol had found him. He quickly scurried farther down the darkened hall past broken tables and chairs and into a chamber on his right. No light shone in the room, not even the moonlight entered. He felt along the walls, anxious and frightened. Slowly, methodically, and desperate to keep his cool, Peter continued to search with his hands until he touched a knob. Another door! The hinges creaked as he opened it, and in the darkness the sound magnified in his ears.

Peter reached into the darkness ahead of him until his hand rested on a cold metal plate. Feeling his way around, he maneuvered to his right and found his way behind the metal object. The depth of darkness in the little room hurt his eyes as he strained to see anything. He could feel the wispy strands of cobwebs caressing his face, but he paid no attention to them. All he wanted was to find a place to hide from whoever was outside.

Then the exterior door creaked open. The noise was so loud that Peter nearly gasped. He ducked down, desperate to control his panic. Steps in the outer corridor grew louder and he watched as a small glimmer of light flashed past him. Muffled voices echoed in the air as the searchers approached.

"Are you sure he came in here?" the first man asked.

"No, but we need to look anyway. The lieutenant won't be happy if we don't take a good look around." The second man huffed and Peter heard the sound of something crashing.

"Be careful," the first man demanded. "We don't want the walls to come down on us."

"Sorry."

A long, ominous silence filled the air.

"What did this guy do anyway?"

"Oh, not much," the first man said. "He left the education center without permission. I guess he's been questioning the teachers and causin' trouble."

Another long pause caused Peter to wonder if they might know where he was hiding.

"I've taken him back to the education compound twice before. He's just a trouble maker."

"What'll happen to him?" the second man asked.

"This is the third time he's tried to escape. Three strikes — you're out. He'll be sent to prison after this, probably McNeil Island."

Peter listened to the conversation with dread. He knew about the island. The rumor was that no one ever returned when they got sent to McNeil. He crouched lower as the two patrolmen searched the rooms. A flash of light passed over his head but then the two men left and entered back into the hall. *I wish they'd just go,* he thought.

"Let's get out of here. This place gives me the creeps." The second man spoke up.

"We need to check upstairs before we leave." The first man said. As the guards moved down the hall, Peter listened more intensely. Footsteps echoed overhead as they vainly searched for him. Minutes passed, though to Peter it seemed like an eternity, before the two men finally gave up the search and came back down the stairs.

"All right, let's go," the first man said.

"Finally," said the second. "But what's going to happen if the guy gets away?"

"Don't worry. No one ever hides forever. This guy is no different than any of the others. They all end up caught in the end."

Their voices trailed off and Peter relaxed as the metal doors scraped shut. He huddled against the cold metal, wrapped in the quiet blanket of darkness. Emotionally and physically exhausted, he decided to remain hidden until daylight. He crouched down upon the cement floor, closed his eyes and wished for the morning light. He didn't know what critters might be sharing his hiding place, but he didn't care. All he wanted was some sleep and to get out of Darrington as quickly as possible.

* * * *

The morning broke in a hazy grey drizzle. Peter stretched his cold, stiff joints and rubbed sleep from his eyes. The gentle sound of rain rapped on the roof and water dripped into the basement and onto his legs. He stretched again and stood up in the cramped chamber, groggy as he stumbled to his feet. A sliver of light filtered in and he could see the ancient oil heater that hid him from the patrol's search. Peter patted the old rusted furnace which was covered in spider webs. A hollow reverberation rumbled in its belly echoing a hunger in Peter's own stomach.

"Well," he said to himself, "Let's see where I am." He moved around the furnace and entered into the room. The walls were covered in mold and much of the sheetrock had crumbled, exposing the framework underneath. A mouse scurried across the floor along the baseboard and ducked into a hole in the decaying wall. Dust filtered through the grey light and he listened to the rhythmic cadence of water dripping in various places.

He stepped out of the room into the hall. To his right a stairwell led to the upper level. Peter looked to his left and noticed the broken pair of metal doors that he had entered the previous night. Several doorframes faced him on the opposite side of the hall. All the doors were broken and off their hinges exposing rooms that had crumbled with age and lack of care. Peter brushed off the cobwebs and dust that had collected on him during the night. His white shirt and blue jeans were stained with dirt.

Looking around, he decided to take the stairs to the upper level, hoping to avoid detection. The cracked steps creaked under the stress of his weight. He walked slowly, careful to keep his feet at the edges of the stairs, fearful of falling through. As he came to the top, he looked to his right and noticed that it emptied into a large room, a meeting hall of some unknown purpose with long, padded benches. At the front of the room was a raised stage with a podium. Overhead, stretched across the entire width of the room, were two metal bars.

The dank, musty smell of the chamber permeated his senses. The room felt abandoned. He stepped carefully into the hall, washed over with a sense of history. Peter didn't know why, but he thought that the room harbored memories, memories of past importance.

Broken and barred windows let the soft breeze of the morning drift in. A bird fluttered and Peter was startled back to the moment. He walked through the room, touching the benches and wondered what the building was used for. Directly in front of him a door stood open and revealed a small office. A broken desk and overturned chairs, along with several fractured bookshelves, littered the small antechamber.

Peter explored the room with his eyes. His attention dropped onto one plain looking book, its pages yellowed and warped from exposure to the elements. With careful strokes, he brushed off the dust from the cover revealing golden letters on its face: *The Baptist Hymnal*. He had never seen a book like it. He opened the pages, turning from one strange looking script to another, uncertain what the odd markings meant. Horizontal lines, permeated with dots and dashes, underscored with words, filled page after page.

Then he stopped. At the top of one page, faint and hard to read, he saw the words: *America the Beautiful*.

"Impossible," Peter said out loud. "America is not beautiful!" He thought about how brutal the educators were at the center. He thought about the forced labor done on government farms and his struggle just to have enough food and water to survive. His eyes scanned the words, *amber waves of grain, spacious skies*, and *alabaster cities*, and wondered what type of propaganda it was meant to be.

Though the words were faded, he read the last line out loud as if he could hardly believe the words, "America, America, God shed His grace on thee, and crown thy good with brotherhood from sea to shining sea." As he read, though he didn't understand why, he choked up and began to weep. Though he struggled to believe it, the thought struck his heart that America was once a place of abundance and comfort.

Then Peter's eyes scanned the next page. The words were hard to read, but he made out one phrase, *God's promise to you is… freedom*. The rest of the words were lost to time, but that statement shocked him. *God*, he thought, *what God*? Years in and out of the education center never taught him about a God. Just the opposite, he was continually reminded that there was no God, that the government provides everything and that it was his sole duty to work for the state.

Peter stuck the book in his shirt, hidden from view. Looking around, he listened to the rain outside and decided to leave. He would keep to the woods and hope that the rain would cover his tracks out of town.

Because the front doors were nailed shut from the outside, Peter went back downstairs and left the way he entered. He cautiously stepped out, fearful that he might be spotted. However, the day had begun and everyone in town was at their assigned duties. He walked around the front of the building. A gentle rain fell from soft, grey clouds. Whitehorse Mountain, which just the night before had shone like a white torch in the moonlight, now hid behind the dismal curtain.

Stepping to the front of the building, Peter's hands trembled with anxious fear, desperately listening for any movement. He had escaped before, but each time he was caught. He knew that prison waited for him if he were caught this time. The street was abandoned. Grass grew from long cracks in the pavement. Peter imagined that the avenue once boasted well kept homes with happy families. However, all he saw was boarded up windows and crumbling structures.

A wooded field lay directly across from the building he had slept in. Looking up and down the road, he made a quick dash and ducked into the brush. Thick, lush undergrowth made walking difficult, but it was perfect for hiding and he needed to remain out of sight. Step by step, Peter moved with cat-like patience, always stopping to listen. His pulse raced and beat in his ears. He decided to try and make it to the Stillaguamish River and hoped to raft downstream, out of reach of the local patrol. He knew well enough that if he made it to the highway he might escape pursuit.

Carefully he walked, fearful that someone might see him. However, as he passed over the broken remains of streets and past the dilapidated remnants of houses, no sight or sound of pursuit ever breached the gentle whisper of rain. With his clothing soaked, he continued.

Peter crossed through the back woods of Darrington without any hindrance. Then, like an exposed artery, he stumbled upon the east-west road, the only road that came up from Arlington, a town about thirty miles west. As he crouched in the bushes, he watched for any sign of patrols. They liked this road. It was easy to spot runaways. He glanced in the trees around him wondering if he was in a section monitored by cameras.

A log transport whizzed past, throwing up a shower of spray. The road itself was only two lanes wide but, because of the patrols, the woods were cut back so that it was at least fifty yards across. He waited as another truck rumbled by, heading into Darrington. He figured that he was at least three miles out of town and hoped that he was far enough away to escape notice.

Taking a deep breath, Peter stood up and lumbered through the undergrowth, fighting with both hands to escape the grasping brush. He broke through, stepped into the open, and ran. His legs burned with exhaustion, but he forced himself to run faster. Fifty... forty... thirty yards to go. Twenty yards, ten yards and then... sirens!

"No!" Peter shouted to the air. He turned and looked to the east toward Darrington. Around a bend in the road sped two patrol bikes, red and blue lights flashing, coming toward him. "Give up now and it's prison for you," he said to himself.

Anger and fear encouraged his legs with renewed strength as he dashed like a wild animal into the brush and trees on the other side of the road. *Get to the river*, he thought. The patrol's bikes were useless in the dense undergrowth but Peter knew that other guards were on the way. Now that they spotted him, they would not rest until he was caught.

Far in the distance Peter heard the town's siren blaring out his predicament. The klaxon warbled its incessant noise loud enough for the entire valley to hear. It didn't matter. He needed to get to the river. Headlong he stumbled through the brush and trees. The book he carried jarred and poked his ribs. He ignored it all. Under power lines and past old, long-forgotten homes, Peter rushed on.

A branch whipped his face, grazing his cheek and soon he felt the warmth of his own blood on his skin. His ribs ached with exhaustion and the constant prodding of the book in his shirt. Taking advantage of an exceptionally dense bit of foliage, Peter stopped to catch his breath. He rubbed his cheek with his sleeve and the white fabric came away stained crimson with a smear of blood. *Great*, he thought, *this is just what I need.*

He tried to crouch lower in the brush when he heard the whooshing sound of a helicopter rotor. He peeked up through the leafy growth to watch a small, black copter slowly move west almost directly over his position. *Don't panic*, he thought, *they can't see you in here.* Peter waited for the minutes to pass as the aircraft continued to search for him. His heart raced and his rain-soaked body shivered with unease. Then it flew away, the rushing noise of its engine faded into the background as the sound of the rain again dominated the air.

He knew that the dogs were next and he had left a trail that even a blind bloodhound might find. Struggling to his feet, Peter continued toward the river. The sirens in town had ended, or he was too far away now to hear it. It didn't give him any peace. His eyes darted back and forth, searching through the trees, fearing every possible movement was a patrol officer. The rain continued, but now the sounds of the forest had changed. In the distance, like the welcome whisper of a friend, Peter heard the river.

He trudged on, feet heavy with the mud brought on by the relentless drizzle. A large patch of thorny blackberry bushes stood in his way, and just beyond the hedge flowed the Stillaguamish River. He noticed that the river was swollen and swift from the summer showers. The muddy water rushed past, meandering like a serpent down the valley. Careful of the thorns, Peter took tall steps to try and smash down a path through the blackberry patch.

The barbed vines were thick, many nearly two inches in diameter and hard to overcome. Often the branches clung to his clothing, tearing at his hands and forcing him to redirect his efforts to find an easier way through. He managed to make headway about ten yards in with twenty to go when he heard a dog's bark. Panic gripped his heart. He forced his feet to move faster, stepping haphazardly through the thickets.

He tripped. Peter's foot caught under a tenacious vine and he fell headlong into the thorns. He thrashed and spun desperate to get back on his feet but the vines clung to him like a spike-laden net. His hands and face lacerated, Peter despised the pain and forced himself onto his feet, blackberry branches clinging to his back. His shirt tore away and the book he had so protected fell to the ground.

He had no time to retrieve it for in the distance Peter now heard the voices of several guards. "He's this way!" one shouted. "No, over here," said another. The voice of the guards, along with the relentless bark of dogs filled him with dread.

Ten more yards, he thought. Peter stumbled through the brush. The dense growth which once served as his shelter from watching eyes now stood as his enemy, a barrier to the river. He wrapped his hands in fragments of his shirt and whacked at the blackberries as if his arm was a machete. Desperation drove him. Blood now freely flowed down his face and covered his arms. His eyes stung with sweat.

"Halt!" the shout rang out not more than fifty yards behind him.

Peter turned. The trooper ran at the wall of blackberries, pulled by a bloodhound on a leash. Peter turned back toward the river, fighting for every foot of distance. He didn't look back. He didn't want to see how many were after him. He didn't understand why they were so desperate to get him.

"Just leave me alone!" Peter shouted to the air. He was almost at the river. He saw the steep embankment and the water rushing past about five feet below it. Just a few more steps and he'd be in the water.

Crack! The sound of a pistol filled the air and Peter pitched forward. Pain wracked his body, his left arm hung limp and the sense of searing fire burned through his shoulder.

Crack! Peter stumbled, as if hit from behind with a two-by-four, and fell into the river. Muddy water engulfed him and mingled with his blood. Every muscle and joint cried out with pain. He quelled the panic for one more moment and forsook the idea of trying to swim to shore. Despising the agony, Peter remained limp, face down, and let the river take him. *Another minute, just another minute*, he thought, *and I'll be out of reach.*

* * * *

The current carried him around a bend. Out of sight of the patrol, Peter tried to swim with his right arm, kicking with his legs to reach the shore. It was no use. His left arm hung limp, worthless and bleeding. He fought hard against it, but the current swept him like a leaf on the water. Waves splashed over him and the river spun him round. In the center of the river flowed a broken tree limb, with branches like gnarled fingers reaching up from the depths. Frantic, he did a mock breast stroke and caught up to the drifting branch.

Peter clung to the limb with the tenacity of a pit-bull. The massive branch must have been from a huge oak. It was nearly twenty inches in diameter and covered with slick lichen. Smaller branches jutted from everywhere and gave him a good chance to hold on. He shivered in the cold grip of the rushing water.

With his right arm wrapped around his gnarled raft, he tried to look at his shoulder and assess his own injury. It looked bad and burned like fire. The bullet had lodged in his shoulder and a trickle of blood continued to ooze from the wound. He knew he heard two shots and tried to diagnose where the second one hit him. He moved his legs and wiggled his hands and toes. Everything worked… everything except his left arm.

Jostling around, he maneuvered to feel his head. His arm still wrapped tightly around a branch, he bent his head forward and felt with his hand. "Owe!" he said as his hand passed over the top of his scalp.

Panic ensued as he thought: *I've been shot in the head.* His heart raced and he desperately felt the wound. His fingers probed and he ignored the sharp pain of every touch. Anxiety filled his thoughts. He feared to find a bullet hole in his skull. Again and again he passed his fingers through his matted brown hair. Though blood stained, he found no breach in his head. *Just grazed,* he sighed in relief. However, Peter knew he was not out of trouble. His shoulder was bleeding, his left arm was useless, his body was exhausted and he was drifting rather swiftly down the river.

He tried to use his legs to maneuver the log to shore. Cold and tired, he gave one last great effort but to no avail. He was at the mercy of the river. As he peered downstream, he feared that his life was finished. Fatigue dominated every muscle and joint. His eyes glazed over and the world looked to be in a heavy mist. He thought he saw a man perched on a log. He didn't even have the energy to cry out for help. His right arm slipped and his eyes darkened as the water engulfed him.

CHAPTER TWO

" He lifted me out of the slimy pit, out of the mud and mire; He set my feet on a rock and gave m a firm place to stand." ~ Psalm 40:2

Peter opened his eyes. Though his vision was blurred, he noticed a chandelier in the middle of a ceiling, gently swaying on its chain. The room was filled with light. Pane windows revealed a lush, green meadow just beyond a large wrap-around deck. Beyond the meadow, full, majestic pine and fir trees swayed in the wind and stood like guardians, a protective forest that hid the quiet homestead.

He lay upon a dark blue sofa, long and plush, with heavy pillows against the back. A colorful quilted blanket protected him from a gentle breeze that entered through an open window. The sweet, fresh scent that comes after a rain wafted in the air. He glanced around the room. Shelves of books lined the walls, though he couldn't read any of the titles. An oval oak coffee table sat next to him. On the table were cloths, bowls filled with water, and an assortment of what he thought were medicine bottles. Several large, white candles stood in sconces, one on each wall.

His left arm throbbed with pain, a sling held it against his chest. Peter glanced down at his left shoulder. A heavy bandage with a spot of blood covered the wound. He tried to move his arm and found that, with some effort, he had regained its use. With his right hand, he reached to feel the top of his head. A bandage covered it completely. He pulled his hand back when pain shot through his scalp like an electrical current. He looked at his fingers and noticed that there was no blood. With every heartbeat, Peter felt his head pound like a hammer against an anvil. *What I wouldn't give for a Tylenol right now*, he thought.

An attempt to sit up sent a wave of vertigo washing through his head. The world spun and he fell back with a thud against the arm of the sofa. Peter took a deep breath and tried to regain his equilibrium. He closed his eyes and sighed.

"I wonder where I am," he said to no one in particular.

"You're in my home," spoke a gentle, baritone voice from behind him.

Peter startled and tried to turn around to see the man who spoke. Again his head spun with throbbing dizziness and he collapsed back onto the sofa.

"Try not to move too much," said the voice, "you've lost a significant amount of blood and you need time to recover."

Peter slumped back into the soft plush cushions and sighed. His head pounded in rhythm to his heart and he kept his eyes closed. "Are you a doctor?"

"Not exactly," the voice paused, "but I am a friend."

"But," Peter stammered, "how... when did..."

"No more questions," said the voice with a sense of compassion. "You need to rest and regain your strength. We'll talk when you're able."

Peter heard the man stand and he caught a slight glimpse of his face. The man seemed tall from Peter's vantage point, with a well trimmed beard and dark brown hair. He noticed the man's eyes wrinkled at the corners like one who was used to smiling, but with lines of worry across his forehead. Then Peter closed his eyes and sleep overtook him.

* * * *

When Peter opened his eyes again, the world beyond the house was dark. Night had fallen and clouds drifted across the pale moon. On the coffee table, a glass oil lamp burned dimly, its wick trimmed low. Shadows danced upon the walls and the room felt cool. He tried to sit up, and though the world still swayed in his dizziness, he was able to maintain his balance. Peter stretched out his arm. It was stiff, sore and throbbed, but he found that, with some exertion, he had gained more motion.

With his feet planted on the floor, Peter rested his head in his hands. He noticed that he didn't have his own clothes on, but wore a set a flannel pajamas. Two slippers rested near his feet and, out of curiosity, he slipped into them. They were a little large, but the soft leather footwear was warm and comfortable. His head was still bandaged, but the pain had dimmed to a dull roar. In his thoughts he debated whether to try and stand.

He didn't know how long he lay on the sofa, but his desire to move overcame the disorientation. He braced his right hand on the arm of the couch and slowly stood. Waves of nausea washed through his head and the world began to spin around him. His legs wobbled and he strained to stand upright. Letting go of the couch, Peter rose to his full height, his left shoulder burned with pain and his head swam with vertigo. Nearly toppling over, he steadied himself and began to feel his strength return.

One step... two steps, and Peter began to walk around the house. He picked up the lamp on the table and turned a small, brass knob to increase its light. As the room grew brighter, he stepped over to the wall of books. A musty odor reminded Peter of being in the education center's library. He lighted his hand upon the tomes, scanning the names of the many and varied copies that filled the shelves.

The books seemed old. Some had cloth covers, some were leather bound, and all bearing titles Peter had never seen. He saw books with titles like *New Testament Commentary*, *The History of Homeopathy*, and *Bioethics*. Shelves of books were devoted to medical sciences, other bookcases housed row upon row of history and philosophy. Peter marveled at the wealth of material. *This man must be about the most educated man in this valley*, he thought. Then Peter started to fear. His thoughts drifted to the possibility that this man was once an educator at the center.

Quietly, Peter walked around the sofa and noticed a stairway just behind a wall. He glanced upstairs and saw a light flicker from somewhere in the upper level. Cautiously he stepped, taking pains to navigate the stairs with silence. He determined to find his host and learn what happened.

Pain filled his senses, but Peter tuned it out. One step at a time, careful to keep his feet from making any noise, he slipped upstairs. *My years of sneaking around the center were good training for this*, he thought.

When he reached the top, Peter turned down his lamp and proceeded toward a light emanating from an open door. He stood just behind the door and peeked in. There, beside a bed, knelt a man with his hands folded in front of him. Next to the man's folded hands lay a leather-bound book. Peter stood motionless and heard the man whispering. Carefully he looked into the room, but saw no one else that the man might be talking too.

"Are you talking to me?" Peter asked.

Startled, the man looked up from his position and noticed Peter in the doorway. "Oh, you're up!" he said. "I'm sorry; I didn't see you standing there."

"Who were you talking too?"

"God," the man said with a smile.

Peter looked upon him bewildered. "What do you mean you were talking to a god?"

"Oh, no," the man replied, "not to *a* god, to *the* God. There is only one after all."

Peter was dumbfounded. *Great*, he thought, *I've been rescued by a crazy man.* Not wanting to insult his host, Peter tried to change the subject. "So, who are you?"

"My name is Joshua. Joshua Eberhardt." The man stood to his feet and brushed his knees. "My family has lived in this house for four generations."

"How is it that I've never heard of you? I mean, you seem a bit, well, peculiar." Peter suddenly stumbled and fell against the doorframe.

Joshua rushed to take Peter under his arm. "We better get you back downstairs. You're still in no condition to move about. I only fished you out of the river two days ago." Together they began the climb downstairs. "I'll make us some nice hot tea and we can have that talk."

Grateful for the assistance, Peter leaned against his host and hobbled to the sofa. He turned the oil lamp up and the room filled with a warm, amber light. Flickering shadows played like children on the walls and a sense of peace came upon Peter's mind. He sat down slowly and leaned his head back against the overstuffed pillows. He sighed as the room stopped twirling in his eyes. He was glad to be back on the couch.

"Now, about that tea, give me just a moment." Joshua went around the corner and disappeared into the shadows. The sound of clanking metal echoed in the darkness. Several minutes later, Joshua reappeared with two mugs, steam rising in gentle wisps from them.

Peter took a sip and the warm liquid singed his lip. He blew across the surface of the rich, brown drink. The tea was strong and warmed Peter thoroughly. For the first time, and he didn't know why, he felt a sense of safety. He watched as his bearded host slid a high-backed, cushioned chair across from him. The coffee table sat between them and both men quietly drank their tea for several minutes.

"So," Joshua asked, "how is it that you ended up in the river?"

Peter glanced over his cup of tea, his brows furrowed as he contemplated telling his story to Joshua.

"I can see that you're concerned. Let me ease your mind a bit. You see, I already know some of the tale." Joshua paused as he sipped his tea. "I heard a radio broadcast that said someone escaped from the Darrington Center. It was reported that the person was shot and killed. The police said that they shot in self defense—that the escapee shot first."

"That's a lie!" Peter slammed his mug on the coffee table.

Joshua smiled at Peter. "I know it is. But why don't you tell me what happened."

Peter nodded, "Alright. You saved my life and I guess I don't have much choice but to trust you." He paused as he picked up his cup and took another sip of tea. "It started ten years ago. I was only twelve and some men came and took my parents. I haven't seen them since. I was told by the educators that they were sent to another center and that I would be sent with them. Two years passed and I determined to escape and find them. I was caught." Peter shuddered as a chill went up his spine. "Then I was punished. They locked me away in a cell for three months. I didn't see another person; I didn't even see the sunlight for that time."

Joshua grimaced as Peter recounted his story. "I've heard about the center and how they treat people."

"Yep," Peter continued, "It is a grueling place. Well, I tried again four years later and was caught again. This time I tried to escape up the Sauk River. I made it about three miles up river and was captured by one of the forest patrols." Peter sighed as he remembered the ordeal. "I was beaten and kept in chains for nearly six months. Then, when they determined that I was finally broken, the guards let me out of the chains. They put me to forced labor and told me that it was my last chance at rehabilitation."

"Why did you try again?" Joshua stood and poured more tea for both of them, then slowly paced in front of the bookshelves.

"I had to," Peter said. "I hate that place. I hate the educators who try to convince me that they have my best interest in mind. I hate the life they forced upon me. I want to be free. So, I spent the last four years trying to get on a lighter detail. When they finally allowed me to work on a neighborhood cleanup crew, I knew that my time had come. I just slipped away when the crew chief turned his back."

"But how did you end up shot in the river?" Joshua's voice remained calm.

"You don't know much about the security guards of the education center. I was hunted down. It was my third escape and, if I got caught, the only thing left for me was to be shipped off to the prison island. I thought I had lost them but they found me when I crossed the highway. My hope was to make it to the river and float downstream until I was out of the valley."

"Well," Joshua said, "in some strange way, you made it. The report is you're dead. No one will be searching for you now." Joshua took his seat again as he looked with thoughtful eyes at Peter. "The question is what will you do now?"

Peter stretched and, with a deep yawn, slouched down into the cushions. "If it's all the same to you, I think I'll get some sleep. I'm quite tired for a dead man," he chuckled.

"Absolutely," Joshua said. "We'll talk again in the morning."

Peter nodded his thanks and stretched his legs on the sofa. The soft pillows welcomed his head and he closed his eyes. He heard Joshua stand up then a squeaky step revealed that his host had gone upstairs. One more yawn and sleep caught up with him.

The morning sun filtered through the window and caressed Peter's face. The gentle warmth stirred him from sleep and as the twilight of dreams gave way to awareness, he heard the clanking of dishes in the kitchen. He lay still for several minutes when Joshua peaked around the corner and looked down upon him.

"Good," Joshua said, "you're awake."

"I just now woke up," Peter replied. "What time is it?"

"It's about nine a.m. If you want to try and get dressed, I've left you some clothes at the end of the couch." Joshua turned away and continued working in the kitchen.

Peter looked at the end of the couch. A pair of khaki pants and a clean, white shirt lay draped over the arm, neatly folded. He sat up and reached for them. His left arm throbbed, but the pain had diminished so that it didn't tax his strength. The bandage on his head was gone, and he touched his fingers to his scalp. He explored the top of his head with care and felt stitches and a bare patch of skin.

"I hope they fit," Joshua's voice echoed from behind a wall. "You and I are about the same size."

"Thank you," Peter replied. "Where can I get dressed?"

"There's a room at the end of the hall. Feel free to clean up in the bathroom and we'll have some breakfast." The dishes again clattered as Joshua prepared a meal.

The scent of bacon and potatoes drifted through the morning air, mingled with the pungent aroma of coffee. Immediately Peter panged with hunger, not knowing how long he had gone without a meal. He still couldn't move well and stumbled to his feet as he maneuvered past the stairway and down a hall. He found a small study at the end of the hallway and dressed himself. He stretched out his left arm, a sense of gratitude washing through his thoughts.

When Peter was dressed, he came back down the hall to the kitchen. Steam drifted out through the doorway and the scent of breakfast grew stronger as he neared. Joshua worked at an island stove, stirring a pan of fried potatoes. Scrambled eggs simmered in another skillet and bacon sizzled on a cast iron griddle.

"Ah, there you are," Joshua exclaimed. "Come, sit and enjoy the morning." Joshua plated a generous helping of breakfast and set it on a marble counter behind the stove.

Peter sat on a tall, wooden stool and slid the plate in front of him. He shook his head bewildered, yet thankful, for the care that his host showed him. "Why are you doing this for me?"

Joshua looked up from his work, "Because you need it." He built a mound of food on another plate and stepped around the stove to join Peter at breakfast. A decanter of coffee sat between them and he poured the hearty liquid into two cups. Both men sat quiet as they ate.

"Tell me," Peter asked, "Who are you?" He paused. "All I know is that your name is Joshua and you seem to know how to mend bullet wounds. Are you a doctor?"

"Let's get these dishes taken care of and we'll talk."

They stood and cleared their places, and then Peter followed Joshua onto the deck outside. The day was bright and warm. A soft breeze carried the sweet scent of pine as a flock of sparrows dodged through the branches of a large Madrona tree. Both men sat on a long bench and stared out at the gentle day.

Peter rubbed the stiffness in his arm. It ached, but the throbbing pain had subsided. The bleeding had stopped and he no longer wore it in a sling. He leaned forward into his hands, thoughtful as he looked into the distance. Joshua leaned back against the house and stretched his legs out, relaxed and appeared to be unencumbered with worry.

Peter broke the silence, "Okay, who are you? I mean, you drag me out of the river, mend my wounds and yet you live alone and isolated from civilization."

Joshua sighed and paused. "What I'm going to tell you will seem strange at first. You've not heard anything like it before. You had asked me why I helped you, it's because I have a different set of rules that guide my life."

"What do you mean, 'a different set of rules'?"

Joshua shook his head and spoke under his breath, "My father was right." He looked straight at Peter, "Have you ever heard of something called a Bible?"

"No."

"Have you ever heard that our world was created by God?"

Peter stopped. He thought back to the book that he had tried to take with him from the strange, run-down building. "I found a book when I was hiding from the patrols. It was called... O I can't remember! But it had strange markings on it and I remember a statement I read. It said something like, 'God has promised freedom.'"

"What kind of markings?" Joshua asked.

"I recall that page after page had these horizontal lines with several black spots. I was sure it was some form of archaic code."

Joshua smiled and nodded. "Come inside."

Both men stood and entered the room where Peter had slept. Joshua ran his hands over the books until he found one. He pulled the tome from its place and handed it to Peter.

"Was it something like this?" Joshua asked.

Peter opened the pages and his eyes widened in surprise. "Yes! This is it. This is just like the book I found at that building." He closed it and looked at the cover. Though faded, the imprint of the title remained visible: *The Baptist Hymnal*. Peter looked back up at Joshua, a tear nestled in his eye. "I read one of the pages that described America as beautiful."

"Oh, yes," said Joshua. "Over a hundred years ago, as I've been told, America was a land of freedom and hope. Then books like the Bible, this hymnal, and any book that referenced God was outlawed."

"Why?" Peter asked, incredulous.

"Because," Joshua said, "if you believe in God, then you believe in an authority that is greater than the government. Our nation was once rich in faith and the values that are taught by the Bible. But the government cannot control a people of faith so they rounded up all who spoke or taught such things. Eventually it became a crime to mention the existence of God and so the truth was lost."

"You seem to know all about it? Why haven't these things been taught at the Center?"

"The Center is there to teach you only what those with power want you to know." Joshua took a deep breath as if he weighed his next words. "But now the Center thinks you're dead. Why don't you stay here, let me teach you the things I know."

"Won't they eventually find me? Don't they know you're here?"

"No," Joshua replied. "I'm off the grid. I live completely self-sufficient and haven't had dealings with others for some time. My grandfather knew that these days would come and prepared for it."

"But if these books, like this one here," Peter said as he held up the hymnal, "are illegal, how is it that you still have them? Shouldn't you obey the law and surrender these books to the government?"

Joshua smiled, "Let me get something for you." He stood and left the room.

Peter reached for his coffee on the table in front of him and sipped on the warm drink. He listened as Joshua rummaged in another room. He couldn't help but smile when Joshua began to hum some unintelligible song. Peter's host returned with a black, leather-bound book in his hand. It looked old. The lettering on the cover had long worn off and the edges of the pages looked yellowed from age.

"What's that?" Peter asked.

"This… this is a Bible." Joshua sat again on the chair and set the tome on the table. "Let's see…" Joshua began to turn pages. The thin, ivory-colored sheets crinkled as he quickly located the page he needed. "Here it is. Let me read this to you, *'We must obey God rather than men.'"*

Peter furrowed his brows as he thought about that statement. "So," Peter said, "you're telling me that this Bible of yours teaches you to thumb your nose at the government?"

"Oh, no," Joshua said. "The Bible teaches that we have to evaluate everything based on what God requires. If the government makes laws and regulations that do not violate God's law and will, then we obey. If the government comes against God and tries to override the Divine authority, then we must choose to obey God — even when it costs us dearly." Joshua grew silent.

"There's something behind that statement," Peter said.

Joshua sighed, "You're right." He took a long sip of coffee before he looked up at Peter.

Peter noticed a pain in Joshua's eyes as a tear hung on his lashes. "What happened?"

"It was thirty years ago," Joshua said. "My wife and I thought we could make a difference. We were both young and foolish. We left here and traveled across the country to Washington D.C. We tried to convince the lawmakers that they had abandoned the principles of this nation. We brought the Bible with us and openly spoke about God but then the state police got involved. They were ordered to eliminate us, so we ran. Deb didn't make it." Joshua stopped as he wiped a tear that trickled down his cheek. "She was shot and died in my arms. Before she died, she begged me to go home. It took months, but I finally eluded the patrols and made my way back here."

Peter looked up from his cup to see tears flow freely down Joshua's face. "I'm so sorry." He didn't know what else to say. His own heart ached as he remembered when his parents were taken, dragged away in the middle of the night. He remembered the feeling of being alone.

"Thank you," Joshua said. "It's been a long time. I don't think I've told that story to anyone else."

"So, you've been here for nearly thirty years?" Peter said to navigate away from such a painful subject.

"Yes, and in that time I have taught myself how to survive on my own." Joshua stood and returned to the wall of books behind him. He picked out several that were worn with age and use. Peter leaned back on the blue sofa as Joshua walked his fingers across the many volumes.

"These books," Joshua said, "with these books I learned medicine, construction, engineering, and a wealth of other needed skills. You asked me if I were a doctor. I'm not. But the knowledge that I used to help you is found right here," he said as he slapped his hands against the books. "Stay with me," Joshua pleaded. "Let me teach you what I know."

Peter rubbed the stubble on his face, thoughtful about what Joshua had told him. He looked at his bearded host and wondered if the kind-hearted man was more than just a strange recluse. He rubbed his left shoulder and could not deny that Joshua must know something. His mind drifted to that strange book called a hymnal and the words he read—*God's promise is… freedom.* "I'll stay with you on one condition," Peter said. "I want you to teach me about God." He glanced up at his host and watched as a smile warmed Joshua's face.

CHAPTER THREE

"They have tracked me down, they now surround me, with eyes alert, to throw me to the ground." ~ Psalm 17:11

Peter stretched out on a rock as he watched the river roll past. A brisk morning breeze blew down from the eastern mountains and the late September sun shone bright as it crested the eastern peaks of the Cascade Mountain range. He welcomed the warmth of the morning light even as he shivered in the chill air, his lightweight jacket little help against the gentle wind.

He closed his eyes and listened. The trees voiced their whispers as the gentle wind blew through the boughs while birds replied with their songs. Water lapped and gurgled over the rocks of the riverbed, and to Peter, all was at rest.

He opened his eyes again and the world rushed into view. Branches waved in rhythmic motion and all the vibrant colors of fall painted the world aflame. Peter had never known such serenity. In his lap lay a black, leather-bound Bible. The thin pages fluttered in the breeze as he recalled Joshua's words, *the best way to hear God is to be silent before Him.*

Peter placed his hands on the book and read the words out loud, "For if you forgive men when they sin against you, your heavenly Father will also forgive you."

"Do you know what those words mean?"

Peter turned to see Joshua standing behind him. He looked up at his friend and mentor and smiled. "You snuck up on me," Peter said with a laugh.

"Yes I did," Joshua replied. "But I wanted to see if you were alright. You've been here for several hours."

"I'm just taking your advice. I wanted to hear God and you told me that I needed to get alone with Him."

"So," Joshua said, "what did God have to say?"

"I'm not sure." Peter paused and thought. "I've been thinking about my time at the Center compared to the months I've spent here. These past three months have been such a change in my life. I've been happy and I have learned more about life in the time I've spent here than all my time there."

"But there's something that nags at you," Joshua said.

"Yes, there is. I feel anger toward those who took my parents and… well… I want to hate them."

"Anger is a natural emotion toward those who hurt you. Remember what I taught you about the 'natural man'?" Joshua sat down next to Peter as he spoke, his feet dangling over the edge of the rock.

Peter thought. "I remember you told me that the 'natural man does not understand the things of God.' It was something like that."

"You're right," Joshua said. "There is a natural way of looking at life and then there is God's way of looking at life. It is natural to be angry, but God wants us to forgive. That passage you just read tells us that forgiveness is the expression of someone who knows God's salvation." Joshua reached out his hand and

Peter handed him the Bible. "Let's see," Joshua continued as he flipped through the pages, "Here it is." He looked at Peter. "Remember what I told you about Jesus on the cross."

"You told me quite a bit. You told me that He died for the sins of the whole world; that God offers to anyone who believes, pardon from sin and eternal life."

"That's correct. Here is one of the statements Jesus made on the cross, 'Father, forgive them, for they do not know what they are doing.' The natural reaction is to feel anger and hatred. Jesus shows us that we can forgive, even when what has happened is cruel and evil."

Peter thought hard about it. "What about you?"

"What do you mean?"

"When the patrol killed Deb, your wife, were you able to forgive?"

Joshua gave a small half-smile. "It took some time, but yes, I did come to forgive them."

"But how could you forgive them? I don't understand."

"Think about it like this." Joshua paused for a moment and then he picked up a small stone. "Let's say that this tiny pebble costs a thousand dollars." He looked around as if searching for something. Then he patted the boulder they sat upon, "And let's say that this massive stone costs the same amount, a thousand dollars."

"Okay, but what are you getting at?" Peter asked.

"Just wait, you'll see." Joshua stood up on the boulder and walked to the edge of the river. "Now imagine that you have all the wealth of the world and you wanted to buy these stones. Which one of them costs more?"

"That's simple… they both cost the same amount."

"But one of them seems so much bigger; the other one seems so insignificant. Are you sure?"

"Of course I am — you're the one who set the price."

"That's right. It's the same way with our sin. Some people seem to have committed great sin and others seem to have committed such insignificant sin. But God is the one who set the price and that price was death. The cost is the same for a small or a large sin, the life of Jesus Christ."

Peter stood up and walked to the edge of the river. He crossed his arms over his chest as he thought over Joshua's words. "So you're saying that because my sins cost the same as their sins then I'm no better or worse than they."

"Yes, keep going."

"And if I'm no better than they are then I can forgive them in the same way God has forgiven me." Peter squinted as the sun rose above the tree line. He raised his hand to shield his eyes and watched as a sparrow darted across the river.

"One of the reasons people hold onto anger is from a point of view that we are within our rights to be angry. And, from a natural point of view, that's true. From a Biblical point of view, however, we must be willing to let God rule our hearts."

"But what if they don't repent? I had to repent of sin to receive God's forgiveness. Shouldn't I require that those who wronged me face the same requirement?"

Joshua smiled as Peter wrestled with his thoughts. "You had to repent to receive God's forgiveness; you didn't have to repent for God to offer it. God offers salvation and forgiveness to the entire world. Those who want to partake of God's forgiveness do so through the experience of repentance and the willingness to humbly receive God's gift."

Peter began to walk away from the river and toward the house and Joshua stepped along side him. He looked up at the ancient home, its storied windows and large deck silently telling a tale of hospitality. He thought about Joshua's generosity and kindness—a kindness that changed his own heart and warmed him to know the Savior. "So," Peter said, "I can offer forgiveness to those who hurt me even if they reject it."

"That's right. And something more: when you do offer forgiveness, you will find a freedom in your own heart. If you hold onto bitterness you are letting the actions of others control your attitude and not letting God control it. True submission to God means that even your attitude belongs to Him."

"I have to admit, it's not easy." Peter chuckled under his breath.

"You're right, but I don't recall 'easy' being one of God's promises to His saints."

Both men walked onto the deck of the house. Strewn about were various tools. Hammers, shovels, gloves and a several crates marked the day's activities. Peter looked up at the sky, a crisp, clear day — perfect for chores.

"I need you to check on the generator," Joshua said. "It's not charging the cells as it should and you seem to have an affinity for things electrical. Later we need to work on the harvest. It's going to be an early winter and I'm afraid we might face frost in the morning."

Peter nodded and picked up the bucket of tools and headed back down to the river. Joshua had told him how his grandfather, Elijah, built a small waterwheel and diverted some of the river's flow to power the device. Now it was old and in constant need of maintenance. He didn't mind. Chores had become a way of life over the past three months, but Peter enjoyed the work. He mainly liked the fact that he was able to receive the fruit of his own work. Remembering the Center, he recalled how all his efforts went to support the educators. All the food and resources went to them and the residents were given mere scraps.

He followed a path along the bank of the river, weaving his way through the brush and trees. In the dense growth the air grew warm. Peter took off his jacket and hung it on a branch. Gnats swarmed in various hovering colonies through the brush and the sun penetrated in long streams of light. Overhead a magnificent canopy of pine and fir branches sheltered the path and kept the air still. He watched as the treetops swayed in the breeze, but no breath of wind ventured to the forest floor.

Several hundred yards away he came upon the generator. Even from the riverbank the waterwheel and generator were hidden from view. A pipe had been set upriver that flowed water to a channel nearly fifty feet from the source. Another pipe was set downriver to provide a constant flowing source of power. Peter knelt down to inspect the wheel. The paddles and the axle were fine. He greased them and continued. The belt to the pulley and generator was taut and the generator seemed to turn with ease. He continued and discovered that the wires on the generator's output were corroded. He cleaned them, and reset the screws that held them in place.

Then something caught his eye. A small metal plate sat directly under the output wires. Peter scraped away some dirt and on the plate was a name, *The Rev. Elijah Eberhardt*. Curiosity filled his thoughts and he took the plate and set it in his bucket of tools. He needed to know and ran back up the trail to the house.

Peter saw Joshua on his hands and knees in the garden. He ran to the garden as Joshua raked with his fingers through the dirt.

"A great harvest of potatoes," Joshua exclaimed. "Come, help me dig these out."

Peter was out of breath, "Yes… but… just a moment." He bent over with his hands on his knees, panting to regain his breath. "I found something… at the generator."

"Oh," Joshua said, "what was it?"

Peter reached into his tool bucket and pulled out a six-inch by three-inch metal plate. "Here," he said, "it has a name on it."

Joshua stood up and brushed his hands on his trousers, "Let's see what you've found."

"It was buried just under the wires at the generator."

"The Reverend Elijah Eberhardt," Joshua read, "now isn't that something."

"What is it? What does it mean?" Peter's excitement trembled in his voice. His eyes grew wide with anticipation.

"I'll tell you all about it," Joshua said, "at dinner."

"You're kidding! You're going to make me wait that long?"

"Yes, yes I am. Don't worry; it'll be worth the wait." Joshua smiled as he knelt back down to rake his fingers through the dirt and uncover more potatoes. He looked back up at Peter. "What about the generator?"

Peter gushed with disappointment but brought his mind back to the work. "The generator is fine, only some corrosion on the output wires. We should have power to spare."

"Good! Now, why don't you help this old man harvest these potatoes and then we'll tend to the animals."

Peter smiled and lent his hand to the task.

The day passed quickly as both men worked side by side. Peter fed the chickens and gathered eggs. He watched as Joshua carefully milked the cow, one task he had never grown accustomed to. Peter marveled at the tenderness Joshua showed to all the animals. Soon the day was over, and both men washed and prepared for dinner.

Before arriving at Joshua's home, Peter had never cooked a meal. Now, three months later, he was an ever-present force in the kitchen. Joshua left the room and then returned several minutes later carrying a jar filled with green beans. He put them in a pot as Peter fried up two hamburgers with sautéed onions. Water boiled in a tea kettle on the stove, whining to be removed. The beans began to boil and Peter turned down the heat as Joshua set their places at a small table in the dining room.

Both men took their seats and bowed their heads in prayer.

"Thank you, our God and Father, for this meal," Joshua prayed. "Ame..."

"And thank you, Lord," Peter continued, "for Joshua who has become my friend and is like a father to me. Amen."

"Amen," Joshua finished.

Peter looked up at his mentor and both men shared a smile. "So," Peter said, "about that metal plate?"

"Okay… seeing that you're so insistent." Joshua sipped his tea and leaned back in his chair. "That plate was thought to be lost a long time ago. From what my father told me, my grandfather was the last Christian leader in the valley."

"What do you mean, 'the last Christian leader'?" Peter asked.

"Years ago, Christians gathered together in groups called churches. When my great-grandfather lived in this house, he took his family to one of these gatherings on a regular basis. These churches had leaders known as 'pastors' and they openly taught about God and the Bible. When my grandfather was old enough he became one of these pastors and actually led the church that his family attended.

"Anyway, it wasn't long after that when the government began to shut down these churches. From what my father told me, Darrington was one of the last holdouts, and my grandfather stood as the last Christian leader in this valley. That plate that you found was the door plate that hung on his office at the church building."

Peter listened with fascination. "Why was it buried at the generator? Why hide it?"

"All I know is that when he led the church, men like him were being arrested in all the big cities. Cities like Seattle and others burned down the church buildings and the government ordered all lands owned by churches seized. I think that when the final blow came to Darrington, he wanted to protect his family. He took his name off the door and hid it in the woods. Perhaps he hoped that someday he might be able to openly preach and teach the Bible, so he put it in a place where he could find it again."

Peter was captivated. "Did you know your grandfather?"

"No, I never had the chance to meet him. My father told me that I was born just before he left."

"What happened to him?"

"I don't know. My dad never told me." Joshua leaned forward and poured another cup of tea. "I think, and mind you this is only speculation, but I think that he went back into town to try and bring Darrington back to the Bible. Towns like Darrington were built on old values and strong beliefs. I think he went back to the church building and was arrested." Joshua looked thoughtful through the large bay windows. The sun had set and only the tip of Whitehorse Mountain glowed with the amber remnants of the passing day.

"So," Peter said, "You tried to pick up where your grandfather left off. Is that why you went to D.C.?"

Joshua scratched his beard, "Perhaps. But it's more than that. I am quite adamant in my belief. When our country gave up the values and faith of our past, I was strongly convinced that I needed to do something to make a difference. I only wish..." His voice trailed off into introspection.

"Wish what?" Peter asked.

"Well, I wish that I had my grandfather's Bible. I would love to read his notes and see his thoughts about the times that he lived. I'm sure that he kept a record of his efforts." Joshua stood up from the table and stretched. He yawned deeply and pushed his chair back under the table. "It's getting late, now. We have a busy day tomorrow and I need to get to bed."

Peter stood with him. "Would you mind if I stayed up and studied for a while?"

"Not at all," Joshua said. "Just remember to turn down the lamps when you're done. We need to conserve the oil." He moved from the dining room and started up the stairs. "God bless you, Peter," he called back as he disappeared into his room.

"Good night, Josh. God bless you as well." Peter stood and stretched then stepped into the study. The night had fallen and the autumn air quickly chilled. He listened as Joshua rummaged around his room. Then, when all was silent, Peter stepped quietly out of the house.

A full moon hung in the brisk evening sky. The silver light illuminated the world with its soft glow. Trees, silhouetted against the sky, waved and swayed in the slight breath of air that blew across the valley. He heard the river's soothing song as it tumbled beyond his sight.

"I'll go and get that Bible," he said to himself. A grin that might have lit up the world crossed his features. He wanted to do something for his host and friend. He remembered the building he had hidden in some months before and believed that it was the same building Joshua's grandfather might have returned to. *It's worth the risk*, he thought, *just to get that Bible for him.*

The tool shed stood nearby. Peter walked to the shed and slid the door open. On a shelf, to the right of the door, was a flashlight. He clicked the switch. It worked! Hiding the small illuminating cylinder in his jacket, he walked out through the fence and onto an old gravel drive.

Overgrown and forgotten, the ancient path led right to the east-west highway. Several sounds scurried around him, but he didn't fear. The road continued; gravel rocks tumbled under his feet as he scampered up a hill. He looked ahead and watched as a streak of light flashed before him. "The east-west highway!" he whispered.

Peter hurried until his foot found asphalt. Darrington was eight miles east and he calculated that he needed three hours to walk there and then three hours back. It might take some time to find the book, but he knew he would be back at the house before dawn. He ducked again when another vehicle whizzed past. He thought about trying to hitchhike, but didn't believe he could trust anyone. He had no identification and without it he faced certain arrest.

So, he walked. His dark clothes and hair blended into the night so that he was simply another shadow in a world of shadows. He had a view of the highway for a mile in each direction and ducked behind bushes and trees when a car or truck passed. However, he began to realize that his constant hiding slowed his progress. He ran. Jogging occasionally, walking when he needed, Peter picked up his pace and continued.

Four hours later Peter arrived at Darrington. The old cemetery sat on his left and just beyond it, a guarded gate barred the highway and prevented anyone from entering the town. Searchlights passed back and forth, scanning the road and surrounding land for any unauthorized people. Guards paced behind the gate, automatic rifles slung over their shoulders. For the first time, Peter saw Darrington from the outside. "It's a prison," he whispered.

When the searchlights passed, Peter rushed across the road and began to walk through the woods west of town. He moved south, careful to remember where the old church building stood. It was midnight and the moon which helped him find his way on the road now served like a searchlight anchored in the sky. Peter sighed and shrugged off his concern. He checked his jacket and made sure he still had the flashlight.

Twenty minutes later, he found himself staring across the street at the broken-down shell of a building. The road was dark, no traffic. He rushed across and quickly pressed against the wall of the old church. He stopped, listened, and heard only the quaint voice of the wind in the trees.

In a crouched run, Peter moved to the back of the building and stepped again down the broken cement stairwell. The old metal door was jarred open, just like he left it. A quick grin crossed his face and Peter ducked into the building.

Inside, Peter began to think about where he might find the Bible. "Upstairs," he said, "probably somewhere important." Walking down the old hallway, Peter avoided the broken and overturned tables and chairs. He climbed the stairs and stepped into the large meeting room. The long, padded benches stood as a timeless reminder of who once met in the building. The air was thick with dust and cobwebs dangled in the air like wispy tendrils.

The moonlight filtered through the broken windows but Peter knew he needed to risk the flashlight if he wanted to find the book. He stood still and scanned the room with his eyes. Then his sight rested on one place, the podium. He walked up the center isle, between the two rows of benches, and stepped upon the platform.

His heart raced. He flicked on the flashlight and it blazed like a beacon in the dark chamber. Quickly he raced to find the Bible. Peter put the light on a small shelf located on the backside of the podium.

He caught his breath. There, amidst a clutter of papers and broken wood, sat a worn, long-forgotten Bible. Peter sat on the platform and cautiously reached for the book. Dust hid the words. He brushed off the cover and gasped. Right on the front of the Bible was the imprint of the owner: *Rev. Elijah Eberhardt*. Peter nearly shouted with victory.

Then he remembered where he was. He doused his flashlight and waited for his eyes to adjust to the darkness. Now he had to get out of town. It was an eight mile walk back to the house and he needed to be careful. The guards are less aware of someone coming in than of someone leaving. Peter put the Bible into his jacket and turned to leave the building.

A light flashed across the windows. "Great!" Peter exclaimed. He waited and listened. However, no other sound was heard so he stepped again down the stairs and left the building. He snuck across the road and made his way through the woods until he arrived at the east-west highway.

A squad-car raced past heading west, blue and red lights flashing their urgency. Peter ducked behind a large patch of brush and waited for the taillights to disappear around a bend. It was nearly two o'clock in the morning and Peter needed to hurry back to the house before Joshua woke. He wanted to surprise his friend with the treasure he carried.

Down the road, in the dark, Peter made his way west and eventually found the ancient drive that led back to his homestead. He ducked across the road and vanished into the trees. He had made it and in his enthusiasm he began to walk faster toward the house.

Peter looked to the east and watched the sky begin to glow as the first light of dawn crested the horizon. Joshua would wake soon and Peter was home just in time to give him his gift. He stepped up the stairs and onto the porch when Joshua rushed out the front door.

"Praise God," Joshua exclaimed, "You're safe."

"Josh," Peter was surprised to see his friend awake. "What are you doing up?"

"I came downstairs early this morning and you were gone. I didn't know where you went or what happened. I've spent the entire night praying to God for you that He would keep you safe."

"I… I'm so sorry," Peter stammered, "I went back into town."

"What! What for?"

Peter reached into his jacket and pulled out the old, weather-worn Bible. He turned it over and showed the cover to Joshua. He smiled as Joshua's eyes widened with surprise when he looked at the name on the front: *Rev. Elijah Eberhardt.*

"How did you find this?" Joshua stood in stunned disbelief.

"Your story reminded me of the building where I hid when I first came here. I figured it must have been the church building your grandfather went back to."

"I don't know what to say... thank you!" Joshua opened the book and the old tome crackled with age as he carefully thumbed through pages.

Peter smiled as he watched his mentor receive the book, but turned when he heard what sounded like thunder from the mountain. "No!" He shouted as a helicopter crested the trees and swooped toward the house.

Joshua looked up, his eyes wide with surprise. "They must have followed you here. Run! Peter, get out of here!" He thrust the Bible back into Peter's hands as he rushed out to the open field where the helicopter landed.

Peter panicked and fled behind the house. On the shore of the river four guards waited, a flat-bottom patrol boat tied off on a tree limb. Peter dashed back to the front of the house, stumbled and fell to the ground just as he heard the crack of a gunshot. He looked up in time to see Joshua fall to the ground.

He tried to stand and run when several guards surrounded him and with a painful crack to the back of his head, he was knocked unconscious.

CHAPTER FOUR

"Many are asking, 'who can show us any good?' Let the light of your face shine upon us, O LORD." ~ Psalm 4:6

Peter opened his eyes. He lay face down upon a cement floor, the acrid stench of urine permeating the air. The room was cold and his hands were bound behind his back. His head shrieked with pain and every heartbeat felt like the blow of a hammer against the inside of his skull. Peter glanced up in an effort to see his surroundings. His eyes were still blurred from the blow he received, but he noticed a thick, glass wall with iron framing. A heavy door with a large lock was the only exit. Twenty feet above his head, florescent lights hung in brackets chained to the ceiling and illuminated the room in a grey, death-like pallor.

His heart sank with despair as he took it in. *I'm back in their clutches again*, he thought.

"Hey, Frank," a voice spoke from behind him. "It looks like this guy's wakin' up."

"Good," said another man, his voice graveled and harsh. "Get him up and we'll take him to interrogation."

Heavy feet echoed against the concrete. Suddenly Peter was grabbed by his arms and hauled up like a sack of trash, nearly wrenching his shoulders out of place. He was slammed against the glass wall, pushed by the tall, nameless guard. Unable to brace himself, Peter crashed against the glass, sending a wave of searing pain rushing through his head. He fell to the ground. As he did, he caught a glimpse of movement down a dark corridor as the shadowed figure of a man stepped through a lighted doorway.

"C'mon! Get up and get movin'," said the one called Frank.

Peter looked through blurry eyes to see a stern, unshaved man reach down toward him. He was again hauled to his feet and left to lean against the cold glass. The other man stood at the exit and turned a massive iron key. The motion of the bolt echoed through the concrete corridors with a dull, mournful tone. Just hearing the sound of the sliding door filled Peter with a wash of memories from his days at the Center.

Clank! The door stopped. Every noise was magnified and only served to remind Peter that he was a captive. He looked down the corridor again, but all he saw was a dim, grey hall with heavy doors and thick walls.

"Get moving," Frank said as he shoved Peter toward the exit.

Peter nodded. He was too dazed to offer a sarcastic retort and simply stumbled into the hall. The door closed behind him with an echo and Frank led him toward the lighted room. His shoulder ached from the wound he received three months earlier and his wrists chafed in the metal binders.

Each step was laborious. Peter's feet felt as if they weighed fifty pounds. As he shuffled along he heard the voices of other prisoners. Some cried out for help, others shouted obscenities at the guards. The air-conditioning unit whirred with an incessant, droning hum that grated against Peter's nerves.

He arrived at the door and the light of the room pierced his eyes. Cinderblock walls, painted white, reflected a large, overhead lamp that burned with intense scrutiny. A solitary stainless steel table sat in the middle of the room with a small, metal stool for Peter. Across from the stool sat a well-dressed man with a blue-green tie and a black, double-breasted jacket. His hair was jet black with small flecks of grey at the temples and he wore heavy, dark sunglasses.

"Sit down!" the escort commanded as he shoved Peter into the room.

Peter stumbled and slammed his knee into the round, metal stool. Bolted into the floor, the stool gave no quarter and he fell to the ground.

"Get up," the stoic, well-dressed man said.

"It'd be easier if I didn't have these cuffs." Peter squirmed and finally maneuvered into the stool.

"You're a prisoner," the man said as if that answered all the questions of cruelty.

"Where am I?" Peter asked. "The last thing I knew some brute struck me on the back of the head and then I woke up in your cell."

"I'll ask all the questions." The man adjusted his tie and leaned forward. "The first thing I want to know is your name."

"I'm Peter Sheridan."

"Interesting," the man said as he wrote some notes on a yellow legal pad. "However, Peter Sheridan was killed three months ago trying to escape. So let's agree not to lie—it won't work."

"I don't know where you get your information, but I'm not dead. My name is Peter Sheridan."

"You're going to make it difficult? Lying will only aggravate your condition."

"I'm telling the truth; I'm Peter Sheridan."

The man sighed in resignation. "Okay, Sheridan, we'll find out eventually who you are. Now, what were you doing with this?" The man pulled out a black, leather book from inside his coat.

Peter's eyes widen as he looked upon the Bible he recovered for Joshua.

"I see you do recognize it. That's good." A sly smile crossed the man's face. "Why don't you tell me about it?"

Peter began to get nervous. The Bible was an illegal book and owning one was a serious offense. He wished he had Joshua with him and prayed in his thoughts for God to give him something to say.

"C'mon," the man pressed, "tell me how you came to have this book!"

"I found it."

"Stole it more likely," the man added. "Do you know what this book is?"

"It's a Bible, the written word of God."

The man flipped through the thin pages. He looked inside the front cover and his eyes narrowed as he read a hand-written note on the inside flap. "Do you know what this means?" The man maneuvered the book so that Peter could read the words:

Find the Shadow Remnant.

"I have no idea." Peter felt flushed; his face grew warm as a sense of fear crept into his thoughts.

"Now I know you're lying." The man stood up and walked behind his chair. "Frank, get in here!"

Frank entered the room, "Yeah, Cap'n?"

"Get this punk out of here until he's ready to tell the truth."

Frank grabbed Peter by his arms and hauled him off of the stool. With one hand on Peter's handcuffs and the other on the back of his neck, Frank turned him around and pushed him toward the open door.

"Wait," the well-dressed man spoke up.

Peter turned his head to look back at his questioner. "What?"

A wicked grin crossed the man's face. "Welcome to McNeil Island."

Frank chuckled and shoved Peter through the door. The noise of the prison filled the hall like the voices of unseen, wretched spirits. Peter groaned as his shoulder hit the wall. Then Frank grabbed his arm and hauled him through the corridor and back to his cell. The burly guard took a loop of keys from his belt hook and fumbled with them until he found the one he wanted.

"Turn 'round and face the wall," Frank ordered.

Peter did as he was told. Frank put his hand on Peter's back and pressed him against the cold, glass. Peter exhaled a sigh of relief when he heard the quick snap of the handcuffs and felt the cold metal slip off his hands. Frank released him from the wall and backed off. Peter rubbed his wrists as he turned around. He looked up at his guard. Frank was a tall, stern man with no compassion in his eyes. He reminded Peter of an ill-tempered grizzly bear.

Maintaining a humble posture, Peter kept his eyes down. "Now what happens?"

"You'll be taken from this holding cell and put in the general population."

"What's that like?" Peter feared his circumstances and his voice trembled with anxiety.

"Keep out of trouble and you may survive. Just mind your own business out there." Frank moved toward the door, grabbed the handle and slammed the chamber closed as he left.

Peter examined the small chamber. There was nothing more than grey cinderblock walls and a glass front. No chairs, no tables, not even a sink. Only a stainless steel commode offered any variance to the room. He watched as guards occasionally passed by the window. Some glanced in as they walked by, but most simply ignored him.

* * * *

Peter wondered if he had been forgotten. Four hours had passed and still no one ventured to open the door and let him out. He was brought no food or water and began to feel the effects. His mind wandered back to his time at Joshua's home. A tear welled up in his eyes as he remembered his friend and mentor lying on the ground. The time he spent with Joshua, and the months of freedom he had enjoyed, was lost forever. He was trapped on the most notorious island in Puget Sound and any hope he had was washed away in the salty surround. A new wave of despair filled his thoughts. He considered pounding on the glass wall, desperate to get someone's attention—even the brute, Frank. But Peter simply shook his head and surrendered to his situation.

Two more hours passed when a guard banged on the door. Surprised, Peter stood on his feet. The guard turned the lock and in a reverberation of sound the door slid open. At the door was a young man, clean shaven and holding a three-foot metal rod. Peter didn't even want to imagine what the rod was for.

"C'mon!" shouted the young guard. "Get yourself moving or I'll have to move you by force."

Peter nodded and moved toward the door. As he passed into the hallway, the guard pressed the stick against Peter's back and his entire body was wracked with searing pain from an electrical discharge. His knees buckled and arms flailed as he fell to the ground.

Struggling to his hands and knees, Peter looked up at his tormentor. "What'd you do that for?"

"You didn't move fast enough. Now get up and get moving." The guard pointed the rod at Peter and waived it in threat.

"Alright," Peter said. "I'm getting up." He legs trembled as he struggled to his feet, hungry and thirsty. "When do I get some food and water?"

"You'll get it when you get into the population, now move."

Peter stood and moved as he was directed. They walked past the interrogation room and followed the hall for almost a hundred yards. He marveled at the scope of the building. It was more extensive than anything he had ever seen. No external light shone, just pallid fluorescent tubes anchored by chains in the ceiling. The long hall, built of pale, grey cinderblock, felt lifeless as a tomb.

The corridor was lined with doors like the one to his vacated cell. Windowed rooms of various sizes housed an uncounted number of men. Peter kept his head down but glanced up through the corner of his eye to look into the various cells. Men sat or stood in assorted poses. Some paced like caged animals in a zoo. He wanted to ask about the men he saw but decided against it. The electrical rod was a strong deterrent.

Ahead stood a pair of double doors, with small slits for windows. Sunlight shone through the translucent panes and provided a warm, yellow glow upon the floor. It was the only warmth that Peter had encountered since being abducted from Joshua's home. Two guards kept vigil at the exit. Dressed in navy blue shirts and pants, the guards held rifles at the ready. Peter glanced up to look the men in the eye and determined that both guards were accustomed to killing.

"Okay," said Peter's young escort. "This is far enough. You wait right here."

Peter stood not more than six steps away from the exit doors. He glanced around, trying not to rouse the ire of the guards but desperate to see what he was waiting on. The two at the door kept their places, no smiles, no scowls, just the grim expression of emotionless men. Time seemed to pass at a snails pace. His stomach growled from hunger. Then, from behind, a black cloth was placed over his head. It was a thick velvet sack, leaving Peter in a world of darkness.

"There," said the young guard. "That'll do."

"Do for what?" Peter interjected.

"Shut up," the guard replied, "or you'll get a taste of this again."

Peter felt cold metal press against the back of his neck. Not wanting to provoke his captor, he simply hung his head in submission and waited. He didn't know if he was to be executed or just left to starve, but his own heart felt the weight of despair and loss so deeply that he didn't care.

"Frank!" the young guard shouted. Peter heard the footsteps of the large man echo up the hall. His gate was unmistakable as he lumbered like an ox.

"Yes, Lieutenant," Frank said, standing right behind Peter.

"Take this prisoner to the population," the young guard said. "Keep him hooded until you get within sight of them. We don't want him finding his way back here. And take these two as escorts."

"Yes sir!" Frank said.

"Now," the young guard said to Peter, "you will do well to behave yourself. No one ever escapes this island. If you try, you die."

"I understand," Peter said.

"C'mon," Frank said as he grabbed Peter under his arm. His fingers dug into the soft flesh just under his armpit.

With a quick step, Peter started to walk with his escort and immediately stumbled. Frank hauled him up and dug his fingers even deeper into his flesh. He heard the doors open and a gentle, soft breeze wafted into the corridor. The scent of pine, mingled with the sweet aroma of mint, served only to remind Peter of what he had lost.

For some time they continued along a rocky path. He began to trust his guide when he realized that the guard steered him away from obstacles. Their pace quickened and soon, Peter guessed, they were nearly a mile away from the exit. He wasn't completely sure, however, as Frank took a variety of turns and twists. All the while, Peter listened to the sounds of the wind blowing through trees.

Thirty minutes passed and they stopped. Frank grabbed the top of the velvet bag over Peter's head and, in a rush of light, the world came into view. He looked upon a sight that was breathtaking. A long, pristine lake sat surrounded by a sylvan forest. The water shimmered and rippled in the breeze like tiny diamonds skirting across the surface. The woods were lush and green yet dotted with orange and red, as autumn took hold of the world. A splash occasionally disturbed the surface of the lake when small trout jumped out of the water after a meal.

Then Peter remembered that he hadn't eaten since the night before and the pain in his stomach returned with a vengeance. "So, Frank, where's dinner?"

"Go find it yourself, punk. This is as far as we go; you're on your own." Frank chuckled as he turned and began to walk back down a winding road, escorted by the two riflemen. The guards disappeared around a bend, swallowed up by the forest.

"Great!" Peter exclaimed in frustration. "Not only am I a prisoner, now I'm alone." He looked down at the water of the lake, his thirst demanding he rush to the shore. Caution, however, dominated his thoughts and he looked all around before taking a step. He knew that many others had been brought here, and he was a far cry from civilization.

Careful and slow, Peter stepped down to the water, his eyes always darting a glance through the trees just in case. Yet, when he spied no others, he gratefully knelt down by the cool lake and spooned up water with his hand. He shook with hunger but he managed to quench his thirst. Splashing water over his head, Peter felt a sense of comfort in his surroundings. He was grateful for the three months that he spent with Joshua, learning how to live and manage off the land.

He looked down the lake. It was nearly a mile in length and from the ripples that appeared it was well stocked with fish. Along the edge of the lake, about fifty feet away, a hedge of blackberry bushes grew with amazing production. He walked down the shore and found the berries ripe and ready for him. Peter foraged and ate until his hands and face were stained purple by the fruit. He walked to the lake and, stripping off his shirt and shoes, he jumped into the water.

"Ah!" Peter gave up a yell as the cold water rushed over his body. He swam and washed and played in the refreshing pool. When his shoulder began to ache, he swam back toward shore. He looked up at the edge of the lake and caught his breath when he noticed movement in the undergrowth. Treading water and desperate to keep still, Peter watched to see whatever had caused the motion. A deer, he thought? Maybe it was a bear. His eyes widened in shock when he saw a boy, no more than ten, dash through the brush and into the woods beyond.

"Wait!" Peter shouted as he desperately tried to swim to shore. His arms tired from the exertion, but he willed himself to swim faster.

He arrived at shore to find that his shirt and shoes were missing. "That little thief," he shouted.

Peter glanced around and noticed a broken branch in the direction the boy had run. His trousers dripped and weighed him down. Without shoes on his feet, the ground cut and bit him with every step. Determined, Peter marched into the hedges and began to walk in the direction the boy ran—away from the lake.

Branches scratched at his exposed skin like the claws of some vicious cat. He tried to find the safest footing, but he often didn't see the ground through the foliage. Occasionally he stepped on a log or over a branch, only to have some sharp, pointy stick waiting for him to place his foot down. Progress was slow and after an hour Peter figured he had traveled about a half mile.

He glanced up and noticed that the day was nearly spent. The afternoon had been warm, but he knew that the nights grew cold and he needed a shelter for the evening. Peter sat upon a fallen tree, looking around to see what he could use to make a shelter. Heavy pine and fir trees were abundant and he decided to break off a few of the more densely packed branches for a lean-to. It took some time, and he wondered where the young boy had gone, but after an hour Peter had constructed a sufficient shelter. It was dry and when he sat down under it, his own body heat kept the shelter warm. He piled a large quantity of fern branches on the ground for bedding and lay down. After an ample yawn, Peter fell fast asleep.

* * * *

The morning dawned grey and cold. Dew had settled upon the surrounding flora but Peter's shelter remained dry and warm. He was hungry, thirsty and anxious to find where the boy had gone. Survival, however, had become his main concern. He didn't have any secure location to call a base camp and wanted to remain close to the lake. He peered out of his shelter and heard the sound of water dropping through the braches. It had rained in the night and no wood was dry enough to hold a flame. The chill in the air bit into his skin and he quickly ducked back under the branches.

Peter tried, to no avail, to make some type of protection for his feet. He gave up the effort and simply slipped out of his shelter and into the morning. The tops of the trees waved in response to a gentle wind but no breeze ventured to the forest floor. He stepped over logs and through dense growth, picking blackberries along a path he hoped would lead to the place where the kid had vanished. He hoped that if a ten year old boy could survive in the woods, then he had resources that might be handy.

The trail led into a sharp ravine. Beneath the brush Peter heard the trickle of water from some unseen brook. He stepped carefully, not wanting to injure himself, and managed to find his way to the bottom. The air was close, heavy with mist and held onto the cool morning. Peter crouched down to pass through some thick growth and stopped when he noticed a small boot print in the soft dirt. A smile crossed his face; the boy was near.

On his hands and knees, Peter crept through the growth and followed the prints deeper into the woods. He happened upon a small stream, its water filtering through the brush and over rocks. He took a handful of water and continued in the direction of the footprints.

After an hour, Peter stopped and tried to get some sense of direction. The sun was obscured by clouds that blew in from the coast, bringing with it a slow, but saturating rain. He shivered in the damp conditions and wished he had some way to make a fire. As he rested, he thought he heard some movement in the brush ahead of him. Though faint, he was certain he heard voices. Shaking off despair, he crouched again in the brush and began to make his way toward the sound.

He neared the voices and stopped. Moving a patch of ferns to the side, Peter peered into a small clearing. The ground was cleaned of all brush and several small shelters made of pine branches surrounded a small campfire. He watched as a dozen people or more milled around the camp. A group of children played on the opposite edge of the clearing and Peter thought he recognized the boy who stole his shirt and shoes.

His eyes widened as he looked upon the scene. "What is this?" he whispered.

"This is our home," a voice spoke from behind him.

Peter whirled around and fell backwards when he saw two men hovering over him. He tried to get up and run, but the men quickly grabbed him and threw him back to the ground. They wore torn, weathered clothing. Some had vests made of animal hide and leather boots of the same material. Each carried a homemade bow with hand-crafted arrows in a leather pouch. Peter stared in disbelief at the men who looked as if they had stepped out of the past.

"Who are you?" Peter asked.

"Right now, we'll ask the questions," said one of the men. "Get up and come into the camp."

Peter stood to his feet as one man led him into the clearing and the other followed. He looked around and noticed that several men stepped from behind trees, bows and arrows aimed right at him. *Great,* he thought, *captured again.* The two men brought him to the fire and motioned for him to sit on a rock near it. The warmth was inviting and Peter sighed with relief as he soaked in the heat of the flames.

The two who escorted him into the camp sat on either side, but Peter could feel the eyes of everyone. He looked around and the young boy who had taken his garments came near.

"It's okay, Paul," said the man on Peter's left, "come here." He motioned for the lad to come closer.

Peter watched the kid approach and smiled as the boy hesitated.

"Sir," said the boy, his voice cracked with anxiety, "I'm sorry for stealin' your stuff." Then he placed the items at Peter's feet.

"Thank you," Peter said as he reached for his shoes. "Paul, is it?"

"Yes, sir," the boy replied. Then he ran off and hid behind a tree.

"So," said the man who had invited Paul over, "who are you?"

"My name is Peter Sheridan," he replied, "and I was taken prisoner outside of Darrington."

"You're Peter Sheridan?" The man said with incredulity.

"Yes," Peter said, "why?"

The man stared down at Peter, brows furrowed in thought. "We've heard of you." He paused and stroked his trimmed beard in thoughtfulness. "You've gained a bit of notoriety."

"Oh," Peter said, "and what kind of notoriety?"

"We heard a report that you were killed, shot in a firefight with guards from the Darrington Center."

Peter sighed in disgust, "That is a lie!"

"The story doesn't end there. Others have said that you escaped and some said that you're a plant for the government." The man paced around the fire. "And now here you are. The question is: what rumor is true?"

Peter shook his head in disbelief. "None of them are true. I was never in a firefight. The guards shot me and left me for dead. If it wasn't for the kindness of... well... of a friend, I would have died. That was more than three months ago and now I'm here."

The man looked back toward Peter with a slight smile. "We do have someone here who will know if you're telling the truth." He motioned for someone to approach.

Peter turned and nearly fell off his rock as he stared up at the man directly behind him. For the first time in ten years Peter looked into the eyes of his father.

CHAPTER FIVE

"You are my lamp; O LORD; the LORD turns my darkness into light." ~ 2 Samuel 2:29

As the surprise wore off, Peter stood on his feet. With his six feet, two inch frame, Peter looked his dad in the eye. A thousand questions rushed into his thoughts, but all he managed to say was, "Hi dad."

The man who stood with him looked Peter up and down. A dim smile crossed his face. "Hello Peter," he sighed, "I'm sorry you're here." He shook his head as he reached out his arms for his son. The two men embraced, tears falling as they reunited.

Peter's shoulders shook as he wept with his father. "Dad," he said almost in a whisper, unaccustomed to that word. He pulled away from their embrace. "Dad, where's mom?"

Before Peter's dad could answer another man came up behind him. "Patrick," the other man said as he put his hand on Patrick's shoulder, "we have to get our camp deeper into the woods. The rebels are sure to have seen Peter come this way."

Patrick shook his head in resignation. "You're right, Jack," he replied and then turned to his son. "We need to get moving.

The rebel gang that lives on the other side of the island is always on the watch for newcomers. They try and recruit people to their cause and usually bring trouble with them."

Peter nodded. "I'll follow you, but then I want some answers."

The colony broke camp and stamped out the central fire. Each person carried their belongings in hand-sewn leather satchels. Peter put his own shirt back on and followed at the rear of the group. He marveled at the condition of the colony. With no apparent technology, the people survived with a frontier mentality. Hand-made bows and arrows, shelters made from tree branches and clothing made from animal hide gave Peter a surreal sense of timelessness. Ahead of him, darting through the flora like a forest animal, Peter watched the young boy, Paul, navigate through the undergrowth.

The group hiked through the trees for nearly an hour when a man at the head of the column lifted his hand to signal their stop. Peter was grateful for the rest. He sat upon a moss-covered log as the people quickly cleared away a patch of ground and stacked up wood for a fire.

Two women came to the firewood with a lantern. They opened a brass panel on the device and lit several small branches, placing them under the stack of wood. Soon the crack of the wood signaled an inviting blaze as smoke wafted up through the trees. The warmth of the fire took the chill from the air as the colony worked to make several small shelters. Peter wondered at the event, curious as to how often the band of seeming refugees had to move.

"Interesting, isn't it." Patrick said as he came up to Peter. He sat down beside him, hands folded on his lap.

"Dad," Peter said, "I don't know where to begin."

"Let's start by getting you into some warmer clothing. I have some leathers that you can wear until your pants dry out." Patrick fumbled through his satchel until he recovered a shirt and trousers. "Go ahead and step behind that tree and get changed. Then come to the fire and we will all enjoy a warm meal together."

Peter did as he was told and when he came back, the entire camp had gathered around the fire. Logs were placed so that the group could enjoy the warmth. Hanging over the flames dangled a heavy, cast iron pot that simmered with the aroma of venison stew. His mouth watered for the hearty dinner. An hour passed when a young girl, no more than twelve, brought him a wooden bowl filled with the hot stew. He stirred the contents and noticed it rich with potatoes and carrots, venison and a deep, savory broth.

"Thank you," Peter said to the young girl who giggled and dashed off to help the others.

When he finished, Patrick looked straight at him. "Peter," he said, and smiled, "Peter, I still cannot believe that you're here."

Peter sighed, "Neither can I." He stood and stretched his legs. It felt good to be warm again and, to his amazement, surrounded by kindness. "Who are these people?"

"These are the people who have been imprisoned for sedition."

"Even the children?"

"No, the children were born on the island. Several of those who were brought here were husband and wife." Patrick gazed out over the colony.

Peter looked around, his heart beat faster and he feared to ask, but knew he needed to know. "Where's mom?"

Patrick placed his hand on Peter's shoulder. "I think you've guessed it already. You're mom is gone."

"When? How?" Peter's hands trembled with anger and pain.

"It was four years ago. We were being rounded up for questioning by the guards. It happens sometimes that we are hunted down and brought into the cells for interrogation." Patrick paused, and tried to hold off his emotions. "One day, about four years ago, a particularly brutal guard, one built like an ox, had a hold of me. I begged for your mother to run but she turned against the guard to try and help me. He hit her with such force that she fell and struck her head against a stone. At that, the guard let me go and he ran off through the woods. I went to her, but it was too late."

"Oh mom," Peter said, over and over again. He held his face in his hands, shaking in grief. Patrick embraced him as both men felt the pain.

A gentle voice spoke, "Daddy, are you okay?"

Peter looked up to see the young boy, Paul, standing just out of arms reach. "Did he just call you daddy?"

Patrick smiled a brief, tear-soaked smile. "Yes he did," he said. "We didn't know it at the time, but when your mom and I were brought here, she was pregnant. She gave birth just over eight months later." Patrick looked over at the young boy, "Yes, Paul, I'm fine. But I want you to come here." Paul rushed into his father's arms and sat upon his lap. "Paul, I want you to meet… your brother."

Peter and Paul looked at each other, eyes wide with surprise.

Peter then turned to his father and shook his head in disbelief. "It seems that you have built a life here. But, why don't you try and escape? It looks like you have the run of this island and if you have access to the shore you might make some type of raft and get off this rock."

"It's not that easy, son." Patrick shook his head in dismay.

Just then, the one Peter knew as Jack came up behind them. "That's right," Jack added. "The moment that anyone tries to escape, they die."

"But why?" Peter asked.

Jack grabbed Peter's shirt collar and pulled it down. Peter lurched as his shirt ripped. "Put your hand here," Jack ordered.

Peter reached behind him and felt a small bump on his spine, just between his shoulders. "What's that?"

"That, my young friend, is the reason why you can't leave." Jack said as he sat next to Peter.

"I don't understand," Peter said.

Patrick shifted his weight. "Peter," he said, "That small bump you feel is a transponder connected to a poison capsule. This island is surrounded by an electrical sensor net that will trigger the device. Two hundred yards off shore and death is guaranteed." Patrick looked at Peter's back. "You have the same scar that we do. They probably implanted it when you first arrived, while you were still unconscious."

Jack spoke up. "That's why they don't guard us too closely because there is no way to leave. So they throw us into these woods and we scavenge and hunt as needed. We're not free, but we try and live as free as possible."

Peter finished his stew and sipped the warm broth with slow delight. A quizzical look crossed his face. "Dad," he asked, "how did you hear about me?"

Patrick smiled. "Well, son, that's a bit of a story as well."

"I'm all ears," Peter replied.

"It was about three months ago that we heard on our radio that someone had attempted an escape from the Darrington camp."

"Wait a minute!" Peter exclaimed. "What do you mean? You have a radio?"

"Oh, yes," Patrick said. "There are several abandoned houses on this island and many more dilapidated buildings. We've scavenged them for all sorts of supplies. You'll see when we get back to our main camp." Patrick stood and stretched. His back cracked and joints popped as he moved.

Peter smiled. "You're getting old, dad."

Patrick sat back on the log. "Forty seven this year," he grinned, "but back to the story. As I said, we heard about the escape and the subsequent shooting. The report was that the escapee was killed. A few days later, while I was fishing by the lake, I spotted a patrol boat on the water. I ducked into the brush, not wanting to be captured for interrogation, when the boat landed. One of the guards stepped onto shore and began shouting my name.

"Anyway, they usually don't call out like that and something inside me was too curious not to find out. I stepped out of the brush and the guard came up to me. I hadn't seen him before. He was shorter than me and something in me immediately grew suspicious." Patrick stopped and stared off into the distance as if looking at the past. He shuddered as he recalled the incident.

"What is it, dad?" Peter asked.

"That man," Patrick said, "that man told me that you were the one who was killed." Patrick's head hung as if he felt the weight of sorrow all over again. He lifted his eyes and Peter noticed a tear on his father's cheek. "Imagine my surprise," Patrick continued, "when you showed up."

Peter stood up, reached his arms above his head to stretch and then sat back down again. "But what about those rumors that Jack mentioned? Where did they come from?"

"Rumors?" Patrick asked.

"Jack said something about it… that I was heard of and he wondered if I were a plant for the government."

"Oh," Peter's dad chuckled. "Jack always worries about things like that. He's been here a long time."

"But what did he mean?"

"Well, about a month ago there was an interview that we heard on the radio. Some old man from Darrington said he had seen you sneak into town and then back out again. According to this man, he had followed you to some old homestead. It was quite an interview. This man went on and on about how you were really alive and working for the government. Most of us thought him to be just some nutcase getting his fifteen minutes of fame. But Jack takes things like that far too seriously."

Peter nodded as he scratched at his growing beard. "I wondered how they found us."

"What do you mean?"

"After I was shot by the guards, I drifted down river for some time and nearly died, when this man named Joshua fished me out of the water. He fixed me up and took me in."

Patrick's eyes widened. "What happened then?"

"I spent about three months there and Joshua told me about his grandfather. He mentioned a bible that his grandfather had used and I went back into town to try and find it." Peter paused as he thought about what happened. "To make a long story short, I did find it. Right after I handed it to Joshua, these black helicopters dropped in on us." He wiped his eyes as he continued. "The last thing I knew Joshua was shot and lying on the ground. Then I woke up here."

The sound of crashing echoed through the woods. Peter looked up to see branches waving and vibrating as a young woman burst through a tall hedge of thick undergrowth. Startled, Peter stood to his feet and was about to run when his father placed a restraining hand on his arm. Her breath steamed as she panted with exhaustion. She motioned for Patrick and Peter's dad stood. He tugged at Peter's arm as he started toward the young woman.

Peter walked with his dad. The young woman, matted blonde hair and with a bow strung across her back, leaned against an alder tree as she tried to catch her breath. He noticed that the woman's shoulder was covered in blood, with a three inch slash deep into the skin.

"Crystal, what happened?" Patrick asked.

She tried to slow her breathing, "I… I was ambushed." She looked at her arm and grimaced with pain. "It was the gang. They're on the way."

Peter watched in amazement as his father went to work. "Get packed!" Patrick shouted to the small group. "The gang is near and we need to get back to the colony."

In a flurry of activity, the small band of islanders rushed to get their gear stowed. Patrick wandered through the site, helping each member gather their belongings and preparing to move out.

Peter looked at the young woman as she nursed her wound. "Crystal, is it? I'm Peter."

"Yea," Crystal said, "That's nice."

"I'm new here." Peter reached out to shake her hand.

Crystal glanced down at his hand then shook her head as she looked up, "I don't care. But I could use a strip off that shirt of yours."

"Oh, of course." Peter ripped some fabric from the bottom of his shirt and handed it to her.

"Do you mind?" Crystal asked. "It's kinda hard to wrap a bandage with only one hand."

"Oh, sure." Peter fumbled with the strip from his shirt and wrapped the cloth around Crystal's arm, careful to make it just tight enough to stop the bleeding.

Crystal looked down at his work and tested to make sure the wrap was secure. "Not bad," she said. "Where did you learn to bandage a wound like that?"

"From a friend," Peter said as he thought of Joshua.

Jack shouted from the camp, "C'mon you two! We're movin' out."

Like a gazelle, Crystal leaped over two fallen trees and dashed into the brush ahead of the group. Peter ran after them, but was stopped by his father who took up the rear of the march.

"Stay with me, son," Patrick smiled. "There's no catching up with Crystal."

"Who is she?"

Patrick gave Peter a quizzical look. "She was ten when your mother and I arrived. Jack has raised her, but I don't think he's her dad. She won't talk about it, though I'm pretty sure that she was orphaned here. But she knows these woods better than anyone else."

Peter gave a slight smile as he followed his dad through the thick brush. Both men walked in silence as they descended down a steep ravine. The day had waxed on and the sun was near the horizon. Shadows filled the woods and appeared to dance as the travelers passed through. A thin mist started to fill the ravine and drifted lazily across the terrain like a soft blanket.

Peter glanced up and marveled at the sight as sunlight filtered its way to the forest floor. Long, thin clouds glowed like a fire in the heavens. As the crimson wisps of clouds drifted across the cobalt background, small pinpoints of light peeked down upon the world. He watched as two lights, flashing red and blue, dashed across the sky. *An airplane*, Peter thought, *I wonder where they're going?* Just as quickly as they came, the flashing lights disappeared.

Peter followed the group as they continued deeper into the woods. They stayed in the ravine, surrounded by massive evergreen trees and thick, dark undergrowth. The cover of the forest prevented any unwanted eyes from looking down on the group as they traveled. The shadows lengthened and soon it was hard for him to see anyone except his father.

"It's not much farther," Patrick said. He stepped carefully around a large, rotted stump.

"It seems that you've found the darkest part of the woods," Peter said.

"We needed to. The gang on the other side of the island has raided us in the past. Besides that, the guards don't come this deep into the woods."

They continued on. The pale moon, occasionally uncovered by the drifting clouds, gave little help to navigate the terrain. Then, as if passing through a vine-shrouded doorway, they entered a clearing with a central fire and dozens of people milling about.

"Welcome to the colony." Patrick said and smiled.

Peter stopped, his eyes widened in stark amazement. Slowly he turned his head as he tried to take in the entire scene. Small, brush-like huts were set into the trees, almost out of the reach of the firelight. Children, ranging in all ages, played about the grounds. Men and women walked in and out from the darkness around the campfire and spoke in hushed voices. Around the campfire a small group of men sat and sharpened knives.

Peter noticed that most of the residents wore the same leather crafted garments as his father. "How have you done all this?"

"It took some time," Patrick said. "When we first arrived, we were thrown into the woods similar to you. Most of the people who had been brought here simply foraged on their own. It was Jack who had the idea of uniting the inhabitants of the island and try to make a life for ourselves." He motioned for Peter to follow him into the center of the community.

"This is amazing!" Peter exclaimed. "But what about the gang you mentioned? Why didn't they join you?"

"That's a good question," spoke a resonant voice. Peter turned to see a familiar face. It was Jack, walking toward them from beyond the firelight. "They're anarchists. Some are actual criminals, thieves and murderers. Others are so jaded by being here that they lost what humanity they had and joined with them."

"Don't you worry that they'll find you?" Peter asked.

"Not really," Patrick said. "There are so few of them and they are unorganized. There are no more than a dozen men and women who are in the gang. They don't venture too deep in the woods. They have their base camp on the other side of the island, on a small islet in Still Harbor. They watch the lake during the day for any newcomer. We've found that if we go out in large enough teams, they usually leave us alone. But it is better not to engage them if we can avoid it."

Crystal came up behind Jack. Her arm had been re-bandaged and she walked with a slight limp. "Jack," she said, her tone almost demanding. "Did I hear you right?"

"About what?" Jack asked.

"You ordered me to stay out of the woods for the night. I was supposed to be on watch tonight!" Crystal shouted.

"You're in no condition to be on watch!" Jack spoke so loud that some birds, resting in branches above them, flew away.

Crystal threw up her hands in exasperation. "That's not fair! I'm better in these woods than anyone in the camp and you know it." She looked over toward Peter with anger flaming in her jade-colored eyes. "Next thing you know, you'll send out this... this newcomer to keep watch!"

"Now that's enough." Jack's words fell like iron from his lips. "You've had your say, but my decision is final. Go fetch me the radio and call it a night. We'll speak about this in the morning."

Crystal stepped away and kicked at a small branch as she disappeared into the dark beyond the campfire. Peter walked with his father to the fire and sat down on a large stone. The flames danced like playful sprites as the wood cracked and popped in the heat. Grey smoke drifted lazily through the branches and vanished as it blended into the night. Jack joined them and reached his hands out to warm himself.

The three men sat quietly for what seemed an eternity to Peter when Crystal returned. Tucked under her arm she carried a small, metallic box that reflected the firelight. She marched toward them, kicking against any unsuspecting plant that dared to get in her way.

"Here!" Crystal thrust the box to Jack who grabbed it. Peter couldn't help but notice the slight grin that crossed the gruff man's face. Without another word, Crystal turned and stomped away, vanishing into the darkness.

"How is it that you've got a radio?" Peter asked.

Jack sat and fumbled with the controls then began to wind a small crank-lever on the side of the device. The machine whined with each turn of the crank. He didn't look up but said to Peter, "Well, there are several abandoned houses on this island. We scavenge at times and came upon this old radio in a rundown garage."

"That should be enough, Jack," Patrick said. "It's charged enough for us to listen to the broadcast."

Jack fumbled some more with the dials as the radio came to life. Static cracked from the small, round speaker as he tuned into a station. Garbled voices muttered from the silver box, unintelligible and useless. Jack continued to turn the dial, anxious for any news from the outside world. "Stupid radio," He lamented.

"Patience, Jack," Patrick offered. "Try the A.M. frequencies."

Jack nodded, and continued down the dial. A high-pitched squeal rang out like a siren from the small box. Then, with one more turn of the dial, a woman's voice came in clear.

"...and that's the seven day forecast. Back to you Brad."

"Thank you Brenda. We're nearing the top of the hour; here are the headlines from today. A farmhouse catches fire in the Skagit Valley cooperative. State police think it's the work of a small group of anti-government activists. The police are working on several leads. If you have any information, call your local law enforcement or dial 911. A report from the Darrington center claims that an escaped offender was sighted near the Arlington-Darrington road. In an interview with a local logger, the report states, the man in question is named Peter Sheridan and was seen less than two-weeks ago. However, the security force at the Darrington center assures everyone that Sheridan is neutralized and asks the public not to believe seditious rumors. And in sports, the Seahawks are set to take on..."

Jack turned the radio off. "There you go," he said. He looked at Peter, "You're mentioned in the news again!"

"What do you mean, again?" Peter asked.

"Well, Peter," Patrick said, "We've listen every night to what is going on in the world outside and for the past week or more, your name has been on the air. Though the Central News Authority keeps close tabs on what is rendered to the public, it seems that there is no end to the discussions about you."

"I don't understand. Just because I escaped from the Center, why does that make such headlines?"

"Because, son, you were able to do what most cannot. If only for a few months, you were free." Patrick stood up and stretched his back, reaching his hands toward the sky. He walked around the fire and tossed another piece of wood into the blaze. Embers erupted into the air and glittered like fireflies before settling down again into the coals. Patrick turned to face his son. "You see, there are very few who even remember what freedom is… or I should say, was. Across the country, only a handful of people hold onto the old ways and most of them keep to themselves and don't speak out."

Peter perked up. "Are you referring to the Shadow Remnant?"

"Where did you hear that name?" Patrick's voice sunk to a whisper and his eyes darted back and forth as if some unseen agent might come out from the darkness.

"It was written on the cover of the bible I found," Peter stammered. "It was the one I tried to give to Joshua."

"What happened to that bible?" Patrick's voice was quick and anxious.

"The interrogator kept it," Peter replied.

"What's the matter, Pat?" Jack moved to stand by his friend.

Patrick shook his head as he looked up at the lumberjack of a man, "I don't know, but I just got one of those sinking feelings."

CHAPTER SIX

"Do not be surprised, my brothers, if the world hates you." ~ 1 John 3:13

Peter watched his father as the shadow of fear crept into Patrick's eyes. The world around him faded from view and all he saw was his dad, silhouetted against the flickering firelight. He fixed his gaze upon him, careful to watch for any sign of hope. There was none.

Before Peter could speak, Jack interrupted. "C'mon Pat! It can't be that bad?" He put his hand on Patrick's shoulder. "What is this 'Shadow Remnant' anyway?"

"The little you know the better," Patrick said.

"Or what," Jack retorted. "We're stuck on an island in the middle of Puget Sound. What more can happen to me if I hear about it?"

Patrick shook his head and moved as if he might speak. He lifted his eyes to look at Jack, "You don't understand. The Shadow Remnant is perhaps the greatest threat to the establishment. The reason my wife and I were sent here, ripped away from our son, was for the simple fact that it was *rumored* we knew about the Remnant."

"Well," Jack said, "don't you?"

Before Patrick could answer, a small boy darted like a phantom out of the darkness and into the light of the fire. It was Paul, his hair matted and clothes rumpled. "Dad," he said, "When are you coming back to the shelter?"

Patrick smiled as his youngest son ran up next to him. "I'll be there in a moment, son. You go and get our beds ready. Don't forget, we have Peter with us also."

Paul's eyes lit up with excitement then he dashed off into the dark. Peter watched the young boy disappear and grinned at the prospect of having a younger brother. His heart languished at the thought of ten years lost without his family and his mother gone before he could reunite with her.

"Paul's correct," Patrick said. "It's time to get some sleep. The morning brings a day of work that will take our minds off of 'shadows.'"

"Dad," Peter said. His voice halted as if he were unused to the term.

Patrick turned away from the flames that danced before him and looked Peter in the eyes. "What is it, son?" He motioned for Peter to follow him and the two men walked in the direction that Paul had disappeared.

"Is there really a group of people that can change things?" Peter asked.

Patrick took a deep breath and sighed. "I hope so."

Peter stumbled through the brush until they came to a small shelter. In the trailing light of the fire, the hut looked to be made of sticks. The chill air was bathed with the effervescent scent of pine. A small flicker of light filtered through an opening at the front of the structure.

He followed Patrick through the small doorway and found three makeshift beds, nothing more than long piles of straw and grass with animal hides thrown over the top. The ground beneath was cleared of all brush and each bed was separated by a small strip of dirt. Inside the shelter it was dry, warm and felt strangely comfortable. A woven canopy of evergreen branches formed the ceiling. Paul sat near the back wall made of several sheets of warped plywood anchored with leather straps that were tied together like shoestrings. Against the side wall sat an old ottoman, stripped of its fabric and padding. It functioned as a table boasting only one small, lit candle. Wax coursed in tiny rivulets from its crater and pooled upon the table like some miniature volcanic landscape.

"It's not much, but it is home," Patrick said.

Peter offered a slight grin, and sat down upon the farthest bed. He noticed that Paul never took his eyes off of him. "What is it, Paul?"

Paul shuffled on his mat. "Well," he said, "I never thought that I would ever get to meet you. Dad told me you died."

"Bless God that he was wrong." Peter smiled at the young boy, who offered a sheepish grin back. "But you need some sleep and so do I. It's been a long, strange day and I hope that tomorrow you'll be able to show me around."

Paul suddenly perked up, eyes wide with excited anticipation. "Yes!" he exclaimed. "I know every inch of this rock and can take you places that..." Paul's voice fell to a whisper and he motioned for Peter to come closer. "I'll take you places that only *I* know. Not even Crystal knows all my secret places."

"That's quite mysterious," Peter leaned toward Paul's ear and whispered in return. "I look forward to it."

Both smiled and Peter returned to his cot, eager and ready for a good night's sleep. He bundled a pile of straw for a pillow, mounded it under his head and immediately fell quiet.

* * * *

Restless dreams plagued his sleep and Peter woke with a start. It was dark. Beside him on the center pad, his dad quietly snored in deep repose. Paul mumbled unintelligible words as he talked in his sleep. He leaned to his left and peered out the small, canvas doorway. The night was filled with the sound of rain dancing through the foliage. Something in the rhythmic pitter-patter soothed Peter's nerves and steadied his fractured thoughts.

He didn't know what time it was. He didn't care. It seemed to Peter that *island* time was not measured in minutes and days but in seasons. The chill air warned that winter would soon arrive.

He lay back down and smiled in the dark. He had lived on the island for over a month and still he marveled at the construction of their little shelter. No rain penetrated the woven barrier of branches and no wind whistled through the chamber. It was dry, comfortable, and felt strangely like home. Lulled by the rhythm of the rain, Peter's eyes grew heavy. With a sigh, he fell back to sleep.

"Pete!" a voice echoed in Peter's ears like the fragment of a dream. He rolled over and ignored the sound.

"Peter, wake up." This time he recognized the impatient voice of Paul.

"Not, yet," Peter complained. "It's too early and I'm tired."

"Too early? You're kiddin'. Dad's been up for two hours and the whole camp is awake. It's time to get up."

Peter rolled back over and stared up at the green needles hanging overhead. The day was cold and he was reluctant to leave the warmth of his bed. Through hazy eyes, Peter looked at his little brother and saw the youthful impatience as Paul paced back and forth, slightly hunched over to avoid hitting his head on the ceiling. With a sigh he sat up. "Alright, already," he said to Paul. "Give me a minute and we'll get started."

"Good!" Paul declared. "You promised to take me fishin' today… and you said rain or shine."

"Yes, yes," Peter replied. "Let me get up and get some breakfast first. Then we'll get going."

Paul rushed out of the hut and vanished into the grey, hazy morning. With a prodigious yawn, Peter stretched his arms and rubbed the sleep out of his eyes. Narrow slivers of light filtered around the door and through the walls. It reminded him of his other tasks for the day, not the least of which was to repair the damage from the previous night's storm. But he had promised Paul, and their dad agreed that they needed to get away and have some time together.

He slipped on his boots and jacket and stepped out of the shelter. The day was subdued with grey clouds like a blanket upon the world. A thin mist hung in the air that only intensified the cold bite of late autumn. Leaves glistened in the damp morning and a large fire filled the center of the campsite.

A warm breath of wind touched his cheeks and carried the robust scent of wood smoke. He walked to the fire and found Paul and his dad standing with hefty ceramic mugs in their hands. A simmering, cast-iron kettle sat on a rock near the fire along with a metal pot of coffee. Beyond the center of camp, through the trees Peter watched as others entered the smokehouse, built like a teepee made of tanned animal skins. Smoke wafted up from the center of the structure and he knew that several trout hung within.

On the air Peter heard the voices of several ladies as they complained about the damp conditions. With a quick grin, Peter picked up an abandoned mug and filled it with the aromatic coffee. He sipped the bitter liquid with gratitude. "Ah!" he sighed. "This is good stuff, but where did we get the coffee?"

"One of our early patrols found an unopened canister in an abandoned house on the south side of the island." Patrick sipped at the rich mixture, steam rising up from his cup like the mist off a hot spring in Yellowstone.

Peter gladly drank the hot coffee and filled a wooden bowl with the mixture from the kettle. He sat down to eat and the hot meal drove the chill from his body. The gruel-like porridge was a blended mixture of ground corn and assorted fruit. Peter enjoyed the thick, rich breakfast. Next to him, Paul fidgeted as if he sat upon an anthill.

"C'mon Pete," Paul complained. "You promised to take me fishing."

Peter smiled, "Don't worry, Paul, the fish aren't leaving the lake." He turned to talk to his father, "Dad," he asked, "do you think that the gang will be near the lake?"

Patrick stroked his beard thoughtfully, "No, I don't suppose they will. It's a bit too cold for them. You and Paul should be set for a good day of fishing. It'll be good to have some fresh fish in camp for dinner tonight!" He waived at Paul and the young boy dashed off through the camp with the eagerness of a puppy fetching a stick. He returned with two fishing poles.

Peter marveled at how quickly his young brother returned. "I daresay that you had those poles stashed away somewhere close!" Paul smiled and turned away sheepishly. "Oh, alright," Peter feigned agitation. "If you're so eager, let's get going."

The two brothers walked away from the campfire and into the dense brush. The trees glistened with the dampness of the morning and small ice sheets covered assorted puddles of water. Paul walked through the trees with the skill of an antelope. He hopped over fallen logs and scrambled around stumps as if he knew every square inch of the terrain.

They walked an hour and the landscape changed. The woods gave way to a wide, pristine lake. The water, as smooth as glass, glittered with a thousand tiny reflections of the morning. Around the entire circumference of the lake was an old dirt road, overgrown and lost to time. Peter and Paul ducked behind a large cluster of ferns as they peered down both directions of the lonely path.

"It looks clear," Peter observed. "I think that we'll be okay."

"Do you wanna go to the dock?" Paul asked.

"It's a bit in the open... But today I doubt that anyone else will be out here."

Paul smiled. Both stepped away from the woods and turned left down the road. The path was occasionally hidden, but Peter pressed through the foliage until they arrived at a small, wooden platform. It floated on the lake about thirty feet away, upon four large oil drums arranged like pontoons, with a small, wooden walkway that reached out to it from the shore. Paul scampered onto the wooden structure with carefree abandon.

Peter stepped carefully. The rotted wood creaked under his weight and the barrels swayed with his movements. The gangplank that reached over the water sagged as he neared the center and he noticed several boards missing. The icy bath shimmered beneath his feet, but he arrived onto the dock.

Paul had his line in the water already, a white and red bobber dancing upon the gentle ripples. Peter dressed his line with a weight and a bobber, placed a worm on the hook, and cast it into the lake as well. He sat upon the cold boards, leaned back and sighed.

"What is it?" Paul asked.

"I'm just amazed at the turn of events that brought me here."

A quizzical look crossed Paul's face. "What was it like at the center?"

Peter looked out over the water in thoughtful remembrance. "It wasn't fun." He turned to face Paul and set his fishing pole down upon the deck. "I was always hungry. We were never given enough time to sleep. The center constantly drilled us with government propaganda and if we didn't comply with their oppressive rules, we were threatened to be re-educated."

"What does that mean?"

"Well," Peter stammered, "it means that if I didn't obey them, they sent me into a small cell with no comforts. I was locked away like an animal if I broke a single rule. I spent a lot of time in that confinement. Sometimes they would beat me, deprive me of food and water, force me to stay awake and listen over and over again to the speeches of the educators."

"Wow," Paul exclaimed. "You're better off here!"

"It seems like it, Paul, but even on this island I am still a prisoner." Peter picked up his pole again and stared back out into the water.

"Yea, but at least you have us." Paul smiled as he looked up to Peter.

Peter nodded thoughtfully. "You are right about that. At the center I was alone and didn't know who to trust. At least here I know the difference between my friends and enemies." He took up the slack from his line. "What I don't know is if we'll get any fish."

A rumbling noise on the water disturbed the peaceful silence. Through the faint haze that sat upon the lake, Peter watched a small, motorized boat approach their position. He looked around, no one else was near. The boat had two men on board and they pointed their craft directly at the dock.

"Let's get!" Peter exclaimed, desperate to keep his voice from echoing across the water.

The brothers reeled in their lines, and Paul was shocked to find a small trout racing across the water, hooked by the gill.

"Pete!" the boy exclaimed, "I caught one!"

"No time, Paul," Peter said, trying to stay calm. "Let it go and we'll come back again later."

Paul jerked the line and the fishhook snapped free of the small catch. The fish darted quickly into the murky depths and Peter dashed with his brother into the woods. They hunkered down behind a thick bush and peered through the branches toward the lake. Peter trembled with anxious nerves and a cold sweat hung upon his brow.

"Do you think he saw us?" Paul asked.

"No, I don't think so. The mist is a bit too heavy this close to shore." He patted his brother on the shoulder. Peter felt Paul trembling and knew the same apprehension. "But keep your voice down. It carries on the water like a megaphone."

Paul nodded in silence and grasped Peter by the arm.

A snap from behind them startled Peter and he nearly jumped out of his hiding spot. He whirled around to see Crystal crouching just out of reach.

"Settle down, newbie," she whispered. "You're gonna get us all caught."

"What are you doing here?" Peter demanded in a hoarse, low voice.

Crystal snuck up to them, keeping well out of sight of the boat. "I'm here to save your life."

"What?" both brothers said simultaneously. Peter braved a glance through the brush and watched the boat circle near the shore. The sound of the motor rumbled as the patrol trolled through the water.

Crystal sighed in exasperation. "You're father sent me to get you. I've spent the entire morning looking for you to tell you that you've been marked for termination."

Peter's eyes widened as he took in the news. "You mean…"

"That's right! They are here to kill you," Crystal finished.

"But how do you know?" Paul asked.

"We caught a couple of the gang getting too close to our campsite," she said, still looking at Peter. "We questioned them and when they finally spilled their guts they told us that the guards were out to get you. They even enlisted the gang and promised the members their freedom if they brought you back. That's when Patrick sent me to find you."

Peter slumped in exasperation. "Why me?" he muttered.

"Hey, I can't answer that," Crystal replied. "But we better get goin' or the only thing we'll be asking is where to bury the body."

"Oh, you're a lot of help!" Paul nearly shouted.

The sound of the boat stopped. All three crouched down even lower, nearly lying on the ground as they peeked toward the water. It was near the dock. The motor was off as they drifted through the shallows. Peter didn't know the smaller man who sat near the outboard, but he recognized the burly man at the prow.

"That's Frank!" he whispered.

Crystal motioned for him to be quiet. The three sat as still as stumps, hoping that the two guards couldn't see them. A slight breeze picked up and the water shimmered with a myriad of ripples. The grey clouds overhead disguised the sun and prevented any shadows from exposing their location. The voices of the two guards carried on the air.

"Aw, Frank!" exclaimed the smaller man. "You must'a been hearin' things."

"Shut it!" Frank ordered. "I know what I heard. There's someone here… or at least there was a moment ago."

"Well that was a moment ago. You know how the population is. They're like ghosts in these woods. By now that Peter fella has learned a few of their tricks. And besides, there's no reason for you to think that he's out on this lake fishin'."

"My sources tell me different. I got word that he and that kid were coming to the lake. So you just get that motor running. We've got a lot of shore to cover."

The smaller man sat back down and began to pull on a cord. The engine sputtered like an exhausted horse. Again he pulled and for a moment the engine rumbled but quickly died. He checked the lines, examined the fuel tank, and gave the cord one more tug. This time the motor roared to life and the smaller man sat at the stern, throttle in hand as he revved the propeller.

Water churned at the back of the craft and the boat bounded against the surface. No sooner had they achieved full speed than the boat suddenly flipped straight up in the air and threw both passengers out. It crashed backward against the water, the keel staring up at the clouds. The motor fell off the back supports and sunk to the bottom of the lake, slicing with its props until it separated from the fuel line.

Without thinking Peter dashed toward the dock. He quickly looked over the scene. The boat was thirty yards from shore. Without hesitation he discarded his coat and boots and then dove into the icy drink. The cold grip of the water tried to force the air out of his lungs. He kept calm and stroked with all his might to get to the fallen men.

When he reached the scene, the smaller man drifted in the water face up, arms splayed and blood oozing from a gaping wound to his neck. His face was ashen, eyes wide open and no breath disturbed his body. Peter shook his head is dismay and began to search for Frank.

Face down, Frank floated about ten feet from the prow. He was tethered to the boat by some small rope that had wound around his arm. Peter wrested the arm from the noose and flipped Frank over in the water. His bulk didn't aide the rescue, but Peter gripped the unconscious man under the arm and across the chest and side-stroked back to shore.

Crystal and Paul ran to where Peter struggled to drag the lifeless guard to safety. They splashed into the cold water and grabbed Frank by each arm, hauling him through the thick brush and onto dry ground. Peter shivered uncontrollably as he recovered his coat and boots from his brother.

"What are you thinking?" Crystal demanded.

Just then Frank began to stir back to consciousness. Crystal backed off and quickly notched and arrow into her bowstring. The large man sat dazed and shivered. Peter took off Frank's shirt and undershirt and put his own coat on him. The cold air bit against his skin like a thousand needles, but he feared that Frank was much worse.

Frank grabbed the coat and pulled it tight against his body as if it were the only hope of warmth he had. He looked up at Peter, puzzled, stunned and motioned him to come closer. "Why?" He asked through chattering teeth. Wh...why d...d...did you s...s...save m...me?"

Peter smiled as he remembered Joshua, "Because you needed it." He turned to Crystal and Paul. "Go and get a fire started. We need to warm up." His stern tone gave no room for discussion and both Paul and Crystal ducked beyond sight and into the woods, Crystal shaking her head all the way.

Peter put his boots on and was glad for the dry fabric. His feet began to warm and he stood, reached down and, with some effort, hauled Frank to his feet. "Come on," he said, "let's get you to a fire and get some heat back into you."

The two men stumbled through the dense undergrowth until they happened upon a small breach in the trees. They found Paul and Crystal with a fire blazing bright and both ran to Peter to help him with his charge. Together they all managed to gather around the fire and helped Frank with his boots and socks, which they placed near the fire to dry.

The day had grown steadily brighter and the noonday sun peeked through the haze and clouds of the fading morning. Strands of sunlight penetrated the canopy of branches and turned their humble vale into a sylvan glade. The smoke from the campfire drifted in lazy motion through the evergreens as a slight breeze caressed the field. All four members of the small campsite sat with their hands held out to the fire, but Crystal sat on the opposite side of Frank, her bow and arrow at the ready.

Frank looked at Peter, his eyes squinted in uncertainty. "Why did you do it?"

Peter smiled again, "Like I told you before... because you needed it."

86

"But you risked your life for me, I… I don't understand."

"Frank," Peter replied, "may I call you Frank? There is an old saying that a good friend of mine told me, 'Do unto others as you would have them do unto you.'"

"What's that suppose to mean?" Frank's gruff demeanor found its way in every word.

"I'll tell you," Peter said. "It means that if I was in a boat that capsized and someone who might have been my enemy was on shore, I would want him to still try and rescue me." Peter paused as he watched Frank try and grip his thoughts around it. "You see," he continued, "there was someone who did something for me once… something that was more than I ever deserved. His actions turned my life around forever. Since that time, I've never looked at life the same."

"But I was coming for you… you're a marked man!"

"I know," Peter said calmly.

"You knew? You knew that I was coming for you and you saved me anyway, I don't understand it." Frank spoke almost as if he spoke to himself.

"That's the nature of the new life I found." Peter glanced over at his brother and Crystal who stared back at him with wrapped attention.

Frank looked down, deep in thought. "This is not what I expected at all."

"You're right about that." Peter paused as he looked up at the sky. "Unless you're planning on doing something else, we need to get back to our camp."

Frank stood. His forehead was marked with a massive bruise from where the rim of the boat struck him. His legs were shaky under him but he found his balance as he stretched to his full height. "No, I'm not going to do anything else. I have to get back and report the accident."

"I understand," Peter said. "Do you remember the book that was brought here with me?"

Frank nodded. "Yeah, I remember it. It was called a... a... bible."

"That's the one. If you really want to know why I helped you, you need to read that book. Find the section called 'The Gospel of John.' Start there. You may be surprised at how much it will teach you."

"I'll think about it." Frank took his boots and socks and put them back on. He donned his shirt and coat and handed Peter's back to him. "But I owe you one... and I'm not a man who lets a debt go unpaid." He stepped away from the fire and disappeared through the trees.

CHAPTER SEVEN

"When a man's ways are pleasing to the LORD, He makes even his enemies live at peace with him." ~ Proverbs 16:7

Peter donned his coat, grateful for the heavy, tanned leathers that protected him from the cold. The fire faltered and no more fuel was added. He looked to his two companions. Crystal stared at him as if she tried to bore a hole through his head with her eyes. Paul sat nearest the campfire and tussled with some dried grasses that nestled between his feet.

"Say it already," Peter broke the silence.

"You absolute idiot!" Crystal shouted. She shivered and Peter wasn't certain if it was from the cold air or her hot temper.

"Should I have let him die? That other man, he was gone, but a life is always worth saving." Peter's retort rang through the air but hit the stone wall of Crystal's stubbornness.

Crystal paced with such ferocity that Peter was certain she would carve a rut into the ground. "You don't survive on this island by being nice! The guards are out to kill you... the gang is out to kill you… and you had to save perhaps the cruelest guard of all."

Peter stood and looked at Crystal with a keen sense of purpose. "Don't you know anything about being a Christian?"

"A Christian!" Crystal slammed those words against the ground. "This is a prison island. There is no such thing as Christianity, especially out here. And you're a fool to think there can be."

He shook his head. "You're wrong, Crystal."

"Your dad talks that way too. But I've seen him fight for his life. He never would have tried to save that… that murderous guard." She turned her back to Peter and began to walk away from the fire. Without looking back, she added, "C'mon, we gotta get back to camp."

Peter patted Paul on the shoulder to get up and both brothers followed after Crystal.

They walked in silence for several minutes, carefully navigating the forest terrain when Paul spoke. "Pete," he said, "what do you think is going to happen now?"

Peter sighed, "I'm not sure." He looked behind him. His eyes squinted as he tried to peer through the dense, green foliage.

"What'cha looking for?"

"Nothing," Peter replied. "I'm just a little on edge after what we just went through."

Paul nodded and stepped over a fallen tree. Moss grew upon the old timber and was guarded by a small patch of blackberry bushes. "You can't get off the island so what are you going to do? If the gang is after you and the guards are out to get you…" Paul let the question trail off.

"When we get to the camp, we'll know more. I trust that dad or Jack will be able to figure out something."

The two continued through the quiet of the forest. They entered the ravine and navigated down the steep embankment until they arrived at the camp. When they passed through the hedge they found themselves staring at a large group who had gathered near Crystal. The central fire blazed its warm, amber glow. Crystal stood with Patrick and Jack, her arms gesturing with great emotion as she talked. Peter heard his name mentioned several times and Crystal's tone told him he might want to just turn around and find a hiding spot.

"Peter!" Jack shouted. "Come here."

Peter sighed again and slowly lumbered over. All eyes were on him. Those who had gathered stood around the fire as anxious and questioning looks passed through the crowd. Murmurings began to resonate and Jack motioned for everyone to be quiet.

"Let's sit and talk," Jack said. He turned to the grumbling group. "The rest of you feel free to get back to your work. Pat and I will talk with Peter."

Crystal sat next to Jack, and Paul rested beside his father. Peter sat on a large rock that was near the fire and faced the four of them. He felt as if he sat before a team of interrogators. The difference, however, was that all eyes on him expressed sympathy — all except Crystal's.

"Am I in trouble?" Peter asked.

Patrick chuckled quietly, "No, son. But the issue has been brought up that you might be implicated in the death of that other guard."

"Is that what you were talking about?" Peter almost fell over in relief. "I thought you were questioning why I rescued that other guard — the one named Frank."

Patrick smiled. "No, Peter, we understand why you did it. It might have been better in the short term if you had simply left the lake, but you upheld a virtue that is more precious than any other."

"Oh, and what virtue is that?" Crystal demanded.

Peter turned to look at the young woman whose eyes glowed with rage and glared at him with unchecked anger. With a subdued temper, he answered her question, "It's the belief that every life is worth saving. If I had to do it all over again, I would."

Crystal fell silent, her brows furrowed in rage.

"What is it, Crystal?" Patrick's voice was soft, but deliberate.

"You don't understand," Crystal said through clenched teeth. "None of you can. That man you rescued is a monster." Though she kept her voice low, anger dripped with every word. She brushed her golden hair back and revealed a stream of tears washing down her cheeks. Jack tried to place his hand on her shoulder but she brushed his affection away and stood.

"Crystal," Jack pleaded.

"No! Don't even try." Emotions burst from her like a thunder storm. "I hate that man—I hate him!" She turned and stared at Peter with stone cold eyes. "And I hate you for saving him." The words fell from her lips like the slow release of poison. She then turned away from them and ran into the woods.

Jack looked toward Patrick, "What should I do?" His voice wavered, filled with uncertainty.

"Just let her go," Patrick said. "She's been angry before."

"Yes, but not like this," Jack returned.

Patrick stood and moved closer to the fire. He reached out his arms to warm his hands. Clouds slowly rolled across the sky, signaling a change in the weather. The cold, November air carried the whispered hints of snow.

"Dad," Paul's voice broke the silence. "What happened that Crystal should be so mad?"

"I don't know, son." Patrick turned to look at Jack. "Do you have any idea?"

Jack looked toward the ground, resting his head in his hands. Silently he nodded. "It was her parents," Jack spoke so quietly that Peter strained to hear him.

"What do you mean?" Patrick asked.

Jack sat up and looked toward Peter and Patrick. "When I first arrived here, Crystal was an orphan. She was maybe six years old and living off whatever she could scavenge. She was wild and fearful of anyone. Though it took some time, as I took care of her, she finally began to trust me. Once, when she was nearly ten years old, she told me what happened." Jack paused and took a deep breath.

"Well," Peter said, his mind rapt on every word.

"Anyway," Jack continued, "she told me that her parents were captured while she watched. She didn't remember the reasons. All she knew was that they were taken from her and she was told that they were marked for termination. The guards didn't even have the decency to try and help her. She was only four when it happened and the guard just left her to the whims of the island."

"I can understand why she's angry," Peter observed.

"Indeed," Patrick said. He placed his hand on Peter's shoulder. "Don't worry," he said, "she won't stay angry forever." He offered a small grin to his son.

The day had worn on and many of the other residents returned to the camp. Some carried bundles of wood; others hefted large baskets filled with various vegetables. The sun was low upon the western horizon and streams of light filtered through the bows and cast long, ghostly shadows through the camp.

Though he tried, Peter could not help but think about Crystal. Her anger toward him beat against his thoughts like a drum. He wanted to go after her, to try and offer his sympathy, but he knew he was no match for her in the woods. Looking up, Peter watched the growing clouds fill the sky with their grey, dreary pallor and his own heart seemed to reflect the mood. He turned to Jack, "Should we go after her?"

"No," Jack said. "Let her cool off. She's held a lot of anger in for years and now it all has come to a head."

"But she's out there alone," Peter protested.

"It won't be the first time." Jack stood and moved toward his small, modest shelter. "Don't worry, Pete. She knows these woods just about better than anyone."

Peter nodded but felt no comfort from Jack's words. He left the fire and entered his shelter. The darkness of the small enclosure surrounded him. It was cold and the damp air acted like the vanguard of winter trying to encroach upon his comfort. He hunkered down under his heavy blankets and barricaded himself from the chill.

* * * *

Peter woke early. He shivered and quickly donned his shirt and coat. The heavy leather easily protected him from the bitter bite of the air. The day had just broke and he peered out into the world to find that the feeling of winter did not disappoint. A light dusting of snow covered everything, sparkling in the crimson dawn. Jack and Patrick stood near the campfire and Paul slept quietly on his bed. He raked his fingers through his hair, scratched at his growing beard, and stepped into the world.

Standing at his doorway, Peter watched as Jack paced back and forth in front of the fire. Flames danced just behind him and he kicked an unsuspecting branch into the blaze. His dad motioned with both hands in some silent, desperate attempt to get Jack to stand still. He debated whether to get into the fray, and decided to join in the conversation.

"I can't believe it... I just can't believe it!" Jack exclaimed.

"Jack, calm down," Patrick said. "Getting all worked up won't help the situation."

Peter stepped into the discussion. "What's going on?"

Patrick took a deep breath, "Crystal is missing."

"What!" Peter shouted.

"It's true," Jack said. "She didn't come back to camp. She's been gone all night long. We've sent several teams to find her — but no luck."

"But she knows this island better than, well, everyone. She could easily hide from anyone trying to find her." Peter immediately thought through a dozen possibilities and scenarios. The guards got her. She's been injured. She's hiding. He rolled these through his mind, but nearly every option demanded that she be less skilled than she was.

Suddenly a man burst through the hedge. He was called "Young Tom" though he was older than Peter. Tom panted in exhaustion, his breath a vaporous fog with each exhale. He stumbled toward the fire, nearly tripping into it when Jack caught him. He tried to catch his breath.

"Speak up, man," Jack demanded. "What do you know?"

Tom sat on a snow-dusted log and leaned his hands on his knees. "I… I found her."

Jack's eyes widened with the news. "Great! Let's go."

Tom held up his hand in reservation. "It's not that simple, Jack. She's been captured by the gang. They've taken her to their camp and are holding her there."

Patrick interrupted, "How do you know this?"

"I was near the old gas station at Still Harbor. I thought to try and get a sense of what the gang might be up to, to get a clue of their activities and hoped they might know something." Tom paused momentarily. Then he continued. "Boy, did they ever know something! One of their guards spotted me and told me to bring a message back — that they are holding Crystal hostage until we turn Peter Sheridan over to them."

Peter stood behind Tom and slowly stepped backward, almost imperceptibly. He had already made up his mind: he would go to the harbor and save her, even if he had to surrender to them. Jack still paced and tried to get more details from Young

Tom. Patrick stared at the fire in contemplation and no one paid attention to Peter as he disappeared through the hedge.

Light snow drifted from the trees as the large evergreens swayed gently in the morning. He had been on the island long enough to know how to find Still Harbor so he quickly made his way through the undergrowth to the old forest road. The road, dressed white by the early snowfall, showed no signs of passage. Rarely did the guards drive around the island, and this late in the season, they never ventured into the woods.

Peter turned to the north and walked. Occasionally a patch of grass or new shrub peaked above the snow in the center of the dirt road. He was unhindered all the way to the harbor. Careful to avoid spying eyes, Peter crouched down and crept through the woods. He snuck up toward the abandoned gas station.

To his left, Peter saw a long building. Its roof was covered in moss and large blackberries grew all around the exterior. A sign had fallen from its side and from what little remained of the faded letters Peter knew that it was once a grocery store. About a hundred yards to the west of the store was the abandoned gas station. Ancient pumps, rusted and useless, sat as a silent reminder of simpler times. Two round metal poles remained where the carport once protected vehicles from the weather. The roof had collapsed and its remnants lay on the ground in fragmented shards of wood and plaster. Stairs led down into a deep hole on the west side of the station.

Peter had no vantage into the interior of the structure. He wondered if Crystal might be kept inside, but he waited and watched for movement. He didn't have to wait long... A group of three men walked around from the back of the building, large clubs of heavy wood in their hands. They gestured and spoke, but their voices were too low for him to make out the conversation.

He looked around for some type of weapon. Several large rocks lay on the ground and a few hefty branches that had snapped off in the last storm were the only possibilities. He was startled by a rustling noise from behind him. His heart raced and breath quickened as he crouched flat upon the ground. Peeking up, he watched as two more of the gang walk past him, so close that he might have read the writing on their shoes.

The first man spoke in a gruff, chiseled voice. "That puny captain promised that we'd get off this rat-hole of an island if we turn over that Sheridan to him."

"You can't trust no one!" lamented the second man, his voice like that of a poorly played trumpet.

"Just you be patient. We'll get Sheridan and then we'll see if they keep their end of the bargain. If not, we'll take care of 'em."

The two men crossed a narrow stretch of road between the woods where Peter hid and the gas station. They opened the door and inside he caught of glimpse of Crystal, tied and gagged, and seated on a chair.

Peter sighed. He saw no way of rescuing her without revealing himself. There was no hiding from the three men that remained outside the station if he tried to approach.

An hour passed as he pondered the situation. The snow of the morning had long since melted into small pools and rivulets. A soft rain fell and the damp condition did nothing for his mood. Then one of the men left the station and stood beside the other three. He motioned around with his hand, pointing in no particular direction, and then let out a screeching whistle. The other man left the building and all five stood and talked.

They were stern looking men. Grizzled features, unkempt beards and matted hair gave them an appearance of being the kind of men who were accustomed to doing wrong. Then, as if they had come to some final decision, all five men walked in separate directions away from the station. *What luck*, Peter thought. One man walked right past him again, not more than twenty feet away.

He waited, listening for the sound of their return. It was quiet. Only the gentle rain disrupted the silence of the late morning with its rhythmic pitter-patter. Peter took a deep breath and carefully stepped away from his concealment.

One step… two steps… and he looked up and down the road. His eyes dashed back and forth in a desperate attempt to see anything. There was no one around, just himself. With a mad dash across the road, Peter flattened up against the wall of the gas station. The musty odor and scent of moss filled his nostrils. He held off a sneeze and then stepped silent along the wall toward the door.

He checked the knob, it remained unlocked. With a creak, he turned the latch and opened the door. The rusted hinges protested loudly. Peter peeked around the door and there was Crystal, tied and gagged upon a metallic folding chair. He slipped into the chamber and moved to help.

"Hang on," he whispered, "I'll get you out of this." He took off her gag first then began working on the ropes that bound her hands.

"You dolt!" Crystal scolded in the harshest whisper Peter ever heard.

"What?"

"You are perhaps the most ignorant person I know," Crystal continued. "Don't you know what their going to do to you if they catch you?"

Peter shot her a look of anger, "Shut up long enough and we'll get out of here, then we won't have to worry about it."

"I'm the bait, you idiot. They left me here thinking that they can use me to trap you."

"And it worked," a gruff, stern voice said from behind them.

Peter spun around to see a tall, bearded man. He tried to stand but the man was quicker than Peter and struck him against the chin with the back of his hand. Peter crashed to the ground, pain shooting through his head. The burly gang member reached down and picked Peter up by the front of his coat. Peter quickly jerked back and both tumbled to the ground.

Then the match was on. Peter spun quickly, striking with both hands against the back of the man's head. The man threw Peter off and rushed at him, but Peter was more agile. He stepped aside and the man crashed into the wall and Peter spun, kicking out the man's legs. The man tumbled to the ground again and struck his head against the doorframe. Peter spotted a metal rod just under a decrepit cabinet. He reached for it, but suddenly was jumped by the man's four other companions. They pinned him to the ground and pressed his face into the concrete floor.

"Get him up!" the man demanded as he stood to his feet.

They jerked Peter to his feet, his body wracked with pain that shot through his joints. His face started to trickle blood from where the man struck him.

"So you think you're a tough guy, do ya?" The man stepped closer. Peter was immobilized by the four others. The man doubled his fist and punched Peter in the gut. Searing, burning pain flashed through his body and Peter crumpled to the floor.

"He's not so tough now," cheered one of the four.

"Yeah, but it took all of you!" Crystal rebuked.

"Shut up," said the man and he backhanded Crystal across the face. Still tied to the chair, she tumbled in a heap on the floor.

"Leave her alone," Peter said through clenched teeth as he tried to force himself to stand against the agony of the blow. He looked over at Crystal who lay unconscious.

"Tie 'em up!" the man commanded. The four others complied with the order and Peter found himself with his body stretched, his feet barely touching the floor and his hands tied to a hook in the rafters. Crystal was strung up next to him, still dazed from the hit she received.

"Get word to the captain. Let him know that we got Sheridan." The leader stood and stared at Peter as he spoke. The other men dashed off down the road and out of sight.

"What are you gonna do?" Peter asked.

The man chuckled, "I'm gonna hand you over to that captain and he's gonna get me off this rock. You're my ticket to freedom!"

"You don't really believe that." Peter panted with the exertion of speaking. Tied as he was, he struggled to breathe.

"Well, if it don't happen, then he'll be sorry. Now you just shut it or I'll…" His words trailed off as a commotion outside the station took his attention. He walked to the broken window and smiled. "It seems we got company."

Peter tried to move in order to see what was going on. His view was limited, but he caught a glimpse of a small band of men on the road. "What do you mean, company?"

The man turned around as he spoke to Peter. "It looks like that Jack fella is goin' try and rescue you." He turned back and called out the window, "Hey Jack, you old dog, is that you?"

"Yeah it's me, Parker." Jack's baritone voice boomed into the old building.

Peter turned to look at Crystal. Her eyes fluttered as she gained more awareness. "Crystal," Peter whispered, "Jack's outside. He's come with friends."

Crystal nodded and offered a brief smile.

"Jack," Parker shouted, "if you come any closer I'll kill 'em both! I got your girl tied up as well—you know that. Now you and your boys back off. All I want is Sheridan, but I'll keep 'em both just in case."

"You're an idiot, Parker. There's nothin' on this island that's worth what you're doin'. Let them both go and we'll get back to our camp." Jack's words rung with authority.

"There's no need for name-callin' Jack," Parker said. "I got me a promise that if I deliver this Sheridan to the guards, then I'm off the island forever."

"Yeah, you'll be off the island forever — in a body bag! Do you think they'll turn off the electric fence for you?" Jack paused. "Think about it, Parker. You'll get on that copter and fly through the barrier and be dead in less than a minute."

Suddenly a rifle shot rang out. The noise echoed across the water and even Parker ducked. The dull rumble of a truck shook the doors and vibrated the ground. The squeal of a megaphone pierced the air. "I hereby order all prisoners to disperse," Frank's voice rumbled out across the area. "This is your only warning. Anyone who does not leave will be shot."

Through the back door, Parker's four companions entered and quickly ran to stand beside their leader. They each knelt down, out of sight of the road.

'"Boy," said one of the four, "you shoulda seen them! They ducked into those woods like scurryin' little rats."

"What's going on out there?" Parker asked. "I thought I told you to get the captain."

"We were gonna," said the first, "but this guard, Frank, met us on the road. He said he knew about the deal and that he'd bring that Sheridan fella back to the captain."

Slow, methodical steps reverberated outside the station. The door flew open and Frank filled the doorframe. He was dressed in his navy blue uniform and carried a pump-action rifle. Behind him, and just outside the door, Peter noticed three other guards with short barreled, semi-automatic rifles. Frank looked around the scene, eyes narrow and glaring. He fixed his gaze on Peter. "Ah, Peter Sheridan, I believe."

Peter almost wished he had left Frank in the lake. He quickly recanted that thought in his mind.

Frank turned to Parker. "Cut 'em down."

"Both?" Parker questioned.

"Yeah, both!" Frank demanded. "I'll take the girl in for questioning. But Sheridan's fate is already sealed. Now cut 'em down and put them in the back of my truck."

Parker quickly obliged. Peter and Crystal's hands remained tied and were dragged out of the station with little chance of resistance. They were thrown like garbage bags into the back of a large truck, olive-drab in color with dual tires on the rear axle. Frank stepped into the cab and the truck lurched to the left from his weight.

"You," Frank called to the nearest guard. The lanky soldier stepped quickly to the cab of the truck and stood at attention. Frank bellowed out his orders. "Get your squad back to the compound. I'll take care of these two," he said as he patted his rifle. The lanky guard smiled with wicked enjoyment and turned away. Frank revved the engine and drove through the assembled men.

About a mile from the station, he stopped the truck, turned off the engine and stepped out of the cab. He walked to the rear and opened the tailgate. Grabbing both Peter and Crystal by the ankles, he hauled them to the back of the vehicle. Crystal's eyes were wide with panic, the first time Peter ever saw her afraid.

Peter stared coolly at his captor. "What'll you do now?"

Frank pulled a large, serrated hunting knife from a leather sheath. "Sit up," Frank demanded. Both Peter and Crystal did as ordered and sat with their legs dangling over the edge of the tailgate. Frank grabbed their arms and cut the cords that bound their wrists. He did the same with the ropes on their feet. He then stowed his knife and motioned for them to step down.

"Now what?" Crystal demanded.

"You're free to go," Frank offered.

"What?" Peter asked.

"Yep, you're free to go. You're camp is on the other side of the lake." Frank turned to walk back to the cab of his truck; his shoulders slumped and head down.

Crystal stepped up to Frank and grabbed him by the arm, spinning him around. "But why… why are you doing this for us?"

Frank offered a quick, humble grin, "Because you needed it."

Peter looked up in surprised amazement. "What did you say?"

"It's somethin' I heard from a man who did somethin' for me once." Frank looked at Peter directly. "I got a'hold of that Bible and read the part you suggested—the one called John." Frank rubbed the stubble on his face. "I read it all last night—the entire section—and I've come to believe." He paused. "I also read a part about freedom and if you want, I'll help you get off this island."

-

CHAPTER EIGHT

"Even though I was once a blasphemer and a persecutor and a violent man, I was shown mercy..." ~ 1 Timothy 1:13

Peter looked at Crystal who stood in stunned silence, mouth hanging open and eyes wide. A cold, soft rain began to fall and the chilled air turned their breath into vaporous steam. Rain dripped from Frank's hat as he kept his eyes set upon the ground. The snows of the night before transformed into brown, muddy slush, streaming along the road in tiny rivers.

The three of them stood like statues for what seemed an eternity to Peter. Only the soft rain gave motion to the world. The silence was broken by the sound of splashing coming up the road. Peter turned and watched as Jack and his father ran toward them. He could see the desperation in their eyes as both men churned against the slippery mess, sending up explosions of mud with each footfall.

Not entirely convinced of Frank's newfound faith, Peter moved toward his father to head off any possible confrontation. He held up his hands to get them to stop and both men panted to a standstill next to Peter. Peter glanced back toward the truck. He had moved out of earshot and could not hear the conversation that Frank and Crystal were having. Both stood leaning against the truck's bed, hands gesturing in the air as they talked.

Patrick caught his breath. "What's going on?" He looked at Peter with bewilderment.

"It's hard to believe," Peter said, "but Frank saved us."

"I *don't* believe it!" Jack exclaimed. "That brute's not one to save anybody."

Peter sighed with exasperation, "I know, I know. But I'm telling you, he saved me and Crystal. You were there. He came in and ordered us into the truck and then drove here and untied us." With a pause, Peter considered telling them more.

"What is it, son?" Patrick asked.

"This might be even harder to believe."

"Spit it out already," Jack said with a hint of frustration in his voice.

Peter looked at the ground as he debated telling the two men. "Well," he stammered, "Frank said that he might be able to help us escape from the island." He glanced up at the two men, hoping to get a sense of their reaction.

Patrick offered a half smile and Jack took a step back in shock. "Now I *really* don't believe it!" Jack shouted as he threw up his hands and shook his head.

"Let's hear him out, Jack," Patrick offered.

Jack paced back and forth across the muddy road, muttering to himself. Several minutes passed when he looked up at Peter and Patrick. "What's next? Are we going to make nice with the gang, too? The reason we survive on this miserable rock is because we have built our lives without them."

Peter took a deep breath. "Jack," he said, "I know that the guards and the gang cannot be trusted, but it is possible that people can change."

"I don't believe it," Jack argued.

Peter took a deep breath, "I have to believe it Jack, or the truth that I've come to know is of no value."

"Look," Jack said, "I've been on this island a long time. These guards don't change—especially that one!" He stopped his pacing and pointed his finger at Peter. "Believing like you do is fine for you and Pat, but it doesn't apply to men like him. They are so brainwashed by their training that they can't think any different."

Peter looked directly into Jack's eyes, "The truth must be applied to everyone—or it has no value for anyone." He looked up to where Crystal and Frank continued to talk. Frank held his head down, his shoulders shook and occasionally he wiped his eyes with his hand. Crystal gently rested her hand on his arm.

The cold, damp weather deteriorated into a steady, dismal rain. Grey clouds hung just above the tops of the trees like a dreary blanket, drifting along with a slight breeze. Peter shivered as water dripped off his hair and down his back. He looked out at the lake. The water pocked and rippled with each raindrop and occasionally a small trout leapt out of the water to snag some morsel.

Patrick began to walk toward the truck and motioned for Peter and Jack to follow. "Come on," he said, "let's find out all that's going on. Besides," he chuckled, "I'd like to get out of this rain and back to our camp."

Peter followed his father with Jack close on his heels. They sloshed through the mud and arrived at the truck to hear both Crystal and Frank sobbing.

"What's going on here?" Jack asked.

"Oh Jack," Crystal said as she held back another round of tears, "Jack, Frank has come clean with everything."

Jack looked down at the emotion-wrought woman who stood before him, her hair drenched in rain and cheeks in tears. "Come clean, eh? We'll see."

Before Jack could press the matter further, Patrick interrupted. "Frank," he said, "what have you to say for yourself?"

Frank stood up straight, almost a head taller than Patrick. But his intimidating size seemed diminished in his countenance. Frank's eyes bore a softer expression and his shoulders slumped. "It's a long story," he said, "but when your son saved my life I was forced to rethink some things. I found that book of his and read it. I'm still not sure what happened, but I saw myself in the same place as those guards who killed the one called Jesus and I hated myself for it. I knew then and there that I needed to change — and that's when it happened. It might seem stupid, but I decided to talk with Jesus. I know that he's not here, but I think he can hear me. I asked him to forgive me." Tears welled up in Frank's eyes as he paused to gather his emotions.

"No, Frank," Patrick said, "it doesn't seem stupid." He moved closer to Frank and placed his hand on the guard's shoulder. "In fact, it's the smartest thing I've ever heard you say."

Peter broke into the conversation. "Perhaps," he said, "we can carry this on at the campsite? The day is nearly gone and this rain doesn't seem to want to let up anytime soon."

"I need to get back," Frank added. "They knew I was coming to get you and the captain will expect a report."

"What are you going to tell 'em?" Jack asked.

"That I have killed Peter Sheridan," Frank smiled. "I'll tell them that I dumped his body in the lake and made it look like an accident. They'll buy it."

"When can we meet up?" Peter asked.

"I'll be on patrol again in two days. Watch for me and when I'm at the south end of the lake we will make plans to get you off this island."

"That sounds good," Patrick said. "We'll be on the lookout for you in two days."

Frank nodded and stepped into his truck. The engine rumbled to life and the ground trembled under Peter's feet. Frank drove out of sight as small wakes of water and mud splashed up from his tires. Crystal stood next to Jack, her eyes red with tears, hair slicked down in the rain. The sun began to set behind the trees. Dipping below the clouds, long streamers of crimson and gold streaked across the sky and shadows set the forest in early twilight.

"Let's get out of here," Crystal said.

The three men agreed and in silence they followed Crystal down the road.

Peter listened to the sounds of the world around him. Trees rustled in the constant rain, a muted, rhythmic cadence that kept time with creation. He walked beside his father as they trudged through the mud. Ahead of them, Jack and Crystal kept pace with each other, slowly gaining ground and out of earshot. Jack gestured with his hands as if he tried to make some expressive point and Crystal rebutted with her own hand motions.

"They're a lot alike, aren't they?" Peter observed.

Patrick took a deep breath and sighed, "More than you know, son."

"How often do they argue like that?"

"All the time," Patrick said. "They both have a determined point of view and it's hard to change it." He paused. "But when they have set their minds to the right thing, they are a formidable pair."

Peter took a deep breath as he set his mind to change the conversation. "Dad," he said, "what do you think of Frank?"

"What do you mean?"

"He was the one who hit mom, right?" Peter's voice wavered, moved with emotion.

"Yes," Patrick said, "he was."

"Do you believe that he's changed… that he's actually become a believer?"

"A man's actions tell the tale. We'll know what the truth is in two days."

"Do you think that he has the means to get us off this island? And once we're off, then what?"

They walked in silence for several minutes as the question hung between them. Shadows lengthened and the pall of darkness threatened to finally overcome the long-lasting dusk. The chill turned cold and rain gave way to a light, soft snowfall. Jack and Crystal were long out of eyesight and both he and his father pulled their shirts tighter around their chests. They began to walk faster, eager to find a pace that kept them warm. But the cold, November night gave no room for warmth.

"Well?" Peter asked.

Patrick cleared his throat, "I just don't know, son. I hope that he will be able to make good on his offer, but too many have tried and failed. If we do make it off this island, I believe I have enough connections still that we can find a place that is safe."

Peter looked his dad in the eye, "You mean the Shadow Remnant, don't you?"

A stern look crossed Patrick's face, "I told you, don't mention them." Patrick's voice almost dropped to a whisper, "Even the mention of the Remnant is enough to condemn our entire colony. The government will send troopers in to wipe out this island if they suspect that we are a part of that group."

As they walked, they passed into the woods. The snows failed to penetrate the canopy of branches. Within the trees the air was warmer but the darkness engulfed them. Slowly they progressed. Peter had grown used to navigating the woods in the dark, having taken several excursions with various scout teams, but even with that experience he struggled to make his way toward camp. His father was just ahead of him, but he only knew that from the snap of twigs and occasional groan when he tripped against some fallen log. Suddenly Peter stumbled into his father who had come to a stop.

"We're near the ravine," Patrick said, "let's be careful."

"I'm right behind you, dad. Lead the way."

Both men stepped with great patience down into the chasm. Out of the darkness, the gurgling sound of the stream echoed with renewed vigor from the day's rain. Branches grasped them like shadowed, bony fingers. Several times Peter had to extricate himself from the tangled web of blackberry vines. In the distance, several hundred yards ahead, a glow emanated through the trees. It beckoned like a searchlight in the pitch blackness of the forest.

"Almost home," Patrick sighed.

Yes, thought Peter, *but for how much longer.*

They passed through the hedge and were greeted by a burst of light from the central fire. The wood cracked and popped its welcome, with an occasional hiss thrown in as snow fell upon the flames. Embers drifted up through the branches and around the fire the colony sat and waited for Peter and Patrick.

"It's about time you two made it back," Jack bellowed. "We've been here at least a half-hour already." The crowd parted and made room for Peter and Patrick to sit by the fire.

"Well, Jack," Patrick said, "we don't have your sense of direction in the dark woods."

"No," Jack laughed, "you don't."

Peter looked Jack up and down, perplexed by the change in attitude. "Jack, what's happened? When we were on the road you were about as happy as a thunderstorm."

Jack nodded in recognition, "I know." He moved to sit opposite Patrick. "But when I had a chance to talk with Crystal, she told me about her and Frank's conversation."

"And that changed your attitude?" asked Patrick.

"Yeah Pat, it did." Jack flashed a brief grin.

Peter noticed that Jack didn't sit long, but paced in front of the fire with the energy of a freed lion. "Jack," Peter interjected, "tell us what she said."

"I will leave that to her." Jack smiled again.

"Fine," Peter said, exhaling his exasperation.

A younger man named Randy stood up in the midst of the others. "Tell us, is it true that we're all gonna get off this island?" His rich southern accent drawled in eagerness.

"I don't know," Patrick said. "We'll find out more in a couple of days."

The one called "Young Tom" spoke up. "But what do you think?"

Patrick took a deep breath, "What I think," he said, "is that we will find out in a couple days. We won't do any good by speculating about this. Frank said that he might be able to help us off this island." Patrick paused as he looked at the eager faces staring back at him. "He says that he's a changed man. If that's true then we'll see it for ourselves. I believe that I've taught you correctly in saying that a man's repentance is more seen than spoken. We'll look at his actions and then make our decision."

Just as Patrick finished speaking, Crystal stepped into the light of the fire. Peter had noticed that she remained in the shadows while the colony listened to those who spoke. A sly smile brightened her face, a dramatic change from the woman who hung from the rafters with him at the old gas station.

One old, gruff man stood up. His body shook as he leaned upon a knobby stick for a cane. "This 'mister goody-two-shoes' routine might just be a trick!" The old man's voice cracked like a rickety door on rusted hinges. "We'll all be captured and taken back to the cells... or worse."

"I don't think so," Crystal said. "I spoke with Frank, and he seemed genuinely remorseful for his actions of the past. I had never seen any of these guards shed tears for one of us. But I believe that Frank was truly sorry."

"Maybe saving his life changed his attitude," said one voice from the crowd.

Peter watched as the colony members grew increasingly hopeful, eyes wide and smiles moving across the crowd like a wave. He raised his hands hoping to still the murmuring voices. "Let's not get our hopes up too soon," he said. "We don't know what Frank has in mind and it might be beyond his power to help us."

"The best thing we can do," Patrick offered, "is to have a good meal together and wait. Nothing will come of us sitting and batting it about like a tetherball."

The colony all nodded in agreement and, though the conversations didn't end, the people began to disperse to their own huts and shelters. Several of the older women stayed near the fire, stirring large pots of stew and broth for the evening meal. Peter hefted several large chunks of wood to the fire. He threw them into the blaze, sending up a shower of embers into the falling snow.

* * * *

Peter, Jack, Crystal and Patrick remained for some time at the fire. Dinner had been served and cleaned and the rest of the colony vanished into their shelters.

Peter looked up at the rugged man who paced in front of the fire. "Okay, Jack," Peter said, "tell us what has got you so pleased."

Jack smiled slyly, "Nope," he said, "I'll leave that to Crystal." He pointed to the young woman who sat with her back to the fire. Before Crystal began, Jack stepped away from the firelight and into the darkness.

Crystal took a breath and looked at Peter directly. "Do you remember when you rescued Frank?"

"Of course," Peter said as he nodded.

"Remember what we heard when they were still on the lake?"

"What?"

"Frank had said that there was an informant in the colony, someone who passed information to the guards." Crystal stood up and rubbed her hands over the fire to warm them.

"I guess I remember that. I didn't pay it much attention, though." Peter's brows furrowed as he thought about that day.

"Well," Crystal said, "to show his good faith toward us, Frank gave up the name of the spy."

Just then Jack returned with a young man in tow. Peter recognized the man; it was Randy. He was stout with thick brown hair and a full beard. He wore the rugged attire like every other member of the camp and Peter recalled having gone with him on a scouting mission.

"Now you see why I am so pleased," Jack said. "I've known for some time that we had a traitor in our camp—and this clinches it!"

Peter grew anxious. He looked right at the young man, "Have you told anyone about Frank?"

Randy grinned with malice, "If y'all think you're gonna get off this island then you're a bunch of fools."

"Shut it," Jack commanded. He thrust Randy to the ground and stood over him like a hunter over a prized game. "I doubt that he's been able to get word to the guards that you're still alive. Since we returned I kept my eye on him. He's not left the camp once so no one knows about Frank or his willingness to help."

"That's a relief," Patrick added. "We'll have to keep him under guard until everything is accomplished. Then we'll let him go."

"Let him go!" exclaimed Crystal.

"Sure," Patrick said, "what good is he to us if we're able to escape from here? Once were gone, his usefulness to the guards is over."

Jack reached down and jerked Randy up off the ground. "I'll keep first watch over him—he'll not get a chance to talk to anyone."

"Alright," Patrick said, "let's all get some sleep and try to wait out the next two days."

* * * *

Two days passed with little excitement. Despite the hope of escape that felt like static in the air, the colony went about their normal course of operations. Scouts hunted for food and those who remained in camp worked on the chores that kept everything in order.

On the second day, Peter woke to the sounds of people milling around the campfire. He had grown accustomed to the constant presence of chatter and felt akin to the members of the colony. He dressed and stepped into the world and was dazzled by the sight of several inches of snow. The previous night brought a constant assault of the wintery weather, but the colony simply moved through its routine with little interruption. He walked toward the fire where Crystal was waiting, enjoying a hot drink. Steam drifted up from the cup she held.

"Good morning," she said as Peter approached. "Get yourself a cup of coffee and some breakfast. We have an early start of it today."

"We?" Peter questioned.

"Yes, we. You and I are going to go to the south end of the lake and wait for Frank. Jack wants us to escort him here so we can hear his plan." Crystal gulped down the remnants of her coffee and stepped away from the fire. "I'll be right back," she said as she left. "I need to get some things."

Peter quickly rushed through a bowl of cornmeal mush. The hot, savory meal was a delight on the cold morning. He poured a hefty cup of coffee, wishing he had the chance to leisurely enjoy the heady drink. Instead, he guzzled it down, burning his tongue, and waited for Crystal to return.

Not more than a minute later, Crystal returned with her bow slung over her shoulder and a knapsack in her hand.

"What's the bag for?" Peter asked.

"We're going to have to keep Frank from finding our hideaway. He might be the genuine article, but Jack doesn't want to take any chances."

Peter nodded his agreement, though he thought that coming back through the woods with a blindfolded man might prove disastrous. "Let's get going, then. He said he'd be there on patrol."

The two walked out of camp and into the woods. Peter's skill at navigating the rough terrain had grown and he was able to keep pace with Crystal who still moved like a jungle cat through the brush. He doubted that the best tracker would find her trail.

They came to the edge of the lake and made their way south, keeping to the woods in fear of gang activity. The previous night's snowfall showed the evidence that several deer had passed across the road, but no tire tracks or human footprints were seen. Then, in a familiar spot, Peter stopped at the same hiding place when he rescued Frank from the lake.

It wasn't long before the sound of a motor thundered through the trees. A large truck, olive-drab in color with massive dual tires on the back axle, emerged through the forest and approached the southern tip of the lake. There was no mistaking Frank's rig; it stood out like a stain on a white shirt. Peter looked at Crystal who kept her eyes ever alert for any sign of trouble. Her keen gaze watched everything, whether on the lake or down the road. Peter was convinced she missed nothing.

The vehicle rumbled to a stop. Thin wisps of smoke rose up from dual exhaust pipes on each side of the cab. The door opened and Frank stepped out into the snow.

Crystal touched Peter's arm, "You stay here," she whispered, "we don't know if he was followed." Without waiting for a response, she dashed out of the bushes and walked up to Frank.

Peter had to chuckle at the comparison. Frank stood more than a foot taller than her and outsized her by twice as much. But Crystal had the tenacity of a badger and stood toe-to-toe with the big man. She gestured and pointed and made a hand reference to the bag she carried, but Peter could not hear a word. Frank simply nodded in agreement. She pointed at the truck and Frank dutifully stepped into the cab and drove the vehicle deeper into the woods, hiding it among the foliage.

Heavy snows continued to fall, and Peter was grateful for he knew that their tracks would be obscured by the constant barrage. Crystal and Frank approached his hiding spot and he stood up, revealing himself to them. Frank offered a quick, simple smile as if he had been out of practice for years and was just learning to rework the muscles. Without a word, Frank reached out to shake Peter's hand and Peter eagerly responded. His hand was swallowed up in Frank's massive grip.

"Okay," Crystal stammered impatiently. "We can hold the greetings for later. Right now we have to get back to camp."

"She's right," Frank said. "I've only a couple hours before I need to report in. I'm the only one on patrol today so no one should discover I'm missing. But if I don't check in by noon they will send a team out to find me."

"Let's get going, then," Peter replied. "Crystal, lead the way."

The three stepped along the road as fast as the conditions permitted. When they arrived at the entrance point of the woods, Crystal handed Frank the knapsack.

"Do I have to wear this?" he asked.

"Jack insisted on it. He doesn't trust you yet and wants to make sure that you can't tell anyone else where our colony is."

"Fine," Frank said. He grudgingly slipped the bag over his head and reached out his hands to feel his way along.

Crystal grabbed his hand. "Now," she said, "you'll have to trust me that I'll get you through these woods without injury."

Frank nodded, though his hands shook with nerves. Peter grabbed the other hand and together the three companions navigated the woods. It was slow going and Frank tripped several times, but with thoughtful steps, their path was relatively free of incident and they arrived at the campsite unharmed.

Jack pulled the bag off Frank's head and pointed to a rock the men could sit on. Peter and Patrick took two other large stones and Crystal on the last one so that all five sat in a circle. Gathered around was the entire colony, eager to hear what Frank had to say.

CHAPTER NINE

"A friend loves at all times, and a brother is born for adversity." ~ Proverbs 17:17

"Before I begin," Frank said, "I have somthin' for you." He looked at Peter and reached into his jacket. Jack quickly stood up and Patrick reached down to grab a nearby stick. Frank pulled out of his coat an old, weather-worn book. It was the Bible Peter had retrieved for Joshua.

"I don't know what to say," Peter stammered. "Thank you." He reached for the ancient text as if it was the most prized treasure of his life. Carefully he turned the pages, rejoicing in the sound of the paper crinkling with the motion. "Won't you be found out? If this book is missing, they'll finally trace it back to you."

"Don't worry about that," Frank said. "It was going to the incinerator and I rescued it without anyone knowing. The captain thinks it's destroyed."

"Why are you doing this?" Jack asked.

"Because it's the right thing to do," Frank said. "I can't change what I did in the past, but I hope that, somehow, what I'm doing now will make up for it in some small way."

"If we can all get off this island, it will be more than enough!" Patrick said.

Frank sighed, "I can't get you all off. There is only a small chance that even one of you can make it."

"What do you mean?" Crystal asked.

"I can, for just a few seconds, turn off the grid that keeps you here. You'll have about ten seconds before I must switch it back on. The system is set so that an alarm will sound if it is turned off for more than twelve seconds. But less than that, the system will think it is merely a power surge and the alarm will remain silent."

"That doesn't give us much time," Patrick observed. "From what I remember, a person needs to be at least five yards away from the grid or else the implant will trigger."

"You're right about that," Frank said. "But you need to be five yards away on both sides of the grid. If you're within five yards on the other side, it'll still set off the device."

"Ten yards in ten seconds," Jack barked, "I don't think it's possible."

"It's a risk," Peter said, "but I'll take it."

"How do you plan on making it?" Crystal asked. "You don't think you can swim across the sound! You'll drown."

Peter offered a brief smile and looked to his little brother who sat near the fire. "Paul, you need to tell them what you have."

"Do I have to, Pete?" Paul asked.

"Yes," Peter said. "I think that everyone needs to know."

Paul took a deep breath and looked toward Patrick. "Dad," he said, "you promise not to be mad at me?"

"Yes, son," Patrick said, his voice soft and low.

"Well," Paul said as he looked at the ground, "I have a boat."

Immediately everyone in the circle sat up and looked at Paul.

"You have a *what?*" Patrick asked.

"I have a boat. It's hidden on the eastern side of the island."

"What were you going to do with it?" Crystal demanded.

"Well, I... um... when I was old enough I was going to row over to the Longbranch peninsula. I wanted to go over there and find somebody to help us escape."

Patrick looked long at his youngest son, "We'll talk about this later. But that boat might be the answer we need."

Frank looked at his wristwatch. "I don't have time to debate this. The tide is at its low point at six o'clock tonight. I will have the grid off precisely at six. You'll need to be ready and in the water before then."

"How will I know where the grid is?" Peter asked.

"There are buoys every thousand yards around the island to mark the gridline. There is one in the channel between the island and Longbranch. Stay just outside of that marker by five yards. There is a signal light on the top of the buoy. When you see that light change—move! You'll have ten seconds, make the best of it." Frank looked at his watch again. "I need to get going or I'll miss my check-in time."

Jack looked at the members of the colony and pointed at two young men sitting nearby. They stood and came closer. "You two," Jack said, "Take Frank back to his truck. Keep this on his head until you get to the lake road." Jack handed the knapsack to the first man.

Frank stood. "Thank you, again," he said to Peter. "I think you saved more than just my life."

Peter stood and shook Frank's proffered hand. Tears welled in Frank's eyes as he turned and stepped away from the campfire. The two escorts handed him the bag and Frank dutifully placed it over his head. With great care, they led him through the hedge and out of camp.

"Okay," Jack said, "we need to make some plans."

"Son," Patrick said to Paul, "can you take us to that boat? We need to see what condition it's in before we use it."

They all stood and the colony began to separate. Several muttered under their breath. "Why does he get a chance to escape?" asked one middle-aged man. "We've been here longer than him!" groused a stoic woman.

Peter listened to the constant reverberations of disappointment. His heart welled up with frustration toward the members of the colony. "Listen up!" he shouted. Everybody stopped dead in their tracks and turned to face Peter. "I don't know why this has happened the way it has. All I know is that, according to Frank, the authorities on this island think I'm dead. If they find out that I'm still alive, it will be the end for Frank. He is enduring the greatest risk of all of us. If he's caught, he's a dead man. Now, I'm going to try and get off this rock and see what I can do to change things from the outside. If I die trying, at least it's for doing the right thing."

The crowd was silenced by Peter's words. From the oldest to the youngest, they all departed.

"Nice speech," Crystal said as she stepped up behind him.

Startled, Peter jumped. He turned to face her, "Thanks."

"I've something to tell you," Crystal said, her voice low and mysterious. "Frank told me why they wanted you... well... dead."

"Spit it out," Peter said, anxious to get going and check out Paul's boat.

"Not unless you take me with you." A sly grin crossed her face. She brushed her hair out of her eyes and shook off the snow that had fallen on her head.

"C'mon, Crystal, you know that there is no time for these games."

"Nope, you'll have to take me with you and then I'll tell you when we're on the water." Crystal smiled and began to walk away.

Just then, Patrick called out, "Pete!"

Peter turned to see his dad standing at the edge of the camp waiving for him. He waived back in reply and walked away from the campfire toward his father.

Jack waited with Patrick. "Let's go get that boat," he said.

Jack, Peter and Patrick followed Paul as he ducked and weaved through the forest growth. Snow continued to fall, but with less ferocity. Gentle flakes descended like small sprites dancing through the trees making their way from heaven to earth. The sun stood high overhead occasionally peeking through the clouds like an eager child playing hide-and-seek. Sullen birds flittered through the branches, eager to find any morsel to feed upon. Through the foliage the four men tramped. They stomped and hacked and fought against large blackberry patches, ducked several branches that greedily reached for their coats and finally made it to the eastern side of the island.

Puget Sound lay before them with a rocky beach and large piles of driftwood littered all about. Just across the water was the Longbranch peninsula. In the center of the channel an orange and white buoy bobbed and wobbled with the waves. A seagull sat upon the marker unaware of the dreaded purpose that its perch represented.

Paul led the three men along the coast, keeping near the forest wall. He stopped occasionally to check some undisclosed mark and then proceeded farther on. Peter's anxiety grew with each step, knowing that soon he would to try and escape from a place that was reluctant to give up its prisoners. He had to try, but death awaited him if he failed.

Without a word, Paul stopped. "Here we are," he declared. He reached up and pulled on a stick. With a whoosh a large canopy of branches flew up, revealing a small, six-foot long, wooden rowboat. It had two oars, two small planks for seats and the hull seemed intact.

"Does it leak?" Jack asked.

"Nope," Paul said with pride. "I've had it on the water twice already and have fixed all the leaks in it."

"It's a fine looking craft," Patrick observed. "It looks like there's enough room for Peter as well as a good amount of supplies."

"Supplies?" Peter asked.

"You can't get over to Longbranch without something to help you afterward. You'll need to have a change of clothes, some food, water, and other necessities. You can't get to the mainland dressed like we are on the island."

"But where are we going to get those things?"

"Don't worry, Peter, we have all that stored away. I've kept my own clothing from when I was captured. You should fit into them just fine. You have your own clothes from when you arrived. The other things we will get from the rest of the colony." Patrick turned to Paul, "Hide the boat again until tonight. We'll come here about five and have Peter launch then."

Paul reached up and grabbed a rope made of woven vines. He pulled hard against the rope and a massive branch bent toward the ground. With a stick, he secured it to a notch in a large, fallen tree. With a few other branches, Paul secreted the boat behind the camouflage.

"I'm impressed," Jack declared. "That's some good engineering."

Paul smiled at the complement, "Thanks," he said sheepishly.

"Now let's get back to camp. Paul, lead the way," Patrick said as he stood with Peter. He reached up and grabbed Peter by the arm. "Wait a minute," he said.

"What?" Peter questioned.

"Shhh." Patrick watched as Jack and Paul moved out of earshot, then he motioned for Peter to follow. "I don't want them to hear what I'm going to tell you."

"What is it?"

"It's about the Shadow Remnant." Patrick's voice grew quick and he lessened his voice to nearly a whisper. He looked around as if he suspected that something might jump out from behind a tree.

"Go ahead, dad," Peter said, "I don't think that anyone is going to hear you out here."

Patrick smiled, "I hope you're right." The two men continued to walk at a safe distance from Jack and Paul. "There was a time when your mother and I were a part of the Remnant. We were with Joshua when he went to D.C. We wanted to take the message we had to the people in power, but we failed to realize that it was the people in power who suppressed the truth. Our efforts failed and we were captured."

"Why are you telling me this?"

"Because I don't want you to make the same mistake I did. I don't want you to try and 'fix' the problems that we have in our country. One man's voice is not enough to get the attention of our government." Patrick spoke with hints of desperation. "Son, if you try to help us, you'll only get yourself killed."

Peter walked thoughtfully along as he mulled his father's words. "So, do you think I should do what Joshua did? Should I just find a place to disappear and live a simple life?"

"Joshua did what he could and he paid a heavy price for his faith."

Peter hung his head, "I'm sorry. It just seems that you're telling me to give up and hide. I don't want to leave you and Paul here in this place."

Patrick looked compassionately at his son. "You need to understand that any chance to change the government won't come from direct intervention with the ruling powers. The only way to change this country and put it back on course is to get the message to the people." Patrick stepped over a fallen tree as they navigated through the woods. Then he stopped and pulled Peter in front of him. "If you make it to Longbranch, find a man called Henderson. He was a part of our team and he can help you disappear. He was the one who set Joshua up on the farm and if he's still around, he can get you set up as well."

The two walked in silence the rest of the way to the colony. The slow-falling snow dotted the air and swirled with every slight breeze. Peter was glad that there was no wind. A rowboat in Puget Sound would be hard enough; to row with a wind against him might be impossible.

When they arrived at the campsite, the colony was buzzing with activity. Men guarded the entrance and several patrols were out in the woods. The campfire blazed with intense heat and many women worked on the evening meal. The air was thick with tension and from what Peter observed, not one person offered a smile or friendly greeting.

Peter and Patrick found Jack standing near the fire with Paul at his side. His hands flailed as he spoke with Young Tom. Tom stood beside Jack, his arm in a sling and head bandaged.

"What happened?" Patrick demanded as he approached Jack and Tom.

Tom turned to speak but Jack spoke up first, "The colony was attacked by the gang! That... that... spy must have told them where we were before he was found out!" Jack's teeth were clenched as he spoke, fighting back his rage. "I should have been here," Jack lamented. "I had no business traipsing through the woods with you when I was needed here."

"How could you know, Jack," Patrick said. "We didn't know that an attack was coming and it looks like the people handled it."

Peter looked around, "Where's Crystal?"

Jack sighed, "I don't know. She was gone when I got back."

"I think she's on a patrol," Tom added.

"I had hoped to say goodbye, but I don't have time to wait for her to return." Peter sighed and went to his shelter. He found his rucksack and grabbed his old clothes—a pair of jeans, his tattered shirt and a pair of tennis shoes. With a heavy heart, Peter looked around the cramped quarters. Now that he intended to leave, he was reluctant to do so. He had come to know his father again, discovered he had a brother, and found he might be able to live his life without the comforts of civilization. Now he had to throw all of it away in the slim hope of escaping.

He sat down and put his head in his hands. The words of his father lingered in his thoughts. *Don't try and fix it.* Now that he knew about his father and brother, his mind raced with the hope of finding a way to rescue them. Sitting alone, he hatched several schemes, but as he mentally traced their potential, each one ended in bitter ruin. Maybe his father was right, maybe he needed to leave well enough alone and find a way to simply live his life. The thought left a bitter taste in his mouth.

"Pete!" Patrick's voice rushed into the small chamber.

Peter stepped out of the shelter and spotted his father near the fire. Patrick waived at him and signaled that he wanted him to come. The snow was now almost six inches deep and he trudged through it with a heavy heart. His feet dragged along, streaking the snow with long troughs after every step. The sun waned into dusk and he knew that his time had come.

"Pete," Patrick said, "we've collected a good amount of food and gear for your trip. We've sent a couple of the men with Paul to load the boat. You have at least a week's worth of food and water, longer if you are careful with it. There is a hunter's knife, some rope, extra clothes, one box of matches and some candles. Longbranch is sparsely populated so you should not run into any patrols."

"What about this man named... what was it... Henderson?"

"I left you directions to his location. He's not easy to find but when you do, tell him you were with me."

"Dad," Peter hesitated. "I think you need to know, I don't want to leave you here. I just got you back! I tried to get to you for eight years and now I have to leave. It's... well... it's just not fair."

Patrick gave him a knowing, sympathetic smile. "I told you, son, don't try to rescue us. Fighting against the ruling powers will only land you in a situation that is unwinnable. The best thing you can do for me is to get into a situation where you can live your life. It will give me great comfort to know that you are free."

"But what about Paul?" Peter's voice trembled with frustration and concern.

"What about him?" Patrick's tone was matter-of-fact.

Peter stepped to the fire and warmed his hands, "Paul should have a chance to live outside this imprisonment. If I take him with me, he and I can find a way to manage our lives together."

Patrick smiled, his love for his son warm in his eyes. "I appreciate that, Peter. But Paul and I have already spoken of this and he wants to remain here. He is still too young. He needs to be in familiar surroundings."

Peter nodded, but his heart raced in protest. "But dad isn't it better for him to have a life off the island?"

Patrick moved to stand next to Peter, placing his hand on his son's shoulder. "Think about it," he said. "He is not much younger than you were when we were taken from you. How did you feel? You told me that you tried to do everything you could to find us. I don't think it would be fair to Paul if he had to grow up without at least one parent."

"No," Peter agreed, "you're right. I guess I sort of hoped that I wouldn't be separated from my family all over again."

"You can choose to stay here," Patrick offered. "There's a chance that they will never find you."

Peter thought about the prospect. Silence filled the space between them like a vacuum. "No," he said with regret. A tear fell from his cheek as he wiped his eyes. "The risk for others is too great for me to stay." He turned away from the fire and threw his bag on his shoulder.

He gave a parting glance at the campsite. The patrols were still out, many others dispersed to their chores and some of the more senior members of the colony sat nearby. The red light of dusk filtered through the trees and emblazoned the clouds with its fire. No wind stirred through the boughs and the stillness brought and eerie calm to Peter's thoughts.

"It's now or never, son," Patrick said.

Peter took a deep breath and resigned himself to the task. "You're right. Let's get out of here." They walked out of the campsite and Peter sensed every eye in the camp watched him as they entered the woods.

With all the people that had gone to the boat, it was easy to follow the clearly marked trail in the snow. Shadows grew through the woods as if the night hurried to fill in the forest. The two men tripped and shuffled their way through the trees. Peter, for fear of being followed, listened intently for any indication of gang activity. Occasionally showers of snow fell from branches and the trees responded in creaks and groans, echoing their displeasure of the wintery covering. With each rush of snow, Peter jumped.

"Don't let your nerves get the best of you, son," Patrick said. "You're going to need all your energy to get across the channel."

Peter nodded in response. Still he listened.

"Son, what is it?" Patrick spoke softly.

"Dad," Peter whispered, "I think we're being followed."

Peter crouched down and pulled his father after him. He looked back and thought he saw the figure of a man dash between two trees about fifty yards away. Peter pointed in the direction of the dark figure. "There!" he whispered, his voice pitched with apprehension.

"I don't see anything," Patrick said. "Are you sure that it's just not the shadows playing tricks on you?"

Peter took a deep, silent breath. "I hope so," he said.

Patrick touched his son on the shoulder. "Let's go. The quicker we get to the boat the better."

The chill air bit like a thousand needles on Peter's exposed skin and the snow caked upon the base of his pants. Both men stood and brushed off the snow from their trousers and moved just a bit faster through the dwindling day. Peter kept his head in constant motion, always glancing back the way they came. Despite his vigilance, he didn't see the shadowy figure again.

They arrived at the shore and was met by the tangy scent of saltwater and kelp. The tide was out, well beyond the massive driftwood and flotsam that had washed up over the years. Old bottles, fishing nets, and a line of dry, green seaweed marked the previous high tide. The sun had set well behind the island and only the trailing, filtered light of dusk illuminated the crimson sky. Long, wispy clouds streaked the heavens like random brush strokes on a dark canvas. One contrail marked the passage of some unseen aircraft.

At the edge of the water Paul stood with three other men. The boat sat near the edge, waiting for the one great launch that would establish its place in history. Peter walked toward them, sloshing through the sandy mud of low tide. Patrick kept pace with him and they arrived at the small craft. Two oars rested against the gunwale and a dark brown tarp covered unseen provisions at the bow.

"You better get in, son, it's time to launch," Patrick observed, his voice wavering.

"I will," Peter said, "It's just hard to say goodbye."

"At least this time, we actually have the chance to say goodbye. And now we both know that we're okay."

Paul rushed up to Peter, arms wide as he nearly knocked his brother over. "Pete," he sobbed, "I love you."

Paul's words gripped Peter's heart and he felt the angst in his chest. Tears fell freely as he held his brother. "You take care of dad, now." Peter pulled away and bent down to look Paul in the eye. He hugged him again and tried to fill his heart with his brother's embrace. "I will see you again," he whispered.

Paul tightened his grip and shook as he wept. "You... you better g-get going," he sobbed. "You don't want to miss the tide."

Peter let his brother go and grabbed the boat's stern. With a heave, he shoved the craft into the water and the small waves lapped at the prow. He splashed in ankle deep then quickly stepped into the boat. With one oar, he continued to shove against the sandy floor. When he could not touch the bottom, he placed both oars into their respective brackets. He sat on the middle plank and faced the stern as the current began to pull him into deeper water.

On the shore, now more than fifty yards away, the small group of colonists waved at him. The sun had disappeared beyond the horizon and only the remnants of daylight remained. The sky deepened into a cold, black cloth marked by the speckled dots of stars. Peter squinted and thought he noticed figures of men rushing out of the forest. The colonists stood like silhouetted statues, unaware of the danger that ran up behind them.

"Look out!" Peter shouted as his voice echoed across the water. He was now more than a hundred yards off shore and began to turn around.

"What are you doing!" demanded a voice from underneath the tarp.

Peter dropped both oars and nearly jumped in the water. The tarp moved, pulled back, and out popped Crystal.

Crystal smiled with a Cheshire-cat grin. "You can't go back now," she insisted. "If you do, you'll miss your chance to get off this blasted island... and so would I."

Peter stammered as his heart raced with the excitement, "I... I have to get back there to help them!" He looked again at the fading island behind him. "They've been ambushed — I'm sure it's the gang."

"Sit down and row," Crystal ordered. "They've been ambushed before. You're dad can handle it. Right now we need to get to that buoy marker and make sure we're across at six o'clock."

"But my brother," Peter protested.

"By the time we get back, it'll be over. You can't do anything for them now — except get off this island." Crystal bundled up the tarp, revealing a treasure of food and provisions for them. She nudged the items aside and sat at the bow, crunched down with her arms around her knees.

Peter returned to the task and glided the small watercraft across the narrow channel. He watched for and spotted the buoy, a brilliant green light flashing at the top. "Won't you be missed?" he asked.

"I don't care," she said. "I've been prisoner on that chunk of real estate for too long."

"But what about Jack, he is going to lose his mind with worry about you. You should have seen him when you were captured."

"Don't worry about him. Paul knew about my plans and he will tell them in due time. He's a good kid, a lot like his dad." Crystal squirmed to find a more comfortable position.

Peter smiled. "Well, you're right about that! He is a lot like dad," he said. He paused, thoughtful about his family. "I've got to do something to save them."

"You can't do anything about it now. But I'll tell you what," Crystal said, "you concentrate on rowing this thing across the Sound and, if we make it out alive, we'll work on it."

He smiled in the darkness. He was glad to have her company, but he didn't want to tell her that. He forced the oars against the current and continued to move the boat to the middle of the channel. *Someday*, he thought, *someday soon*.

They neared the marker. Peter heard the water splash against it as it bobbed and dipped in rhythm with the waves. The green light flashed with a piercing glow in the deep darkness. "What time is it?" he asked.

"Soon," Crystal said. "It's nearly six o'clock." She looked up over the bow. "I think this is close enough."

Peter fought with the oars to keep the boat from drifting. "I need your help," he panted, "I can't keep it steady."

Crystal immediately sat up behind him and placed her hands on the oars. Together they waited for what seemed to Peter like an eternity. Suddenly the light on the buoy turned bright red.

"Now!" Crystal shouted.

With great effort both Peter and Crystal fought the oars against the water. One second… two seconds… three seconds and they were side-by-side with the marker. Four… five… six and the boat was past. Seven… eight… nine…

Ten! Suddenly the light turned green again.

They continued rowing until they were at least fifty yards away. Panting with exhaustion, they let down the oars and both slumped down. Peter looked back at the bobbing green light in the water. "Well," he said, "I guess we made it."

CHAPTER TEN

"The enemy boasted, 'I will pursue, I will overtake them...'" ~ Exodus 15:9

Water lapped softly against the hull of the small boat. The craft swayed in gentle cadence to the motion of the waves. The rhythm of the water, coupled with the great exertion it took to get off the island, made Peter very sleepy. Now, in the middle of a narrow channel of Puget Sound, a cold breeze whispered across the surface and sent chills over his sweat-soaked body.

The clouds had drifted to the west and exposed the night sky in glorious splendor. Stars beyond count filled the great expanse of heaven as if the diamond mines of all the earth erupted in one great expulsion of brilliance. In the distance, and growing closer with every stroke of the oars, the Longbranch peninsula stretched out like a dark shadow surrounded by a reflection pool. An occasional light pierced the night from some unseen home or a passing vehicle.

Crystal returned to the bow and hunkered down as low as possible to get out of the frigid breeze. Peter heard her shivering and was determined to get her to land and get a fire started. He heaved on the oars, muscles burning in pain. The cold sapped his energy, but he forced himself to continue.

"I th-th-think we're almost th-there." Crystal spoke through chattering teeth.

"I know," Peter said, "hang on a bit longer and we'll be on shore." He turned and looked toward the peninsula. He guessed it was less than two hundred yards away.

His hands ached and he wondered if they might not be permanently curved around the oars. It felt as if every muscle in his body screamed against the cold and the effort to row. He shifted in his seat to try and keep his legs from growing stiff. Ice chinked off his trousers and rattled on the floor of the boat. Oh great, he thought, I'm freezing up.

"Wh-what's that?" Crystal asked.

Peter looked up and watched as a light flashed back and forth, reflected upon the water. The whir of an engine echoed through the frigid air. To his untrained eye, he guessed that the searchlight was about a thousand yards away on the island's side of the barrier.

"It looks like a searchlight," Peter said. His heart raced with the possibility of a patrol boat on the water looking for them. "I don't think they're after us," he said, desperate to still his own nerves. "They're still close to the island, moving along the perimeter—as far as I can tell." With renewed vigor, however, he rowed harder, eager to get to shore.

"We w-won't be able to l-light a f-f-fire when we g-get to sh-shore." Crystal's words trailed off as she stuttered through the cold. Her teeth chattered and whole body shook.

"Nonsense," Peter replied. "We'll get inland and hide in the woods. No patrol boat will find us once we're on shore." He looked back over the water and noticed that the light had gone farther north. Waves began to grow with intensity, rocking the boat like a cork as he fought to keep a steady rhythm. He glanced over his shoulder to the shoreline of Longbranch and, under the watchful glow of a billion stars, he saw the beach.

He then looked down at Crystal. Her eyes were closed and legs pulled tight against her chest. She held her legs, wrapped in her arms, and leaned her head against a small bundle of provisions. Peter's heart skipped a beat as panic welled up in his throat like a fire. "Crystal… Crystal!" he demanded. He dropped an oar and reached for her. "C'mon, wake up!" he commanded as he shook her leg. Her trousers were cold and stiff with ice.

Waves slapped against the boat as Peter forsook the other oar and spun around to face her. Unresponsive, Crystal lay in the bow with no more movement than the provisions she nestled against. With both hands he stretched her legs over the middle seat. Desperate and now fearful that Crystal had succumbed to hypothermia, he rapidly tried to rub warmth back into her limbs.

Her eyes fluttered and body trembled. She looked up at Peter with a glazed, confused stare, eyes sluggishly looking back and forth. "Where are we?" she asked, her voice a mere, hoarse whisper.

"We're almost on shore," Peter's voice cracked with worry. Then, without warning, the boat ground to a stop. Peter glanced up and realized that the current had pushed them almost on shore. Water beat against the stern and with each wave's crest they inched closer to the sandy beach. He looked over the starboard edge and saw that they had grounded on a small spit of sand nearly thirty yards from the forest.

Without thought, he jumped out of the vessel and splashed nearly knee deep in the salty currents. He felt the tide pull against him, but as adrenaline rushed through his veins, he was not going to be deterred. Sloshing through the water, he grabbed the bow and forced the boat through the sandy shoal. Exhausted and cold, he stepped onto dry ground, the boat tight in his grip.

Crystal had roused enough to understand her situation. "I... I can't seem to move my legs," she said.

Peter scanned the surroundings, eyes wide as he studied the situation. Across the water a light flashed back and forth. The patrol boat had returned. He was too far to hear the motor, but knew instinctively that they were on the prowl for him. *It won't be long*, he thought, *before they figure out what happened*. He looked down at Crystal who slowly crept back to life from some frostbitten half-death she experienced. The forest was still twenty yards away.

Without thinking, he stepped to the side of the boat and hefted Crystal in his arms. She didn't protest, but leaned her weight against him and wrapped her arms around his neck. "Don't worry," he whispered, "I've got you." She offered a faint smile as Peter stepped as quickly as possible to reach the protection of the forest. His heart beat like an iron hammer against the anvil of his chest as his mind raced with prayers.

He stepped through the sand and made his way toward the woods. The brilliant starlight gave dim illumination. He spotted a path that wound into the forest and disappeared behind a large fallen tree. Exhaustion stole his balance and he stumbled as he tried to step over a thin branch of driftwood. Together they tumbled into the thick undergrowth, whipped by frozen limbs and dusted in snow.

Peter drug himself to his knees. Crystal lay beside him, face down as she struggled to try and regain some control of her limbs. She pressed against the hard ground with her hands and her arms shook as if she suffered through her own personal earthquake. Branches and vines arched over them like a canopy. He crawled over to Crystal and helped her to her knees. With laborious motion, they inched their way to the shelter of the fallen tree.

"Stay here," Peter said. "I'm gonna get our gear and try to build a fire."

Crystal nodded and Peter climbed over the trunk and moved as quickly as his sore muscles allowed back to the boat. The night had grown colder and though he thought it might have been only seven o'clock, the evening darkness had deepened. The small silver crescent of the waning moon offered little illumination.

He managed to get to the boat. Several bags were tightly pressed against the bow, each having a strap, so he hoisted the items onto his shoulder and pushed the boat back into the water. The small craft drifted with the incoming tide and disappeared beyond his sight. He hoped that wherever it landed might mislead any search party.

Then he glanced out over the channel. The lights on McNeil Island reflected against the still waters of Puget Sound. The island sat over a half-mile away, but even at this distance Peter noticed several lights rushing back and forth upon the beach. The boat that had scoured the channel earlier had crossed beyond the buoy. Its spotlight flashed against the water, scanning in every possible direction. With each passing second the boat moved closer to Longbranch.

Peter's heart raced as he kept his eyes on the spotlight. It moved closer, still panning back and forth across the water, and he knew they searched for him. He had to disregard his own panic and get back to Crystal. He hoped the incoming tide would dispel his footprints as he clambered back to the tree.

Crystal sat leaning against the fallen log. He sat down and ravaged through the packs until he found what he wanted, a box of wooden matches. With as much haste as he could muster, Peter scavenged branches, twigs and dried leaves. He scraped the ground clear of snow and ripped out a small patch of undergrowth to form a bare spot on the ground. With eagerness, he piled the tinder into a heap and took out a match. His entire body shook in waves as the cold bit against him. Focused by desperation, Peter calmed his trembling hands and struck fire to the match.

He protected the small flame with his hand like a hen guarding her only chick and slowly lowered the miniscule blaze to the pile. It sparked, flashed and finally ignited into a small fire. Peter bent down and gently blew against the glowing embers. *Whoosh!* The tinder caught and erupted into a brilliant campfire.

Crystal looked through half-closed eyes and offered a slight grin. "Well, you did it," she whispered.

Peter nodded, "C'mon now, get closer to this fire and you'll start to warm up." He added more fuel to the blaze. The fallen tree helped to contain the heat in their small campsite and both Peter and Crystal sat with their backs against it. Soon the warmth of the flames broke through the icy layers of clothes and touched his skin.

Crystal began to move with greater ease and stretched out her legs. "I hope I don't have frostbite." She pulled at her boots and freed her feet from their frosty confines.

"Well," Peter asked, "can you feel your toes?"

"Yeah," Crystal sighed with some relief. "They hurt, but they're okay." She rubbed her legs vigorously, "I just want to be warm."

"I know," Peter agreed. "But once you're able, we need to get off this spit of land and move farther inland. There was a patrol boat on the water, and I think they're looking for us."

"Figures," Crystal lamented. "Just when you think you're safe."

"I set the rowboat adrift. It might be that they'll find it and not us."

"Perhaps," Crystal said as she moved to sit up. "But I don't think we ought to count on it."

Peter nodded. He decided to take a look over the tree. With care, he crept to the top of the log and peered through the heavy branches. The crescent moon gave little light, but he was able to see the beach and the reflective water. The tide had come in more and it seemed to him as if half the beach had been washed away. The channel reflected the flashing buoy as waves lapped against the shore. Far to his left, perhaps a mile down the channel, a dim flash of light crossed the water.

"Well," Crystal demanded.

Peter stepped down from his perch. "I think they're on the far side of the island right now. There was a flash of light, a spotlight, about a mile away."

Crystal took a deep breath and sighed, "Well that's a relief."

"How are you feeling?"

She stretched her arms and legs, nearly putting her feet in the small campfire. "I'm stiff, but I think I'll live."

Peter didn't say it, but he feared that his campfire might act as a brilliant beacon to expose their location.

"Peter," Crystal said, "you worry too much."

"Oh, and you can read minds?"

"Nope," she chuckled, "just expressions. When your brows furrow like that and your eyes get narrow, I know you're worried." She sat up and reclaimed her boots from near the fire. "Ah," she said, "these are warm." She turned her head toward the packs that lay in the snow. "What's in them… anything to eat?"

Peter grabbed the bags and rummaged through them. "Let's see," he said. He pulled a wrapped bundle out of the first and unrolled a large quantity of dried meat. Another bag contained an assortment of cold vegetables: carrots, beets and potatoes. The third bag held some small cooking pots. "I think we can cook up a bit of stew," Peter observed. He quickly gathered some large stones for the pot while Crystal packed the cookware with snow. Peter then cast more wood upon the campfire and a shower of embers rose up in response.

Soon the fire was strong, warm and filled their little camp with a gentle, flickering orange light. The snow in the pot had melted and began to boil. Peter offered the provisions to the water and almost immediately the savory scent filled the air. While their dinner simmered, Peter rummaged through the packs and found two wooden spoons and two serrated hunting knives with leather sheaths. He handed one of the knives to Crystal and strapped the other to his belt.

The meal was ready and they ate together the hardy, rich stew. Peter savored the warmth as it coursed down his throat and radiated through his entire body. "Ahh," he declared, "that's good." A heavy breeze wafted up from the Sound and sent the light of their campfire dancing upon the trees.

"So," Crystal observed, "what do we do now?"

Peter fished through the bags again. "Clothes, matches, cooking gear," he muttered to himself. "Where is it?"

"Where is what?"

"My dad said that he left information for us. We need to find a man named Henderson; he can get us to a place of safety. He did it for Joshua and my dad thinks he can do it again."

"What good is that going to be?" Crystal demanded. "That won't help the people we left behind!"

"I know, I know." Peter sat up and looked at his travel companion. "But it gives us a start. Dad said that this man belonged to a group called the Shadow Remnant. From what I understand, they wanted to change things… to restore freedom."

"Well," Crystal said, "I don't know much about that. I've been trapped all my life. All I know is that Jack and the others are still prisoners and we are the only ones to make it off of McNeil alive." Crystal stood and stretched her arms above her head.

"Is the stiffness gone?" Peter asked.

"Yeah," she took a deep breath, "I feel fine." She walked around the fire, warming her hands. "Perhaps this Henderson will have an idea of how we can rescue our friends."

Peter continued to rummage through the packs. He grabbed his own knapsack and pillaged through it as well. He touched the old Bible and the words of his father ruminated through his mind, *don't try and fix it.* "I have to try," he said to himself.

"Try what?" Crystal raised an eyebrow.

Peter pulled out the book, pages yellowed and crisp. He carefully thumbed through it and found the text he sought. He looked up at Crystal, then back down at the pages to read, "It is for freedom that Christ has set you free."

"What's that suppose to mean?" Crystal asked.

Peter glanced back up at her, "I'm not sure, exactly. But we have been set free and I believe that it is because of Jesus. Frank became a Christian and now we're free. If we have been set free by Christ, we've been set free for a reason. I should have been dead when the patrol shot me. I should have been killed on the island and we should not be standing here, escaped from the one place no one ever leaves." His eyes narrowed as he thought. Then, as if a revelation struck him, he turned to Crystal. "Tell me, what was the reason the guards wanted me dead?"

Crystal took a deep breath. "Frank said that rumors of a Peter Sheridan were rampant. Your name was in the news. The tale of your escape from the Darrington Center was growing. From what the guards had mentioned, they believed you were some great instigator of rebellion, a leader in this thing you call the Shadow Remnant. They wanted your dead body to prove to the people that no one escapes their judgment."

Peter smiled a simple, clever smile. "If that's what they expect, perhaps that what I need to be," he said. He continued to flip the pages of the Bible when a loose piece of paper slid to the edge. Looking down, Peter turned to the page and discovered a note. He unfolded the stained parchment and began to read:

Peter,

If you're reading this note, you have made it off the island. I want you to know how absolutely proud I am of you. I am sorry that our time was so short, but you made the right decision to escape. It gives me great joy to know that you will have the chance to live beyond the confines of this prison. To that end, I know what you're thinking. You want to do whatever it will take to free us and you think that Henderson might be able to help. Remember why I'm here. Any effort to change the mind of the government is futile. You will find Henderson near the beach. There is a small island between McNeil and Longbranch. Henderson lives about a mile north of that location. Get there and have him help you set up your life outside of watching eyes. One more thing, tell Crystal that Jack knows she is with you – he knew all along that she would stow away. I love you, son.

Crystal looked up at Peter, her eyes moist with tears. "I could never fool him," she said.

Peter found his own heart gripped with sorrow. He cast the note in the fire and it instantly flamed into ash. Just then the sound of a motor rumbled up from the beach. Peter crawled over the fallen tree and watched a patrol boat skimming across the water not more than three hundred yards away.

"What is it?" Crystal demanded.

"A boat," he voiced his strongest whisper. "Keep your voice down and douse that fire."

Quickly she kicked snow and dirt upon the flames. Smoke and steam hissed in the cold and drifted lazily through the overhanging bows. As the flames died, she grabbed all their provisions and pressed them into the bags. The sound of the motor grew louder as the craft neared the shore. Peter put the Bible back into his knapsack and picked up another of the three bags. Crystal picked up the remaining pack and both jaunted deeper into the woods.

"Do you know where we're going?" Crystal asked.

"No, but away from the beach can't be a bad start. We'll make our way north when we're inland a bit." Peter didn't turn to look, but he heard Crystal's footsteps close behind him.

The slim moonlight was no help in the dense forest. Peter stumbled and shuffled through the snow-covered flora. He thought he spotted an old animal path that turned north and began to follow it. It ended at an insurmountable wall of blackberry briars. He turned to the left and tried to circumnavigate the barrier.

Together they plodded, slow and steady. The terrain opened up a bit and Peter glanced down to see that they walked upon an old, paved road. Overgrown and abandoned, it provided easier travel for them. Long-forgotten houses lingered along the road like ancient skeletons of earlier times. Their failed and rotted wood still sat upon concrete foundations but no house remained intact.

"This reminds me of Darrington," Peter observed.

"Oh," Crystal said, "what a miserable place."

"It was, but the signs of better times still haunt the old houses and buildings. Like here," he pointed to one, dark blue two-story home. A rusted, chain-link fence surrounded the property and a massive willow tree draped its swaying branches nearly to the ground as if it covered its own face in shame. The grass was overgrown and briars dominated the southern portion of the front yard.

"I don't see what you're looking at?" Crystal said.

"Well, just imagine it," he said. "This house used to be the home of some family. Children played in this yard and laughter was heard across this fence. I can imagine that there were some good times that this house might remember."

"Perhaps you're right," she said. "But I've never known a life like that and I know that you haven't either."

Peter nodded and they both walked on in silence. They passed the ghostly houses that whispered in eerie voices as the wind blew through the broken windows and frames. Shutters slapped and an occasional hinge creaked in despair. Peter thought that if houses could talk, this might be what abandoned ones would say.

"I think we need to get back to the beach," Peter said. "We've walked far enough to be near that island." He was reluctant to leave the easy passage of the road they followed but turned to his right and began to step through the trees. Branches slapped at him and released small showers of snow. Crystal followed close behind as they made their way back to the rocky shore. The scent of salt permeated the air and the breeze grew increasingly colder. Through the trees Peter spotted the glint of water sparkling in the moonlight. A hedge stood before him. He crouched behind it and peered over the top to see if he might spot the patrol boat.

"It seems quiet," Crystal observed.

"Yes, but I'm not letting up my guard just yet. That boat was close to the beach when we came inland and I'm sure they must have seen the campfire. I just hope that they don't know how to follow someone through the woods." Peter stood up and walked around the hedgerow.

The tide had nearly made it to its highest point. A gust of wind wafted up from Puget Sound and bit into his skin. He shivered in the cold and wished that his recent circumstances had taken place in summer. Waves lapped against the shore and both he and Crystal stepped onto the beach.

Just north of their location, more than a thousand feet into the sound, sat a small island. McNeil Island was farther beyond and the channel opened up to the north. "Okay," Peter said as he looked out at the island, "we keep moving north."

Crystal remained silent as she stood like a statue, staring at McNeil Island.

"Crystal," Peter said. "Crystal, what is it?"

"I just never thought that I would look upon the island from this side," she observed. "I always wondered what I would feel if I ever escaped."

146

"Well," Peter asked, "what *do* you feel?"

"It's strange," she said, "but I feel homesick."

"Wow," Peter exclaimed, "that is strange."

"I lived there since I was four years old. Now I'm looking at it from the outside. I was brought there with my family and then I lost them. Jack took me in and now I've lost him." Crystal wiped a tear from her eye. "I've got to get them off that rock," she whispered.

Peter reached out and touched her arm. "C'mon, Crystal, let's get moving."

They stepped onto the beach and turned north. The coarse, pebbly beach hindered their speed, but was easier to navigate than the rough, wooden terrain. Peter kept his eyes searching the channel for any sign of pursuit, but he saw no boat on the water and no sound carried on the air.

They had traveled about a mile when the beach curved inland and opened up into a small cove. Clouds drifted in from the west and obscured the moon in a hazy, wispy blanket while soft snowflakes fell in lazy descent. The snow lighted upon Peter's cheek like the silent touch of Jack Frost. In any other situation, Peter might have delighted in the winter-like weather. But on an unknown beach with the possibility of being recaptured, he simply grumbled under his breath.

"Well, well," Crystal observed, "are you loosing your temper?"

Peter took a deep breath. "No, it's just this unrelenting cold." He looked toward the forest. "We should be near the place dad mentioned. Henderson has to be around here somewhere. Maybe we need to get back to the woods."

"Okay," Crystal said. "At least we will be away from the water and under some cover."

They turned inland and clambered over several large pieces of driftwood. A small path wound through the debris and they followed it into the thick stand of trees. The snow began to fall heavier and the moon was completely hidden behind thick clouds. Peter struggled to see his way through the woods and found that the branches and dense foliage grasped his clothes and tangled his feet.

Without warning, a bright light blinded Peter and Crystal. Dazzled by the intensity, he covered his eyes and fell backwards into her. They both tumbled to the ground as he tried to reach for his knife.

"Keep your hands in sight," a graveled voice said from behind the light. "Don't make any sudden moves."

"Who are you?" Peter asked.

"None of your business," the shadowed voice said. "I've put up with trouble makers long enough to know how to deal with the likes of you. Now tell me who you are and what are you doing on my property?"

"My name," Peter stammered, "is Peter... Peter Sheridan. My father, Patrick, told me to find a man named Henderson who lived near this cove."

"You're lying!" The voice rebuked. "Patrick's gone and Peter's dead."

"No," Peter replied, "I am Peter and we just escaped from McNeil Island. My dad's there... he's been there for ten years." Peter stood to his feet and helped Crystal up. "He told me to find a man named Henderson who helped a friend of mine—Joshua Eberhardt."

The light went out and Peter was once again blind to the environment. He heard footsteps draw closer. Then the light came on again, this time not as bright and pointed at the ground. Before him stood an old man, wrinkled on every inch of skin, with eyes set like stone. He was shorter than Peter by four inches and held a small handgun in his fist, pointed at the ground.

"Do you know where we can find a man named Henderson?" Peter asked.

The old man took a deep breath. "Yes," he said, "yes I do. In fact, young man, you're looking at him."

Peter's eyes widened. "Mr. Henderson?"

"No," the old man smiled, "it's Dr. Henderson."

CHAPTER ELEVEN

"Do not forsake your friend and the friend of your father..." ~ Proverbs 27:10

The glow of Henderson's flashlight moved in arrhythmic motion as the old man stumbled up the narrow path. Peter and Crystal followed at a slight distance, careful to navigate around the driftwood that bordered the edge of the forest. Between two massive logs that had washed up on shore some years before, the trail disappeared into a dense copse of trees.

Peter marveled at how quickly Henderson moved through the woods. "Hey," he called out, "give us a chance to catch up."

Henderson turned around and pointed the light at Peter. "Be quiet," he demanded in a hoarse whisper. "We're not safe yet." He turned and shone the light again on the trail as he moved deeper into the woods.

Peter sighed in exasperation but did as he was instructed. He kept his eyes upon the ground, careful to step along the path. The snows that had fallen gave the scene a soft, tranquil glow as

151

he continued to follow. He looked up and did a double take when he watched Henderson disappear from sight! No light, no glow, no sign of his passage. Henderson was gone.

Crystal ran up to Peter. "Where did he go?"

"I... I don't know," Peter stammered. He stared ahead at where he had last seen the old man. Henderson's footprints were clearly marked in the snowy path where he stood. However, as he looked intently up the pathway, the footprints simply stopped. Curiosity mixed with anxiety as Peter carefully walked ahead.

Snow crunched under his feet as he studied the trail. Then Henderson simply appeared out of thin air. Crystal gasped and held back a scream while Peter jumped back. The old man looked at the two, brows furrowed and eyes narrowed. He carried the flashlight low and pointed its beam at the ground. Peter regained his composure and tried to calm his racing heart.

"Would you two hurry up!" Henderson whispered. He turned and walked away, and disappeared.

Peter and Crystal looked at each other in bewilderment. With care, Peter stepped up the path to where he had seen Henderson. With one hand he reached out in front of him. Fingers, hand and then his arm vanished as if they never belonged to his body. With a start, he drew his arm back and his hand and fingers were whole. He wiggled his fingers in front of his face just to make sure that all was in order. With a deep breath, he stepped forward.

A brilliant shimmer, with all the colors of the spectrum, dazzled his eyes. It lasted only a fraction of a second, then, in contrast to the dark, dense forest, he found himself standing on an open path with a ribbon of light on either side of a narrow, winding walkway. At the end of the path a large, two-story house rose in regal splendor. A gabled double door stood open, surrounded by a large, pillared deck. Lanterns, held upon thin, round poles, burned with a gentle white light at each corner of the deck. Snow-covered trellises were wrapped with thick vines at the far end of the house. Two out-buildings stood separated by at least thirty yards from each other and the main home. Between the out-buildings the remnants of a garden lingered, with rows of old corn stalks standing like spears in the earth and four large tripods wrapped with the remains of some unknown vegetation.

Without warning, Peter was hit from behind. He pitched forward and fell, catching a glimpse of Crystal as she tumbled to the ground beside him. His reached out his hands to brace himself and struck the cold stone path sending a shockwave of pain up his arms. He rolled, and then lifted himself to his knees. "What were you doing?" he demanded.

Crystal had landed on her side and tried to stand with as much dignity as she could muster. She brushed her trousers and then her hands. "You… well… you just vanished! I thought you had gone farther up the trail and I ran after you."

"You panicked," Peter said.

"I don't panic!" Crystal huffed. "You might have been in trouble and needed me to rescue you."

Peter brushed off his hands as blood oozed from abrasions on his palms. "Yeah… that must have been it." He looked at her from under his brow and shook his head.

Henderson stood on the deck of the house, waving eagerly for Peter and Crystal. Peter stood to his feet and walked toward the house. Crystal followed behind. He grinned as he listened to her protesting her innocence under her breath.

The wood creaked as Peter stepped onto the deck. The door stood open and a warm breath of air brushed his cheek. Memories of Joshua's home flooded his thoughts as he looked upon the pleasant house that stood before him.

Crystal stepped up and nudged him aside as she pressed her way to Henderson. "Okay, doctor, what is this place?" Her words were sharp as she stood with her hands on her hips.

"I'd prefer it if we'd go inside," Henderson said with little concern. "But if you want to remain on the porch, you're welcome to do so." He turned and walked through the door into the house.

Peter followed him in and gave Crystal a disapproving glare as he passed her. She rolled her eyes and followed.

The room was warm and bright. A long counter filled the back wall, ending at a stainless steel sink in the corner. An island cook-top made of brick stood in the center of the kitchen. An oval oak table with four matching chairs sat separated from the rest of the room. Papers were strewn across the surface like fallout from a clerk's office. An archway that led into the remainder of the house stood on the opposite wall.

Crystal entered behind him and dropped the pack she carried. "Wow," she said. "This place is amazing."

Henderson stood at the table, stooped over as he examined some of the papers that littered the top. He glanced up at the two travelers. "Why don't you two get cleaned up and rest a bit. You're safe here, for now." He motioned for them to follow as he walked through the archway.

Peter set his pack down but slung his knapsack that contained the Bible over his shoulder. "What is this place?"

"It's a safe-house for those who are 'off the grid,'" Henderson said.

"A safe-house?" Crystal asked. "Safe from what?"

"From prying eyes," he said.

"But how did you... I mean, how does it work?" Crystal continued.

"Not now," he replied. "There'll be time enough to answer your questions. Right now you've both been exposed to the elements and need to get out of those leather clothes and get some rest. After you've cleaned up, we'll have a late dinner. Then you can rest a bit."

Henderson pointed Peter to a stairway down a narrow hall. The passage was dimly lit and decorated with assorted pictures of men and women. The stairs led to an upper level that boasted of three bedrooms and a bath. Peter entered the first bedroom, a small chamber, simple and quaint. Dark curtains hid shuttered windows and a small chest of drawers sat against the wall next to a closet door. A single bed filled the center of the room, nestled against the far wall, just below the windows.

Peter cast his knapsack onto the bed and stepped into the bathroom. A white bathtub and shower stood to one side with a toilet hidden behind a vanity wall. Opposite the tub was a porcelain sink with a gold-framed mirror hung above it. He leaned against the rim and looked at himself in the mirror.

The man looking back at him was a stranger.

He had never seen himself with a beard. Now his face was covered with a full growth and he looked ten years older. His eyes were sunken and cheeks hollow. Lines of worry crossed his forehead like narrow furrows in a garden. Dirt and grime darkened his face and hair, and exhaustion issued from every pore. He turned and moved the shower curtain aside and noticed a fresh bar of soap, razor and washcloth. Hung on a small metal bar attached to the wall was a large towel. Peter sighed at the prospect of a hot shower and clean clothes.

* * * *

After he showered, Peter descended the stairs, freshly shaved and eager for the promised dinner. He had discarded the leather garments acquired from the island and donned his father's clothes. It was strange to wear a normal shirt and pants after spending so many months in the rugged gear from the colony. He rubbed his face, grateful for the clean-shaven feel and made his way to the dining table.

Crystal sat at the table with Henderson. The papers had been cleared and the table was set with an assortment of bowls, cups and plates. Ham slices, bread and butter and a large cook pot of vegetable soup lined the center of the table. Steam wafted up from a carafe next to Henderson and bore the heady scent of fresh coffee.

"Come," Henderson said. "You need a rest from your ordeal." He slid a chair out and motioned for Peter to sit.

Peter took the offered seat and felt the heaviness in his chest subside. He sipped at the coffee which had been poured, and took several slices of ham and ladled a steaming bowl of soup. "I'll tell you," he said between bites, "these have been the strangest months of my life."

"Oh," Henderson said.

"Yes," Peter continued, "these have been the strangest months ever. I've been shot, left for dead, recovered, caught, sent to an island, reunited with my dad, discovered I have a younger brother, escaped from the island and now I'm here." He paused as he took another sip of coffee. "And," he continued, "I've learned about faith, became a Christian, made some strange friends, heard about something called the Shadow Remnant and am now considered a threat to the state."

"You've had a busy season," Henderson quipped. "But for now, you're safe. This is, as I said before, a safe house and I've been telling Crystal that it's been some time since I've had the opportunity to use it as such."

"So, were you a part of this Shadow Remnant?" Peter asked.

Henderson smiled, "Wrong tense."

"What do you mean?" Crystal asked.

Henderson took deep breath, "I mean, young lady, that I *am* a part of the Remnant."

"You mean that there are others who still fight against the government?" Peter wondered.

The doctor shook his head, "You've got the wrong idea about the Remnant. It's not an army or a fighting force. The Shadow Remnant is, even now, a network of those who still hold to the ancient principles of liberty and freedom." He stood up and walked into the kitchen. Shaking, he grasped a cup from a wall-mounted cupboard and filled it with water from the faucet. "I've not seen another member of the Remnant, for, I suppose, over ten years — since before your father was taken."

"What happened, what happened that my dad would be captured?" Peter asked.

"Peter," Henderson moved back to the table and looked intently at him. "I'm just amazed at how much you're like your dad. I'd swear that he's sitting here but for your age."

"Don't change the subject," Peter injected. "What happened that he was caught?"

"I wouldn't be off base if I told you that your father was captured because he tried to fix the wrong problem."

Crystal intersected the conversation. "Are you going to speak in riddles?"

"No," Henderson said. "But I'm not going to go into the depths of the past tonight. I'm old and need my rest as well. I will tell you all tomorrow. There is much that will need to be done." He spoke the last statement under his breath, as if he spoke some mystery to his own thoughts.

Crystal was about to speak again when Peter motioned for her to be still. "I think that a good night's sleep will do us all some good. What arrangements should we make, Henderson?"

"You noticed the rooms upstairs," Henderson said. "Those are my guest rooms and you're welcome to them. I lodge in the master suite downstairs and will call upon you in the morning." He stood and moved down the hall, opposite the way of the stairs. Then he turned and faced the two at the table, "By the way, you don't have to be so formal. You can call me, Marcus."

Peter called down the hall, "Good night Henders... I mean, Marcus."

"What now?" Crystal asked.

Peter glanced up from his plate of food. Her blonde hair was pulled back away from her face and glistened, damp from her shower. She wore a denim shirt with a gold necklace that boasted an amethyst pendant in the shape of a cross. Her cheeks, lightly freckled, seemed to glow with rosy warmth.

"What are you staring at?" Crystal asked.

"I, well, I never noticed you had freckles." Peter smiled as she blushed.

"Fine," she said, "but if you make fun of them I'll slug you!"

Peter gasped in mock fear. "You were asking about what we do now. I don't know. I think the best thing for us is to get a good night's sleep. I don't know about you, but I'm exhausted. My next move is up to bed."

"Do you think we can trust this guy?" Crystal paused as she thought. "I just don't know. Maybe he'll turn us in and then this game is over."

"Look," Peter said, "I'm too tired to worry about it. There's a warm bed and some sleep waiting for me upstairs and I'm going to find it. I've not slept in a real bed in some time."

"Well I've never slept in one!" Crystal retorted.

"Good, then go pick a bedroom and get some sleep. I think we're safe for now." Peter gulped down the last dregs of coffee in his cup and stepped away from the table. He walked down the hall and up the stairs, Crystal close behind. Without looking back, he entered his room and shut the door behind him. He heard another door close in the hall and readied himself for bed.

* * * *

Peter woke early. The room was dark and only a slight glow from the frosted window offered any illumination to his chamber. He relished the warmth of his bed and hunkered lower under the covers to absorb all the comfort it offered. As he lay he listened to the sounds of the house. Boards creaked and groaned as a wind whispered through the trees. Over the din of the old house's voice, he heard Marcus rattle around in the kitchen. Grudgingly, he rose up out of bed and placed his feet on the hardwood floor. A chill ran up his leg from the cold wood and he shivered. He stood and moved to the window.

The frosty window glowed with the iridescent light of the world outside. He rubbed the pane with his hand and gazed out at the scenery. Lamps on the deck burned with a soft, white radiance. The air shimmered with the halo of camouflage that surrounded the property. The path toward the beach was lit with two strands of glowing rope, one on each side. Like dancing silhouettes, trees swayed in the breeze and put the world in motion. To the east a faint sliver of amber light caressed the horizon.

From his second story vantage point he looked out over the water more than one hundred yards away. Peter watched as the wind rippled the water in a shimmering dance. Slowly and steadily the sun peered over the horizon like a child peeking out from hide-and-seek. Then, in an expansion of brilliance, the world was bathed in scintillating majesty. He was reluctant to leave the window until the aroma of bacon drifted through the door like the beckoning of a long-lost friend.

Peter opened the closet to retrieve his trousers and, to his surprise, found a terrycloth robe hanging on a hook inside the door. He wrapped himself in the robe and stepped to the doorway. He took the Bible out of his knapsack that lay against the dresser and held it close to his chest. Then he turned and opened the door to the hall. At his feet in front of the doorway a pair of slippers waited. He shook his head in wonder and slipped his feet into the proffered footwear. The soft, cushioned shoes were warm and comfortable. In silence Peter walked down the stairs and into the dining area.

He found Marcus working the kitchen like a professional chef. Pots boiled on the stovetop, bacon sizzled on a griddle and a rich warmth of hospitality glowed upon the old man's face. Without a word, Henderson signaled for Peter to take a seat at the table. Peter did and poured himself a cup of rich, black coffee from a carafe nearby. He sipped the pleasant, hot drink with the delight of real civility.

"Where's Crystal?" Marcus asked as he stirred a pot of steaming breakfast.

"I guess she's still asleep."

"Good," he said. "It'll give us a chance to talk. There's some things you need to know about your father — things that will affect you, I believe."

"I'm all ears," Peter leaned back in his chair as he drank his coffee.

The old doctor moved to the table, a stainless steel pot of oatmeal in his grasp. He set the steaming meal down and went back to retrieve the bacon. When he returned to the table, he sat directly across from Peter, poured himself a cup of coffee and looked up at the young man. "I'm not sure where to begin. There is a lifetime of history that your father experienced that I'm sure you would like to know."

"You talk like my dad was a major player in the past."

"He was. In fact, it was your father who tried to organize those who still held the ancient beliefs."

"But where are those people now?" Peter's brows furrowed as anxiety crept into his mind.

"I'll get to that later. Your father's story begins about thirty years ago," Marcus said. "Patrick was a member of the political arena. He was just like all other political pundits, educated in the state schools and brought up believing the propaganda. Then one day he came into my office and I asked him if he ever read any of the old documents." He paused as he looked off in the distance, thoughtful.

"What is it?" Peter asked.

"I was thinking about that moment," Marcus said. "Your dad was going to have me arrested for even suggesting that he read something forbidden by the government."

"You've got to be kidding!" Peter's eyes widened with surprise.

"No, I'm not. He was engrossed in the doctrine of the government. As a member of the party, he did everything he could to bring down anyone who opposed the sanctioned beliefs." He took a bite of oatmeal and a sip of coffee.

Peter shook his head in disbelief. "But my dad is a strong believer! He lost his own freedom trying to secure it for others. He thinks that those in power are oppressive and, perhaps, downright evil. I can't imagine him ever being a part of it."

Marcus nodded, "You must allow for a person to change, Peter. But I tell you that your father was a leader in the government and a powerful man. He was persuasive and, at times, violently so. He didn't think it wrong to arrest and imprison those who spoke against the government; that is until the day he walked into my office."

"What happened then?"

"Like I said, I asked him if he had ever read any of the old documents, the real history of our country. He was appalled at the idea, but I pressed the matter further. I recall asking him what he was so afraid of. That if the current system was the best for everyone, what was the risk in simply reading the 'forbidden' books."

"Then what?" Peter was engrossed in the tale.

"He took me up on the dare. I gave him some information to read and he began to come back for more. I finally introduced him to a man I knew, a historian who knew the ancient documents from memory. What your dad learned in those few months changed his point of view. He began to look at the world he lived in with an open eye, not with the view of a government agent. He saw the oppression and rampant poverty of our nation and turned to the Remnant to help him."

"Help him with what? What did my dad plan?" Peter had long forgotten about his meal as he listened intently to Marcus' tale.

"Your dad thought that, with his influence in the government, he could change the minds of the political elite. He tried to persuade those in congress and talked with many outside the chambers. He was relentless as he showed detailed accounts of how the government was oppressing the people." Marcus stood and stretched his legs. He poured a second cup of coffee and sat back down.

"What happened next?" Crystal asked as she stepped out of the darkened hall into the room.

"Oh, good morning," Marcus said. "Come, sit down. Get yourself some breakfast."

Peter looked at her with a suspicious eye. "How much did you hear?"

"Just about everything," she said. "I've been up for about an hour and heard your conversation even upstairs. Someone had left these slippers for me at the foot of my door so sneaking down the stairs was not too difficult."

"Well, come on then," Marcus said. "Now that you've heard most of it, you might as well listen to the rest."

"Are you sure?" Peter asked. "My dad seemed to think that it was dangerous for people to know about it."

"Too late for that," Marcus replied. "She already knows more than most."

"Besides," she added, "if you want my help, you need to tell me everything."

"Alright," Peter said. He motioned for Crystal to sit down, eager to get back to the story.

Marcus continued, "What your dad did next was a risk. I thought it might be too dangerous, but he felt that if he could show the administration the truth they would be moved to change. So," he paused as he considered his words, "Patrick brought together members of the Remnant from all over the nation. Your friend, Joshua, was one of the many who gathered in Washington D.C. to show the government exactly what was happening around the country.

"As you guessed, it didn't work. Joshua's wife was killed, several members of the Remnant were captured and your mom and dad fled back here to try and avoid the military police. It wasn't long before they were captured and taken to the internment center in Darrington. Then you were born."

"That's a bit ominous," Crystal said. "What happened after Peter was born?"

"Well," Marcus said, "Patrick kept in contact with the Remnant. He had seen first hand the oppression of the government and tried to organize local pockets of those who would resist the enslavement. He was a fighter and wanted people to fight for their freedom. The problem he found was that people felt isolated. There were not enough people willing to risk it."

"But why?" Crystal asked.

"Because the government controls all the outlets of information," Marcus said. "People were inundated with the political propaganda and never listened to him." Marcus looked Peter right in the eye, his expression stern and deliberate. "He worked for twelve years trying to get people to understand that they could be free. Then he was taken away from Darrington and never heard from again." Marcus sighed. "Most of us thought he was dead, that they just simply killed him and your mother."

"Well, I'm glad you were wrong," Peter said.

Marcus sipped his coffee again. "Then I heard about you — that you had escaped Darrington and was killed in the attempt. But reports from sources other than the media came in and said you were alive, even taking your dad's place as a leader of the

Remnant. The myth of your life began to grow among some of the members and they began to believe that you were the one man who had the ability to thwart every government attempt to capture you. But the broadcast news continued to report that you were dead."

"Well, I'm glad they got that wrong too!" Peter exclaimed.

"You'll understand my surprise, then, when you showed up on my beach," Marcus added.

"So, what do we do now?" Peter asked. "My dad sent us to you because he said you might be able to set us up like you did Joshua."

"No," Marcus said. "I can't do that for you."

"What?" Crystal demanded.

"That's not why your dad sent you to me. He sent you here because he knew that I have all the contact information for the members of the Shadow Remnant. He sent you to me because he wants you to try and do what he couldn't."

"Oh, and what is that?" Peter asked.

"He wants you to take the message of freedom to the people. Your dad tried to fix the wrong problem. He thought that he could change the government. He realized, too late, that what he needed to do was get the message to the people."

Crystal began to fume. "Look!" she demanded, "I don't care about any of this 'Shadow Remnant' stuff. I just want to get my friends off that blasted island!"

"Your friends are there because the government thought they were dangerous. They were considered dissidents, enemies of the state. It was for that reason the island was reopened."

Peter pressed the issue, "Why not just kill those who were dangerous?"

"Because," Marcus said, "they wanted to try and gain information about the Remnant. They also wanted to show the population that the 'reeducation' centers were hospitable and humane." He turned to Crystal, "There's only one way to rescue your friends. You need to bring liberty back to the nation."

CHAPTER TWELVE

"Whether you turn to the right or to the left, your ears will hear a voice behind you, saying, 'this is the way; walk in it.'" ~ Isaiah 30:21

The sun broke through the morning mist and bathed the world in light. Snow covered the ground and sparkled as tall pine and fir trees gently swayed together. Peter stood and walked to the double door and stared blankly through the pane-glass windows. His mind raced with doubts and troubled thoughts drifted through his wandering imagination. He sipped at his coffee, absentminded to the two others who sat at the table.

"What is it, Pete?" Crystal's voice, soft with concern, broke the silence.

"Why me?" Peter asked, frustrated. "All I wanted to do was find my parents. Now here I am—a fugitive. How did I get here? I... I just can't do this." His voice wavered, "What can one man do to change a nation?"

"Peter," Marcus said, "one man can't change a nation. But one man can begin the process. You can be the voice in the minds of millions."

"Oh, great!" he snapped. "How in the world am I supposed to do that?"

"Well, funny you should ask. When your dad abandoned the notion of changing the government, he began to explore how to speak to the people. Before he was captured, we were working on a way to get the message to as large an audience as possible. It was ironic what he discovered."

"What was that?" Crystal asked.

Marcus took another long sip of coffee. "He realized that it's possible to tap into the Federal Communication Network and use the government's own weapon against them. They have had control over the dissemination of information for over a hundred years and Pat learned that it was possible to break into that network and speak to the whole nation at once."

Crystal stood up and carried the dishes to the kitchen. "So," she said, "are you saying that the government controls all the media?"

"Absolutely," Marcus said. "What poses as multiple media sources is actually controlled by a central network. Internet, television, radio, all the major communication outlets are under party control. From what Pat told me, every news story, every talk show, even cartoons and sitcoms must be approved by the FCN."

"So how did you plan on doing this?" Peter asked.

"The FCN is headquartered in Colorado. We almost breached the location once, but had to abandon the effort."

Crystal was at the sink, clanking the pots and plates as she washed the dishes. "What happened? Why did you abandon it?"

"We were pursued by federal agents. They found out what we were planning and led us into a trap. We managed to evade them but our tech specialist was taken. None of us who remained had the technical skills to do what we needed." Marcus poured himself another cup of coffee and stood next to Peter. He put his hand on Peter's shoulder and looked into Peter's eyes, "Answer me this: do you want to pick up where your father left off?"

"I don't know that I have a choice," Peter said. "It seems that his legacy is my destiny, whether I want it to be or not."

"What do you suggest we do?" Crystal asked.

"We?" Peter remarked. "I can't let you take this risk."

"Well you're not going to do this yourself," she huffed. "You wouldn't last a week without me!"

"Oh, that's right," Peter mused sarcastically. "It was you who rescued me from the gang and you who carried me off the rowboat when we got to Longbranch."

Crystal lowered her eyes and blushed. "Well, you shouldn't try to do this alone. And if this is the only way to rescue Jack and the others, then I'm in."

"Alright," Peter said, reluctantly. He turned back to Marcus. His heart pounded in his ears as his blood raced with trepidation. He lifted his cup of coffee to his lips, hands trembling with anxiety. "You need to know, neither one of us have been anywhere. I was in Darrington all my life and Crystal was on McNeil. We don't know where to go from here."

"Well," Marcus said, "these next few days should be spent in preparation. If you're going to take on your dad's mission, you'll need to know some things, things that I can teach you." He stepped to the table and sat down again. "Right now, why don't you both go and get changed. Robes and slippers are not quite appropriate attire for what comes next."

Peter nodded and Crystal dried her hands off with a towel. As Peter passed the table, he reached for the Bible he had set down.

"Just a moment," Henderson said. "If you don't mind, I'd like to read a bit of this while you get dressed."

"Sure," Peter said. "But be careful because it is very old. I rescued this from an abandoned church in Darrington."

Marcus reached for the book. He brushed his fingers across the cover and looked at the faded inscription on the front: *Holy Bible.* A tear fell from his eye. He fingered the pages with the gentleness of one who caressed the wispy locks of a newborn baby. "This is a rare treasure, Peter."

Peter watched as Marcus fanned the pages. "Do you know the Bible?"

"Oh, yes, quite well," he said. "Books like this were outlawed over almost a hundred years ago. There are still some out there, mostly in fragments. I've only seen one other completely intact."

"When was that?"

"When I was a surgeon in Washington D.C.," he replied. "It's been, let me think, over forty years ago. A patient came in to my office. He belonged to a small group in the capital and he spoke to me about things he had read. I was curious and asked him to bring me more. When he came back, he had a complete Bible with him. I remember him shaking as he held it out to me. I think he was scared that I might turn him in." Marcus grew silent as he thought.

"What is it?"

"Just think how much courage that man had to bring the Bible to me, even when he thought he might be arrested. The truth was more important than his life. It was that courage which prompted me to learn more. Eventually I became a believer and not ten years later, met your dad."

"Amazing," Peter said.

"What?"

"That the man who came into your office might be the reason why I'm here today... that his courage is the catalyst for this mission," Peter said. He turned and started down the hall to the staircase, "and he doesn't even know."

When Peter came back down the stairs he found Crystal and Marcus at the table discussing the Bible. The table was again littered with papers as if an office had exploded and Marcus eagerly sorted through the pile as if he searched for a treasure.

Marcus looked up to see Peter standing in the archway. "Good," he said, "I'm glad you're ready. I have much to show you. You'll need to be brought up to speed on many things."

"Up to speed, what is there that we don't already know?" Crystal asked.

"History, for one," Marcus said. "You need to understand what happened to our society. It's been over a century that freedom was lost. And for you to face what's out there, you'll need to learn about it." Marcus stood from the table and pointed down the hall away from the stairs. "If you'll follow me, I'll show you."

Crystal stood with him and Peter filed behind as Henderson led them down the passage. The walls were decorated with scenic pictures of pristine landscapes. One large picture of Mount Rainier, five feet tall and just as wide, hung as the centerpiece to the motif. Peter stopped to stare at it for some time. The volcanic mountain stood in the background with a pristine lake set in the fore. Tall evergreens surrounded the lake like sentinels and wispy clouds caressed the sky.

"What is it that you see?" Marcus asked as he stood beside Peter.

"I don't recall ever seeing Mount Rainier like this," Peter said.

"Really, that's how it used to look before the war. It was the tallest peak in Washington."

"It's amazing. That was a beautiful mountain," Peter remarked.

"Perhaps now," Marcus said, "you begin to understand that not everything is as it seems. The things you know as truth need to be viewed from a more informed perspective. You cannot simply trust what you've learned—especially when the facts don't support it."

"But how are we going to know what is truth and what is not?" Crystal said as she came along side them.

"Observation," Marcus said. "Open your eyes and see. Our rulers say you must trust them, but watch to see their actions. The system of education says that they have the truth, but look around and see if what you've learned is based in reality. Historians say that we're better off under government control rather than free. But learn what freedom is and discover for yourself if it's better to be free or to be systemically enslaved."

"But I've lived isolated from the world, without all this 'education' that you're talking about," Crystal said.

"Then you have an advantage," Marcus observed. "You will be able to learn without the burden of having to filter out pre-biased propaganda." He moved away from the painting and walked down the hall.

Peter followed with Crystal close behind. The hall ended at another arched doorway with a heavy metal door. It had one small window in the center of the upper panel and a massive lock that reminded Peter of the prison cell. Marcus fumbled through his pocket until he pulled out a flat, jagged key and, with a clank, unlocked the door.

A low hum issued from somewhere in the blackness beyond. Musty and cool, the portal opened upon a stairwell that descended into darkness. Peter's heart echoed in his ears as it beat with renewed apprehension. He half-expected a squadron of bats to burst forth from the cavernous hall before him.

"Come," Marcus said and stepped into the dark corridor beyond.

Peter and Crystal jumped back when the passage was filled with a rush of light.

"Come on," Marcus said again, "I'm not getting any younger."

They entered the hallway and followed the old man down the stairs. The walls were dazzling white, unadorned by any picture or ornament. A cool breath of air gently stroked Peter's skin as a chill went through his body. The low hum grew louder the deeper they descended. Twenty steps... thirty steps... forty-two steps later and they were at the bottom. Again they faced a grey, heavy metal door with a small window and massive lock. With the same key, Henderson snapped the lock open and the door creaked with an eerie welcome.

"What is this place?" Crystal whispered to Peter.

"It's the brain-center for this house," Henderson answered with a smile. "We're almost there."

They followed Marcus through the door and again a burst of light exploded before them. It revealed a large room. Lining the walls were twelve tall metal cabinets. Each cabinet had assorted lights that flashed in sequential patterns. In front of each cabinet stood a metal table, adorned with a computer monitor and keyboard. At the far end of the room hung a massive display screen that was ten feet wide by six feet tall, with a checkerboard display of the surrounding area. Peter observed the beach, the road, the perimeter of the house and property and several other locations he did not recognize. In the center of the room was a round table with several chairs. The center of the table had a conical-shaped metal cylinder with thousands of dark specs on its surface.

Peter's eyes were wide with wonder. "Did you build all this?"

Henderson chuckled. "No," he said. "Remember, we had an expert in electronics. He created this room and prepared this house to be a safe house. Each of the computer banks on the wall handle the camouflage, perimeter security, monitoring and other defensive measures. From the large screen," he pointed to the massive monitor on the far wall, "I can see anything that might enter the property long before it arrives. That's how I knew you were on the beach. I had a perimeter warning and came down here to monitor your passage."

"So, why don't you just use all this technology to speak to the nation?" Crystal asked.

"Because, we're off the grid," he said. "If I were to tap into the Federal Communications Network I'd be immediately discovered and shut down. This house is safe because no one can trace it. Even our power is self-generated." He moved to the central table. "But I didn't bring you down here to simply show you this room. I want you to watch something. Come, sit down."

Peter moved to the table with Crystal and both sat down opposite Marcus. With a flash, the table erupted in light and the conical cylinder burst forth with a radiant glow. Peter's mouth hung open as he watched a holographic display come to life right before his eyes. Men from ages past stood before him wearing long waistcoats and colonial garb. Pictures flashed before his eyes of men in a great debate who were overwhelmed with a sense of duty.

"Have you ever heard of the 'Revolutionary War'?" Marcus asked.

Crystal shook her head but Peter nodded. "Sure," he said. "It was during the colonial times when the people of America rebelled against the king of England because they didn't want to pay taxes anymore. That despite the king's protection and oversight, the people revolted. The king of England didn't want to destroy them so he allowed them to form their own country."

"Well," Marcus said, "that certainly makes the king of England appear as the good guy."

"That's what I was taught in my history classes," Peter said.

"I have no doubt about it. But it isn't accurate. The revolution was fought by men of good conscience who deemed liberty more important than life. These men debated long and hard about the call to freedom. They pleaded with the king to stay his hand of persecution but their requests went unanswered. So, for the sake of liberty, they formed a government and declared their independence from Great Britain. Two hundred and fifty years later, our government became the persecutors of liberty rather than its protector."

Peter and Crystal watched the scenes flash before their eyes. Days of long ago played out in cinema-graphic horror as they peered into the window of history. World War One, World War Two, The Gulf War, The Second Korean War, all paraded across their view with unrelenting perseverance. The hours ticked away with no disturbance as Peter and Crystal watched the past unfold.

Then World War Three burst onto the scene in nightmarish violence. Massive explosions rocked the world and cities were vaporized in seconds. They watched in silent horror as people fled for their lives from the assault of thousands of troops, all dressed in black with heavy face-shields.

Then the scene changed and they observed a man who sat behind a palatial wooden desk, surrounded by a dozen or more on-lookers applauding with each stroke of the pen. As quickly as it appeared, the projection ended and it was once again nothing more than a round table before them.

Peter sat, shocked to silence. He looked up at Marcus, who stood on the opposite side of the table, and watched as tears ran down the old man's face. "What is it?"

Marcus wiped his eyes, "I hate wars and I hate violence," he said as he choked back his emotions, "but those wars were fought to secure liberty. Yet, with one stroke of a pen, our leaders surrendered liberty without a fight."

"What do you mean?" Crystal asked as she tried to catch her breath from the moment.

"That last scene you watched," Marcus said, "was in 2032, one hundred years ago, when our president signed a bill into law that ripped freedom from the hands of the people. With that single action, he outlawed anything that was not government sanctioned. Food, clothing, literature, everything was placed under the direct control of the government and has been ever since. He said it would only be temporary, a necessary measure to bring order back to our country after the devastation of World War Three. But once that law was passed, freedom died."

"But why didn't people protest? Why didn't people fight against it?" Crystal questioned.

"At the time the people were reeling from the war. Whole cities were lost and in some locations the very air was toxic. People clamored for help. They were desperate for anyone to tell them that they were going to be alright, and desperate for someone to lead them out of the decimation that took place. So, they turned to the government and surrendered their freedom for perceived security."

Peter stood up and walked over to the large display that glowed with the images of their surroundings. He stared at the screen absentmindedly. "What I don't understand," he said, "once the crisis had passed and people were okay, why didn't they simply elect more liberty-minded people to the government?"

"Because," Marcus continued, "once the regime had power to control information they had the power to change history and what people knew. It took only a generation before people forgot what liberty looked like. Political speech was forbidden and any action taken to try and bring the truth to light was immediately crushed. That's when those who knew the truth went into hiding; that's when the Shadow Remnant was born."

"Well," Crystal said as she stood, "all I know is that I was imprisoned for years and for no other reason than that someone thought my mom and dad were dangerous to society."

"There are many others around the country who are in the same situation. If they can't be re-educated, then they are sent away. That's what happened to Patrick and his wife. They were sent to be re-educated in Darrington and it didn't work."

"Why would it?" Peter asked.

"Pressure and pain can be quite persuasive. Your father had something that many don't, however. Your father had faith." Marcus moved toward the door. "Let's go back upstairs and get some lunch. We've been down here a while and I'm getting hungry. We can continue this conversation over a hot bowl of stew."

Peter smiled at the idea as his stomach growled in anticipation. He and Crystal followed Marcus upstairs and all found themselves, again, at the dining room table.

The day had expanded and a brilliant, shimmering sun peered down through the boughs. Cold, blue skies graced the winter world while crystallized shadows danced across the house with the swirling wind that moved through the trees.

Marcus busied himself in the kitchen as he extricated various pots from the lower cupboards. He pulled out a wooden cutting board and, with an assortment of produce garnered from the refrigerator, began to slice and dice a vegetable stew. Crystal poured water into a pot and added the carrots, celery, onions, potatoes, and leeks. Peter watched the two navigate around each other like some choreographed dance. To help the preparation, he gathered utensils and bowls and began to brew a strong pot of coffee.

The table was still littered with various papers. Peter shuffled and piled them into an orderly state when he caught a glimpse of a document with his father's name.

To: Maj. Patrick L. Sheridan

You are hereby ordered to infiltrate the organization known only by the name: "Shadow Remnant." Make contact with a known operative and associate of the organization: Dr. Marcus Henderson. Gather pertinent intelligence and uncover the names of key personnel.

By order of: Maj. Gen. Samuel A. Connor

"What's this?" Peter asked.

Marcus looked up. He left the kitchen with a nod to Crystal and came to Peter's side. "Let's see," he said. "What have we here?"

"It seems to be some type of military order given to my father," Peter observed.

"Oh, yes," Marcus said. "That order was what brought Patrick into my office the first time. He had originally come to me to expose the entire operation. I guess the General didn't plan on Patrick having an ear to the truth. Once he began to learn how corrupt the government had become and how oppressive the system was, he became a strong believer in liberty." Marcus stopped and went back into the kitchen. He waved at Peter to follow, "Come here for a moment."

"What is it?" Peter asked.

"Come, taste this."

Peter gave a quizzical look, "Okay."

"Now," Marcus began, "you have never tasted my stew."

"No," Peter replied.

"I promise that once you do, you'll want more." Marcus smiled as he pulled a heaping spoonful from the pot.

"I'm sure it's wonderful," Peter replied. "But what does this have to do with anything?"

"Well, you haven't tasted my stew yet. Right now, all you know is that it might taste good. You're so used to eating processed food from the government that anything else is something foreign. But just wait until you taste my stew."

"Sure," Peter said. He gingerly took the spoon from Marcus and sipped at the hot broth and vegetables. The warm, smooth liquid, with a hint of garlic and salt, coursed down his throat like a drop of pure delight. "This *is* delicious," Peter exclaimed.

"You see," Marcus continued, "now that you've tasted it, you know it's good. It was the same with your father. He had never tasted liberty. All he knew was the processed life given by the government. Once he tasted freedom, however, he was startled at how good and right it was. He began to want more and soon he became an advocate for liberty."

Peter smiled at the object lesson. "I know what you mean. When I was with Joshua I enjoyed my own freedom for the first time. I did what I chose, not what was required by my director. I lived for myself for the very first time, and it was wonderful."

"Yes," Marcus said. "You got it. Liberty is addictive. Once you taste it you want more. And once you've experienced it for the first time you never go back. But, let me ask you, did you use your freedom to harm or to help?"

"Well," Peter said, "I guess to help. I wanted to help Joshua with the work and use my skills to keep the farm going. But I benefited from it too. The food we grew, the work we did, all provided for my life as well as his."

"Your right," Marcus said. "The government wants people to believe that freedom only provides the means for causing harm. They promote the notion that a free person will strike against others, cause destruction, perhaps even kill. But a free society, built on a moral foundation, will become a prosperous and generous people."

"But what is that 'moral foundation'?" Crystal asked.

"It's simple... the foundation of faith in God and adherence to His moral law." Marcus picked up the Bible and carefully thumbed through the crinkled pages. "Here it is," he said. Then he read, "You, my brothers, were called to be free. But do not use your freedom to indulge the sinful nature; rather, serve one another in love."

"So," Crystal asked, "what does that mean?"

"It means that a person who is set free by God has the responsibility to use that freedom to benefit others. What Joshua believed, what Patrick believes, and what I believe is that the best way to benefit others is to offer them the same freedom we've found."

Crystal picked up the pot of stew and hefted it over to the table. "Well," she laughed, "I had a hand in this stew as well, so don't take all the credit." A smile crossed her face as the two others moved toward the table.

They all sat down to enjoy the meal. Peter ladled large portions for each bowl and poured coffee for everyone. The warm, savory scent carried in the air like comfort food and Marcus bowed his head in prayer. "We thank you, Lord, for freedom and for the friendships that help us. We pray that this food will warm and fill our bodies as you warm and fill our lives. Amen."

Peter lifted his head and looked at Marcus, "Perhaps," he said, "each of us will have a hand in it after all."

CHAPTER THIRTEEN

"The Lord will rescue me from every evil attack..." ~ 2 Timothy 4:18

A noise in the kitchen roused Peter from a deep sleep. He had been with Marcus for three weeks and had grown used to the old man's habits, but the senior member of the home never clattered around in the kitchen before seven a.m. He glanced at the glowing timepiece that sat upon his dresser. The red, digital display showed 6:17 a.m. Careful not to make a sound, Peter slipped out from under his covers and stood upon the hardwood floor of his room. Slowly he opened the door.

Voices emanated from below. He listened intently, desperate to make out who was speaking. He recognized Henderson's graveled, mid-western accent. The other voice was muted and low and completely unfamiliar. Hesitant, Peter put on his slippers and stepped down the hall to the stairs. The low whirr of the furnace clicked on and covered the sounds from the kitchen.

With care, Peter crept down the stairs and listened as Marcus talked with the unseen visitor. As he neared the dining room, he pressed against the wall beside the arched doorway, and listened to the conversation.

"No, Marcus," said the stranger, "it's already too late." His low voice rumbled and set an ominous tone.

"But you don't understand," Marcus said, "Peter is not ready yet. He doesn't have his father's training and the plan is just too dangerous."

"Marcus," boomed the stranger, "whether he's ready or not, the fed's have already gotten wind of this. Before I left, I got word from an insider that they're close to finding him—even in this safe house."

"But how?" Marcus' voice wavered with emotion.

"It's that blasted implant," the stranger said. "Peter got one while on McNeil and they're tracking him."

Peter startled to feel a touch on his arm. Crystal stood beside him, her finger pressed against her lips to keep him quiet. He took a deep breath and tried to calm his racing heart.

"But this house was supposed to hinder those kinds of tracking implants!" Marcus protested.

"Doc," said the stranger, "your twenty years behind the times in technology. Your dispersal shield will not keep them from finding this place as long as that tracking device remains."

"But…" Marcus paused. "Can't it be removed?"

"From what we understand of those devices, if you try and remove it the poison is immediately triggered."

"How is he going to make it to Colorado, then?"

"There's only one way… but it's got to be now or never. The word in the Remnant is that Sheridan is free and it has stirred up both panic and hope." The stranger's voice trailed off.

"You don't understand," Marcus spoke with staccato deliberateness, punctuating each word. "Peter is not his father. He's a good kid, and he has the courage and tenacity of Patrick, but he doesn't have his experience."

Crystal suddenly pushed Peter aside and shot around the corner. "Who cares!" she shouted. "We've come this far and we'll make it the rest of the way."

Peter stepped around the corner as well and got his first look at the stranger in the house. He was tall, perhaps two inches taller than Peter with dark skin and curly black hair, grey at the temples. The man was older, but not as old as Henderson and walked slightly hunched over and with a limp. He wore wire-framed glasses that aided dark brown eyes more used to reading than spying.

The man turned and looked right at Peter. A broad grin filled his features as he reached out a massive hand. "I'm glad to meet you, Peter."

"Oh," Peter said, "and who are you?" Peter reached out and shook his hand.

"My name is Earl Buchanan. I was an associate of your father's and I've come to help you." His tone carried a quiet authority, deep and resonant.

"Well Mr. Earl Buchanan," Crystal said, "you don't know anything about us, so how can you help us?"

A broad smile crossed Earl's face. "I know more than you might think, young lady." He hobbled to the table and sat down. "Come, sit for a minute." Crystal and Peter followed him to the table and sat on the opposite side.

Crystal folded her arms across her chest and looked hard at the man across from her. "Okay, what do you know?"

As if in slow motion, Earl leaned back, his chair creaking under the strain. "Where should I begin... perhaps at the point where you were taken to McNeil Island?"

Crystal's eyes widened. "What do you know of it?"

"I know," Earl said, "that you were very young, perhaps three years old, when you were taken away."

"What about my parents," She demanded. "What do you know of them?"

Marcus stepped to the table and interrupted. "Perhaps, my friend, you need to let the past rest." He turned his attention to Peter and Crystal. "Why don't the two of you get dressed for the day, we'll have some breakfast when you're ready."

Peter nodded and stood from the table. Crystal, reluctant to go, gave way to the moment and followed Peter out of the room.

"There is no reason to bring up those things right now," Peter heard Marcus whisper to Earl, his tone cautious and angered.

"She needs to know sometime," Earl replied. Their voices faded as Peter went upstairs.

He came back down and entered the dining room to find Earl still seated, with Marcus beside him and Crystal on the opposite side, pounding her fist on the table.

"Wait just a minute," Crystal said. Her face flushed with anger as she looked at both men. "If there is something about my parents that I need to know, you tell me!"

"In time," Earl said. "There are other plans to make and our time is short. The holographic camouflage around this house will not hide you forever. If we are to put our plans in motion, we'll need to leave soon."

"Plans, what plans?" Peter asked.

Before Earl could answer, the sound like a massive whistle whined from hidden speakers in the ceiling. Marcus stood; his eyes wide as he looked out the window toward the beach. "Hurry," his voice cracked with anxiety, "we must get downstairs."

Without question, Peter followed him down the stairs, Earl and Crystal right behind him. They entered the main computer center. The lights flashed on and Marcus locked the door behind them. He quickly moved to the multi-display on the far wall and typed on the keyboard just beneath it. Blue and red lights flashed on a panel next to him and the screen pixilated then resolved to display only the beach.

"What is it?" Crystal asked. She stood near the central table, her hands clenched like fists.

"It's the proximity detectors. The alarm indicated that there was motion on the beach, but I don't see anything." Marcus continued tapping and clicking at the keyboard and with each entry the screen moved and zoomed in and out.

Peter stood with Crystal. His heart raced in the moment and he felt a tinge of apprehension. "Maybe it was just a stray animal," he said. He hoped for it, but in his heart Peter feared the worst. Earl pulled out a chair at the central table and sat down. Peter looked at him with amazement. "We might be facing federal agents and you can sit? How can you be so calm about all this?"

"Because there's nothing I can do about it," Earl said. "If they are agents then we'll need to evacuate, and if not, there's nothing to worry about."

Marcus turned his head to face the table. "Peter, come over here. Earl doesn't need you to help him hold down that chair — he can handle that himself."

"Funny," Earl said.

Peter moved to the screen. "What can I do?" he asked.

"I need you to keep an eye on this monitor to tell me if you see anything — and I mean *anything* — moving." Marcus turned to one of the computer banks on the wall and began to type at its keyboard. Suddenly the screen displayed in shades of red and blue. Trees that once were green showed on the large monitor as a pale orange. The beach looked like a wide swath of mottled blue carpet and the bay was done in deep blue.

"What is this?" Peter asked.

"This is a thermal image of the beach. If there is anything out there, it will show up." Marcus didn't look up but continued tapping on the keyboard.

Peter gasped. "Wait!" he said. "There is a bright red glow on the left hand side of the screen." Everyone looked up as Peter pointed to the area. It looked like a pinpoint of red emblazoned on one of the pale orange trees. Then the object moved. Marcus rapped on the keyboard and the screen zoomed in to the upper left quadrant of the display.

"It looks like a... a hand," Crystal said. As she spoke a bright red figure dashed across the screen.

"That hand is attached to an entire body," Earl said. "We need to get out of here." His usually calm, resonant voice wavered for a moment.

Peter's heart raced as the fear of capture entered his thoughts. "What are we going to do? We don't have a way of escape."

"We might," Marcus said. "Peter, I want you to go to the central computer bank and press the center red button three times."

Peter looked away from the monitor and noticed a bank of buttons of various shades. He hurried to the metal cabinet and in the middle of a set of flashing lights a single red button waited. Peter lifted his hand, hesitant to do what was instructed. "What's going to happen?"

"Just press the button—three times!" Marcus' words raced from his mouth.

Peter did it. Suddenly the entire cabinet moved to the left. Old bearings screeched against one another as a small tunnel was revealed behind the computer.

"Look!" Crystal shouted and pointed at the large screen.

Peter's eyes fixed upon the display. It was still set to look out upon the bay, but Marcus had switched it to show the world in real light. The bay was subdued grey as clouds shrouded the sky. Green fir and pine swayed in a fractious wind, their once shining needles pallid and dull. In the far distance, McNeil Island,

and halfway between, a black helicopter hovered over the water. His heart sank as he looked at the screen.

A flash of light burst from the helicopter, followed by a streak of fire through the air. Suddenly the house shook as if struck by a massive earthquake. Dust fell from above, and the room rocked with such violence that large cracks split the concrete floor. Two computer banks fell over and the room immediately went dark, with only the glow of the large monitor providing any light. Peter watched the screen in horror as another flash from the aircraft sent another missile streaking toward the house. A second later and the sound like thunder rocked the underground bunker.

"Get in the tunnel!" Marcus shouted as he moved to the only remaining exit. He grabbed a flashlight hanging on the wall and with a quick snap, the way was lit. Everyone followed the wizened man just as another explosion shook their world.

Crystal stumbled and Peter instinctively reached to catch her. He hauled her to her feet and both chased after the bobbing flashlight ahead of them.

"They're firing missiles at us Pete!" Crystal's voice cracked as she tried to keep on her feet. Every minute another explosion rumbled overhead.

Peter listened for anything behind him. They hurried down the narrow passage, each footfall echoing against the concrete walls. He looked back and watched as the computer room, now more than two hundred yards behind them, flashed in a brilliant fireball. Heat rushed through the tunnel and with it a wall of flames. His eyes widened as if they intended to jump out of his head. "Run!" he shouted.

He grabbed Crystal by the arm and both made a mad dash down the tunnel. The heat intensified and he felt the searing temperature on his back. Ahead, the hallway emptied into a large room and a wave of air pressure threw them both into the chamber. They tumbled across the floor as flames burst forth in a violent rush then disappeared. Marcus and Earl heaved against a massive metal door. It swung closed with a dull thud that echoed in repeated vibrations.

"Okay," Crystal said, gasping for air. "Where are we now?" She stood to her feet and brushed her hair away from her face.

Marcus wiped his hands off on his trousers and slid a thick, grey bar across the doorway. "We are actually across the street from my property. Just above us is an old, abandoned house." He handed his flashlight to Earl and moved to the far wall.

"What's your plan?" Peter asked.

"We need to get above ground" Marcus said as he ran his fingers along the wall. "Earl, bring that light over here."

"Get above ground!" Crystal demanded. "Those feds are up there looking for us."

"It's better than them finding us down here," Peter said. "At least we have a running chance."

"They're not looking for us—at least not yet," Marcus said.

"What... why?" Crystal asked.

Marcus didn't turn around as he continued to glide his hands against the wall. "Because," he said, "I blew up the house. I had explosives rigged to go off if anyone ever discovered me. There is nothing left of that place except a crater and a pile of debris."

Peter's eyes widened. "You destroyed everything?"

"Yes," Marcus said. "Now, if you'll help me, I need to find a panel on this wall to unlock a hidden door."

Peter moved to the wall. The flashlight reflected against the grey-white stone so that the entire room glowed with an eerie quality. Dust drifted in the air and the specks sparkled in the beam. He began to run his hand against the wall as well, hoping to find some catch or deviation in the smooth stone. Crystal joined him and all three frantically searched the wall.

"I've found it," Marcus declared. With a quick snap that echoed like a firecracker in the square room, Marcus pushed against a panel and a narrow door opened, exposing a cast-iron, spiral stairway. Dust and cobwebs drifted through the air and a mouse scurried through a small hole on the back wall of the stairwell. Earl stepped in with the flashlight and aimed the glowing beam into the darkness overhead.

Peter glanced up from where he had crouched and peered into the shaft. The stairs vanished into darkness overhead, winding up through strands of webs and coated in years of dust. He stood and brushed off his hands then cautiously stepped through the door. Placing his foot carefully on the first rung of the stair, the entire structure creaked in rebellious consternation. His hands trembled when he clutched the rail, leaving his prints in the grey dust. One step... two steps, and Peter began to walk up the stairwell.

Earl stepped behind him, shining his light up through the dark, cavernous hole. Flecks of dust drifted in lazy disarray, momentarily coming to life in the light. Peter brushed away heavy strands that stuck to his clothes and looked back down the well to see the others step onto the spiral escape. With each step, the metal registered a new groan and Peter felt the stairs tremble under his feet.

"How long have these stairs been here?" Crystal asked, as her voice echoed through the shaft.

"I built this a long time ago. In fact, this entire escape route was planned when the safe house was developed. I honestly never believed that I would need to use it," Marcus said.

Without warning, a massive explosion shook the ground. The cast-iron vibrated in the quake and Peter held tight to keep from falling. "What's happening?" he shouted.

"I don't know," Marcus said. "Just hurry."

Another explosion rocked the chamber and the metal began to squeal in desperation. Peter noticed that the frame began to pull away from some anchor points on the wall as he stumbled up the stairs. He tried to hurry but the staircase swayed, loosed from its support and overwhelmed with the weight of four climbers.

Peter looked down at Earl. "Shine the light up here." Earl had kept the light squarely on the stairs but moved the beam to shine toward where Peter pointed. Peter looked up and noticed a wooden ceiling five feet above his head. "We're at the top!" he declared. He pressed against the wooden barrier with his back and tried to force it open.

"You can't get in that way," Marcus said as he stood behind Earl and Crystal. "There's a latch on the left hand side of the…" he stopped when another shockwave rumbled the stairs.

"Left side… left side," Peter muttered to himself. He looked at the ceiling and reached up to explore it with his hands. He felt along the tongue-in-groove wood and brushed away several dark webs when his hand rested on a small knot. It was a hole just big enough for his finger. He pushed his index finger into it and felt a small button press in with a snap. A fraction of an inch was all the ceiling moved but it was enough. Peter shoved against it with his shoulder and the hatch gave way, opening into a dark room.

He slid the trapdoor aside and scrambled into the open space. The musty scent of the unused house drifted through the dust-filled air. Except for the dim, filtered light that entered through the boarded up windows, darkness was all he saw. Then Earl scampered up the stairs into the room and scanned their surroundings with the flashlight.

They stood at a junction point between a long hall that disappeared into blackness and two rooms, empty of any furnishings. Then another shockwave rattled the house. Peter heard the stairs grind against the strain as Crystal and Marcus scrambled to get to the top.

"Hurry!" Peter shouted.

Crystal nearly ran up the remaining stairs and leapt into the room just as the cast iron shifted and with a metallic snap pulled away from its upper support. Peter nearly jumped back into the hole, restrained only by Crystal's quick reflexes.

"Marcus!" Peter called into the void as grating metal screeched against the walls. He snatched the flashlight from Earl and scanned the darkness. The spiral stairs had twisted and now leaned against the wall. Long scratches, like claw marks, scarred the drywall and revealed the last desperation of the circular steps. Ten feet beneath the trapdoor, Marcus hung onto the rail with one arm and shielded his eyes from the light with the other.

"I'm okay," Marcus said.

After a collective sigh of relief, Peter reached his hand down toward the older man. "Can you make it up?" He asked.

"Yeah, yeah… just give me a minute." Marcus tried to catch his breath. "I'm old, remember. It's been a while since I've had to do things like this." With labored steps, he began to climb up the ancient staircase. He reached the top and was still nearly three feet shy of the trapdoor.

Peter looked at Crystal and Earl, "grab my legs." He leaned in and reached down to Marcus. "C'mon, Marcus… let's get out of this place." Marcus stretched and grabbed Peter with both hands. Peter looked at his older companion and noticed blood on his face and arms. Crystal and Earl pulled on his legs, dragging both out of the gaping hole. All four fell back against the wall, exhausted.

Another rumble ripped across the earth. The stairs groaned again, collapsing in a twisted heap, grinding and screeching as it gave its final cry. Peter nudged to the edge of the hole and peered into the cavernous well. He shone the flashlight into the depths and shook his head as he looked at the mangled bundle of metal that used to be the stairs.

"Well?" Crystal asked.

"I've seen spaghetti less tangled," Peter said. "I'm glad we got off that thing when we…"

"Peter." Earl's soft voice turned Peter around immediately.

He flashed his light toward Earl and Marcus. Both men leaned against the wall; Earl hovered over Marcus, tending to the older man. Marcus barely moved and his breathing was labored. Blood stained his checkered white shirt and dripped in a slow rivulet upon the carpet. Earl pressed ripped fabric against Marcus' shoulder as Peter rushed to old man's side.

"What happened?" Peter asked as his voice trembled with fear.

"I… I fell against the rebar," Marcus whispered, gasping for air.

"Don't try and talk," Earl said then added, "You're dull enough when you're not hurt."

"You," Marcus offered a grin before he tried to sit up. "You're still annoying." He slumped back down against the wall and looked at Peter, his hands motioning for him to listen. "You need to get out of here." Marcus took a deep breath and grimaced in pain. "You and Crystal… there's transportation in the garage of this house."

"I can't leave you here," Peter protested. "I need to get some help for you."

Marcus shook his head, "No, that's not the plan."

Peter began to argue but Earl held up his hand, "Marcus is right. Your tracking devices will pinpoint you and they'll find you both. If you don't get going soon, you'll never get out of here. Don't worry, I'll look after Marcus."

"But what about you?" Crystal asked.

"Once you're gone, they'll quickly forget about us. Besides, Marcus and I have been at this a long time. We'll be okay."

Peter stood and ran his hands through his hair in frustration. "I don't even know where to go from here?"

"South," Marcus whispered. "Find a man named McKenna. He has part of the plan with him, and you'll need it to complete your task." He tried to reposition himself but groaned as he shifted. "Look for him at an abandoned military base in California." Marcus' eyes closed.

Earl pulled his hands away from the wound. The bleeding had slowed, oozing like sludge through his clotted shirt. "Go," he said, "I'll look after him. Marcus and I have been friends a long time."

A rush of noise blasted over the house and Peter looked up at the ceiling, half expecting to see the roof cave in.

"A helicopter," Earl observed.

The sound faded into silence. Peter stood quiet, cocking his head to one side as he listened for its return. But the threat had passed and he relaxed.

"You're safe for a moment, but not for long," Earl said. "Believe me, if they find your signal, they'll find you."

"How do we avoid being detected?" Crystal asked.

"The car," Earl said. "While you're in the car, it will shield you from their tracking ability."

"But where do we go from here?" Peter asked.

"You can take the bridge south of here to Johnson Point. From there, head to the interstate and then down to California."

A rush of noise burst over the house and the entire structure shook violently. Peter fell to his knees and Earl held Marcus close, protecting the unconscious man from falling debris.

"We gotta get out of here, Pete!" Crystal's voice trembled.

"Go," Earl said, still calm. "The car is in the garage at the end of the hall." He pointed down a long corridor that led away from the stairwell. "You'll find instructions in the car, but get going. The car will hide your signal."

Peter and Crystal moved down the hall. He looked back once more to see the shadowed figure of Earl leaning over his friend. Crystal grabbed him by the arm and both entered the garage.

Peter shone the light upon the vehicle, a metallic-silver, two-door coupe with black-wall tires and tinted windows. The doors lifted open and Peter sat on the left side behind the wheel, closing the door after him. Crystal slammed her door down and hunkered in the seat as if it were a bunker.

Without touching anything, the dash lights flashed on and the car came to life. The gravimetric engine hummed as the machine's magnetic coils began to cycle. A dashboard computer flashed on, and a navigational screen silently slipped out in the center of the panel. Peter's eyes widened as the car spoke.

"*Welcome back Major Sheridan,*" said the computerized voice from hidden speakers.

Peter smiled, "This was my dad's car."

"Well I hope he doesn't mind us borrowing it," Crystal said. The whirr of a helicopter rushed overhead again. "Maybe it knows the way out of town."

"Earl said south," Peter whispered.

As if on cue the computer spoke, "*Please enter navigational coordinates.*"

Peter looked at the navigational screen and began to push buttons on the side of the panel. Soon he figured out the system and located California on the display screen. "Earl said something about an abandoned military base," Peter spoke to himself. Suddenly the house rocked with a massive shockwave.

"I don't think we have time to figure it out now," Crystal said. "Let's just get out of here."

Peter stepped on the accelerator and the engine revved. In his excitement, he threw it into gear and they launched out of the garage like a missile just as another explosion hit the house. The fiberglass garage door shattered into a thousand fragments and Peter frantically steered.

The streets were dark and no life stirred on the peninsula other than the two of them. "Look behind us," Peter said.

Crystal leaned back, and peered through the rear window. "I don't see anything," she said. "It's dim and the clouds are low so that black helicopter is gonna be hard to spot."

"Let's hope that we are as well," Peter said. He drove for a mile when he pulled off the road.

"What are you doing?" Crystal asked.

"Let's wait a while. If this car can mask our signal, we'll be better off if they stop looking for us. We can leave in a couple of hours. Right now, let's get some rest." He backed the car under a tall grove of trees and sat quietly. He found a switch on the dash by the speedometer. With a flick, he turned the vehicle off, anxiously waiting to make his way south.

MICHAEL DUNCAN

CHAPTER FOURTEEN

"Trust in the LORD and do good..." ~ Psalm 37:3

Time lingered as if the world had ground to a halt, so Peter took to studying the various panels and devices of the car. An array of information displayed on the video panel. The pale, grey-blue glow illuminated the cabin and reflected off of Peter and Crystal in ghostly relief. He pressed a button on the right side of the display and switched from a rear-view camera to weather and temperature data. Various selections were of navigational maps and strategic charts. One, however, piqued his interest.

"Look at this," Peter said.

Crystal, still hunkered down, kept her head lower than the windshield. "What is it?"

"It looks like a map of the country with pinpoints marked all over it." Peter touched the screen and it centered on the place where his finger had landed. He slid his finger across the screen and it moved with it. A quick smile crossed his face.

"Well, you've found a new toy. What's the big deal?" Crystal, however, sat up and began to watch Peter move and slide the map of the country across the screen.

"I think I understand what these marks indicate," he said. Peter continued to move the screen until he landed on the Pacific Northwest. "Here, look at this."

Crystal watched as Peter pointed to various markers on the display. "I don't understand what you're driving at."

"Well," he said, "here is a mark near Darrington. This has to be Joshua's house. And here," he moved the screen a little south and west, "this must be Marcus' home. I think that this map shows the location of the members of the Shadow Remnant."

"No wonder they hid this car," Crystal observed. "If the feds got their hands on this map, they could find every member." Her voice wavered as she asked, "Does he have McNeil marked on the map?"

"Let's see." Peter moved the screen and centered on the small island in Puget Sound. He tapped the screen and it zoomed in on the island. A small, red flag marked the little isle. "Yep," he said, "there's a mark on the island."

"Who do you think was a member of the Remnant on the island? Do you think it was my parents?"

"I don't know; I wish I could tell you." He moved the screen off McNeil and tapped it twice. It zoomed out and showed the entire west cost of the United States. He scrolled down the coast and zoomed in on California. "Now I wonder which mark represents the man named McKenna." There were fourteen flags in the Golden State, many set near the southern border with Baja Mexico.

"Which one is it?" Crystal asked.

"I think your guess is as good as mine," Peter said.

"What did Earl say?" She paused, thoughtful with her eyes closed. "Didn't he say that McKenna is located on an abandoned military base?"

"Yes." Peter continued to scan through the various flags in California. "There is one, here." He pointed to a flag in the central part of the state. "It shows an airport runway and a reference: *Castle A.F.B.*"

"Well, let's get going." Crystal sat back and strapped herself into the black, high-backed, leather bucket seat. She gazed at Peter, her eyes wide with excitement and anticipation. "Do you really think we can pull this off?" She paused as she adjusted the seatbelt. "I mean, think about it, just a month ago you and I were living on an island and survival was our highest priority."

"I don't think our priorities have changed much," Peter mused. "I just think that survival has become a whole lot more difficult." He flipped the switch on the dash and the car hummed to life. The tachometer revved above two-thousand rpm's and the pale blue glow of the dashboard lights illuminated the cab in its subdued hue. He looked back over at Crystal and sighed. "Do I think we can pull this off? I don't know, but I think we're gonna find out."

Peter put the car into gear and pressed his foot on the accelerator. It jumped like a rabbit out of a hole and they were off. The engine hummed softly as he drove. Clouds hung low, caressing the trees and masking their passage from any aerial agents. As Peter drove, Crystal manipulated the display screen and scanned through the various data that appeared.

"Find anything you like?" Peter asked.

"Nothing that I understand," she said. "This car... this device, these things are all so different than what I've ever known."

"What are you looking for?"

"A radio," she said, her brows wrinkled in frustration. "You would think that with all this technology, this car would have a radio. I'd like to hear what's going on in the world."

Peter smiled. "You've never been in a car? Not even on the island?"

"Little reason for it," she said, "you can't drive a car into the woods."

"Try the control panel above the display screen." Peter pointed at the digital panel, with numbers lit in bright green. "You might want to hit the button marked, 'power'."

Crystal smirked at him. "Ha, ha," she said and pressed the flat button marked: *pwr*.

The stereo cracked with static. Crystal pressed a button labeled, *scan*, and the digital display rapidly changed as it rushed through the various frequencies in search of a clear signal. It landed on a station playing the music of a soft acoustical guitar accompanied by a gentle piano.

"That's kinda nice," Peter observed.

"You just drive," Crystal ordered, "I'll find a station that will give us the news." She pressed the scan button again and it raced along until it hit another clear station.

A radio announcer came on, voice clear and passionate as he spoke at length. *"On the outskirts of Portland, today, another band of criminal dissidents exploded a make-shift bomb at the international airport. No one was hurt but the airport was shut down, tying up flights. It is believed to be the work of a rogue group, and insider information gives them the name: Shadow Remnant."*

Peter shook his head and reached over to the stereo. He pressed the power button and it went silent. "I don't think I want to listen to the news."

Crystal looked at him and raised her right eyebrow. "What's the problem?"

He sat quiet for nearly a mile as trees and old, abandoned houses whisked past. "I just wonder if they were really a part of the Remnant. I mean, from what dad told me, the members didn't want to terrorize but to teach."

"There's only one way to find out."

"Oh," Peter said, "and how's that?"

"We need to get to Portland and find one of those 'Shadow Remnant' people. They'll certainly know your father and might be willing to talk with us." Crystal gave a quick smile. "Who knows," she added, "they might even know about *you* already!"

Peter gave a half-hearted grin at the idea. "I don't think that I've become a national figure." He ran his fingers through his hair and stared through the windshield as if he tried to gaze into the future. "In fact, I hope we can do what my father wants without anyone getting wind of it. I would rather remain anonymous until we're done."

"I don't think that's possible any more." Crystal sighed as she spoke. "You and I are now fugitives. I don't think being anonymous is an option."

Peter remained silent as the miles slipped quietly beneath them. They arrived at a bridge connecting the Longbranch peninsula to Johnson Point. Clouds hung heavy over the bay and shrouded the span in a dense fog. He stopped as they neared the edge of the ghostly bridge. As far as he could tell, it simply vanished into the grey mist. In the veiled distance a foghorn bellowed out its warning as some unseen ship navigated through Puget Sound.

"What am I doing here?" Peter spoke to himself. His heart languished in a sea of doubt, shrouded in the grey haze of uncertainty.

Crystal answered, "You're here to finish your dad's work and, hopefully, rescue them from that blasted island." She swiveled in her seat to face Peter directly. "Look at me," she demanded.

Peter turned, his face set with lines of worry. "What?"

"I'm going to tell you something that your dad told me. It was a couple years ago. I was so upset and my life seemed so senseless. He said, 'Crystal, you might never know why you're here on this island or why your parents are gone. One thing you can trust is that God knows.' He told me that I could trust God to do for me what was best, even when it didn't feel best at the time." She paused and took Peter by the hand. "I'm telling you now: God knows why you're here. I don't know if I am ready to believe all that stuff about Jesus. But one thing I do know is that your dad never lied to me and if he believed that God had some plan or purpose to all this, that's good enough for me."

The rush of a helicopter interrupted her as it passed overhead. Peter's heart leapt in his chest and glanced up through his window. The heavy fog prevented him from seeing any aircraft but swirls of air waked through the clouds like small cyclones.

Crystal crouched down in her seat. "Peter, we gotta get across this bridge," she said as her voice quivered.

Peter looked back at Crystal, eyes wide with apprehension, and then he stepped on the accelerator. The engine hummed to life and the car rushed forward. Peter tapped his fingers on the steering wheel and beads of sweat coalesced on his forehead. He peered out the window, cautious and anxious, fearful to see the black helicopter whirring overhead. All was grey. In every direction, fog had enveloped the world.

The long, straight bridge rushed beneath them as the car rapped each seam of the conduit in rhythmic cadence. Anxiety welled up in his thoughts. "I'm such an idiot," he said. "That's a government helicopter… I was stupid to think we could hide from it."

"Well," Crystal stammered, "doesn't this car have any defenses?"

"What… like a jamming system?" Peter asked.

Just then the computerized voice said, *"Radar jamming system on."* A slight flicker occurred and the blue dashboard lights turned a subdued crimson.

Peter grinned and stepped harder on the accelerator and the car sped along the bridge. The engine hummed as if it had longed for use when they suddenly rushed off the bridge and into a canopied forest. The road turned left and Peter slammed on the brakes to navigate the sudden change of direction. Tires squealed, then screamed and they came to a sudden stop. On the right side of the car a tall Douglas fir tree stood no more than six inches away from the mirror, with a heavy green branch draped across the hood.

Shaking, Peter sat in silence behind the wheel as Crystal stared blankly out the window, eyes wide in fear. Heavy fog drifted through the trees, lazily moving with the air. Small needles fell upon the windshield, dotting the surface of the glass. Peter took a deep breath and let his shoulders relax.

"That was close," Crystal said as she stared out her passenger window, the rough, jagged bark of the fir tree only inches away.

"Too close." Peter said as he wiped his brow.

A whoosh of wind rushed overhead followed by a massive explosion. Peter looked behind him to see a large fireball followed by another rush of wind as the shockwave shook the car. Needles jumped off the tree as if they had been scared out of hiding and covered the vehicle. Branches swayed and vibrated with the concussive force.

"What was that?" Crystal demanded.

"I think that the bridge was blown up," Peter said, rather cool and detached.

"How can you be so calm?"

"Well," he said, "if they blew up the bridge instead of us, then they don't actually know where we are."

A slight smile crossed Crystal's face as her eyes widened in recognition. "I understand. They can't find us."

"Nope," Peter returned. "The only problem is, when this fog lifts, they'll spot us without using their detectors."

"I wish we could camouflage the car like we..."

Crystal was interrupted by the computer voice, "Camouflage engaged."

A shimmer rippled over the exterior skin of the car and it vanished, blending in with the surrounding flora. Only the small fir needles gave any indication of where the hood was located.

"This thing is amazing," Crystal remarked. "I wonder what else it can do."

Peter paused, thoughtful as he pondered what to say next. "Display instruction manual."

The dashboard screen flashed and a menu file scrolled onto the display. "*Please select from the following items: Tactical, surveillance, stealth, diagnostics.*" The female computer voice droned out her monotone selections.

"Well, this will make it easier," Peter observed. He pressed the screen selection, *tactical*, and a new menu appeared: *environment, global positioning, tracking, infrared*. He selected tracking, and the screen shifted from an icon display to a radar sweep with green, concentric circles. A white bar whirled around and two red dots flashed every time it passed over them.

"What's that?" Crystal asked as she pointed to the two red indicators.

"My guess," Peter said, "is that we are the center of the circle and those two marks are helicopters."

With each sweep of the bar, the two dots moved away from the center of the circle. Eventually both indicators fell off the screen.

"I wonder what the range is for this thing," Peter said.

On cue, the computer voice responded, "*range setting three miles.*"

"It looks like they've gone," Crystal said. "Let's get out of here."

Peter stepped on the accelerator, but nothing happened. Again he tried, but the car remained motionless. "I don't know what's wrong." His face flushed red with frustrated embarrassment as he slapped the steering wheel with his hands.

"Don't break it!" Crystal said as she smirked. "Maybe there's a book or something that will help us out." She pressed a button in front of her and a panel fell open to expose a small compartment. Inside was a sealed envelope, yellowed with age and crisp. She pulled it out and turned it over. Her hands trembled as she examined it. "Peter," her voice almost a whisper, "this letter is for you."

He took it from Crystal, shocked to find his own name written in faded letters on it. Carefully he slid his finger along the seam of the seal and the flap cracked open. One sheet of paper waited within the envelope, crisply folded. With the care of an archeologist, Peter slid the rustic parchment from its container and slowly unfolded the document.

"Well?" Crystal demanded.

Peter continued to stare at the letter, hands trembling as he held it. "It's from my dad," he whispered.

"What does it say?"

He cleared his throat, as emotions welled up from deep within, and read:

Dear Peter,

I don't have time to explain to you all that has happened these past few years. If you're reading this letter, then I have failed in my mission and it has fallen to you. I knew, even from the day you were born, that God had set you apart for a special purpose. If you're reading this, that time has come.

As I write this, the agency is closing in on us. Kyle and Samantha were taken two years ago, but I fear their capture was a ruse. I'm convinced they betrayed us to the government and used their capture to cover their tracks. If you meet them, don't trust them. We have eluded their traps, but we can't escape them much longer. And, if you are reading this, then our capture, perhaps even our executions, have already happened.

By now you have met up with Marcus. Listen to him. He will help you to understand what we — the Shadow Remnant — were trying to accomplish. He is a key member and a good friend. There are others you

205

can trust, but be careful. Our mission was a simple one: restore America to the ancient wisdom of the past. You'll learn about it along the way, but be certain that the only hope for saving our country is to rekindle the fires of liberty in the hearts of her people. The truth has lingered in the shadows for a century and the members of the Remnant have kept it. Now it's time to bring it back and let the citizens of our land remember freedom. God has called all men to be free. I hope you have discovered this for yourself.

This car is a prototype, the only one like it, and is equipped to help you. The computer will respond to both vocal and tactile input. It has a multi-faceted defense system and is equipped with navigational and tactical computers. In the trunk I've left extra clothing. I guess, if you're driving my car, you might actually fit into my outfits. I was a major in the special ops. It might serve you well to wear my uniform when you have to cross state-line checkpoints.

Do not let this vehicle fall into the hands of those who stand against the call for freedom. It contains all the locations of the members of the Remnant. Your first destination is to make your way to California. Find a man named Dr. George McKenna. He has taken refuge on an old military base, Castle Air Force Base, to be precise. McKenna is a historian and he has the document that is central to our plans.

Hold onto hope and do not give in to fear. God has called you to this and he will accomplish it through you. Remember: what you've heard in the shadows, proclaim from the rooftops. People need to remember freedom, and even from your birth I was convinced that you might be just the man to remind them.

Know that your mother and I love you very much. We are sorry that you're alone in this. Don't concern yourself with us. By the time you read this, if you do, we are gone. Our hope is secure and our fate is in the hand of God. The Holy Scriptures say to trust in the Lord and do good. Our time has passed, now is your hour to rise up and do the good that God has given you. Always remember, our love goes with you.

Peter looked up from the letter as tears streamed down his face. Through reddened eyes, he looked at Crystal who, herself, wept silent tears. "Wow," he said, his voice hoarse and muted.

"It's dated, July 17th, 2114. He wrote this letter eighteen years ago, on my fourth birthday."

Crystal nodded and wiped a tear that trickled down her cheek. "How… how could he know that you might be here? And why didn't he tell you any of this before they were taken to McNeil?"

"I don't know. I think that Marcus might have told us more if we had the time." Peter took a deep breath and gained his composure. He looked at the display screen and touched the panel, going back to the radar display. The sweeping bar circled round and round, but nothing appeared in the concentric rings. "I want you to watch this screen and let me know if you see anything appear on it."

"Why?"

"Because I'm going to get into the trunk and I don't want to be outside if those helicopters come back. Remember, they can track our implants." Peter took a deep breath and opened the door.

"Be careful," Crystal stammered. "This feels dangerous."

Peter smiled and stepped out of the vehicle. The door shimmered in its camouflaged state. When Peter stepped outside, the car looked like it was a part of the scenery, reflecting the flora of their surroundings. He had to feel his way along the edge of the vehicle but quickly found the trunk. "Okay," he said to himself, "if this car responds to verbal commands, let's try it." He bent down to the level of the car. "Open trunk."

A snap and a click and the car shimmered like the ripple of a pond then the hatch over the trunk opened about an inch. He lifted it the rest of the way and inside the compartment was a large garment bag and two boxes.

"Well," Crystal called out as she stuck her head out her door. "What's in the trunk?"

"Just a minute," he said. The two boxes were sealed with simple tape, and Peter cut through them with his knife. Inside the box was a large assortment of packaged food items, carefully preserved. The garment bag was hermetically sealed and he cut through the outer layer of plastic. Inside was the dark-blue uniform of his father: pants, coat, shirt, shoes and a wide hat with a patent-leather bill and an eagle medallion made of silver. He quickly tried the coat on for size, and found that it nearly fit perfectly, with just a little room. He tilted his head toward the passenger side of the car. "Anything on the screen?" he asked.

Crystal ducked inside the car and a second later came out again. "Pete!" she shouted. "There is one small red marker at the top of the screen. It's faint, but it's there."

"We gotta go," he said. He threw the items back into the trunk, slammed the hatch closed and ducked back into the car. The skin of the vehicle shimmered again when he closed the door.

"But the car won't start," Crystal said.

"I know, I know. I just wish this car would tell me what's wrong." He rapped his fingers on the steering wheel again, impatient as he watched the red blip on the screen move closer. "They must have honed in on my signal. They won't need to see us to know where we are." He sighed, exasperated. "Why won't this car move?"

"*Car disabled when camouflage engaged*," the computer voice said.

Peter and Crystal looked at each other, eyes wide. "Well disengage the camouflage!" Peter demanded.

A shimmer of light and the car returned to normal. He stepped on the accelerator and the car leapt forward. Needles flew off the hood like sticks in a hurricane. The dashboard lights were still subdued crimson and Peter hoped it meant that the jamming device was operating. With care, he kept them on the road, driving as fast as the winding street allowed. They navigated through dense trees, passing an assortment of houses, some abandoned and others occupied. He managed to average about thirty miles an hour along the residential, rural roads.

"What about that aircraft, is it following us?"

Crystal kept her eyes on the panel, "I don't know. It's still hovering over where we were. I don't know if they spotted us."

Peter pulled to the side of the road, out of sight from any houses. "Engage camouflage."

"*Camouflage engaged,*" the computer replied.

"What are you doing?" Crystal asked.

"We need to wait until that aircraft is gone. If they see a car along these roads, they'll jump down on us like a pack of wolves. When they are off the screen, we'll go. Once we're on the highway to Portland, we will simply blend in with the rest of the traffic."

Just then the whirr of a helicopter rushed over and, in the lifting fog, Peter watched the black aircraft. It flew north, hovering occasionally until it moved on again. This lasted an hour, and with the fog burned off a brilliant blue sky opened up.

"Just go, already," Crystal whispered to the radar screen.

As if on cue, the helicopter rushed overhead again and vanished out of sight, slowly moving to the edge of the screen until it disappeared completely.

"You ready?" Peter asked.

"Absolutely," Crystal said as if she exhaled for the first time.

"Camouflage disengage," he commanded. The car responded and Peter stepped on the pedal. The engine hummed to life and they were off.

They wove their way through the vacated streets of Johnson Point until they arrived at the interstate. The day had grown bright and clear, and the sun drew near to its zenith. Traffic on the highway buzzed along like ants in a line, all speeding in synchronistic motion. Peter took a deep breath, pressed on the accelerator when the traffic light turned green and merged into the menagerie.

He found himself in the middle of three lanes of traffic, all moving south. Large cargo trucks and flatbed carriers shifted from lane to lane, looking like fish navigating in a stream. Surrounded by vehicles, he relaxed his vigilance and focused on the road before him. The miles passed beneath them and occasionally a black, unmarked helicopter flew overhead, but nothing indicated that they were discovered.

"Do you mind if I turn the radio on now?" Crystal asked.

"No, I don't mind."

Crystal pressed the power button and the news station they had previously heard cracked to life. "*...and that's the sports report. The weather today is expected to remain clear, with a high around 45 degrees and a low tonight in the mid 20's. The week ahead will grow milder as clouds come in from the southwest, bringing with it a 70 percent chance of rain. Traffic conditions in Seattle are still bottled up on Northbound I-5 from Southgate to Lynwood as police are still investigating a possible terrorist attack when a chemical truck exploded near the 405 interchange. It's now 11:30am and time for the headlines. Federal investigators are still looking into the reported escape from McNeil Island detention center. Two fugitives, a man and a woman, are on the run and should be considered armed and extremely dangerous. The Portland bombing is still under investigation, but reports say that the saboteurs will soon be found. In sports...*"

"Turn it off," Peter said.

Crystal looked toward him and rolled her eyes. "Peter, you're going to have to get over it. Let's face it, we are the fugitives they are looking for and the Shadow Remnant might not be as peaceful as your father once knew."

"If that's the case, then they're no better than the people that rule here. Freedom can't be won through terror."

Crystal smiled. "Listen to you," she said, "you're beginning to sound like your dad."

Peter returned her smile and turned his attention back to the road.

They let the miles pass in silence as they drove through the towns of western Washington. They passed through Vancouver and the scars of the old war still hung upon the face of buildings. Towering skyscrapers, now unused and fractured, dotted the landscape as they neared the Columbia River. One old structure, nearly thirty stories tall, with widows blown out and a gaping hole in the center, stood as a marker to the devastation that people knew. Signs on the highway spoke of detention centers, reeducation camps, and government controlled lives at every exit.

They passed broken cars, abandoned on the edge of the highway, and came upon the remains of a bridge that once spanned the massive Columbia River. Now broken, with twisted iron and fractured cement that crumbled into the waterway, the ancient passage was replaced by a ferry terminal and boat. Peter drove right down to the water.

Crystal shrieked, "Pete! We don't have any travel papers!"

It was too late. They were in line to drive onto the ferry and encased by cars and trucks on all sides.

"Let's have faith," Peter said. "We need to trust God now."

As they neared the ferry ramp, a soldier in a grey, unmarked uniform, checked each vehicle as it approached. Peter took a deep breath and opened his window when his turn had come.

The soldier standing outside the window showed little concern for his duty as his eyes were watching the traffic. "Travel papers, please." His voice was monotone, as if he had said that same line all day.

"I beg your pardon," Peter barked. He spoke loud, with authority.

The soldier turned and his face whitened when he looked into the car window and stared at the insignia on the jacket Peter wore. "Oh, major, sir, my apologies."

"What's your name, soldier?" Peter commanded.

"Langston, sir… Corporal Langston."

"Pay attention, next time!" Peter stared down the corporal.

"Sir, yes sir!" Langston waved them through without another word.

Peter rolled up the window and looked at Crystal who stared back at him with her mouth hung open. He offered a quick smirk and felt rather pleased with himself.

"Okay," she said, "how did you know to do that?"

"I just remembered how the guards treated me at the center, and how they were on the island. When I realized I still had my dad's jacket on I thought it might work. I had hoped that dad's rank was still enough to stir up a bit of anxiety." He touched the computer screen and navigated back to the display that showed the flagged markers on the map. "Now," he said, "we'll need to find that Remnant group in Portland."

"Tell you what, you drive, I'll find the group."

The river crossing took less than ten minutes and they were in Oregon. Crystal pressed the screen and scrolled across the pages to find the singular red flag that marked the location of the Shadow Remnant. Peter followed the car in front of him and as he passed the lone soldier at the ramp, the young corporal gave a salute. Peter returned it and drove up a steep hill and back onto the interstate.

"Well," he said, "where do we go from here?"

"It looks like the flag is located in the eastern part of the city, somewhere near the junction of a road marked '84' and '205'. It's on some street called, 'Glisan.' You'll need to go east on '84'."

He followed her directions precisely and less than an hour later they found themselves on an abandoned campus. A broken sign, covered over with brush and weeds, no longer displayed the name of what the sight used to be. Peter pulled through the deserted parking area and up to one of the larger buildings. No movement, no sound, not even the breath of wind stirred the ancient structures. Peter stopped and looked at the navigational map. Their position rested right on top of the red flag.

"Well," he said, "this is spooky."

"Maybe if you drive around a bit, we'll get someone's attention."

"That's what I'm afraid of," Peter said. "Too much attention might be bad for us." However, he did as Crystal suggested and navigated around the buildings. Slowly he drove, eyes scanning the cracked windows and doors that stood off their hinges.

"Pete," Crystal stammered, "we're going to have to get out of the car and look around."

"I know," he said, "but I want to see one more thing first." He parked the car near a broken, moss-shrouded building. "Engage camouflage," he commanded. The car responded and shimmered before it disappeared.

"What are you doing?"

"Just a minute," he said. "Engage infrared." The display screen flashed and took on a bluish hue. The buildings were depicted as large, black silhouettes and the trees as a less deep green. He slid his fingers over the display and moved it so that he might scan the entire compound. A red dot appeared. Peter held the screen in place and tapped it twice to zoom in on the location. There were now three dots, located in a building behind them, moving between rooms. "Infrared off," he commanded and the screen returned to a topographical display of the campus.

Crystal stared with wide eyes. "That's amazing."

"I think the Remnant is located in the building right behind us." He looked through the rear glass and determined to take the chance. "You should stay here, Crystal. There's no reason for both of us to risk getting caught."

"You're kidding, right?" Crystal said. "There is no way that I'm stayin' here. You and I are in this together and, besides, you'll need me, I'm certain of that." A smile flashed across her face.

"Alright, let's go. But don't forget where we've parked. We won't be able to see the car when it's hidden like this."

Peter and Crystal stepped out of the car, and when the doors closed, it looked as if all that stood there was the old, decrepit building. Peter buttoned his dad's jacket and they made a quick dash across the parking lot to the other building.

It was a brick structure with moss and ivy growing all along the walls. Windows were boarded up and the door hung precariously on its hinges. They entered the structure and the first level was vacated. Broken sheetrock lay strewn across the floor, revealing the framework like exposed bones of an old skeleton. They tried to walk quietly, stepping lightly and careful not to kick anything. Filtered light poured in through wooden slats covering the windows, shimmering in the dust and casting ghostly shadows upon the walls.

From a distant room a faint sound echoed through the silent hall. Muted voices spoke and Peter walked toward the noises. The sound carried from below as they found a broken stairwell that emptied in the basement of the building. With patient steps Peter and Crystal hugged the sides of the stairs and made their way to the bottom floor. The voices, though dim, were louder and Peter followed them to a door, slightly ajar. He peeked inside. A man in a wheelchair and two others, talked just low enough so that Peter didn't make out what they were saying.

Then he was tapped on the shoulder. "Crystal, not now," he whispered.

"Peter," she said, full voiced.

He turned to see a tall, scraggly bearded man with dirty-blonde hair holding a pistol in one hand and Crystal's arm in the other. "C'mon, you," ordered the man with the gun. "You're comin' to see the boss." Peter was pushed through the door into the room where the three others were talking.

The man in the wheelchair slowly whirled around. Peter's eyes widened and knees buckled when he saw the man in the chair. It was Joshua.

"Hello, Peter," Joshua said in his warm, familiar voice. "Welcome to the Shadow Remnant."

CHAPTER FIFTEEN

"The LORD is my strength and my shield; my heart trusts in Him, and I am helped." ~ Psalm 28:7

Peter didn't know what to say as he looked at Joshua. Questions swirled through his thoughts like a hurricane as he stared at Joshua in the wheelchair. It felt to him as if time had come to a crashing halt, and the motions of those around him were in slow motion. He wanted to rush to his friend, to tell him all that had happened, but all the words that came out of his mouth were, "What... how?"

"Steady, Peter," Joshua said. "We'll have some time to catch up, but right now we should get out of here. This location is safe, but I think we can find better accommodations."

"But... but," Crystal said, "They're tracking us! We have these stupid implants in our backs that they can follow."

"Oh my," Joshua said. "That's a problem." He turned to the man with the scraggly beard, "William, I think you can let her go."

"But we don't know who they are! What if they're here to spy on us? They might be from the feds," William said.

"Nonsense," Joshua said. "This is Peter Sheridan."

Suddenly the two men who stood behind Joshua turned to face Peter, their eyes wide in surprise. William immediately let go of Crystal and put his pistol in his belt. He walked over to Peter, "I'm sorry, I didn't know it was you."

Peter turned to Joshua and raised his arms in question. "What's this all about?"

"Well, Peter," Joshua said, "you've become somewhat of a known figure. Your name is being passed around the Remnant as a person of consequence."

Peter shook his head, bewildered. "Why?"

"Not here," Joshua said. "Let's get to our safe house and we'll talk there." He pushed on his wheels and rolled toward Peter. "So, how did you two find us? We were just about to leave our meeting when you showed up."

"It was the car," Peter said.

"Car, what car?" Joshua asked as he cocked his head to one side.

"My dad left me a car, near Marcus' house on Longbranch. Dad told us to find him when we escaped from McNeil Island."

"Well, you have been busy," Joshua observed. "Some of what was heard in the Remnant I thought was mere hyperbole, but you have had some adventures." Joshua continued to roll toward Peter. "I'm glad to hear that your father is still with us."

"He's trapped on McNeil Island," Crystal said. "He and Jack and all the others are stuck on that blasted rock. We escaped with the hope of finding a way to rescue them."

The one named William moved closer to Joshua. "Boss," he said, his voice lowered to just above a whisper. "We should get outta here. We've been here for over an hour and you know the rules."

"Certainly," Joshua said. "You are right." He turned and waved the two others away and signaled for William to follow. "I'll go with Peter and his friend. He doesn't know where the safe house is and will need me to show him the way."

William nodded and disappeared down a darkened hallway with the other two. Peter watched them, listening as they muttered under their breath. Crystal stood just behind him, arms folded across her chest.

"Come," Joshua said, "let's get to this car of yours and make our exit as well."

The day had waxed late and long shadows cast ghostly images across the overgrown campus. Peter pushed the wheelchair and Crystal followed close behind as they made their way to the car. His heart pounded with the excitement of seeing Joshua again. As they neared the old, vine-covered building Peter moved from behind Joshua and, with his hands before him, felt for the car. There was a small thud and a rippled shimmer when he found it.

"Amazing," Joshua said.

"Just wait," Crystal offered with a smile.

Peter hurried to find the door handle and with a click, opened the vehicle. The interior glowed with the subdued crimson of the dash lights. "Take Joshua to the passenger side," he said to Crystal.

With a quick jaunt, Crystal moved to the right and had the passenger door open and Joshua inside, comfortable in the high-backed leather seat. "I'll take the back seat," she said, folding the wheelchair and tucking it in with her.

With the doors closed, Peter felt as if he could breathe again and exhaled a heavy gasp of relief. "I'll tell you this," he said, "these implants have grown beyond an inconvenience."

"What are they?" Joshua asked.

Crystal broke into the conversation. "Everyone brought to McNeil Island was given these implants to keep from escaping."

She took a deep breath. "If you crossed through the electronic barrier it triggered the release of a nerve agent into your spine and killed you."

"What we didn't know until we made it to the mainland was that these things were also tracking devices. They give off some sort of radio signal so that the guards can keep tabs of you," Peter said.

"So," Joshua said as he stroked his beard in thoughtfulness, "we need to disable that radio signal."

"Well," Crystal said, "when we're in this car they can't track us. And this car has some pretty cool stuff to keep us safe as well."

"That won't be good enough," Joshua said. "We will need to disable them permanently, and perhaps have them removed."

"That's not possible," Peter said. "These devices will release their poison if anyone tries to remove them."

"We'll see," Joshua said. "But, we must have faith." He strapped his seatbelt across his chest and waist. "Now, let's get going."

Peter disengaged the camouflage and drove out of the campus to the highway. He maintained the ever-vigilant radar jamming system and followed Joshua's instructions as they navigated down the thoroughfare. He had never been to a city and the magnitude of humanity that coursed through the veins of the metropolitan sprawl overwhelmed him. Bleak, stark houses lined hillsides with towering skyscrapers lurking in the distance like approaching Visigoths. Cars streamed past him with passengers and drivers all keeping their eyes from peering into the vehicles of other travelers.

Crystal took note of this. "What's up with all these people?"

"What do you mean?" Joshua asked.

"They're zombies," she said. "They just stare straight ahead and don't even notice the world around them."

Joshua chuckled. "No," he said, "they're not zombies but they are spiritually and emotionally dead on the inside."

"What do you mean?" Peter asked.

"They exist, but most have lost the will to truly live. The government controls just about every aspect of their lives. They go from work to home and back again, ever living to make sure that they don't do too much to get noticed by anyone." Joshua shifted and pointed out the window. "Take that exit."

"But they're free!" Crystal exclaimed.

"It's been over a hundred years since anyone has truly experienced freedom. The powers in Washington D.C. have stripped our lands of freedom and now control everything." Joshua shook his head and sighed. "There are those of us who still believe that we can be free again. I'm convinced that if people knew what they were missing, what they've lost, they will demand it."

"Why don't you just tell people what they're missing?" Peter asked.

"It's not that easy. We've tried it before but the government monitors everything. Here in this car we are invisible to them, so to speak. But every radio, television, internet connection all feed back to the central net and if people openly spoke about freedom they would be arrested for dissidence."

"So why not just take a few people at a time to these 'safe-houses' and tell them individually? It would take more time, but it might be worth it," Crystal said.

"Which people?" Joshua pointed to a small road to the right. "We could never be sure that the people we talk to aren't informants. One slip and the Remnant would be uncovered and destroyed."

"But..." Peter said.

"No more for now," Joshua interrupted. "We're almost at the house and my first priority is to get the both of you free from those implants." He pulled a flip-phone from his breast pocket and looked at the display. "No signal," he said, "must be this car." He looked toward Peter, "Can you turn off the jamming device so I can make a call?"

Peter sighed. Reservation and doubt crept into his thoughts but he complied, "jamming off."

"*Jamming system disabled*," the computer responded. The dash lights turned an iridescent blue.

Joshua looked at his phone again, "Ah, good," he said. With a brief beep and several pressed buttons, Joshua put the device up to his ear. "Parker, this is Joshua. No, not for me, I've a couple of friends that will need your help. No, not over the phone, just come to number three and I'll let you know. Yes, number three. You know where it is. Okay, I'll see you in a bit."

Peter reengaged the jamming protection in the car when Joshua clicked the phone closed. Guided by Joshua, they drove upon a lonely, two-lane road that wound its way through the hills south of Portland. Houses were sparse, and no other vehicle drove along the way. The sun had drawn close to the horizon, sending fingers of amber and golden light streaming across the sky. White, tender clouds seemed to erupt in flashes of fire as the night approached. A solitary aircraft, thousands of feet in the air, reflected the sun and left a shadowed contrail on its way.

"Peter, I want you to take the next left," Joshua said. "We're almost there."

Peter did as requested and turned down a dusty, broken road, slightly overgrown with ferns and other brush. They entered a wooded glen and soon all the world vanished behind the barrier of trees. It was dark under the reaching boughs, but the road continued on for several hundred yards. In the distance, the amber glow of houselights shone with warmth and welcome.

"Joshua," Crystal said.

"Yes."

"I was meaning to ask you, what was that place where we met you? It was marked on a map that this car has, but now you're taking us to another location."

"It was a school."

"Oh, like one of the education centers?" Peter asked.

"No," Joshua said. "It used to be a college where you could study the Bible."

"They had those!" Crystal exclaimed.

"Yes, they did. People would come from all over to study and learn. They trained to be preachers and teachers, missionaries and servants. There was a time when our country had Bible schools in every state. But, like that one, when it became illegal to own a Bible, they all shut down."

They approached the house and Peter pulled the car alongside the back of the building. Wisps of smoke drifted lazily out of a brick chimney near the peak of the roof. Through a large, plate glass window, he watched several people move about. Two other vehicles were parked behind the house, nearly obscured by brush and branches. When he stopped, he engaged the camouflage and the car vanished. They stepped out of the car and Crystal grabbed their packs that were almost forgotten in the back seat.

"That's just amazing," Joshua said almost breathless.

Just then an older, rotund woman came out of the house, blue apron around her waist and grey hair on her head. Peter thought she must have been the epitome of every grandmother. He marveled at the sight as her hair bounced when she walked and she wiped her hands on her apron.

"Who's that?" Peter asked as he pushed Joshua in his wheelchair.

"Martha!" Joshua exclaimed. "How are you? I didn't think that you'd be here tonight."

"Now, you know better than that," Martha said, her high voice and Midwestern accent gently stroked the air with kindness.

"Since you were bringing in some new folks, I wanted to make sure they were fed proper. They need home cooking, not what you serve."

Joshua gasped in mock offense. "I say, I've cooked for myself for years and not one complaint. Peter here can testify for me."

A broad grin crossed Martha's face. "Don't you hide behind these kids. You just wheel yourself into the house and get cleaned up. Supper's on the table." She turned to Crystal and Peter. "You kids come with me. I'll show you the house in a bit. But you need to freshen up." Martha pointed to the back porch. "Head on into the kitchen and you'll find a sink and some towels." Peter and Crystal smiled in unison at the kind hospitality that Martha showed.

"You make me feel at home," Crystal observed.

Martha reached to Crystal and embraced her with a tender, grandmotherly hug. "That's the idea, dear," she whispered as she patted Crystal on the back.

Peter joined Crystal and received a similar embrace then both walked toward the stairs at the back of the house while Martha and Joshua followed.

"They make a cute couple," Martha whispered to Joshua.

Peter looked down at Crystal and smiled as her face flushed red with embarrassment. He kept pace with her as she walked faster to the back door. They passed through the door and stepped onto the tiled floor of the entryway. It was a covered porch, completely enclosed with a coat rack lining the left wall. Several heavy, winter coats hung in disarray, along with a battalion of boots and gloves scattered against the wall. To the right was another door that opened into the kitchen. They entered the kitchen to find William and the other two men sitting at a table, sipping what smelled like coffee and enjoying a quiet moment.

"Hey!" William shouted. "It's Peter and, well, and I didn't get your name."

"Crystal," she said with little emotion.

"Peter and Crystal," William continued. "Tell me: is it true that you killed a guard to get away from that place up north?"

Peter's eyes widened with horror. "What!"

"Yeah," said a red-headed man who sat to William's left. "We heard that you took out a guard, killed him with his own gun."

"You said it, Ken. That must'a been one heck-uv-a fight," William said with a grin from ear to ear.

Crystal stepped in front of Peter. "Look," she said, "I don't know where you get your information, but you're just... you're just... well, you're just wrong!"

"Look, now," the third man said, "I know you're trying to keep a low profile, but you can trust us. We're all in this thing together."

Peter placed his hand on Crystal's shoulder before she had the chance to voice her next thought. "We might be in this together," he said, "but I'm not sure that we're working in the same direction."

"Aw, c'mon," William said. "It was all on the news how you escaped from up north and then battled the guards on McNeil until you made your escape. Heck, we even heard that you blew up a bridge just to keep 'em off your trail."

A creak at the door and Joshua wheeled his way into the kitchen. "You know the news is not the best source of information, William." He maneuvered to the opposite side of the table. "Those broadcasts will only tell you what they want you to know, and it doesn't always involve the truth. You can't trust it."

"Yeah, I know, you keep sayin' that. But some of it must be true." William scratched at his scruffy face.

Martha walked into the kitchen. "True or not, none of that matters right now. You three boys set the table for dinner while our guests freshen up." She turned to Peter, "Honey, why don't you and your wife head on upstairs to get cleaned up."

Peter's jaw dropped open and his pack hit the floor. "We're not... I mean, we... well..."

"What he's trying not to say is that we're not married," Crystal said. The look of surprise was not lost on her as she, again, flushed with embarrassment. Even her ears glowed red beside her golden, blonde hair.

"I'm so sorry," Martha said. "I didn't mean to embarrass you." She twiddled with her fingers. "But that does change things a bit." Then Martha looked up at Peter and Crystal, "Okay, Crystal, you can stay in the room with me and Peter can bunk with Joshua." With a final 'humph' that seemed to settle the matter, she shooed Peter and Crystal off to wash up, a gentle tune humming on her lips.

The household had gathered around the table in heavy conversation when Peter came back downstairs with Crystal. When they entered the kitchen, the room fell silent. The table boasted an assortment of pots and bowls, many languidly offering wispy strands of steam from beneath their respective lids. Porcelain plates were set before each chair, with two vacant chairs waiting for them. Peter felt his stomach rumble with anticipation and realized that he had not eaten all that day.

"Well, come in," Martha said. "Sit down and let's have supper."

Peter did as he was told, followed by Crystal. The covers were removed from the pots and bowls and a wealth of steam issued forth to Peter's great delight. A large baked ham sat within a round, cast-iron Dutch oven. A dozen ears of corn were in a large metal bowl and another pot held such an ample amount of potatoes that Peter was sure they had raided the markets of three different towns.

"Where do you get so much food?" Crystal asked.

"Oh, we grow it ourselves, dear," Martha replied.

"You won't find food like this down at that local store!" Ken said as he reached his freckled hand to pick out the biggest corn-on-the-cob.

With lightning quickness, that amazed Peter, Martha reached out and slapped Ken's hand. "Now don't you go grabbing anything 'till we've given thanks." She turned and faced Peter. "Young man, would you do the honor of offering our thanks to God."

Peter smiled and nodded. "Dear Lord," he began, "I want to thank you for this day. I never thought I would ever again share a meal with Joshua. Yet, Lord, here I am and here he is too. You've blessed me beyond reason, and I am more than thankful for what you've done. Thank you, also, for the friendships that I have found, for Crystal, for finding my father and meeting my brother. Thank you for your protection and guidance when we've least expected it. And thank you for this meal, and for Martha who is a faithful and kind host. Amen." He wiped a tear from his eye and looked up. Everyone at the table was silent, emotions filling their features.

"That was a lovely prayer, dear." Martha said.

With the silence broken, the food was passed around and every plate was piled high with delight. The conversations swirled through the air in a cacophony of voices as if each in turn tried to out-volume the other. Crystal visibly relaxed and began a verbal joust with William who took the gaffes with the humor of a pit bull.

"What I want to know," Peter said, loud enough to silence the entire table, "what I want to know is how you made it down here, Joshua! When I was captured, the last thing I saw was you being shot by an agent." Behind his own levity, however, Peter felt a deep grief and guilt over his friend's condition.

Joshua smiled as he wiped his mouth from his last bite of corn. "It's a story unto itself," he said. "I must have lain there unconscious for some time. When I came too, the helicopter, the agents and you were all gone. I began to realize that the bullet had missed my vital organs, but had nicked my spine. My legs were paralyzed." Joshua took a deep breath. "So I crawled. I forced myself onto my hands and drug my limp body into the house." He shook his head as he remembered. "Getting up those stairs was no easy thing. I had to drag myself up to my bedroom and find this," he held up his flip phone.

"What then?" Crystal asked, engrossed in the tale.

"Well, I hadn't used this thing in years, but it was my only connection with someone on the outside. I turned it on and, to my delight, I had just enough battery life to call my friend, Parker."

Joshua was about to grab his plate and clean up the dishes when Martha stopped him. "Now," Martha said "you just leave all that be. I'll get it taken care of. You just roll on into the living room and relax."

"I've learned not to argue with you," Joshua said. He moved around the table and through the doorway into the living room. Peter and Crystal followed, with the three others standing to do the same.

"Now, William," Martha said. "You, Ken and Mark can all stay right here in this kitchen and help me get these dishes done." The three men offered their protests, but relented with the threat of desert being withheld.

Peter flopped down on a soft, plush, deep-blue sofa and Crystal collapsed beside him. "That might be about the most I've eaten in a month," he said.

Joshua smiled, "It sure brings me back to when we were at the river house."

"About that," Peter said, "I want to say I'm sorry."

"For what?"

"I should never have gone to get that Bible. I'm sure it's my fault that they found your house and now," Peter choked back his emotions. "Look at what I did to you."

"You didn't do this to me," Joshua said. "And you should never second guess a good deed. Remember what I taught you, 'anyone who knows the good he ought to do, and doesn't do it, sins.' You were doing a good thing; I don't hold that against you. In fact, it might have been the greatest act of generosity I ever received."

"But," Peter continued, "Will you ever walk again?"

Joshua took a deep breath and exhaled a sigh. "I don't know. Parker, the man I called, is a surgeon and he repaired the damage. But it will take time for the nerves to re-grow, if they're going to. But this is in the Lord's hands, too. Who knows, if I didn't get injured like this, I never would have come down here and we would never have reconnected. I may have been brought to McNeil with you and I'd still be trapped there."

"I guess that's something," Peter said.

"You've got to trust that there is a higher plan, one that only God sees. Don't let these circumstances keep you from doing what God wants. You mustn't feel guilty for what happened to me."

Suddenly Crystal shot off the couch. "I'll be right back," she said as she dashed up the stairs.

Peter and Joshua looked at each other, bewildered.

Just as quick, Crystal bounded down the stairs, sounding like a herd of deer, and burst into the room holding her knapsack. She reached inside it and pulled out a large, black tome. "Joshua," she said, "I believe this is yours."

Joshua reached toward her and took the book. He cradled it in his hands like a treasured antique and ran his fingers over the faded gold letters on the cover. He looked up at Crystal, "I don't know what to say… thank you."

Crystal beamed with a smile that lit up her eyes. "I took it when we had to leave Marcus' house. I forgot all about it until the two of you began to talk."

Just then Martha came into the living room. "Oh, what have you there, Joshua?"

"This, my dear Martha," Joshua said with all the pomp he could muster, "this is my grandfather's Bible."

"My, oh my!" She exclaimed. "I haven't seen even a page of the Holy Word since I was just a girl. My grandmother had a few torn pages she kept hidden when I lived in Minnesota." She looked at Joshua, "Would you favor us with a reading tonight?"

"As you wish, madam," Joshua said and bowed his head to her.

Martha gave a polite curtsy, "Why thank you, kind sir."

"If this get's any sweeter, you're both gonna be sugar-coated!" Crystal exclaimed.

A flash of light crossed through the living room from outside. Peter glanced out the large, pane-glass window to see a vehicle drive toward the back of the house. Martha darted out of the living room as an older man, stooped and with a cane, stepped out of a brown sedan.

"I think," Joshua said, "that Parker is here."

CHAPTER SIXTEEN

"Consider it pure joy, my brothers, when you face trials of many kinds." ~ James 1:2

The back door to the kitchen creaked open and shut with a bang. Peter watched as Martha escorted Parker into the house. Though stooped with age, he was tall with grey hair, flecked with black strands, which peeked out from under the brim of his fedora. He carried himself along on his cane, slowly walking into the home with the gallantry of simpler times. Peter thought that the newest house-guest must have been some type of professor.

Joshua wheeled around and coasted to the kitchen table where Parker sat and sipped on a steaming cup of tea prepared by Martha. Their voices carried low upon the air and Peter strained to hear more than muffled tones. William and Ken entered the living room and flopped upon two chairs, opposite Peter. Mark, however, left the kitchen through the back door, disappearing into the night beyond. Peter glanced out the window and watched as headlights popped on, followed by a motor revving up. In a stir of dust, a car drove off.

Peter looked back toward William, "Where's he off to?"

"Aw, that's just Mark," William said. "He's gone to watch some broadcast or somethin'. We ain't got a T.V. here so he goes down to Portland to see what's happenin'."

"Peter," Joshua called from the kitchen. "Peter, will you come in here for a minute?"

Peter walked into the kitchen and sat down at the table. The grim expressions on the faces of Martha and Joshua shocked him a bit. "What is it?"

"Well," Joshua began, "it has to do with your implant."

"Yes... and," Peter said. His mind raced with the possibility that he might live with the device the rest of his life. "It can be removed, can't it?"

Parker spoke up, "Oh, yes, my boy. It's not a problem to remove the device. It'll hurt, but the implant is only subcutaneous. The painful part is from the tubing that runs into your spinal canal."

"Well, if it can be removed, then remove it." Peter's voice grew in anticipation.

"You don't understand," Joshua said. "The problem with your implant is not that it can't be removed, but that the signaling device has already triggered an alert in Portland. They know you've crossed the border, and they're looking for you."

Martha rubbed her hands together. "Oh, dear," she sobbed. She pulled up her apron and wiped the tears from her eyes.

Peter's eyes crinkled up in perplexed thoughts. "How do you know this? What information did you find out?"

"I work for the government," Parker said. "I overheard two agents talking outside my office today. They said that they picked up your signal in Portland, but lost it again. They know you're near and will send their tracers to find you."

Peter's eyes widened at the idea that the man across from him worked for the very people who were hunting him. "What do you mean, you work for the government?"

"I'm a doctor," Parker said as if that were explanation enough.

"What's that suppose to mean?" Peter asked.

Joshua spoke up. "Peter, no doctor is allowed to practice medicine without being a government employee. If you're caught doing so, it's an automatic twenty years in prison. Parker here is actually Dr. Parker Chamberlain. He has been with the Remnant now for a long time."

Peter stood up when he heard Parker's full name. "You!" he exclaimed. "I've heard of you! You were the one who used people like laboratory rats. We talked about you when I was at the center. The guards would keep us quiet with the fear that you might come and take us away for your twisted experiments."

"That's enough, Peter," Joshua said in a calm, stern voice.

"It might surprise you that my reputation is less than deserved," Parker said. "One of the tools used by the government is well-honed propaganda." Parker stood up and stumbled to the pot of coffee on the counter. He poured himself a cup of the warm drink and turned to lean against the cabinets. "I think you might understand what I mean. I've heard much about the exploits of Peter Sheridan."

Peter nodded in realization. "I suppose I need to learn to be careful not to believe everything I once thought true."

"Enough talk," Martha spoke up. Her eyes red with tears, she replaced her apron and stood up. "Dr. Chamberlain, you need to help these young people. They've been through enough and if you can help them, then please do."

"But how do you know how to remove them?" Crystal asked as she walked into the room.

Parker hung his head. "Well," he said, "I was the one who invented the device in the first place." All eyes widened at the revelation, all except for Joshua who simply nodded.

"What?" Crystal demanded. "Why would you make such a horrible device?"

Parker took a drink of coffee and settled back down again in his chair. "It was about thirty years ago," he said. "I was a biochemist and was commanded to develop a way to keep the most violent people under control. Knowing that they already data-chipped every dangerous criminal, I simply developed a serum that would be injected into the spinal canal, triggered by a specific electronic impulse. I never thought that they would use the device to control political dissenters." Parker shook his head as he thought. "It was then that I decided that I'd do what I could to change things. When I discovered there were others with the same discontent, I joined with them."

"I hate to change the subject," Martha interrupted, "but shouldn't you just do what you need to? You can use a room upstairs."

"You're right, of course," Joshua said.

"I know I am." Martha smiled and stood up from the table.

Parker stood up as well. "Peter, if you're ready, we can do this now."

"What does it entail?" Peter asked.

"It's actually quite simple. All I'll need to do is cryogenically freeze the solution in the vial under your skin. Then, with it frozen, I will simply remove the device."

"You said it will hurt," Crystal observed.

"I have to freeze the liquid while the tube is still inserted in your spinal canal. It will be excruciating." Parker paused, as he reached for his cane. "After you," he said, and gestured toward the stairs.

Peter stood and, followed by Crystal, ventured upstairs with Parker. They entered into a small room with a high-stacked bed. The ceiling was slanted so that on one end of the room Peter had to crouch down to stand. Several dressers lined the walls and a closet was hidden by a simple curtain.

"Peter," the doctor said, "why don't you lie face down on this bed? It should be good enough for what we need." He opened a twin-handled leather bag and removed a rolled up assortment of tools. A bottle of alcohol and several sealed packets also were removed from the bag. Then he removed what looked like a can of spray paint.

"Are you going to paint my back, doc?" Peter asked.

"No," Parker chuckled. "This is a coolant, to freeze the device under your skin."

Peter took a deep breath, removed his shirt, and lay face down. "Let's get this over with."

Parker stepped to the bedside. "Crystal," he said, "you might want to wait outside the room while we do this."

Without a word, she nodded and left the chamber.

"Okay, Peter," Dr. Chamberlain said. "This will hurt."

"Just do it," Peter said as he clenched his jaw, waiting for the pain. He felt a cool wash touch his skin as Parker cleaned the area with alcohol.

"Joshua did a good job on your gunshot wound," Parker remarked. "But what are all these other scars on your back?"

"Just evidence of where I grew up," Peter said. "After my parents were taken from the center, it wasn't easy for me."

A sharp sting pierced his skin and Peter winced.

"That was the first incision," Parker said. "I'm going to pull back the skin and expose the cylinder."

Peter gave a slight nod and felt a burning tug against his skin. He shuddered as Parker washed the wound with a cold liquid. "Was that it?"

"No, just need to clean the area to get a good look at how they implanted it."

"Warn me when it's gonna get worse, doc." Peter grimaced through the burning sensation, as if his skin was being torn.

"I will."

For Peter time passed in slow, painful tics of the clock. Seconds seemed like minutes as he waited. The doctor continued to move and shift unseen muscle and skin and every touch brought a new sense of agony.

"Okay, Peter," the doctor said. "I've isolated the device and have separated it as much as I can from the surrounding tissue. Now, this is going to be painful." Dr. Chamberlain paused. "Are you ready?"

"Go ahead," Peter said reluctantly as he grabbed the edge of the mattress.

He heard the whoosh of a steady, vaporous spray and smelled the scent of stale air. It was cool on his skin, uncomfortable but not painful. Still the steady stream blew on his back, and he felt the chill touch his shoulder blade.

Then the cold reached along the cylinder, down the tube and into his spine. The pain hit him with such violence that he screamed. Ice filled every inch of his body and he thought that his hands and feet might explode with the sheer force of his surging nerves. He crushed his eyes shut and gripped with all his strength, tearing into the fabric of the mattress. The rushing sound of the propellant filled the room, like a hurricane that might never end.

"Just a little longer," Parker said.

His words were little more than a whisper to Peter who again shrieked in desperate agony. Time had stopped and he knew that his life was over. Then the rushing sound ended.

"Okay, that's done. You're going to feel a little tug now," Parker said in a soft, friendly tone.

Peter nodded, relieved that it was almost over. His body quivered with the stress. A new pain wracked his body. The little tug felt as if Parker tried to rip his spine out. He convulsed in agony, as if a massive spike was thrust into his back then ripped out again.

"Done," Doctor Chamberlain said. "I just need to clean and close up this incision."

"Th... thank... y... you, d...d... doc." Peter trembled and slowly relaxed as the pain subsided into a dull ache.

"I wish I had something for the pain," Parker said as he placed a sterile bandage on the wound, "but I can't get the pain killers out of the building. In about an hour you will begin to regain your strength. Try not to move around too much, you will need to let your body adjust."

Peter gave a nod and listened as Parker left the room and clicked the door closed behind him. He lay there for what seemed like an hour or more, drifting in and out of consciousness. His hands and feet tingled, especially at the tips and he wanted to shake life back into them. He hadn't moved in all that time and tried to roll over. Every muscle ached as if he had run a marathon. His joints screamed in protest but he forced himself to turn, and cast his gaze upon Crystal.

"Good evening," she said.

"Hi," he replied, his voice hoarse. His throat felt as if he had inhaled a bucket of sand.

"Don't try to get up. Doctor Chamberlain said you should stay in bed the rest of the night."

"I can't just lie here all night," Peter protested.

"Why not, you've been here for the better part of three hours already." Crystal smiled her usual, Cheshire-cat grin. "I just came to look in on you and see if you needed anything."

Peter offered a half-cooked smile. "I could use a glass of water."

Crystal disappeared out the door and returned a short time after with a large plastic glass filled with cool water. He reached out and took the proffered gift and sipped on the refreshing liquid.

"Well," Crystal said, "you've taken my room so I guess I'll have to sleep downstairs." She placed her hands across her chest in mock anger.

"But what about you?" Peter asked, not responding to her humor. "What about the device in your back? Isn't the doctor going to take it out?"

"No need," she said. "I never had one of those things."

Peter sighed with great relief. "I am so glad," he said. "I'd hate to think of you going through that agony." He shifted to try and find a comfortable position. "But I thought that everyone on the island was forced to have one of those things."

She smiled. "No," she said, "just those who were brought to the island. Those like me and Paul—those who started off as children on McNeil—don't have those things." She stepped into the doorway. "You get some rest. Joshua said that we'll talk more tomorrow."

* * * *

Peter woke with a start. His room was dark, and the sound of a slight breeze whistled through the single-pane glass windows. A pale moon peeked through the trees and cast silver light that flittered like spirits on the walls. His back throbbed, and the place of the incision stung like needles piercing under his skin.

The door was closed, but just beyond in the hallway he heard footsteps try to sneak past. Though his body ached in protest, Peter rose from his bed, keeping quiet so he didn't alert the one in the hall. He felt like he was back in Darrington, trying to avoid the guards. Cautiously, he placed his ear against the door and heard whispers from beyond. He cracked the door open a fraction and peered into the dark, with only the dim glow of a solar charged light to offer a faint illumination. In the room opposite, he heard low voices talking in hurried whispers. With patient steps, while his heart seemed to beat in his ears, he drew next to the other door.

"We'll do it tomorrow." Peter recognized William's voice.

"Are you sure we can pull this off? It might be the biggest target we've ever had," said another man. Peter thought it was the one named Ken.

"Look," William said, "we went after the airport and that didn't even stun anyone let alone get 'em to listen. We gotta get this one to make our point."

"But, to kill a man," the other said, "I mean, that's serious. It's one thing to scare people, but to actually kill someone... I don't know."

"We're in this together," William retorted in a harsh whisper. "Mark, where did ya say that the government guy was gonna be?"

"He's holding a rally and speaking down at the mall. Tomorrow afternoon, the federal communications director will be there."

"But, William, that's not the way we set this up. We're just trying to scare them so that they listen."

"Ken," Mark said, "if you don't take this to the next level, you'll never be heard."

"This guy is one of the biggest liars in our country," William added. "Take him out and we might be taken seriously."

"But what about Peter and the others?" Ken asked. "They might be of some help. He did make it off of McNeil. You've heard what he's done. Let's ask him and Joshua to help."

"No," Mark's voice was adamant. "Joshua believes differently and Peter will listen to him. We can't trust that they will take such a risk. They don't have the same desire for change that you do. Words won't bring this country back, only action."

"When will that fella be there?" William asked.

"He speaks at two in the afternoon. You need to be ready by then. Have the diversion set up and then come to the central courtyard where you will kill the communications director."

Peter nearly gasped, but stepped quietly back into his room, shocked at what he just heard. He shut his door and listened as the three men snuck down the hall. They stepped down the stairs, the third stair squeaked and Peter knew they had departed. *I've got to stop them,* he thought. *If the Remnant is known for murder, people will never believe that we speak the truth.* Peter lay back down in bed. The soft mattress lulled him into a renewed drowsiness. He had some time, and he needed some sleep.

* * * *

He woke again, this time to a morning canopied with clouds and baptized in a gentle rain. Through the window, Peter noticed that two cars were gone, Parker's and William's. His back itched, and he needed to change the dressing, but he wanted to get to the mall before the three men had the opportunity to execute their plan.

Quickly he dressed. As he entered the hall, he thought of the conversation from the night before and wondered what type of diversion that they planned. His first task, he knew, was to save the life of the director. A brief glance into the other room showed no one left. The bed was disheveled and the room carried the pungent scent of gunpowder. He slipped down the stairs, avoiding the third one so he didn't wake anybody, and tiptoed through the living room. Crystal slept on the blue, plush sofa and the two other bedrooms had their doors closed.

Desperate to avoid detection, Peter stepped through the kitchen, only to find Joshua waiting at the table. "Good morning, Peter." His calm, baritone resonated softly in the quiet morning.

"Hi, Joshua."

"And, where are you off to this morning?"

"Joshua, did you know that those three men were the ones that set a bomb at the Portland Airport?" Peter spoke rapidly, hoping to get a head start on the three men.

"Sit down, Peter, please."

Peter gushed with anxiety, hurried in his thoughts. His respect for Joshua overrode his agitation and he took a seat. "Joshua, I don't know that I have much time for this."

Joshua sighed, "Patience, tell me what you know."

Peter took a deep breath to calm his racing heart and told him what he had heard in the night. "And, so," he concluded, "they're going to kill him!"

Joshua shook his head in dismay. "I should have known," he lamented. "Mark is the one you need to watch out for. I wondered about him. He joined us just three months ago and connected quickly with William and Ken."

"What should I do?" Peter asked.

"With your implant out, you will be able to walk the mall without difficulty, but you'll never get close enough to the director to warn him." Joshua stroked his beard as he thought. "Go get your father's uniform. Come back and put it on."

Peter did as he was told. He rushed upstairs and donned the uniform. It was a good fit, if slightly loose. He looked at himself in the mirror and was shocked to see a soldier looking back at him. His heart raced with anticipation as he dashed down the stairs and found Joshua still at the table.

"Okay, Peter," he said calmly. "The only way you'll get close enough to warn him is to pretend to be on the security detail. You are now a major in the special ops. You'll need to act like it."

"How will I know who the director is?"

"He'll be the one surrounded by guards," Joshua said as he smiled and rolled back toward the living room. He glanced back and said, "I'll be praying for you, Peter."

Peter rushed out the door to the car. It was easy to spot as the rain had left a glistening sheen on the surface, though it still remained in its camouflage mode. He opened the door, tossed his father's hat to the passenger seat and jumped in. With a quick flick of the ignition switch, the engine hummed to life and he sped off down the gravel drive.

"Show Portland," Peter commanded. A flash and the street map of Portland showed on the screen. "Show current location," he said again and the map scrolled until it rested on a small flag in motion. "Show route to nearest mall," and a red line appeared that traced along the roads until it arrived at a place titled: *Clackamas Mall*. Peter glanced at the map and followed the path given by the computer.

Thirty minutes later, Peter entered into the main thoroughfare of the city. Arterial streets were wider and dozens, if not hundreds of cars and trucks ventured along their routes, bound for unknown destinations. As he drove, he crossed under the main highway and the map pointed him to the right. He looked and saw a massive building, sprawled out over several city blocks. All manner of vehicles filled in the asphalt lots that surrounded the structure. A large video display sat perched above the main entrance, flashing its instructions to all who ventured to go inside.

Peter drove around to the north side of the center and found a massive warehouse complex. He wove his way through the maze of buildings and found a quiet location to park. He stepped out and looked around. No one was in sight and he commanded his car to engage the camouflage. It vanished with a shimmer.

With that done, he stepped across the street and walked toward the mall complex. People milled around the entrance, coming and going and yet giving Peter a wide berth, diverting their eyes from catching his gaze and purposely avoiding any potential contact with him. It was an eerie feeling to be so feared and it struck him with a sense of dread. Conversations stopped as he passed, only to be resumed when they thought he was out of earshot.

"Did you see him," a young woman whispered to her companion.

"Yes, shhhh, he might hear you," said the other.

"He seemed young to me."

"They get these boys younger all the time. Just let him alone."

Peter continued on, the two girls out of earshot, and walked up to the main entrance. Several lines had formed at least twenty people deep while guards checked identification cards before people were allowed to enter.

"C'mon," shouted one guard three lines over from Peter, "keep this line movin'!"

"Make sure you have your cards out where we can see 'em," said another as he pushed a young man out of the line. "Go home boy, and bring your momma back with you next time." The young man, no more than thirteen, dashed away as several others mockingly laughed.

Peter reached the front of the line. The guards suddenly snapped to attention when they saw the insignia on his coat. "Major," said the tall, scruffy soldier who guarded his line. "I didn't expect anyone from Ops to be here."

Peter braced himself and spoke, "What are you doing here?"

"Just protecting the mall, sir," he said. "No one is allowed in to shop unless they have their purchasing card with them." The guard looked around as if some spy might be listening, "I'll tell you, just between you and me, those shadow-folks won't be gettin' in here! That gang will have me to deal with, especially that leader of theirs."

"Oh, and who is that Sergeant?"

"You musta heard of 'em already, that fella which broke out of Darrington and then escaped McNeil up in Washington. But he'll not get past us!"

The line behind him began to grow anxious as he waited to be let in.

"Sergeant," Peter said, "you might want to let me in and get these people moving."

The guard stood erect, "Sir, yes sir!" He pressed a remote button and opened the door, letting Peter into the building.

"One thing," Peter said, "where is the director holding his speech?"

"Lower level, sir, center rink."

Peter nodded and returned the salute, then walked through the door.

The mall was an expansive circus of vendors, with a wealth of humanity stirring around like ants in a nest. A cacophony of sounds emanated from everywhere at once, but Peter focused on finding his way to the lower level. As he walked about, people who noticed him still moved away from him. Most people, however, seemed lost in their own minds, like distracted androids that moved in and out of the shops.

He found an escalator which descended downward, and beside it was a kiosk video board. He stopped to watch the display. A kind, slender woman appeared on the screen and with a gentle voice spoke to the passers-by. "Have you someone in your life that is hungry? Do you know people that try to live outside the system? Your purchasing card is your protection, but there are those who have rejected it and are hurting our society. Do yourself a favor and turn them in. If they are found guilty, you could receive a reward up to ten thousand dollars."

Peter shook his head at the notion as he remembered Joshua and Martha's great hospitality. It seemed to him that those who lived outside the system were by far better off than all who he witnessed ambling about the mall. He walked onto the escalator and descended to the lower level.

A large, open space was transformed into an amphitheater, with bleachers surrounding a platform and podium. Some guards were present but either ignored him or steered away from him. He determined to approach one guard who stood by the dais. The lone soldier snapped to attention at Peter's approach.

"Soldier, your name," Peter commanded.

"Corporal Samuel Green, sir!"

"Okay, Green, when is the director going to arrive?"

"Mr. Kyle Johansen's arrival time is classified, sir, but he is scheduled to speak at fourteen-hundred hours."

"I need to know where he is, I have very important news for him," Peter tried to sound as authoritative and demanding as possible. He saw in the young soldier's eyes a quick glance to a door just beyond his post.

"I can't tell you, sir," the corporal replied. "You will need to get clearance from the squadron commander, Captain Mathews."

"Then go and get your captain, and I will deal with him."

Corporal Green saluted then disappeared behind the bleachers. Peter moved toward the door that Green had glanced at and quietly tapped on it. Nothing happened. He tapped on it again.

The knob moved and Peter slammed his shoulder into door. Rushing in, he quickly closed the door behind him and assessed the room. Two men were standing by the opposite wall and one lay on the ground.

"What's the meaning of this!" demanded the man farthest away. He was blonde with a touch of grey at the temples, cut short and clean shaven. He stood just a little shorter than Peter, and his look of surprise captivated Peter's attention.

"At ease," Peter commanded, and helped the fallen man up.

"What is the meaning of this, major?" the man asked again, this time with less emotion.

"Are you Director Johansen?"

The man hesitated, "Yes, I am."

"I need to speak with you," Peter looked at the other two, then back to the director, "alone."

Johansen looked at the two other men and waived them out the back door. They appeared reluctant, but quietly obeyed and closed the door behind them. "Alright, major, we're alone, what's this about?"

Peter took a deep breath and listened at the door he entered. "I'm not in the army," he said. "I'm not a major, and I've come to warn you that your life is in danger." Peter raised his hand, "Don't think of calling your guards; hear me out."

"Who are you?"

"My name," he hesitated to say it. "My name is Peter Sheridan."

The director's eyes widened in disbelief, "You!"

"Yes, me," Peter said. "I'm here to warn you that there are three men who are coming to take your life."

"You're lying! No one could get past my guards. They're the best security money can buy."

"Yeah, no one like me," Peter shook his head. "Look, they're in the mall already. They're setting up some type of diversion that will take the guards away from you, and then they will kill you."

"Why are you telling me this? You're the leader of those terrorists, that... that Shadow Remnant."

"I'm telling you this for two reasons. One, because you need to know that the Remnant is not a terrorist group."

"And two?" Johansen asked.

"And two," Peter said, "because your life depends on it."

"You know, you're the most wanted man in America right now. You'll never leave this mall alive."

"We'll see," Peter said.

A violent shock, like an earthquake, shook the room. Peter and the director fell to the ground. Sirens blared and the sound of people screaming filled the halls beyond the door.

"Looks like the diversion has happened," Peter said as he stood. "I'll be going now." He rushed out the door into the melee of people. From behind him he heard the director shouting for his guards, but he didn't look back.

Smoke rolled through the mall along with the chaotic rush of humanity. Peter filtered into the maelstrom and made his way along the corridor, trying to get to the upper level. Out of the corner of his eye, he caught a glimpse of who he thought was Mark. He turned, and looked down the concourse where the bleachers were set up. As he watched, a dark-haired man ducked behind the wall.

"Great," Peter said out loud, and turned to go back to the director.

He pushed and shoved his way against the current of human traffic, spinning and moving as fast as possible. He crossed the open section behind the stands and saw Corporal Green unconscious on the floor. He checked the corporal's pulse and found him still alive.

"Guards!" shouted the director from inside his room.

Peter ran to the door and slammed into it with his shoulder. His back jolted from his wound, but he again slammed against the door. The frame cracked and the door flew open, striking a body behind it.

Eyes wide, Kyle Johansen stood against the far wall. He looked at Peter, his face pale and body shaking with the shock.

On the floor lay Mark. Dazed, he looked up and squinted. "You!" he said. Mark tried to reach for the gun that had slid from his grasp, but Peter picked up the revolver and dumped out the cartridges, then threw the weapon against the wall.

The director looked back at Peter. "You came back, why?"

"Because you needed it. Now quit spreading your lies about me." Peter ducked out of the room and disappeared into the crowd. Guards filed through the people, forcing their way back to the director's chamber and gave no notice of Peter's passage.

He glided up the escalator to the second level, and found his way back to the main entrance. People near the doors seemed little concerned for what happened on the floor below them. He smiled as he exited the complex, walking across the parking lot to his car. "Now," he said, "I think I should head for California."

CHAPTER SEVENTEEN

"They repay me evil for good, and hatred for my friendship." ~ Psalm 109:5

Peter raced back to the farmhouse. He drove as fast as traffic allowed and, guided by the computer, found his way to the woods and up the gravel drive. The day had brightened and he noticed Martha working in the greenhouse that was in an open area of the backyard. Crystal was in the woodshed, chopping several large, round sections into usable firewood. He thought that she must finally feel at home, doing work that she was used to. Then he noticed, out of the corner of his eye, nestled behind a small copse of trees, William's car was back.

With a cloud of dust following, Peter stopped his car and stepped out into the warming day. All seemed peaceful, but a certain dread had crept into his thoughts and he wanted to find Joshua right away. Crystal waved and he returned the gesture, but then quickly ducked into the house. It was eerily silent as he stepped into the kitchen. He peered through the arched door into the living room. There sat Joshua in his wheelchair, with William and Ken on the blue, plush sofa.

"Peter," Joshua's voice was somber, "come in here."

He walked in and took a chair beside his friend. "What is it? You look like you've seen a ghost."

"No, not a ghost," Joshua said. "We've been listening to the radio. There is an all-out alert for you."

"Yeah, so what?" Peter tried to sound nonchalant about the news. "That director told me that I was a wanted man."

"Ya' don't understand," William said. "You've been fingered as the guy who tried to kill the communications director."

"What?" Peter's voice rose with incredulity. "I saved that guy's life! This is how he repays me?" He shook his head in disgust and despair.

"It was that no-good, double-crossin' Mark," Ken said. His face flushed with anger, so that even his eyes looked bloodshot-red.

"What do you mean?" Peter asked.

Joshua held up his hands to silence the conversation. "Peter, tell me everything that happened. Don't leave out a detail." He turned to face William. "You need to get Crystal and Martha in here, we'll need to go to a safe house that Mark is unaware of."

William jumped up and dashed out the door.

"Now, Peter, tell me what happened."

Peter told Joshua the story from when he entered the mall to when he left, leaving out no details, explaining how he had saved the director's life. As he spoke, Crystal came in, followed by Martha who fanned herself with her apron.

"You did what?" Crystal demanded.

"I went to the mall and saved the man's life," Peter said again. Her furrowed brows said she demanded more of an explanation. "Crystal," he said, "I discovered last night that Mark was planning on murdering the Director of Communications. I went to stop him... and I did."

Martha pressed past Crystal and William to enter the living room. "So, what's the problem?"

"You don't understand," Joshua interrupted. "Mark nearly did kill him and Peter was able to stop him. Now, however, Mark has sold us out for his own life. Just a few minutes ago, on the radio, the director said that Peter was the one who tried to kill him and that Mark came in at the last minute to save him. It's a good bet that he will lead the federal agent's right back here."

Martha grew flustered with the thought and sat down on a chair near the archway. "Joshua, what will we do?"

"It's not a hard decision, Martha, we need to leave this place and go to a location that Mark knows nothing about." Joshua wheeled around in his chair to face Peter. "You and Crystal ought to go. You need to get to California and find McKenna. With that device gone, they can't track you. But Mark knew some of the plan and will be after you. He knows that you're going south, and I'm sure if he was willing to sell you out, the authorities will know everything he knows."

"But what about you?" Peter asked. His heart raced with nervous energy and he felt like prey sensing a predator. His eyes continually moved back to the large, pane window, fearful that he might see a helicopter or van approaching.

"Don't worry about us," Joshua said. "We will take William's car and find a safe place to disappear. We have a head start on them. Mark was live on the radio just before you arrived so that should give us about thirty minutes before anyone gets here."

Peter stood and moved toward the window, gazing into the distance as if he sought his future. "It's not fair," he said as he ran his fingers over his head.

"What's that?" Joshua asked.

"I save his life, and I get repaid with lies."

Joshua nodded. "Remember what you were taught," he said.

"What's that?"

"There are those who will persecute you and say all kinds of false things against you," Joshua said. His voice was low and comforting. "Peter?"

Peter turned around and saw Joshua holding out the ancient Bible. "What?"

"I want you to take this. You need to trust what it says, but to do that you need to learn it." Joshua wheeled his chair and parked next to the window, staring out into the distance. "This book will help you."

Peter stared at the old, leather cover with its faded gold letters. "I can't take this from you. This belongs to your family... why give it to me?"

Joshua smiled, "Because you need it." He raised it up just a little higher.

Peter reached and received the proffered book. "I'll take it," he said, "but only if it's on loan. It belongs to you and when all this is done I will bring it back."

"Fair enough," Joshua said. "But you and Crystal must get going." He turned and faced the young woman who stood behind Martha as if needing to hide. "Crystal, gather your things. And you, Peter," he continued, "You better change out of that uniform. You'll find that there are people in the rural areas of this land that don't, how shall I say it, that don't appreciate those in uniform."

Peter nodded and dashed off upstairs. He returned just minutes later, changed into a pair of blue jeans a white, button-down shirt and his backpack in his hand. Crystal ambled down the stairs behind him with her pack draped over her shoulder. He looked down at his mentor and friend as a tremor wracked his thoughts. "I can't believe this," he said.

"What?" Joshua asked.

"Once again, you and I part ways because I'm being hunted." He walked to the window where Joshua waited. "I just hope the next time we see each other I won't be on the run."

"Me too," Joshua said.

Both men embraced and Peter looked up to see Crystal and Martha having a quiet discussion in the kitchen that ended with an emotional, tear-filled hug. Crystal looked back at Peter and he saw a new awareness in her eyes, as if she had settled something in her thoughts. The carefree look was replaced with a determination that Peter had never seen in her before. He moved to the kitchen in time to hear the end of their conversation.

"Now, dear," Martha said, "You remember what I told you. You'll see that it's true."

Crystal nodded and embraced the matronly woman. "Thank you," she whispered as she choked back a tear. "Keep us in your prayers."

"Always," Martha said with a smile. "You and Peter have a great task before you. Just don't forget to keep your eyes open. You'll see that God is with you."

William ran into the house. "We gotta go!" he said. "I got my car set and you all need to get movin'. Ken's waitin' in the car if you'd just hurry up!" His voice wavered as he spoke and he panted to get out every word.

"He's right," Joshua said as he wheeled up. "You two go and we'll follow close after."

"Okay," Peter and Crystal said simultaneously. Both walked out of the house to the car. The sleek, silver vehicle waited like a patient thoroughbred, and hummed to life when Peter switched on the engine.

With a cloud of dust behind them, Peter sped down the gravel drive and through the small forest of trees until they came to the main road. Tires squealed on the asphalt as he turned toward Portland. He hoped to simply take the highway south to California. With the jamming system on, he switched on the radar and frequently glanced down at the screen for any sign of approaching vehicles. They drove for several miles when a small blip appeared on the screen.

"What's that?" Crystal asked.

"I don't know?" Peter replied. "What's the range?"

"*Range set, six miles,*" the computer voice said.

Peter pulled the car off the road and backed onto a small dirt trail, just wide enough for the vehicle. He engaged the camouflage and the car shimmered and vanished. "Now we wait."

They had stopped for only a minute when a black helicopter rushed over the top of a small hill and flew across the landscape toward the farmhouse. Two minutes later six black sedans and one van sped past them on the road, sirens blaring out their warning cries.

"That was close," Crystal said.

"Yes," Peter agreed. He looked in the direction of the house and watched the federal vehicles disappear beyond a rise. "I just hope that the others made it out in time." He disengaged the camouflage and found his way back to Portland.

The roads were barren of traffic until they arrived on the outskirts of the city. As they neared Portland, the streets slowly filled with other travelers until every road was swarmed with cars. He moved along with the rest of them, hoping to blend in with the motorized menagerie, and couldn't help but feel that the other drivers were little more than ants that moved through the streets, carried along by instinct rather than any great purpose. Ten minutes after arriving in the city he located the on-ramp to the highway. With a deep breath, as if plunging into an icy river, he turned south and merged onto the interstate.

The traffic flowed along with little hindrance. At staggered intervals, patrol cars lined the side of the road. Some had other vehicles pulled over, others waited like wolves ready to leap. Each one, however, gave Peter a sense of dread. He wondered if they waited for him, watching to see if they could trap him in some clever scheme. Yet, Portland passed behind them with no challenge as they coursed their way south to California.

The miles passed in silence as Peter and Crystal watched the scene change from urban sprawl to a more rural spread of farms and houses. A fine mist fell upon the earth and draped the car with its watery vapor as the wipers kept time to the rhythm of the highway.

"Seems calm out here," Crystal observed.

Peter shook out of his own daze, "What, oh, yeah. It reminds me of the farms that I had to work at in Darrington."

"Was it rough for you? I mean, I've only known life on the island, and with Jack and the other colonists everyone pitched in to make it a home."

Peter thought back to the days he spent at the center and shook his head. "No," he said, "it wasn't home. We were often beaten and it never seemed like we had enough to eat. We slept for only five hours a night and were working seven days a week. My life was completely controlled by the guards. That's why I tried to escape so many times, and got shot for my troubles." He reached over and rubbed his shoulder.

Crystal offered a sympathetic grin. "I wonder if we'll actually be able to change things."

"I don't know," he sighed. "But I don't have much of a choice now. Unless things change, I'll be on the run forever. I doubt that I could live as a hunted man for the rest of my life."

"We could always sneak back onto the island and live with the colony," Crystal smiled.

Peter's thoughts turned to his father. "You know, it doesn't seem fair."

"What's that?"

"Just weeks ago I was back with my family. It seems every time I find a place that I might be able to call home, I'm put back on the road."

"Well," Crystal said, "according to Martha, 'that's just the way it is, dear.'" Crystal chuckled trying to imitate Martha's accent.

"You're a lot of help," Peter said, his voice lilted with sarcasm.

"That's what I'm here for." Crystal leaned back in her seat and put her feet up on the dashboard. A grin crossed her face as she closed her eyes.

Peter shook his head again and turned his attention to the world beyond the car. The mist had given way to low, drifting clouds that occasionally sprinkled the window. A large truck rolled ahead of him and blasted a wall of spray off its tires. Rolling hills rushed past, dotted with communities and solitary houses and Peter wondered about the lives of the people within. The hours and the miles seemed to merge into one monotonous blur. Peter glanced over to see Crystal sleeping, her head resting against the door.

"Crystal?"

She stirred and shook her head, "Huh... where... what?"

"Good morning," Peter quipped.

"Shut up," she said and rolled her eyes. "Where are we?"

"Still in Oregon," he said. "We've covered a lot of ground. We passed through a town called Medford and are nearing the border with California."

"Any chance we could pull off and stretch our legs a bit?"

"Sure... there's nothing between here and the border, so I don't think we'll see anyone." Peter slowed the car down and stopped on the side of the road. He opened his door and the cold, damp air bit against his skin. "You may want your jacket," he said.

"Yeah, it's a bit cold, but I gotta stretch my legs for just a minute." Crystal stepped out of the car and reached her arms up as if she tried to grasp a passing cloud. "Ah, that's better. Sitting in a car for this long is tiring. Give me a hike across the island and a swim across the lake instead of this cooped up means of traveling."

"Well," Peter said, "it is better than walking to California."

Crystal squinted with her eyes, "I'm not so sure about that." She bent forward and then side to side. "C'mon," she said, "let's take a walk."

"Where?" Peter questioned. "We don't know this area and as far as I can tell there's not much around but trees and hills."

"What's that sign say?" Crystal pointed toward a large green sign that hung over the highway.

"It says Siskiyou Lodge Treatment Center next right."

"Well," She said as if her thoughts were obvious.

"Well what?" Peter asked.

"Let's go check it out."

"Why?"

"I don't know. It's something to do and it's better than being cooped up in that car for another five hours without a break. Besides, you could use the exercise." She smiled and began walking toward the sign.

Peter put the car in camouflage mode and followed after her, jogging occasionally until he finally caught up. "Why are we going there again?"

"Simple," Crystal said, "because I need to stretch my legs and you need the exercise." Her voice dripped with sarcasm.

Peter just nodded and kept pace with her. They walked for several hundred yards, cutting across the asphalt highway and through some sparse trees until they happened upon a small valley that sheltered an old, three story building. The structure was lined with windows, though a good many of them had been boarded up. A chain-link fence surrounded the compound with razor wire at the top, twisted into concentric circles. One gate in the center of the fence was open and a square guard station sat in the middle of the road.

No guard was visible, but Peter knew better than to trust it. He had been tricked before and the entire scene stirred painful memories. "Crystal, why are we here?"

"Just to stretch a bit and to feel the ground beneath my feet…"

"Get down!" Peter said. He crouched low upon the ground and pulled Crystal down with him as a black car drove up to the gate.

The car stopped at the guard shack and the driver got out. He was a gruff looking soldier with chevron-stripes on his arm. He gestured in the air with his hands and motioned as if he ranted, but he was too far away to be heard. A shorter man ran out of the three story building, hurriedly buttoning his olive-green jacket as he neared the car.

Both men walked about and appeared to shout at one another, looking like two lions measuring up the competition. The driver relented, hands cast down at his side, and opened the rear door of the car. Like a shot, a man rushed out and ran from the area, racing up the hill—right toward Peter and Crystal.

"Great!" Peter lamented. He ducked lower and peered through the grass as the man drew closer. "Would you get down!" he demanded.

Crystal lay upon her belly, eyes wide. "What should we do?"

Shots rang out from the compound as the man neared. The sound of bullets whistled through the air. Peter could see the runner's face, as sweat glistened from the man's olive-colored skin. His hair was matted and eyes wide with panic as he dashed toward the two who still lay in the grass.

"Crystal," Peter said, "can you still run?"

"Yeah," she said.

"You're faster than I am. I want you to run back to the car and turn off the camouflage. I'll be right behind you." Peter slowly moved to his knees, careful to keep a keen eye on the approaching runner.

"You're going to rescue this guy, aren't you?"

Peter ignored the obvious statement, "On the count of three, I want you to sprint to the car. Do you remember where it is?"

She nodded, "Just past the large green sign, and parked off the road."

"Okay," Peter said, "One... two... three!"

Crystal stood up and dashed across the field like a cheetah. Dust kicked up from her shoes, and soon she was far ahead.

The man with the Mediterranean skin just about stepped on Peter when Peter jumped up and grabbed him, tackling him to the ground. Peter pressed his hand over the man's mouth and motioned for him to be quiet. "If you want to get out of here," Peter said in his sternest voice, "follow me." The man nodded and both stood, Peter in the lead as they ran for the car.

Shots rang out from behind them, and Peter glanced back to see the two guards in staggered pursuit. Through the sparse trees, almost to the highway, he saw the car. Peter's thoughts rang out in his head with praise for Crystal. The man with him kept pace, stride for stride, and soon they were over the interstate and in the car. Peter switched the engine on and stepped on the accelerator. Dust and rocks kicked up from the tires and they sped off down the highway.

Past the onramp for the treatment center, Peter looked to his left to see the driver running back to his vehicle. "This is not going to be good."

"What," Crystal said.

"The guy's coming after us. Let's just hope that he gives up the chase before we get to the border."

"He will not," said the man in the backseat, his voice rich with a middle-eastern accent. "He will pursue us until his car burns up. He will call for his backups. That was how he caught me."

"Who are you?" Crystal asked.

"My name is David Cohen."

"So, why were they after you?" she asked.

"You saved my life, so I owe you," David said, "but I do not trust anyone, especially strangers."

"Look," Peter said, "right now all of us are in some rather hot water. We have a patrol car behind us, and probably border guards on alert in front of us. We don't have much of a choice but to trust each other."

"Yes, you are probably right," David said. "I hacked into the federal communications network to find a way to shut it down. They found me, but I eluded them many days. But these guards are like hounds and will not give up so easy."

"So we've noticed," Crystal said.

"I was captured and sentenced to 'treatment'," David continued.

"What kind of treatment?" Peter asked.

"I have heard many rumors of what they do. It is some form of injection that targets the brain and gives you a chemical lobotomy." David shuttered. "It was either run and be killed or surrender and become a lab experiment." He took a deep breath, "I chose to run."

The road twisted and wound its way through the rugged, mountainous terrain. Peter kept the speed up as fast as his own skills allowed and just hoped that the driver of the other vehicle was having as much difficulty as he was. He commanded a rear view on the display screen and noticed a black government car several hundred yards behind.

"We are not going get away from him," David said.

"You may be surprised," Crystal replied. "We've already escaped more challenging situations."

"But who are you?" David asked.

"My name is Peter," he was hesitant to disclose his last name. "This is Crystal," he said as he motioned toward her.

"But who are you? This car, your appearance at just the right time, it is all too coincidental for my taste."

"It seems we have a habit of doing that," Crystal said. "But, if you want, I guess we can drop you off here."

Peter gasped and it grabbed the others attention. He fixed his eyes upon a blockade waiting for them at the California border. Several cars were parked at angles in the road and at least a dozen men waited behind them. "Great!" he lamented and slammed on the brakes.

"Peter! What are you doing?" Crystal asked.

He didn't answer but cranked hard on the wheel and spun the car to face the other direction. With his foot on the accelerator he pushed the vehicle faster and suddenly rushed past the car that followed him. With a look at his rear-view screen he watched as those who had blockaded the border jumped into their cars. With tires smoking against the asphalt, the border was emptied.

Peter gave a quick grin and wound his way around a sharp turn in the road. Then he slammed on the brakes again. A quick look around and he maneuvered into a small patch of dirt that led up to a gated fence. He parked, and engaged the camouflage.

Crystal looked at Peter with a quizzical smirk and raised her eyebrow, "Again? Didn't you try this trick once before?"

"I like to stick with what works," he said with a smile.

"What do you mean?" David asked. "Why are we just waiting here?"

"Just a moment," Peter advised, "You'll see."

A minute later and the first car rushed past, then the next and the next. Soon seven cars had raced by, moving north to try and catch them.

"Can we go now?" Crystal asked, holding back a chuckle.

Peter disengaged the camouflage and backed into the highway, turning south toward the California border. He pressed the accelerator and rushed along, eager to get across.

"Who are you?" David asked again.

Crystal turned to Peter, "I think you can tell him."

Peter took a deep breath, "My name is Peter Sheridan."

David's eyes widened and a smile crossed his face. "You cannot be? What are the odds that I should find you?"

"What do you mean?" Peter asked.

"I had heard about you and when I learned that you were leading the Shadow Remnant I had hoped to find you."

"Why?" Crystal asked.

"Because, I know of your exploits and wanted to join you in fighting against the government."

"But I'm not here to fight against the government," Peter sighed.

"Watch out!" Crystal yelled.

Peter looked again and turned the wheel sharp, narrowly avoiding a car that was parked in the middle of the highway. It was the black government vehicle.

"I told you!" David said. "Did I not tell you that he was relentless?"

Peter raced past the trap and drove for the California border. The black sedan followed, but lost ground. He looked ahead and saw the guard house at the border, with its crossing arm lowered over the highway.

With renewed determination, Peter didn't slow down and crashed through the red-striped arm. Splinters flew like shrapnel and the road ahead was straight and long. He looked at the screen and the car behind him faded in the distance, lost in the growing twilight. The three travelers took a collective sigh of relief.

"I guess," Crystal said, "that we're in California."

"It seems so," Peter agreed. "But I doubt that we're done with trouble."

"You can be sure of it," David said. "We have not seen the last of that man."

CHAPTER EIGHTEEN

" When you pass through the waters, I will be with you..." ~ Isaiah 43:2

With no pursuit behind them, Peter slowed the car to just under seventy-miles-an-hour and drove through the night. The empty road passed beneath them as David and Crystal slept quietly in their seats. Their gentle breathing almost kept time with one another as Crystal's head leaned against her door and David lay sprawled on the backseat. They passed through several quiet towns, like small outposts of humanity in an otherwise barren landscape.

Clouds had parted and the night sky shimmered with millions of stars. A pale moon emanated its soft glow and bathed the world in sheets of silver. An occasional car in the northbound lanes passed by, but no sight or sound of pursuit disrupted the momentary peace. Peter's head felt heavy and his eyelids started to sag in the hypnotic rhythm of the road. He shook his head to try and wake up, but exhaustion began to win against his will.

"Peter!" Crystal shouted as she slapped him on the arm. "Peter, wake up!"

"Huh... what?" he said and bolted upright. He gripped the steering wheel in his hands and swerved left and right. The car fishtailed but he brought it under control. His heart raced and he slammed on the brakes.

"Calm down," Crystal said, "You were starting to doze off."

He exhaled, trying to calm his heart rate. "I must have been more tired than I thought."

"Why not just pull over? You need some sleep," Crystal said.

"We're only a couple hours away from McKenna's location. I had hoped to get there before morning."

"Just pull over," she insisted. "None of us will get there if you fall asleep at the wheel."

Peter did as he was told and maneuvered the car to the edge of the road, far enough out of the way so as not to be struck by an oncoming vehicle. "Engage camouflage," he said.

"*System error*," replied the computer. "*Camouflage system disabled.*"

David stirred in the backseat. "What... where are we?"

"Somewhere in central California," Crystal replied.

"What was that voice I heard?"

"It was the computer," Peter said. "It just shared some bad news."

"Oh, what was that?" David asked.

"We can't hide the car; the camouflage system has been disabled. It probably happened when we crashed the border."

"What'll we do now?" Crystal asked.

"I guess we'll have to do this the old fashioned way." Peter took a deep breath and opened the car door. "Okay, everyone out and look for branches and brush to hide the car."

They stepped out into the chilled air. Each went a separate direction. Peter walked away from the front of the car and stepped into the rugged brush, looking for any that was loose. The bright moon illuminated the scene and caused faded shadows to dance with each breath of wind. He piled some brush into his arms and walked back to find David and Crystal standing nearby. He added his cache to the gathered brush from the others and spread it across the surface of the vehicle.

"I hope it's enough," Peter said as he examined their work.

"You worry too much," Crystal said with a smile.

"If we are done," David added, "I would like to go back to sleep." He opened the door and slipped into the back seat, curling up and, with a sigh, closed his eyes.

Crystal looked at Peter and rolled her eyes, and then both stepped back into the car. The amber glow of the dash lights provided subdued illumination and, with her head against the door, Crystal was fast asleep.

Peter reclined his seat and put his head against the car door. He looked out through the window to the south and a dim glow hovered upon the horizon. The navigational screen was on and he moved his finger along the display, slowly dragging the image until it rested upon a large metropolitan area, Sacramento. According to the map, the city was sprawled out and covered several square miles. Many other names were listed, suburbs of the main hub of the city. Peter looked again at the orange glow on the horizon and wondered what he might find.

* * * *

The morning dawned bright as a cloudless day presented itself with a dazzling sun. Piercing blue skies spanned to the horizon. Peter stretched his arms and rubbed the sleep from his eyes as David quietly snored in the back seat. Crystal lay curled up on her chair, hair draped over her eyes and hands folded under her head. He rubbed the growing stubble on his face and determined to find a place to clean up a bit.

He opened his door and a breath of cool air danced into the car. Crystal mumbled some unintelligible words as she rubbed her eyes and stretched out the night's muscle cramps. David also woke, complaining under his breath. Peter smiled and, glad to have the company, stepped outside and began to uncover the car.

Despite it being winter, the morning was warm. Peter discarded his jacket and moved to the hood of the car where he saw the damage done when he crashed through the California border. A long gash cut across the front bumper and the radiator grill was cracked, with one piece missing. He also noticed a slight dent in the hood, with a wrinkle in its outer skin.

Crystal stepped out of the car and stretched. "Well," she said, "what's the damage?"

"Not good," he said. "The grill is cracked and there is damage to the front bumper. I don't think we will be able to use the camouflage until we get it repaired."

"That's not possible," Crystal said. "Didn't that letter say that this car is a prototype? Who would be able to fix it?"

"I doubt that there is anyone who we can trust enough to work on this car."

David stepped out of the back, rubbing his eyes. "Good morning," he said. "What are the two of you discussing?"

Peter looked at his newest companion, uncertain how much he should share. "Just the damage done to the car," he said. "It's not bad... not bad enough to stop us... just some cosmetic damage."

"What was it that you said about, 'camouflage'?" David asked.

Peter was hesitant, but Crystal huffed as she rolled her eyes and spoke up, "This car is equipped to become invisible. I don't know how, but when we ran the border crossing we damaged something and the car can't become invisible again."

"Ah," David said, "That is an interesting problem."

"Do you know something about it?" Peter asked.

"I know electronics," David said. "I might be able to help. Show me the damage."

Peter took him to the front of the car and David ran his hands over the grill, bumper and hood. He explored the damage with his fingers and his eyes widened with each pass. "Well," Peter asked, "can you do anything?"

"This is amazing technology," David said. "This skin on the car is like a layer of paint, yet you can see here the electrodes throughout the covering." David pointed out some flecks that had small, silver beads imbedded in them which were no larger than the tip of a sharpened pencil. The paint was thoroughly filled with these small silver specks and when Peter looked closer he could see them with ease.

"So, why can't the car go camouflage?" Crystal asked.

"My best guess is, with the paint damaged, the surface of the car cannot conduct the needed signal to enable the bending of light. Without the proper paint, I do not think that the camouflage mode will work again." David stood and brushed off his trousers. He looked up at Peter, "I am hungry. Any chance there is something to eat?"

Peter smiled at the directness of his new companion. "Actually, there is," he said. He went to the trunk and pulled out a box filled with military rations.

* * * *

The sun rose above the horizon, sending down long streams of light that filtered through the dusty air. Traffic began to increase on the highway some thirty yards away and elevated the noise of the morning so that the three companions had to try and talk over the din.

"Where are you two going?" David asked.

"We're heading south," Peter said. "We're looking for a man named McKenna."

"Why?"

"We hope that he is in possession of a document that might change the nation." Peter replied.

"Oh, and what document is that?" David sipped at his canned juice and nibbled again at the dried beef.

"We haven't a clue!" Crystal said through bites. "Every time we had the chance to sit down and learn something, we've been run off by whoever is chasing us at the time."

David nodded, "I see. So, with this document, what is your plan?"

"We need to get to Colorado and try to tap into the federal communications network. The plan is to share the information with the entire nation." Peter leaned back against the car as he watched the traffic flow by. "My dad and others believe that if the people hear the truth, they will want it."

"Do you not think that it would be better to take down the network?" David asked.

"No," Peter said, adamantly. "We need to use the network in order to reach as many people as possible. The more people hear the message, the better. The federal network controls every media outlet so if we can hack into it, we will be able to reach the entire nation at once."

David stood up and paced beside the car. "I can help you. I know how to hack the network and..."

Crystal interrupted, "No offense, but you got caught the last time."

"That is only because I had limited access and they were able to trace my profile to my location. If I had direct access, I can override their tracking capabilities and you can share your message." David said.

Peter considered David's offer. "I've grown a little cautious these last few months, so I hope you understand when I ask, what's in it for you?"

"What is in it for me?" David asked. "I am the same as you, I am a wanted man. You have been able to avoid capture, and I hope to be able to do the same thing. Besides, you rescued me from a fate worse than death. I am in your debt. If I can, I want to help you."

"Crystal," Peter said as he turned toward her, "what do you think?"

"Let's take him with us," she said. "But let's go now. We've been out here too long and I'm sure they're looking for us."

Peter nodded in agreement, "Let's get out of here."

They all climbed back in the car. Peter revved the engine and pulled back onto the highway. Trucks and vans rushed past. The sun crept slowly up the sky, making its way toward its zenith. In the distance the city of Sacramento slowly grew as they neared.

"I wonder what we can expect there?" Crystal asked as she stared with wide eyes at the looming city.

"I can tell you," David said. "It is not a pleasant town. There are many different factions and anarchists that control sections of the city."

"I thought the feds control everything," Crystal said.

"No," David said. "California is a dangerous state. It is under martial law, but there is little control."

"What do you recommend?" Peter asked.

"Recommend? I recommend that we do not stop at all. We need to get through it as quickly as possible."

"How do you know so much about it?" Crystal asked.

"Because," David said, "I was a member of the Folsom Gang. I was used by them to do electronic spying and sabotage. I hacked into the Federal Communications Network in Sacramento and when I was caught, the gang cut me loose. We will find no safety there."

"It also sounds like we will find no federal agents," Crystal observed.

"There is no guarantee of that. They monitor everything even if they do not control it." David said.

"But what about this highway?" Peter asked. "Can't we simply stay on it until we get through the city?"

"The river bridges were blown up a long time ago. There are few ways to get through the city. Let us hope that we can get through unnoticed." David offered a half-hearted grin.

"Isn't there a way around the city?" Crystal asked.

"Not really. We might go west and try to get around it, but no matter which way we take, we will have to cross the river. And every crossing is hazardous." David shifted his position in the back seat and lay down. "Let me know when we get close to the city."

"Do you have contacts there that we can use?" Peter asked.

"I might, but it will not be safe. If a person is captured by federal agents they are always suspected of being a plant if they return. My old gang is just as likely to kill me as anything." David again smiled, "And that is something I would like to avoid."

"Well, maybe there is a Remnant safe house in the city?" Crystal said. She pressed the screen and moved the picture back and forth over the map of the city. No flag appeared except the one much farther south—the one at Castle A.F.B.

David didn't sit up, but with his eyes closed shook his head. "There is no such thing as a safe house in Sacramento. We will do well just to pass through and keep going south." Then he sat up as if a thought was trying to force its way out. "Do you have any money?" His voice trembled with urgency.

"Not that I know of," Peter said.

"Why?" Crystal asked.

"Because we will need it to get across the river," David said. "Every portage is controlled by whatever gang is in power at the time. The one thing they have in common is the cruel habit of demanding payment from anyone and everyone."

"What do they take if you can't pay?" Crystal asked.

"You do not want to know."

"Well, maybe your dad planned for this," Crystal said to Peter. "He may have something stashed in the trunk for such an emergency."

Peter pulled the car onto the side of the road and all three stepped out to check the trunk. Boxes filled with provisions and clothing was all they found. Peter glanced up at the sun which had passed its noon zenith and began its descent to the western horizon. They repacked the trunk and stood silent as the highway roared past.

"I could put my dad's uniform on again. It worked to get into Oregon. It might work here."

David scanned Peter up and down. "The moment that uniform is seen they will fill it full of bullets. I do not recommend you be in it at the time."

"Then we will have to trust ourselves to God's providence. We must get to Castle, so we must go through Sacramento. A way will be made," Crystal said.

Peter's eyes widened at Crystal's words. "When did you take on such faith?"

Crystal smiled but gave no reply.

"Well," Peter said, "let's go and see what turns up."

They got back into the car and entered the flow of traffic. Road signs pointed to various industrial sites as they passed through a city called Woodland. The highway bent and twisted past industrial buildings like a thread woven through fabric. Smoke billowed from large, conical stacks on each side as trucks entered and exited the highway. In the distance Peter watched the growing city before him. Massive skyscrapers came into view as they peeked over the horizon. The interstate widened and, for no reason Peter could determine, a myriad of vehicles filled up the extra space on the road.

He merged into the flow of traffic and kept a steady pace. On they went, drawing ever nearer to the city. His own anxiety grew even as the towers of Sacramento grew in his view. The clear day provided an ample view of the looming metropolis. From his vantage, Peter thought the city to be a brilliant vista, filled with scintillating skyscrapers of glass and steel that reflected the afternoon sun.

They approached the first barrier. The Sacramento River wound its way down from high in the mountains and cut its path across the state of California. Now it was directly in front of them, with broken bridges and another makeshift ferry system to cross over.

The line of cars waiting to cross was long and they waited for more than an hour, creeping closer to the water. When they were next to board the ferry barge, someone dressed in black, wearing a hood and sunglasses to cover his face, approached the car. Peter looked back at David, hoping for some clue to his next action but David simply shrugged his shoulders in uncertainty. The stranger tapped on the driver's window and, with a deep breath, Peter opened it.

"Whatcha doin' comin' 'er?" the stranger asked.

Before Peter could answer David spoke up, "Don't ya talk to my driver. You got questions, you talk to me."

The man moved to the back window where David was sitting up tall and wearing Patrick's coat. David rolled down the window and looked up at the stranger standing over him.

"Where'd ya get that coat?" the man asked.

"I got it off a fed, what's it to ya?"

"It ain't nothin', man. But I gotta check before you cross." The stranger's voice quivered for a moment.

"Well, you checked. Now we got business to get to so you betta let us pass."

Without another word the man signaled for them to drive forward.

Peter closed his window and pulled the car onto the barge. They were the first one on and the boat filled up with several more cars and trucks behind them. Peter shifted into park and turned around. "What was that?"

David smiled, "I know how these men think. If we seem important they will let us cross into the city."

Crystal nearly broke out in laughter. "The way you handled that was amazing! I think you scared that young man half to death."

"But your accent," Peter observed, "you didn't sound like yourself."

"No," he said. "I lived with these men long enough to know how they talk. I can imitate them."

"You seem a little worried still," Peter said.

"I am. Getting into the city is the easy part; the hard part will be getting out." David removed Patrick's coat and slumped back into his seat.

They crossed the river as water slapped against the hull of the craft. The boat rocked in the waves and Peter watched as the hooded man threw a rope to another man waiting on the dock. Then the same man approached the car.

He tapped on the rear window and David opened it. "Now, if you wanna get off this boat, you gotta pay."

As the boat was pulled toward the dock, three men, clad in black and armed with automatic rifles, stood in a line to guard against any who tried to drive away.

"Whatcha mean, pay?" David asked with as much authority as he could muster.

"If you got business, then you know you gotta pay." The man snapped his fingers and the three on the dock raised their rifles and aimed right at the car. Peter noticed that they were still several feet from the dock and wondered if they held the boat until payment was made.

In a rush of motion the three men with rifles aimed their weapons into the air and began to fire. Then sound exploded in the air around them as three black helicopters swooped down from above, firing massive rotary guns. Wood splinters exploded off the dock like shrapnel and everyone near the shore ran for cover.

One of the rifle men fell, clutching his chest. Peter revved the engine as he watched the barge drift closer to the dock. Six inches away and he thrust the car into gear and squealed his tires as he raced off the boat. The tires slammed against the dock but his forward momentum carried them and they were on dry land. Gunmen and bystanders jumped out of the way, desperate to avoid being hit by Peter or the weapons' fire from the helicopters.

"Do not stop!" David shouted. "Now that we have crossed into Sacramento you need to get us outside the city. No matter what happens, keep driving."

Peter did as instructed and raced down the highway, weaving in and out of traffic. He glanced at the rearview display and his eyes nearly popped out when he watched as two trucks chased after him, slamming against the guard rail and pushing cars as they forced their way down the interstate. To Peter, it was complete chaos behind them.

He turned his attention back to the road before him. He passed everyone, hands gripped on the wheel as if he held on for dear life. Then, out from behind a towering skyscraper, two helicopters came right for them.

"We're not going to get out of this!" Crystal shouted. The sound of gunfire erupted and the road behind them exploded with asphalt debris.

"They are not after us," David said. He turned and pointed at the vehicles that were chasing them, "Look!"

Peter glanced down at the display and watched as the two trucks screeched to a halt and spun around, speeding back the way they came. "What's going on?"

David exhaled as if all his tension escaped at once. "I told you, this town is under martial law. We are not safe, however.

Those who worked the barge will have reported that we are in the city."

Peter slowed down so that he drove with traffic instead of forcing his way past them. "Which way do we go?"

"We cannot take the mainline out of the city, so we will need to get off the highway and move through the streets," David said. "Take the next exit off the highway and I will direct you to, what I hope, is a safe escape from here."

Peter did as instructed and left the highway. They navigated through the heart of Sacramento. From a distance it looked like a pristine metropolis, but up close the buildings took on a different appearance. The towering structures were scarred with massive holes and fractured walls. Debris littered the sidewalks and in some places entire buildings lay collapsed and shattered on the ground. Peter found the journey difficult at best and had to drive slowly to avoid the city's wreckage.

They entered what might have been considered a residential neighborhood as David directed them. Houses lined the streets and they approached an open area, overgrown and littered with piles of rubble. Nobody moved about the streets and most houses had windows and doors broken or boarded up.

"Keep your eyes open," David said. "This is the neighborhood of another gang. They control this area and I promise you that we are already being watched."

As if on cue, two cars pulled out of hiding and began to tail them. They were four-door sedans, both of them dark brown and each had four people inside. Peter watched them in the display screen and began to increase his speed. From the lead car behind them, two men crawled out of the windows, sat on the rear doors and aimed small rifles at them.

"Pete," Crystal shouted as she stared out the rear window. "We need to go faster!"

Gunfire erupted behind them. Peter rammed the accelerator to the floor and sped down the cluttered road, desperate to avoid the broken bits and pieces that littered the streets. The two cars followed, weaving through the wreckage as they fired their weapons. Bullets screamed through the air, exploding into various objects as they passed. Peter's heart raced faster than the car. He looked at the display and his hands shook when he noticed the cars closing in on him.

"Take a left!" David shouted.

Peter slammed the steering wheel and raced down Fair Oaks road. The lead car that followed spun out of control and rolled, glass and metal shattering in every direction... The second car swerved to avoid a collision and continued the pursuit.

"Right!" David barked. "Take a right!"

Peter felt sweat course down his forehead as he screeched the car around the corner. His eyes were on the road ahead and he noticed that a broken bridge lay before him, No cars were on the road. He slammed on the brakes, coming to a stop.

"What are you doing?" David demanded.

"What am I doing?" Peter said. "You brought us to a dead end!"

"That bridge is out," Crystal said as she pointed out the windshield.

Peter looked in his rear display and the lone pursuit had stopped as well, the four men stepping out of their car and trained their rifles right at Peter and his companions. He looked back at the bridge and shook his head. "Hang on!"

He pressed the pedal to the floor and the car sped down the road. Faster and faster... eighty... ninety... one hundred miles an hour! They hit the broken bridge at a hundred-and-ten miles an hour. All three screamed as the car flew across the gap and slammed hard on the other side.

"Woo-hoo!" Crystal shouted.

Peter stopped the car and spun around to look out the back window. Their pursuers stopped at the edge of the bridge and jumped out of the car with their weapons in hand so Peter gunned the engine and soon their attackers were long behind them.

"Are we safe, now?" Crystal asked.

David continued to watch out the back window. "Safer," he said. "We need to get back to the highway and get outside the city limits. But the greatest danger is behind us."

David's prediction came to pass as he directed Peter through the southern part of the city. They navigated through broken, dilapidated communities as the sun fell toward the western horizon. Occasionally they would see a person on the street or in close proximity to a house, but as they neared, the person would hide or disappear behind a door.

"I just can't believe how miserable people seem," Crystal said.

"Of course they are miserable," David said. "They live without hope."

"Maybe we'll change that," Peter said.

Twenty minutes passed and they found the highway south. Hours rolled by in silence as the sun sank below the horizon. Darkness shrouded the world and hid the despair seen in the broken cities they drove through. Mile after mile disappeared behind them. Crystal called up the navigational map on the display and pinpointed the location marked as Castle A.F.B.

"According to this map, you'll need to take the next exit," Crystal said.

Peter complied and left the highway. The road was a fractured and potholed thoroughfare, with tufts of grass growing up through the cracks. An occasional car passed by, but they made their way through the town unhindered. It was a straight road that led to a dark corner.

Peter stopped and checked the map on his navigational display. "To the right," he said, absentmindedly. He turned and followed the road to another cross street. No lights, no street signs, only an occasional flashing beacon from some distant tower gave any sense of life. He turned right again. The spinning airport light flashed green then white. As the beacon passed, Peter spotted an abandoned gate with a broken guardhouse on his left. He stopped the car.

"Now what?" Crystal asked.

Peter didn't say a word, but stepped out of the vehicle. The two others quickly exited the car as well. He walked up to the old gate, with Crystal and David close behind him. A broken metal sign lay on the ground by the guardhouse, covered in the overgrowth of time. Peter carefully brushed the dust off the sign.

It read: *"Welcome to Castle Air Force Base."*

CHAPTER NINETEEN

"I will instruct you and teach you in the way you should go; I will counsel you and watch over you." ~ Psalm 32:8

"I guess we are here." David said.

Crystal came up beside Peter and placed her hand on his arm. "What do we do now, Pete?"

He took a deep breath and looked down at Crystal, "I suppose we ought to go in and find this guy, McKenna."

"How do we find him?" David asked.

Peter looked beyond the broken guard shack and fallen gate. A fog began to settle upon the world and obscured his view so that he could only see a dozen feet ahead. The flashing light in the distance became little more than a pin-prick of illumination and offered no help. An old metal barrier barred the road and Peter walked up and placed his hands on it. The rust-covered barricade creaked with age as it swung ever so slowly inward. Peter gave the arm a shove and it grated against its metal swivel but moved until it was parallel to the road.

"Well," he said, "it looks like the door is open."

They returned to the car and took their seats. The amber glow of the dash lights illumined the car with ghostly light. Peter switched the car on and drove through the gate and onto the ancient military base.

"So," David asked, "where do we look?"

"I don't know," Peter said. "There are so many buildings on this base that one man might hide anywhere."

"What about this car?" Crystal asked.

David looked puzzled. "What do you mean?"

"I nearly forgot," Peter said. He reached to the panel and pressed through the menu until he found the heat sensing program. The screen flashed and took on a bluish hue and displayed the world in negative relief. Buildings were deep black, cold and lifeless. Trees showed up in varying shades of blue and no red was on the screen.

"This is one amazing car," David observed. "Is that a heat-sensing scanner you are using?"

"I believe so," Peter said. "But I think this fog is interfering with it."

"It is my opinion that the range is rather small. We will need to drive around if you are looking for a warm body." David sat back and watched the screen.

Peter took his advice and began to navigate down the road. Overgrown and marked by potholes and cracks in the asphalt, the street forced Peter to be careful as he drove. He made his way past several decrepit buildings, broken and overrun with weeds. Old, gnarled trees stretched their branches over the road as if they reached to try and snatch the car. Moonlight filtered from above and cast long shadows through the misty fog that now clung to the ground like a cotton blanket.

"I wonder," David said, "can we see an overlay of the road on this screen?"

"I don't know," Peter replied.

Just then the computer voice stuttered, *"r-r-road overlay."* The screen flickered and white outlines appeared marking the road that they drove.

"What's wrong with the computer?" Crystal asked.

Peter shook his head, "I have no idea." He looked down at the screen as if just looking at the device might bring it back to working order.

"I believe that jumping the bridge in Sacramento must have damaged the device," David surmised.

"You're probably right," Peter said. "I just hope that it'll work long enough for us to find this McKenna."

They drove through the center of the base, avoiding fallen tree limbs from some long ago storm. As they wove through the streets, Peter tried to pattern his search so that he didn't back-track on himself. Hours slipped away in slow motion.

"Where are we now?" Crystal sighed with exasperation.

"We're close to the backside of the base. The old runway is just in front of us," Peter said as he looked at the display.

"What do we do if he is not here?" David asked.

"I don't know," Peter said. "He's the only one who has the information we need."

"Pete!" Crystal shouted and pointed to the display. A red dot appeared, only for a moment at the top of the screen, and then disappeared.

"That's got to be him!" Peter exclaimed.

"He might have seen our headlights," David said. "It looked like the red dot was on the move."

Peter switched the lights off and used the display to find his way across the tarmac and onto the runway. The red dot appeared again, this time clearly visible and working its way toward an old building on the other side of the airfield. He drove slowly and neared the building when the red dot disappeared.

"Now you see me now you don't," Peter said to the screen. "I'm not buying it."

"What are you talking about?" Crystal asked.

"These buildings somehow shield our sensors," Peter said. "I think our McKenna is inside this one." He pointed at a square, black spot on the map and then stopped the car.

"What are you doing?" Crystal asked.

"We might want to walk the rest of the way." Peter stepped out into the fog, the cool air heavy with the musty odor of the vaporous covering. Without the headlights or the interior illumination, the world was plunged in darkness.

"I can't see five feet in front of me," Crystal said.

"It is definitely a challenge," David agreed.

"C'mon," Peter urged. He walked toward the old building, hands in front of him to fend off any unwanted barriers. His fingers fell on a metal pole, the frame of an old fence that had long rusted useless. The old obstruction now lay strung along the ground, little more than jagged bits of metal wire. Peter stepped over the rusted strands and continued on, listening to Crystal and David walking close behind him.

They approached the building, a concrete structure with narrow, barred windows and a single door with a ramp leading up to it along the edge of the building. A metal rail, rusted and broken in several places, followed the edge of the ramp. The grey, lifeless edifice had more in common with a crypt than a home, but Peter was certain that the man they sought was hiding inside.

"Peter, be careful," Crystal said as they neared the entrance.

He nodded and walked up the ramp. The entry was solid steel, narrow and had no window. No handle protruded on the surface so Peter pushed on it. There was nothing—no movement, and no indication of how to enter. Peter leaned against the fractured rail and ran his fingers through his hair, frustrated at the barrier.

"Maybe you should knock." David said.

Peter rolled his eyes in annoyed acknowledgment and rapped on the door. Still nothing happened.

Crystal came up, moved Peter out of the way and pounded on the steel entrance. The hollow echo reverberated within the concrete structure. "Hey, you in there!" she shouted. "We're not gonna hurt you. We just want to talk!"

"Yeah, that'll work," Peter said. He shook his head and moved back to the door. "See if you can find some lever or device to open this thing. That guy had to come in here somehow." Peter ran his hands along the edge of the doorframe while Crystal and David searched along the ramp.

"Peter," David said. "I think I found something."

He turned and saw David standing at the bottom of the ramp. "What is it?"

"This pole, it's loose," he said.

"Crystal, come away from there," Peter commanded. He went and stood with David as Crystal joined them. With a quick thrust, he pushed the round, metal pole. Almost imperceptible, Peter heard the click of a latch. He slowly walked back to the door and gave it a slight push. It swung inward, revealing a large open chamber, dark and hollow. He turned back to the others and motioned for them to come.

A flash in the dark and the crack of a gun echoed within, followed by the sound of a ricochet against the concrete wall. Peter ducked behind the wall and Crystal and David fell to the ground. Another crack resounded in the dark as the hidden gunman fired from the shadows.

"Stop shooting!" Peter shouted.

"Step in the doorway with your hands on your head," a wavering voice spoke from the darkened building.

Peter looked down at Crystal and David who still lay on the ground. Both shook their heads at Peter, but he stood and slowly approached the open entrance, his hands on his head. "We're not from the government," he said, "and we're not here to hurt you." Peter stared into the dark, his heart pounding like a hammer. He tried to steady his nerves, but felt extremely exposed. Gazing into the room, he thought he saw a darker shadow move through the blackness before him.

"Who are you?" asked the voice.

"My name is Peter Sheridan."

"Never heard of you," the voice said. "But you look like you might be an agent."

"We're not agents," Peter protested. "But we were sent to find you, that is, if your name is McKenna."

"Who sent you?"

"Marcus Henderson," Peter said.

"Marcus is still alive?"

Peter hesitated. "I don't know," he said with some reservation. "We escaped an attack but when I last saw him he was wounded."

"You left him alone and he was wounded?" the voice demanded.

"No, not alone," Peter said. "He was with a friend of his… someone named Earl."

"So Earl is alive too?"

"I don't know. Like I said, when we escaped, the house we were in was under fire. I don't know if they made it out."

Just then a light flashed on and Peter squinted in the bright glow of the florescent illumination. At the back of the room, holding a semi-automatic rifle, an elderly man stood beside a wall switch. He had grey hair, balding on the top. He wore a dark blue overcoat and dark pants and shirt. His eyes seemed always on the lookout, glancing back and forth. "So, why did they send you here?"

Peter slowly lowered his hands to his side. "Do you think we could come inside to talk about this?"

The man nodded and Peter signaled for Crystal and David to come in. The room was bare, with a metal door on the wall to

Peter's right. A stairwell in the center of the room descended into a darkened basement. Crystal and David entered behind him and raised their hands when they saw the man holding the gun.

"Close the door," the man commanded.

Peter obliged him. "So, are you McKenna?"

The man hesitated. "Yes, I'm George McKenna."

"Well," Crystal said, "do you think you could put away that gun?"

"After I find out who you are," McKenna said.

"Peter already told you who we are," David added.

"No, he told me who he is and now I see that he brought two confederates with him." He lifted the rifle barrel so that it pointed at David and Crystal. "I've not lived this long by trusting people and I'm not ready to start now."

"You must've heard about us already!" Crystal demanded. "We've been in the news for months."

"I don't have a radio or any other means of learning what's going on in the world. There is nothing I need to know from the outside." He lowered the barrel of his gun slightly. "What I do need to know is who you are."

Peter stepped closer to McKenna. "Like I told you, my name is Peter Sheridan, my father is Patrick and we escaped McNeil Island up in Washington to come down here and find you. I was told that you were a part of the Shadow Remnant and that you had a document of such significance that it could change the course of our nation." He moved a little closer. "You're right about these two, they are my confederates. Crystal," he motioned his hand toward her, "escaped with me from McNeil, and we rescued David here from a torture center in Oregon."

"So you're fugitives," McKenna said. He pointed the gun at the floor and rubbed the stubble on his face. "Well, I guess you can't be all bad if you're working with Marcus and Earl. Let's go downstairs and we can talk."

"Are you a part of the Remnant?" Crystal asked.

"Let's go downstairs and I'll answer your questions." McKenna moved to the stairwell and started down the stairs. He turned back to the three who still waited near the entrance, "Are you coming?"

Peter followed him and motioned with his head for Crystal and David to come. McKenna led them down a concrete stairwell that switched back halfway down. He turned the corner and the cold, grey walls ended at a steel door. To the left, a lighted keypad hung on the wall. McKenna tapped out a series of numbers and the entrance clicked open.

Peter walked in with him and his eyes widened as he looked upon the room. Lining the walls were row upon row of shelves filled with books reaching up to the ceiling twelve feet over his head. In the center of the room, standing back to back were two rows of dark, oak cabinets that contained thousands of documents, some hung loosely out of drawers or were pinched inside of doors.

Crystal entered behind Peter. "What is this place?" she asked, turning in a circle to try and see everything.

"This is my library," McKenna said.

"How did you get such a collection?" David asked as he entered behind Crystal.

"I have spent the better part of my adult life collecting these. I took it to be my own personal mission to save the literary works that the government declared forbidden. For the last thirty years I have scoured the country looking for these," he said as he pointed to the books on the shelves, "and I've brought them all here to be kept safe."

"But how did you get around the country without being caught?" Peter asked.

"Simple," McKenna answered, "I walked." He moved away from the shelves and pointed toward the back of the room. "Come join me in the back, I've set up my living quarters there."

Peter followed him, exploring with his eyes the books that lined the shelves. He reached out and ran his hands over the titles, amazed at how many volumes the man owned. "So," he asked, "how many do you have?"

"I think that my collection now numbers over seven thousand books and twelve thousand documents."

"What books do you have?" David asked.

"I have all types, all of them forbidden by the government."

"Do you have any bibles?" Crystal asked.

"Yes," McKenna said. "I have twenty-seven copies of the holy book, three in their original languages. I also have an entire section of commentaries, lexicons, and a host of other study aids. All in all, my collection of biblical literature might be my most extensive."

Peter came into the living area which consisted of a narrow bed, a small table with four chairs, a refrigerator and stove on the opposite wall and a small sink. The area was cluttered with papers scattered on the bed and table, many of them rolled up like scrolls. Peter picked up a few documents that crinkled when he moved them. The parchment was yellowed, old and the writing done by hand. He looked at McKenna who moved some papers off a chair and sat down. "How old are these?"

"Many of them are several hundred years old. Some of these papers were smuggled out of Washington D.C., out of what once was called the Library of Congress. When the government began to crack down on what they considered illegal literature there were those who knew that if they didn't try to preserve our history, it would be lost forever. When I learned that these documents were scattered across the nation I purposed my life to collecting them." He motioned for the three of them to sit.

Peter sat at the table, arms resting on piles of documents. "So, what are you?"

"I guess," McKenna said, "that I am somewhat of a curator. I was a professor of history many years ago. But when I began to discover that the history they wanted me to teach was so revisionist I decided to embark on my own to find out the truth." He moved from the table and began to thumb through a stack of well kept papers.

"What are you looking for?" Crystal asked.

"You'll see."

Peter absentmindedly glanced at the manuscripts near him and read titles like, *The Federalist Papers*, *The Gettysburg Address* and *The Star Spangled Banner*. "What are these?" he asked.

McKenna glanced up, "Oh, those," he said as he turned his attention back to his search, "those are very important papers from centuries ago. They are, of course, copies of the originals. But I can assure you that they are true to the text and trustworthy." He pulled a large sheet from the pile. "Here we go." He looked back at the table, "Peter, I want you to read this." He motioned to a paragraph on the hand-written document.

"Okay," Peter said and began to read: *"We hold these Truths to be self-evident, that all Men are created equal, that they are endowed by their Creator with certain unalienable Rights, that among these are Life, Liberty and the Pursuit of Happiness -- That to secure these Rights, Governments are instituted among Men, deriving their just Powers from the Consent of the Governed, that whenever any Form of Government becomes destructive to these Ends, it is the Right of the People to alter or to abolish it, and to institute new Government, laying its Foundation on such Principles and organizing its Powers in such Form, as to them shall seem most likely to effect their Safety and Happiness."*

McKenna's eyes glossed over with tears as Peter read. "That, my friends, was from a document called the Declaration of Independence." He took the document from Peter and carefully returned it to the stack. "Years ago, the founders of this nation knew that liberty was preferred over tyranny. They wrote such documents to declare with one voice that they no longer would yield their liberty to the government that ruled the colonies. So they formed a new system and created the United States."

"It is not like that now," David said.

"You're right," McKenna agreed. "But it can be again! If people will learn that liberty is given by God and secured by courageous faith, that it is better to be free than enslaved, I believe that they will cry out for it again."

"Is this the document that Marcus and the others were referring too? Is the... what did you call it... the Declaration of Independence what we came here to find?" Crystal asked.

McKenna took a deep breath. "No," he said. "There is another document that I keep carefully hidden. Again, it is not the original, but it is a word-for-word copy of the original. Marcus, Earl and the others, including a man with the last name of Eberhardt, all believed that if people heard it and believed it, that it would change our nation." He sat back down at the table.

"Well," David asked, "where is this amazing piece of paper?"

"I have it hidden away and will not allow anyone to know its location. I will get it for you, but only if you're intention is to share it with the nation. I knew of the plans that the others had made, plans to rekindle the fires of liberty, and if that is your mission, then I will retrieve it. Otherwise, it stays hidden."

"George," Peter said. "Can I call you George?" McKenna nodded. "George, we are here to try and set our loved ones free. The only way I know to do it is to do what was asked of me. If people cry out for freedom again, and can change the way things are, perhaps those who are held as political prisoners will be set free. My father and brother, Jack and the others all are held against their will for no other reason than that they wanted freedom. I'm on the run because of this mission and have no other hope of securing my own freedom than to try."

McKenna nodded. "I understand. I will get it for you in the morning. When you drive out tomorrow..."

"That will be a problem," David said. "I do not believe that the car we came in will endure the long drive to Colorado. It has received quite a beating since we have been in California and the computer is malfunctioning."

"Can't you repair it?" Crystal asked.

"No," David said. "I do not have the equipment or the skills to repair such a technically advanced machine as that car."

Peter shook his head in despair. Doubts crept through his thoughts, and the sense of anguish at having come so far only to fail filled his imagination. "So," he said, his words dripping with the distress of failure, "here we are, a thousand miles from where we started and no closer to our goal."

"There must be another option," David said.

"Sure there is," Crystal agreed. She looked at McKenna, her eyes narrowed. "You didn't really walk across the entire country packing books and papers. You don't strike me as the type. How did you really get around?" Her eyes stayed narrow as she crossed her arms over her chest.

"What do you mean?" McKenna asked, his voice quivering.

"You know what I mean," Crystal demanded. "You have a car or some other transport. Fess up! We're in this thing together so you might as well get in the game."

Peter and David watched Crystal hammer George with her accusation. Peter recognized the look she gave the historian. It was the same look he saw often on the island, when she and Jack were in some heated dispute. "Aren't you being a little harsh, Crystal?"

Crystal glared at him, but before she could answer, McKenna spoke up. "You're friend is right," he said. "I do have transportation. But I'm not an adventurer. I don't have it in me to take these risks. When I retrieved these documents, I had the entire Remnant working with me to collect them. They would take them to secure locations then I would gather them up."

"Fine," Crystal said, "but how did you get around?"

"I," he hesitated, "I have an airplane."

"You have a what?" Peter's eyes widened with hope.

"I have an airplane," he said again. "This is an old military airbase after all." He offered a slight grin.

"How long has it been since you have flown?" David asked.

"Many years," he said. "I've not taken the old bird out for, I guess, almost fifteen years. You see, I found a good supply of fuel left here on this base, and used it as a place to make my home. After the last world war this area was left desolate and abandoned. It seemed the perfect place to store all my finds."

"So you could simply fly us to Colorado?" Crystal asked.

"No, it's not quite that simple. If I were to take off now I would be spotted in minutes. Before, I had a government pass to travel by personal aircraft. But that was a long time ago. Besides, my plane does not hold enough fuel to fly to Colorado. I'd have to find a place to stop and refuel, and those are hard to come by now." McKenna stood up and paced near the bed.

Peter's brows furrowed as he thought about their situation. He held his head in his hands and mumbled under his breath as he tried to talk himself into a solution that he thought might be doable. "What if," he said at last, "what if you're plane was invisible to radar?"

"How would that be possible? It's only a small aircraft but it's not undetectable."

"No," Peter agreed. "But my car has the capacity to hide from radar detection. Perhaps we can integrate the system from my car into your plane." Peter quickly looked at David, his eyes wide, silently pleading with David to agree.

"It might be possible," David said, hesitantly. "I will have to examine the schematics of your car and look over the airplane as well. It will take time."

"Peter, are you serious?" Crystal asked. "Are you really going to dismantle your dad's car?"

"I figured it this way," Peter said. "If my dad were here, I don't think he would treasure that car more than the mission he was on. If dismantling the car gives us the best possible chance to succeed, then that's what I intend to do. Let's get some rest. Tomorrow we have a big day."

"I hope you know what you're doing," Crystal said as she stood up from the table.

"So do I," Peter sighed.

CHAPTER TWENTY

"Do not take revenge, my friends, but leave room for God's wrath..." ~ Romans 12:19

Peter woke the next morning completely alone. The night before, at McKenna's request, he had moved his car out of the open and into a darkened hangar. Afterward, he had found an isolated corner of the historian's library and with the Bible from his backpack, he read until he fell fast asleep. Now he looked around and all he saw were his Bible that lay open on the floor and a myriad of books and papers collected by the recluse.

He stood and tried to stretch out the aches in his muscles and joints. His neck felt as stiff as a board and head throbbed with every beat of his heart. *Next time,* he thought, *I get the bed.*

"Hey, sleepy," Crystal said as she walked around the corner. "I didn't think you'd ever wake up."

"Where are David and George?"

"They're at some hangar to check out the plane. George sent me back to find out if you woke up yet."

Peter stretched again. "I wish I could get the kinks out of my back. Sleeping on this concrete floor didn't do me any favors."

"It's your own fault," Crystal chided. "If you didn't stay up so late reading, you might have had a better night's sleep." She came around behind Peter. "I used to help Jack when he was hurting," she said as she reached up and began to press the heel of her palms into Peter's back. "Now just a minute and I'll get those knots out of your back."

The back rub felt good, but Peter turned around and gently took Crystal's hands in his. "I appreciate that," he said as he looked into her deep, green eyes. "But right now, I think I still need a little tension to get through these days."

Her face flushed red as she pulled her hands from his. "I was only trying to help," she said then turned away and walked back toward the living quarters.

Peter's heart sank as he watched her. Then he remembered that he wanted to find David. "Crystal, wait!" he called out.

"What!" she snapped as she turned around. Her narrowed eyes glared at him.

"Weren't you supposed to take me to George and David?"

Crystal huffed and crossed her arms. "Fine, follow me."

She led him out of the basement and back into the upper level of the building. They exited through the security door that they had entered the night before and stepped into a bright, clear morning. The fog had long burned away and though a chill still hung in the air, Peter was glad to feel the gentle warmth of the sun.

It took some effort on his part to keep up with Crystal. Her rapid pace told Peter to stay at least an arm's length away. She led him across the tarmac and into another large building, rounded at the top, with massive sliding doors at the front. The steel building was rust colored, weathered through time and exposure, and hosted a nest of tumbleweeds that had parked against the windward side of the structure. At the back of the building a barbed-wire fence that once isolated the hangar from the grassy field beyond now had little more than broken strands attached to rusted metal poles.

They entered in through a single, windowless door at the rear of the building. The hinges creaked to announce their arrival. Inside, the building was spacious. The high, rounded ceiling and cement floor made the room echo with every sound. Light filtered in through broken windows and missing sheet metal. Adrift in the air, millions of dust specks flickered as they passed through the ribbons of light, while stray birds flittered and nested in the metal rafters.

In the center of the building, a single engine Cessna 206H waited like an aerial chariot to carry Peter and the others to Colorado. The cowling was propped up, exposing the engine. Near the rear of the craft, the clamshell door hung open and David stepped out. He carried a small handful of tools as he moved away from the aircraft.

Next to the plane sat the car. The hood, trunk and all doors were open as George walked around the machine. He held a clipboard and made several marks as he scratched his head, a bewildered look in his eyes. "David," he said, not looking up from his clipboard. "I don't know how you're going to integrate this computer system into my airplane. The technologies look completely incompatible."

"No, no, no!" David said, exasperated. "You do not understand. We do not need to integrate the entire system, just the radar jamming system. The power supply of your airplane will be sufficient to run the equipment; we can cannibalize the car for anything else we need." David looked up and noticed Peter and Crystal standing in the doorway. "Peter," he said as he motioned for him to come over.

Peter walked over, with Crystal close behind. He continued to glance at the car then back at the plane, his thoughts filled with dread at what they were attempting. The plane was old, and Peter wondered if it was more suited to be in a museum than a working aircraft hangar. "How far along are you?"

"Worried?" George asked.

"Yes," Peter nodded. "I'm a little worried. This plane is ancient. How do you expect that we will fly this thing to Colorado?"

George crossed his arms and narrowed his eyes as he stared at Peter. "I'll have you know that I've logged over two-hundred hours in this," he said as he patted the aircraft.

With a troubled, questioning glance, Peter looked at David who stepped away from the car. "Dave?"

"Ah, yes," he said. "This plane is quite safe. I looked it over very carefully and believe that it will carry us to our destination. We are only having a little trouble adapting your father's technology to it. But I think that I have worked it out."

"How long before we leave?" Peter asked.

"Not long," David said. "Perhaps an hour, maybe two and we will be ready to fly away from here."

"Do you think that the radar jammer will work?" Peter's voice wavered as he hesitated to ask.

"Who is to know," David said. "We can only try, and leave the rest to fate."

"Peter?" George said. "Maybe you can use this time to patch things up with Crystal. She left in a huff and the look on her face told me that you're the reason."

Peter turned around and noticed, for the first time, that Crystal wasn't standing behind him. He rolled his eyes, threw his hands in the air and nodded in agreement.

"If I didn't know any better," George chuckled, "I'd think the two of you were already married." This brought a laugh from David as both men returned to the car and leaned over the engine.

"Is there anything I can do to help?" Peter asked, reluctant to face Crystal's anger.

David looked up from beneath the hood with a mischievous smile, "No."

George popped his head out from under the hood as well, "Just make sure you and Crystal patch things up before we leave!"

Peter shook his head and turned away from the men. He stepped out of the hangar and looked out over the day. High overhead an airliner left long streaks of vapor in the clear blue sky, like ribbons of cloud trailing from the back of the plane. The sun crept across the sky, with a bright halo that encircled it. He looked across the tarmac and watched Crystal walk from the hangar. She was over fifty yards away and kicked at a rock as she marched back to McKenna's quarters.

Peter stepped up his pace to catch her, until he was nearly jogging. Crystal disappeared through the door just as Peter reached the building. Panting with the exertion, he entered to see Crystal standing just inside. Her face was turned away from him and she held her head in her hands. He stood in the doorway and watched her as she sobbed.

Crystal turned around and wiped her eyes. "What do you want?" she demanded.

His heart sank to see her in tears. "I... well... I wanted to let you know that we should be leaving in a couple hours."

"Fine," she said.

Peter stepped closer to her. "Crystal, what is it?"

She lifted her head as if she wanted to speak, but turned away. "It's nothing."

Before Peter spoke again, McKenna rushed through the door. "Hey, good," he said. "You're both here. I want to show you what all this is about." He moved toward the stairwell and waved his hand for them to follow. "C'mon," he said. "You two need to learn more about what the Remnant wanted to do."

Peter sighed and followed Crystal and George downstairs. They entered his library and passed through his living quarters into a small antechamber. The room was dimly lit and a slight draft circulated the cool air. There was just enough room for all three to enter the small space. At the back of the room an old wine rack held an overflow of assorted scrolls and papers, with an antique oak chest-of-drawers, stained dark brown, in the middle of the back wall.

McKenna opened the top drawer and pulled out a large folder and set it on the top of the dresser. He motioned for Peter and Crystal to step closer. "This is what your dad was after," he said as he touched Peter on the shoulder. "This is what people have forgotten."

Peter stepped up to the dresser. With great care he opened the folder and looked down at the ancient document as if he feared that the paper might disintegrate if he gazed too hard upon it. His eyes moved back and forth as he drank in the words. The weathered manuscript, with slightly faded letters, couldn't hide the meaning of what Peter read. Crystal moved to stand next to him and he absentmindedly wrapped his arm around her shoulder. She drew closer to him and placed her arm around his waist and leaned her head on his shoulder.

"George," Peter said, "if people actually believe this, it *will* change the nation."

"That's why it was written," McKenna said. "Freedom was forged a long time ago and the goal of the Remnant is to bring it back. If we can get the population to listen to this, it could change not only our country but the world." He rolled up the document and put it in a tube that he had taken from the second drawer. "We will need to take it with us." With the tube tucked under his arm, McKenna sighed. "Let's get ourselves packed and ready. Your friend, David, must be nearly done and we ought to be going."

They spent the next thirty minutes gathering their gear. Peter had his backpack slung over his shoulder, and double checked to make sure that the Bible was secure. George strode out the door and Peter followed with Crystal by his side as they left the building and moved toward the hangar.

The sun had risen to almost midday and caressed the earth with its warmth. Despite the brilliant day, a dread fell upon Peter's thoughts. Perplexed by his apprehension, he looked up at the hangar again. Nothing seemed out of the ordinary, but he reached down and took Crystal by the hand. "Wait," he said.

"What is it?" She looked up at Peter with a puzzled, quizzical expression.

"McKenna," Peter whispered hoarsely to the historian who walked about ten steps ahead of him. The older man turned around and Peter motioned for him to return.

"Pete," Crystal said, "What's going on?"

"Something's not right," Peter said.

"What's not right?" George asked.

"I don't know, but I've got a bad feeling that we're not alone on this base anymore." Peter glanced around, half expecting to see federal agents spring up out of the ground like prairie dogs. Then he heard what sounded like the dull thud of a car's door closing. McKenna's eyes went wide and Crystal spun to face toward the hangar.

"Get out of sight," Peter whispered. They all ducked behind a small shack between the hangar and McKenna's shelter. "You two stay here. I'm going to get a closer look."

"Are you nuts?" McKenna demanded. "If the feds are here, you won't stand a chance."

"Look," Peter said, "David's in there. I have to see what I can do."

"You can't take them on alone," Crystal said.

"I'm not going to. I'm just going to check out what's going on." Peter motioned for them to be quiet. "Now stay out of sight."

"You better be careful," Crystal demanded. Then she added, "Or else."

Peter nodded and slipped around the backside of the small shack. A narrow ditch crossed behind it, all the way to the back of the hangar. Tall grass grew along the edge of the channel and Peter kept his head low as he approached. He looked back and saw Crystal looking toward him as she crouched down behind the small building.

He turned his attention back to the task. "Keep your head in the game," he whispered to himself. There were multiple places where the exterior wall of the hangar had been breached through time and rust. Peter peeked up from his hiding place and tried to get a glimpse into the structure. From his vantage point he saw movement, but could not identify any individual. He crawled closer until he heard what sounded like muffled voices. He inched his way even nearer, so close that he was no more than two feet away from the back wall.

Peter lifted himself up from the trench and peered into the hangar through a small breach in the sheet metal. David sat on a chair, his hands tied behind his back and a gruff soldier standing over him. The guard was a brute of a man, with a curly beard and chevron stripes on his arm. Peter couldn't believe his eyes, it was the same guard that David had escaped.

David's face was bruised and his head hung limp. Blood trickled from his lip and nose and his clothes were torn. The soldier backhanded David across the side of his head and David and the chair tumbled to the ground. He reached down and manhandled the chair to set David upright and then struck him across the cheek.

"Now talk!" the gruff man barked.

David gasped for breath, "I have told you, there is no one here."

"You're lyin', punk. Someone helped you escape. You didn't make it here by yourself and I'm gonna bring you and your partners in." The guard leaned on the chair so that his face was in David's. "Now tell me, who was on the road waitin' for ya?"

302

"I do not know who they are," David said. "I found them parked on the highway and when I had the chance I took their car and left them stranded."

The gruff soldier backhanded David again. "Now I know you're lyin'!" He moved to the car. The hood was up and both doors were open. "If you were able to steal this car, then the owner was an idiot."

David tried a brief smile but grimaced in pain. "I am an expert in electronics," he said. "It was not hard to figure out the controls on this vehicle."

Peter watched the encounter, horrified at the brutality. He glanced at the door that stood about fifteen feet away. His first thought was to rush the man, and try to overpower him. But the guard seemed built to fight and Peter doubted he could beat him. He was impressed at David's determination to endure the man's cruelty without telling him about the others. With no other options, he returned to where Crystal and George remained hidden. They sat, crouched behind the small building and George jumped when Peter rounded the corner.

"Well?" Crystal asked.

"He's tied up and beaten. It's just one man, and I think it's the same guard that had him at that treatment center." Peter glanced back around the shack.

"Now what?" George asked.

"How close were you to getting the plane ready?" Peter questioned McKenna.

"We were nearly done. All David said was left to do was connect the power supply to the system." McKenna gave Peter a puzzled look. "What does that matter?"

Peter ignored the question as he considered a plan. "Is there fuel in the plane?"

"Yes," George said. "It's completely full."

"Okay, this is what we're going to do," Peter said. "We're going to sneak up to the building. You two will hide in the grass and I'm going to get that brute to chase me. I want you to get into the hangar, get David into the plane and start toward the runway. I'll be running in that direction, so get as close to me as possible and leave the door open. I'll jump in and we can take off."

"That's crazy!" George exclaimed. "Why don't I just go get my gun and we can kill that guy?"

Peter exhaled his exasperation. "No," he said defiantly. "We're not in the killing business. The Scripture warned that if we live by the sword, we'll die by the sword. If we try to finish this business with violence, that's how it will end. And," he added "I don't want it said that I started a blood-soaked revolution."

"But Peter," Crystal said, "what if it doesn't work? You'll be here and we'll be flying away."

"I know," he said. "If that happens, you'll need to finish this mission. We've come too far now and there is too much at stake."

"But... but," Crystal stammered. "Let me be the one. I run faster than you and..."

"No," Peter interrupted. He looked into her deep green eyes as tears began to run down her cheek. He wanted to tell her, wanted her to know how much he cared but the words failed. "I... I just can't let you do that." Then he looked at McKenna. "You make sure that you get that plane moving. We'll only have one chance at this, and the life you save might be my own."

He took Crystal by the hand and the three of them ducked into the tall grass of the ditch. They crept along, moving closer to the hangar and could hear the brutal guard as he berated and swore at David. Peter stepped up to the back of the building and peered through the small opening in the sheet metal. David was still tied to a chair, beaten and bruised, but alive. David gave a slight glance toward Peter, and a glint of recognition sparked in David's eyes.

"What!" the guard demanded. "Who are you looking at?" The soldier started walking toward the back of the hangar. "Is it your accomplice?"

Peter glanced back and George and Crystal and gave them a nod. He then stepped to the side door and flung the barrier open. "Here I am!" he shouted. "You were looking for me? Well you found me."

"And who are you?" The guard swore at Peter.

"I'm Peter Sheridan." Peter appreciated the double-take the guard did as a look of astonishment, mingled with a touch of fear crossed through the soldier's eyes. With that, Peter ducked out the door and disappeared beyond the hangar.

"Wait! Halt! Stop or I'll shoot!" The guard shouted in the air as he tore through the door and started chasing Peter.

Peter looked back to see the lumbering hulk of a man pursuing him. He ran into the open and aimed his feet for the runway. As fast as he could, Peter rushed across the cracked pavement. Weeds brushed his legs as he made his way down the tarmac, occasionally looking back to see that his pursuer was still behind him.

Crack! The sound rang out as a bullet whizzed past his head.

Oh, great, he thought. *How many times in one life can a man get shot at?* Then he heard a sound that filled him with hope. The rumble of a prop engine roared to life and he looked back to see the Cessna pull out of the hangar, the clamshell door still hanging open.

Then a fearful thought gripped his heart as he turned. The guard had turned back and now was running toward the hangar, his black pistol in his hand. *He's going to shoot the plane!* Rage welled up in him like a torrent so that he rushed headlong at the guard. He took no thought for his safety as he watched the plane move closer. The guard had his back to Peter and was stopped, weapon at the ready.

Ten yards… five yards… and at a full sprint, Peter crashed into the guard like a freight train. The gun discharged harmlessly into the air as it flew from the soldier's hand. Both men tumbled on the concrete and scrambled to get to their feet.

Peter was first to his feet and he kicked the legs out from under the guard. He quickly scanned the ground and saw the gun lying about fifteen feet away. He rushed to get the weapon when the soldier grabbed Peter by the ankle and tripped him.

He fell and rolled over to see the guard standing. Peter hopped up quickly and jumped on the back of the brute, driving his elbow into the man's spine and slamming him to the ground. Both men rolled over each other in an asphalt wrestling match, desperate to reach the pistol. Peter, just a bit quicker than the guard, grabbed the gun, spun and cocked the hammer as the soldier lunged at him.

"Stop!" Peter shouted.

The guard pulled up short and lifted his arms in the air as if he surrendered. "What, now you gonna kill me?"

"Not if I can help it," Peter said, out of breath as he stood to his feet, keeping the weapon trained on his opponent. "Now stand over there." He waved the gun to move the soldier away from the runway. Just then the plane pulled up and Crystal ran out the door. David was close behind her as he limped from the aircraft.

"Are you okay?" She demanded. "This isn't the way you planned it."

"Yeah," Peter said. "I'm okay, just a little bruised and scraped from wresting this guy."

"So," David said as he stood next to Peter, "Did I not tell you that he was relentless?"

The guard's eyes took a hard, narrow look as he stared at Peter. "Sheridan," he said, "you won't get away with it."

"With what?" Peter asked. "What do you think we're tying to do?"

"What does it matter," the guard said. "You're just a punk criminal and you'll get yours."

David leaned over and spoke under his breath to Peter. "Let us do to him what he did to me."

"What?" Peter said with incredulity, amazed that David suggested it. "We're not like him."

David looked at Peter. His eye was nearly swollen shut and dried blood still crusted the edge of his mouth. He was bruised from his black eye to just above his neckline. His mouth was clenched in anger and his eyes were set like granite. "He did this to me," David said. "He hurt me and I want to repay him – an eye for an eye." Tears fell from his eyes as he spoke through his anger.

"David, that's not what we're here for. Don't let *his* brutality shape your character." Peter placed his hand on David's arm. "Let's just get out of here."

David nodded and limped back to the aircraft.

The cockpit window opened and George called out, "Hey! Let's go – we're burning gas here."

Peter cracked a brief smile but kept his eye on the guard. Then he spoke to Crystal. "Get back on the plane; I'll be along in a moment." Then he turned his full attention to the guard.

"Now what?" The soldier barked.

"You've hurt my friends," Peter said, "and you threatened our lives. We could have killed you while you beat on David."

"Then you're a fool," he replied.

"Perhaps I am," Peter said. "But I'm not a murderer. If you don't get anything else, I hope you learn a little mercy." He backed up toward the plane until his stood at the doorway. With a quick snap, Peter released the clip from the handgun and threw them in opposite directions.

"I'll find you, Sheridan."

"You may," Peter said, "but circumstances might be different when you do."

Peter stepped into the plane and closed the door. George throttled up the engine and the aircraft taxied down the runway until it built up speed. With a slight tug against gravity, the plane lifted off the ground and Peter slumped back in a chair.

Just in front of him, Crystal treated David's injuries with the leftovers of a first aid kit. Peter glanced up at George who sat in the cockpit and maintained control of the craft. He felt the fatigue of tension as he looked out the window and watched the guard and the old Air Force base shrink in the distance. The sun reached its zenith and a brilliant blue sky welcomed the small aircraft as they soared through the atmosphere toward their next destination.

CHAPTER TWENTY-ONE

"If I go up to the heavens, You are there..." ~ Psalm 139:8

Small rivulets of condensation streamed across the window as Peter watched the world rush beneath them. They sped their way east over the Sierra Nevada Mountains and he finally relaxed. Thousands of feet in the air, the land beneath them stretched out in every direction and contrasted with the rich, blue sky. They had flown over a vast swath of brown, barren earth before they reached the foothills of the mountain range. Now, as if it were painted upon the ground, great rolling hills filled his view. Lush pine forests spread out as far as the eye could see, but finally gave way to large snow fields and towering peaks.

Hours had passed when Peter leaned back in his chair and retrieved the Bible from his backpack. He thumbed through the pages, careful not to crease the old paper. The musty scent of the book opened up a flood of memories as he thought back to his days before he left Joshua's home on the river. His eyes stopped upon a page and he read out loud, "If I rise on the wings of the dawn, if I settle on the far side of the sea, even there your hand will guide me, your right hand will hold me fast." A quick, contented smile crossed his face as he thought of the text and looked out at the wing of the aircraft that carried him.

"What was that?" Crystal asked.

Peter stirred back to awareness and looked up at Crystal. "Oh," he said, "It's a passage from the Bible. It seems to speak about what we're doing right now."

David breathed quietly as he slept, and Crystal moved back to sit beside Peter. She brushed her hair from her eyes and plopped herself in the seat next to him. "What do you think it means?"

"I think," Peter said, "that it means we are being guided by God all the time. No matter how far we go, He is always there."

Crystal sighed, "Does it help you to think that?"

Peter rubbed his hand on his chin in thoughtful musing. "Yes, it does. I'd like to think that God's hand has led us and kept us safe."

Crystal took Peter's hand, "Me too." She smiled at him and cast her eyes down. "You know," she said, "it's been only a few weeks since we left the island but it already seems like a lifetime ago."

"I know what you mean," Peter agreed. "Just a few months ago the only thought I had was leaving the education center and now I am cruising across the sky on some mission my dad started." He paused and sighed as he squeezed her hand a little tighter. "Sometimes it doesn't even seem real."

"Do you wonder how they're doing?" Crystal asked.

Peter nodded, "I do," he said. "I think of my dad and little brother a lot. When we left…" He let his words trail off.

"Pete," Crystal said, as her voice grew a bit sterner, "you can't worry about them. For goodness sake, your dad was special operations in the army! Jack and the others know how to take care of themselves. By now they probably have taken over the island

and the gang is broken." She reached up and gently touched his cheek and caused him to look her in the eyes, "and if we hadn't left when we did, I doubt that there would have been a second chance."

Peter nodded. "You're right, of course," he said with a half smile. "But Jack and dad and… and even Frank and the others may have paid a very high price for our freedom."

She smiled as she turned to face the front of the aircraft. "If there is anything I learned from knowing your dad it was that if he thought the cause was just and right, then it was worth the sacrifice."

Before Peter could respond, George called from the cockpit. "Peter! Why don't you come up here?"

Squeezing Crystal's hand one last time, he stepped up to the front of the plane. He scooted between the pilot and copilot's seat, careful not to disturb any of the levers that sat between them. A digital display filled the front, center panel of the cockpit and flashed as they flew over the rugged terrain. He sat in the copilot's seat and looked out the window. Mountains loomed around them, closer than Peter thought they would be and in the distance growing clouds filled the horizon.

The whir of the engine made it difficult to hear so Peter took the proffered headset from George. He placed the large, cushioned domes on his ears and lowered the microphone to his mouth. "What is it, George?" He could hear his own voice crackle with the electronic distortion.

"We have a couple problems." George's voice cracked through the headset.

"What is it?"

The historian pointed out the windshield to the looming clouds. "First," he said, "we can't fly high enough to get over that storm and second, we are coming into a no-fly zone that is not only monitored by radar but by military spotters. If we cross into the salt-flat region of Utah, we will be seen."

"Then we'll have to fly through the clouds," Peter said.

George's eyes widened, "Have you lost your senses? There's no way this little airplane can handle the winds and air currents in that storm. We'll be torn apart!"

"God's hand will hold us!" Peter declared. "If the clouds are our only hope of passing unseen, then that's where we go."

George shook his head but kept the aircraft pointed right at the clouds. "You better get back there and make sure that the others know what we're about to do." Peter nodded and removed his headset.

He weaved between the seats and sat back down with Crystal. David roused, his wounds were cleaned and dressed, and he sat up in the forward passenger seat. Crystal sat by the window and stared with wide eyes at the growing storm.

"Where are we?" David asked in his rich, middle-eastern accent.

Peter took a deep breath to calm his nerves before he spoke. "We are, currently, just about to fly over the salt flats of Utah."

"So, why does George seem so nervous?" Crystal asked.

"Well," Peter said, "to get to where we need to go we have to fly directly into a storm."

"Why?" David's voice wavered.

"Because the plane can't fly high enough to climb over the storm, and if we try to fly beneath it, George is convinced that we will be spotted." Peter tried to sound nonchalant but his own apprehension got the better of him and his voice quivered with anxiety.

Crystal looked at him, her eyes sparkled with hope. "Don't you remember the scripture you read? It said that God's hand will hold us fast. Well I believe that God will protect us through this."

"Peter!" George shouted from the cockpit. "We're entering the no fly zone. We'll know in a moment if that radar jamming device of yours is gonna work."

"Why?" Crystal asked.

"Because this area is constantly monitored by the feds," George replied. "It's been under surveillance since the great uprising of 2075, when the government crushed a rebellion with targeted nuclear strikes." George's voice grew louder as the plane began to shudder.

Peter looked at David with a glance of apprehension. "David?"

David smiled, and then winced in pain. "It will work."

Peter glanced out the window and the canopy of blue sky vanished in a haze of clouds. Water streamed across the glass and small vortexes, like miniature tornadoes of water vapor, spun in radical motion off the wing tips. The aircraft fought against the turbulence as it rocked and vibrated through the clouds. Rain pelted the windshield and drummed against the skin of the plane. David and Crystal sat with eyes wide, strapped into their seats with their seatbelts tight against their waist.

Lightning flashed. Thunder rolled across the heavens and shook the plane so that Peter wondered if the craft might fly to pieces. He pulled his seat belt tighter and bent his head in prayer.

"Peter!" George shouted.

Peter lifted his head and looked toward the cockpit. George gripped the wheel of the aircraft, knuckles white as he fought against the ever increasing strain. "What?" Peter shouted in return.

"We have to set down! If we stay in this storm we'll fly apart!"

"How close are we?" Peter yelled.

"I don't know – that last flash of lightning took out our GPS. My last reading is that we were still two miles from the landing strip." George's hands shook as he wrestled the controls. "I need you up here! I can't let go and need you to help with the controls."

Peter unbuckled himself and stumbled against the rocking motion of the plane. His stomach churned with the turbulence but he fought the queasiness. He braced his hand against the ceiling and stretched his leg over the floor controls between the cockpit seats. A jolt struck the plane and Peter fell into the co-pilot's chair. Squirming around, he righted himself and strapped in to secure against the rough conditions. He gave George a quick glance, and hoped that he didn't convey his anxiety with his eyes.

"It's too late to worry now," George said.

Peter donned the head gear and spoke into the microphone. "What do you need me to do?"

"Just a moment," George replied. He pushed the yoke forward and the plane began to descend through the clouds. Rain spattered against the windshield and another flash of lightning illuminated the sky. Thunder rocked the atmosphere. "That was close." George's voice cracked through his microphone.

"How close?" Peter asked.

"You don't want to know," George replied. "Suffice it to say, if we were corn, we'd be popped right now."

"What do you need me to do?"

"We're gonna land," George said. "I'll need you to control the throttle as well as monitor our descent. It's taking all I have to keep this thing from spinning out of control." He pulled back and the plane shifted upward.

They passed through the cloud wall and found themselves flying in what looked to be a hole or cavern of air surrounded by massive, dark thunderheads that stood in billowed pillars. The winds struck the aircraft with sheering force and the aircraft shifted to the right. George fought the controls and managed to keep the plane from flipping upside down. Peter watched the world outside as they approached the leading edge of another wall of clouds.

"Pete," George's voice cracked in his headset.

Peter turned to face him.

314

George glanced at the throttle controls that sat on the front panel, between the two seats. "When I tell you, I want you to throttle down."

Peter nodded; his heart raced with anticipation as George pushed on the yoke and the aircraft descended. He looked out the window to see the world again enveloped by clouds. He tried to see the ground—nothing. It looked to Peter as if they flew through a turbulent grey soup with currents of wind that desperately tried to rip their transport apart. "God help us to land safely," Peter whispered into the air.

"Amen!" George replied.

Suddenly they dropped below the clouds and the ground rushed beneath them. Only a few hundred feet above the earth, George followed a valley between two massive mountain ranges. His eyes were wide and alert, darting out the window then down at the gauges as he pushed and pulled the yoke and turned the aircraft to keep from brushing against the trees or slamming into a hill.

Pallid grey, the world was a dismal swath of scorched and shattered houses and buildings. Burnt trees, flattened by some massive wave, lay strewn across the hillsides like matchsticks, all felled in the same direction. No life moved in the region.

"Peter!"

George's voice crackling in the headset brought him back to the moment.

"Peter, I need you to throttle the engines back. The winds are too strong and I need both hands on the wheel."

Peter reached up and pulled the throttle cable and the engine slowed, humming lower as it reduced speed. He looked up again and before them stretched a long runway lined with fractured buildings. Peter glanced back at George who had his eyes set upon the single strip of land that seemed capable of supporting their landing.

The wings drifted up and down and the plane shifted side-to-side in the swirling currents. The constant cascade of rain pelted their aircraft, mingled with the hint of snow that spotted the windshield.

A grim expression crossed George's face. "You better pray that the runway is not iced over. It is winter after all."

Peter looked back at Crystal who had her head bowed. He couldn't tell if she were praying or simply crouched in fear, but he guessed it was both. He quickly recited a prayer in his own thoughts as his fate waited before him. David clutched the armrest of the seat as he cinched his belt tighter against his waist.

THUD! The wheels of the plane touched the ground.

"Throttle back!" George crackled.

Peter pulled the throttle cable and the engine slowed to a mere whisper of its capability. George pressed on the foot brakes to slow the aircraft and lowered the flaps. The wheels rumbled against the rough asphalt as they approached what used to be a line of buildings on their left. Fractured, skeletal remains of burned structures dotted the runway and silently spoke of perilous times. George intermittently pressed on the foot pedals and guided the aircraft to the shell of a hangar.

"This is where we needed to come?" Crystal asked.

George didn't turn around, but nodded in agreement. "This is the safest place to be if we want to refuel and make it to Colorado." He took control of the throttle and brought the aircraft to a stop. "The feds watch the no-fly zone, but they don't enter into the area. We'll need to find some fuel and this is the most reasonable location."

"Why are the feds reluctant to enter here?" David asked.

George shut down the engine and unbuckled from his seat. He turned to face his passengers. "Because," he said, "they think that this place is a radiation hazard. Remember, they crushed the uprising with nuclear weapons."

"But," Crystal asked, "How do you know that it's safe?"

George smiled, "Because I know people who have been here, and who have lived here."

"So what do we do now?" Peter asked.

"This place is similar to the location where I lived. It's an old military base and there must be some residual resources located here. Right now, it's getting late and we need to secure the plane and make camp." George opened his door and a quick flash of cold air rushed into the cabin.

"Are there people living in this area still?" David asked.

"Oh, yes. But I doubt that we'll see them. They are very reluctant to show themselves, fearful that the government will come back to wipe them out." George stepped out of the plane and opened the clamshell door for the other three.

With Crystal's help, David stepped out the door and hobbled onto the cracked cement. Peter followed them out and shut the door behind him. The latch snapped closed. When Peter turned around he found himself surrounded by twenty rifles being held by people in dark blue trench coats with hoods and masks hiding their features. All Peter saw were their eyes— twenty pair of eyes, piercing and stern. Crystal, David and George all stood in front of him with their hands held behind the backs of their heads, shivering in the growing cold.

"What's this?" Peter asked.

"You'll come with us," a grim voiced captor spoke.

Peter looked around and noticed one of the members of the hooded squad motion with the barrel of his gun. George moved out first, with Crystal helping David and then Peter followed behind. Each of the party had two guards that escorted them with their weapons at the ready. They led them out of the fractured hangar and into the open air.

Snow fell like feathers and cast an eerie glow across the old, broken military base. The beams of several flashlights sparkled in the swirling menagerie of flakes. Peter glanced around, hoping to think of some means of escape, but they were too well guarded. White drifts began to pile against buildings and his feet ached in the cold march through the gathering winter.

"Where are you taking us?" Crystal demanded.

"No talking!" the gruff voiced captor spoke.

With deliberate steps, the members of the squad marched in silent cadence, with the precision of trained military. They neared a bivouac of piled sand bags with two masked guards behind it, automatic rifles slung over their shoulders. As they passed, the guard stood erect and saluted with a return salute from the lead captor.

Great! Peter thought. *We're captured by some crazed militants.*

They approached a door that was halfway in the ground with a short flight of stairs that descended to it. Around the door stood a large cement frame and just beyond it a rounded mound of concrete. The lead captor escorted them through this door and into a well-lit, underground bunker.

A long hall stretched before them and reminded Peter of his walk toward the exit of the McNeil Island prison. Everything was cement. The walls, the ceiling, the floor all resonated with the dull echo of each footfall and made the tunnel sound as if a thousand marched down the passage. A heavy, metal door, grey and slightly rusted, stood before them and their escort stopped at the door and knocked twice.

Peter didn't hear anything, but the door swung open, grating against the rusted hinges. His body shuddered as the noise reminded him of nails scratching against a chalkboard. Then the guard urged him forward with a nudge from the butt of his rifle.

The room glowed with the blue-grey light of flickering fluorescent tubes hung from the ceiling. Desks lined the walls and a rectangular conference table filled the center of the room. A stern man, with salt-and-pepper hair sat at the end of the table and glanced over his spectacles to gaze at Peter and the others.

Papers were scattered across the table in front of the solitary figure who returned his attention to the documents.

"Captain," the lead guard said, "I've brought them as you ordered."

"Very well, sergeant, you can return to your post." The man's voice seemed relatively calm and he spoke with a genuine disregard to the entrance of the others. The lead escort raised his hand in salute and departed, followed by his squad.

Crystal clenched her fists and her eyes narrowed in agitation. "Who are you?" she demanded. "Why did you bring us down here?"

The man glanced up from his reading again and took off his glasses. "I'll be with you in a moment," he said with indifference.

Peter reached for Crystal's hand to stop her from entering into a tirade. He looked at her and her eyes flared with anger and frustration. With his eyes, he motioned for her to glance back at the two guards who stood beside the entrance with rifles in their hands. Crystal nodded her capitulation and ever-so-slightly relaxed her fists.

The captain stood from his seat and casually walked over to Peter and the others. He looked over each one and put his glasses in his shirt pocket. "Which one of you is called, *Sheridan*?"

"I am," Peter said.

"Yes, I thought so," the captain said. "You look a lot like your dad."

Peter and Crystal shot each other a glance, eyes wide with surprise.

"Please," the captain said, "come and sit down. You're safe here for the time being and I'm sure you could use a rest." He pointed to the conference table where each one took a seat. Peter sat so he could face the captain who took the head of the table.

"How," Peter stammered. "How do you know my father?"

"I doubt that there is a person in the Remnant who hasn't heard of Major Sheridan. But I was privileged to serve with him. Back then, however, he was Captain and I was a lowly second lieutenant."

"What's your name?" George asked.

"I'm Randal," he smiled. "However, it's Captain Miller to the men who serve with me on this post."

"But Captain," George continued, "I didn't expect that we would see anyone in the zone, least of all on this base."

"There are a few of us. We have gathered here at the command of Major Sheridan. He told us that the Remnant would be safe here because the rest of the population will try to avoid this place." Randal paused and leaned back. "He was right," he chuckled. "They even put a no-fly zone around this region."

"Then how did you know that I was, well, that I was me?" Peter asked.

"We monitor all government broadcasts from here and we caught the name *Sheridan* being mentioned. So, when we heard that a guard had reported your escape from California in a small aircraft – and then no surveillance tracked you – I was interested. Then our perimeter guards reported that a small plane had landed. I was amazed because there was no indication that any aircraft had crossed the boundary warning stations. I assumed that it was Patrick who had found a way to escape. Imagine my surprise when you showed up."

"But what are you doing here?" David asked.

"We're waiting," the captain said. "I had traveled to Washington years ago, before the major was taken to McNeil, and he told me about his plan. He ordered me to gather any who still trusted the ancient ways and bring them here. Well, when I arrived, I found an abandoned regiment of troops that were on this old Air Force Base. They had survived the cataclysm thrown at them from the feds and took me as their commander. I told them the major's plan and they agreed to help put the plan to action."

"So what was my dad's plan?" Peter asked.

"He told me that eventually someone would come through with the documents that could change the course of the nation and bring it back to the way it used to be. He didn't tell me who, but I suspect that he believed it would be you."

"Why?" Crystal asked.

"I don't know, but the last time I saw you," the captain said as he looked at Peter, "you were three years old. Yet, your mother and father both believed that you had a destiny set before you."

"Well," Peter said, "here I am."

"Indeed," Randal agreed. "But I must ask... do you have the documents with you?"

Peter grinned, "We do."

"Are you really going to try and finish your dad's mission?" Randal sounded hopeful.

"I am, but I'll need help. These three are going with me," Peter said as he looked toward the others.

Randal stood and moved toward the heavy metal door. "Well," he said, "right now let's get you and your friends situated. We have provisions and there are bunks available for you. We are here to help fulfill this mission."

"I appreciate it, captain," Peter said. "Ever since this crazy adventure began I have had the startling experience of finding help and support where I least expected it." Peter thought about Joshua, then Frank and the others who moved through his life. Without thinking, he reached down and took Crystal's hand. She eagerly squeezed it in her own.

Randal smiled, "That's the way of God. His help often comes disguised as caring people."

A sudden rush of motion drew their attention to the hall beyond the door. The rapid echoes of someone running down the corridor came to an abrupt end when the door flew open. A pale, thin soldier stood panting, his rifle slung over his shoulder and steam wafting off his overheated body. Snow covered his hood and dotted his dark blue overcoat.

Peter stepped back, not sure what to expect and put himself between Crystal and the door. But Randal clasped Peter on the shoulder as he passed to stand next to the young soldier who gasped for breath.

"Calm down, airman," Randal said. "What is it?"

"Sir," the soldier huffed, "the radio room sent me. They intercepted some terrible communications from outside the zone."

Peter glanced at Crystal and the others as they listened. "Terrible... how terrible?" he asked.

"Sir," the airman continued to speak to the captain. "I think that they know Sheridan is here."

CHAPTER TWENTY-TWO

"But those who hope in the LORD will renew their strength." ~ Isaiah 40:31

Peter felt as if his heart wanted to leap out of his throat. He looked at the young soldier who delivered the news, steam still wafting off the man's back. The sense of dread filled the chamber and a quick glance at his companions provided no measure of encouragement. George and David both hung their heads and Crystal tightened her grip on Peter's hand.

Captain Miller, however, kept his composure. "Airman, return to the communications room. I'll be along in a few minutes."

"Yes, sir," the young man said. He saluted and departed, allowing a chill gust of air to briefly enter the room.

Peter shivered, either from the cold blast or the troubling information. He looked toward the captain, "What now?"

"First," Randal said, "we need to get you some better clothing. It's winter after all." With a smile, he moved to the door and led Peter and the others up the long corridor.

They exited the hall and stepped into the day. Snow cascaded down, luminescent, fluffy flakes that filled the atmosphere, dancing through the air as they tumbled to the earth. Several soldiers rushed past, dressed in heavy winter coats, with their faces covered by woolen ski masks. Their tracks from when they arrived had long since been filled with snow, even as the footprints of the many soldiers vanished, covered by the winter storm.

"This is good." Randal exclaimed.

"G-g-good?" Crystal shivered. "How is this good?"

"This storm will prevent any satellite surveillance. But come; let's get you some warm clothes." The captain turned and walked past the tunnel, in the opposite direction from the hanger where George's plane waited.

Several buildings, like a silhouetted backdrop, grew larger as they approached. Soon they stood in front of a three-story edifice, gazing up at the mammoth brick-and-mortar structure. Several large sections were missing, exposing rooms to the open air, and holes appeared in various locations on each of the levels, but Randal led them in.

"Why do you still use this building?" David asked. "It seems to be rather, well, unsafe."

"We're limited in our resources. We use this building for non mission-critical supplies. We should find some warmer gear for all of you, however." He navigated through the broken building to a large, back room. Dust filtered through the air and sparkled in the glow of Randal's flashlight.

"Captain?" George spoke up.

"Yes, what is it?" Randal turned to look at the senior member of the party.

"Well, aren't you worried about the message from that airman of yours? You seem rather indifferent to the whole thing."

"Sir," Randal replied, "I have perimeter guards who are fully equipped. There is constant surveillance of outside communications and a blessed storm that will prevent any movement outside the zone for at least a day. You can relax, we are quite safe. For now, let's get you and your friends some decent winter gear and then go to the radio room."

Captain Miller flashed his light around the door until he found a switch, about chest high. He pressed it and a dim, central fluorescent light flickered and hummed as it began to glow. Peter's eyes widened at the cache of supplies that filled the chamber. All neat, and in order, rows of coats and shirts hung in uniform procession. Stacks of blue and khaki trousers lined the wall on one side, with a wealth of camouflage pants on the other. Leather and mesh military boots stood in racks at the very back of the supply room, organized by size and style.

"Get some parkas and gloves," Captain Miller commanded.

Peter and the others did as he said and found sufficient protection against the winter storm. Peter's parka fit perfectly, with sturdy waterproof gloves that were lined with some type of soft fabric. He glanced up at the others and all of them were examining their new garments as if they had never seen or worn such items. Crystal held the clothes as if she modeled the latest in military fashion, beaming with a warm smile. Peter watched her, delighted to see her happy.

"Peter." Randal stepped up from behind him, startling Peter back to the moment.

"Yes," he said as he turned to face the captain.

Randal walked up to him and placed his hand on his shoulder. "I'm amazed at how much you remind me of your dad."

"How so?" Peter asked. He wanted to hear as much information as possible about his father.

The captain gave a quick smile and nodded. "Besides bearing a strong resemblance, you carry yourself as he did." He gestured toward the three others who still moved through the racks of clothing. "Take these three," he said. "They will follow you to the very end of this mission. You give them someone they can trust, someone they can rely on to lead them. Your dad was very much like that."

"How long did you serve with him?"

"For years," Randal said. "When I was a lieutenant, your dad was a captain. Not long after, he was promoted to major and he asked me to serve with him."

"What'd you do?" Peter asked. "From what I understand, dad was not a believer until *after* he became a major."

Randal gave him a sideways glance. "You know more than I thought." He paused and took a deep breath. "We both were assigned to expose those whom the government considered insurrectionists. When Major Sheridan learned the actual truth, he shared it with me. We both devoted ourselves to recovering the old documents and restoring them to the country. That was our mission – and that is why the Shadow Remnant exists."

"Hey!" Crystal interrupted, "When can we get something to eat?"

"Come on," Randal said. "We'll go to the mess hall. I'm sure we can find you something to eat."

Peter laughed and moved toward the door, following Randal.

"Peter," Crystal ran up to him and grabbed his arm, nearly knocking him over.

"What?" he asked, feigning annoyance.

"I wish we could send about a hundred of these back to the island," she said as she pulled the parka tighter.

He offered a slight smile, "So do I."

David and George pressed ahead of them, following after the captain while Peter and Crystal causally walked behind. They stepped out of the broken building. Snow fell from the heavens with such force as to fill their tracks even as they walked. Crystal hooked her arm in Peter's and ducked her eyes from the onslaught of winter.

Hardly visible ahead of him, Peter kept his eyes on the glow of Randal's flashlight. With Crystal in tow, he kept a steady pace until they arrived at another building. It was a single-level structure with boarded windows. Red brick framed a metal, double door. With a clank, they pressed through the door and stomped their feet on the tile floor to knock off all the snow. Steam wafted off their backs as snow fell from their hoods.

David, George and Randal sat at a round table in a sea of round tables. The room was a long, rectangular structure, functional and with little décor. Several lesser-ranked soldiers entered and delivered trays of food, one for each of them—except Randal.

Peter took a seat and looked at the captain. "Aren't you going to eat?"

"No," he said. "I took my meal earlier at the command post and need to get to the communications room. Be at peace for now and enjoy your meal. I will return shortly and let you know more." Randal stood and pulled his coat on. With a perfunctory wave, he left the building.

"Well," David said, "this is interesting." He fumbled with his fork as he absentmindedly pushed his food around his plate.

"What I want to know," George snapped, "is how they found us!"

"I don't have a clue," Peter said as he shook his head in bewilderment. "Randal said that he didn't detect us until we were spotted by people who saw us land. I can't figure how someone in California knew where we went."

"Who knows," Crystal said. She poured herself some cool water out of a ceramic pitcher. "Maybe that device you installed didn't work as we thought."

"It had to," Peter said. "They didn't detect us and no alarms were raised when we crossed into this no-fly zone."

"It was m…" David whispered.

"What?" Peter asked. His eyes narrowed as he looked at his companion.

"I said," David took a deep breath, "I said it was me."

"What do you mean?" George demanded.

David stood. "When I was captured by that brute of a guard, they implanted a tracking device in my arm." He looked at Peter. "I thought that if I was able to get far enough away they would be unable to track me. I told you!" He paced out his frustration as he threw his hands up in the air. "I told you that he was relentless, that he would never give up."

"Nice," George said. "Just when we thought we were safe."

"So, what do we do now?" Crystal asked.

"I don't know." Peter stood and moved away from the table, aimlessly wandering through the room. His thoughts were awash with a tide of ideas, but none of them seemed plausible. He dare not leave David behind, but to take him farther on only guaranteed that they would be found. He thought David might hide in the aircraft, but he needed his expertise to hack into the communications network. He stopped when he reached the far wall, where a singular window remained intact.

Outside, two guards were posted about fifty paces away from the building, hunkered down behind a barrier. The snow fell in steady flurries. Large, white flakes flittered past the window, and a single light shone from high atop a post. The world was bathed in the sparkling glow of winter.

He startled when someone tapped him on the shoulder. Peter turned around to see Crystal standing behind him, her green eyes piercing into his.

"Peter," she said, her voice was calm and steady.

"What?" He didn't mean to sound so sharp, but his frustration filled that single word.

"Don't snap at me," Crystal said, her voice growing a bit harder. "I wanted to suggest that the captain of this base might have an idea on how to help."

As if on cue, Randal entered the room and walked over to Peter. "Sheridan," he said, "There's been some more news."

"By the sound of your voice, I don't think it's going to be good," George added.

"No, it's not. You all need to come with me."

Peter moved to follow the captain. A dread fell upon his heart as he pondered the ominous words of his benefactor. Crystal moved to walk beside Peter as David and George followed close behind.

He led them through the blizzard. The wind had increased so that the flakes now attacked them like miniature spears, pricking their skin with a biting cold. Crystal, again, anchored her arm in Peter's and kept her eyes down as they trudged through the bitter night. David struggled, limping through the snow. A young soldier suddenly appeared from out of the darkness to walk beside him and help him along. George grumbled under his breath, his voice barely audible in the whistling wind.

Stumbling along, they entered into another single-story building not far from the hanger. Large, satellite dishes stood like shadowy sentinels on the roof and an eighty-foot tall radio tower kept vigil on the opposite side of the structure. Randal led them down a dimly lit corridor with doors spaced every twenty feet on either side. The whir of some unseen machine kept the air filled with its dull noise as a constant breath of warm air blew down from square vents in the ceiling.

Through a door on the left, they entered into a large room with two rows of computer terminals in the center of the chamber, and what seemed to be a large, back-lit map of the region that filled the far wall. Several blue-clad soldiers sat at the computers, furiously clicking away at their various keyboards.

"What's this place?" Crystal asked.

"This is the communications room," Randal said. "From here we monitor all available information from our perimeter stations to the government channels and satellite communications."

"How?" David asked.

"We use key-word algorithms to scan broadcasts, internet transmissions and satellite feeds in order to know what the outside is up to. Along with that, we receive coded messages from regions around the country so that we can keep up with what is happening with the Remnant."

Peter stood amazed at the organization. "This is incredible! Who set this up?"

"Well, there were many early on, but this," Randal moved his hand as if to point to the entire room, "this was your dad's idea. He believed that if there was to be a restoration of the old ways, then there would need to be a central place where the members of the Remnant could communicate."

"Why hasn't the government shut this down?" George asked, his voice pitched with surprise.

"Because they don't know about it," the captain replied. "You see, all this functions on principles long since abandoned. They don't even have the means of monitoring our frequencies, and I doubt that anyone is around who would even know how."

"But this — this is incredible!" George exclaimed.

"I was a bit apprehensive at first," Randal said with his usual detachment. "When Major Sheridan discovered these ancient communications techniques, and that we could use them without discovery, he began collecting the equipment and storing it here. Well, not long afterward, he was captured. But he was able to establish this center and build bridges of communication with other cells. Since then, we have tried to maintain contact with various locations, biding our time until the mission was accomplished."

Peter was apprehensive. "So, Captain, we're here. What's so urgent?"

Randal turned to a terminal and picked up a square touchpad tablet. "We intercepted this text message sent from a federal marshal. They are on the way."

"What do you mean, *they're on the way?*" George asked. "You said that no one would try to enter the zone during this terrible storm."

"Yes," Randal said, "that was my assumption. But I didn't take into account how important Sheridan is." The captain handed the pad to Peter. "He has been classified as a dangerous insurrectionist and a top fugitive under the current state of martial law."

Peter looked at the pad as the screen glowed with faded light. He shook his head as he read the words beneath his own name: *wanted – dead or alive,* signed by someone named Frederick P. Gallagher, Commanding General of the federal marshal service. "From what this says, this General Gallagher has given orders to the civilian army corp. to enter the zone and get me. But," Peter asked, "Who is this *General Gallagher?*"

"He may very well be the third most powerful man in Washington D.C." Randal said.

"Oh," Crystal said, "and who are the first two?"

"That's easy," Randal said. "President Cunningham and the Director of Communications, Kyle Johansen, are the two most powerful men. And," he added, "Between the three of them they control the entire country."

"This is why the document is so critical," George added. "Once the country learns about how things used to be, then there will be change."

"You cannot guarantee that," David said. "The people of this country have become dependent on the government for everything. You might find that they will reject your words and betray you."

Peter handed the pad back to Randal. "We have a more pressing problem, right now."

"Yes, like how do we escape from here?" George said.

"No, that's not it. We're going to fly out of here, but we need to take care of another problem," Peter said.

"What's that?" Randal asked.

"David has a tracking device implanted on him. He needs to have it removed."

Randal nodded his understanding. He turned to one of the soldiers, "Sergeant, take David to the infirmary and see what they can do."

"Captain," Peter said, "would it be alright if I go with him?"

Randal offered a rare smile, "Certainly."

Peter and David followed the sergeant out of the communications room and back into the snow-bound world. Flurries rushed past them and the wind made it seem as if the snow fell sideways. The rugged soldier led them past the entrance to the underground command bunker and navigated their way through broken streets. The rubble of broken and fractured buildings, laced with snow, lined the roads as they made their way to a central complex. It was a three-story building with boarded windows, surrounded by a wall of trees that acted as a protective barrier against the wind. They walked through the trees and entered the main doors.

The long corridor that stood before them was electric with activity. Peter did a double-take as he watched blue-clad medical personnel walk about the well-lit hall. Patients in white gowns meandered in and out of rooms or were wheeled along on rolling stretchers. The steady hum of an unseen air conditioner provided the background chorus to the scene.

An orderly walked up to the men. "Sergeant, who are these two?" he asked.

"The captain sent them over," their guide said as he pulled off his hood, sending a cascade of snow to the floor. "Seems like this one's got a trackin' device that needs to be removed," he said as he pointed at David.

"Alright," the orderly said. "Come with me." He led Peter and David down the long corridor. They stopped at an elevator and waited as the carriage arrived.

"How is it," David asked, "that so many buildings are destroyed on this base, but this one is still fully functional?"

"I'm not sure," the orderly said. "It's been this way since I arrived on base."

"When did you get here?" Peter asked.

"I've been with the captain for two years," he said.

"Where did you come from?" David asked as the doors to the elevator opened. They stepped inside to the soft sound of classical music.

"I was up north, in Montana to be precise. I escaped from the Deer Lodge education center and ended up here. I was making my way south, to warmer climates, in hopes of trying to live on my own. When I arrived on base, the captain took me in and asked if I would join him." Just then the door opened to the third floor and the orderly escorted them out into the hall.

"You're story sounds similar to mine," Peter said.

"I don't think so," the orderly said. "For me, it was as simple as walking away. I haven't been tracked or hunted or wanted by the government. In fact, I would say that there is no one looking for me." He led them to a set of double doors that swung open when they arrived. It led into a well-lit room with a single surgical table in the center, surrounded by all manner of assorted trays and monitors.

David began to show signs of apprehension as his breathing quickened and his eyes explored the room. "What is going to happen?" David asked.

The orderly picked up a hand-held scanning device. "Well," he said, "the first thing to do is find out where that tracking device is implanted in your body. If you could stand next to the table, I'll begin the scanning process." He smiled, "Now this won't hurt a bit."

David stood next to the foot of the surgical table and flinched when the orderly moved the scanner near his head. Peter rested his hand on David's shoulder as he remembered the pain he suffered when his own device was removed.

However, the orderly simply moved the scanning device just above David's skin, listening with an earpiece that was connected to it. He passed over his back, scanned his legs and finally explored David's arms with the device when his eyes widened. Peter watched as the orderly slowly moved the scanner up and down David's right arm. Then, with a gleam of delight in his eyes, he declared, "I've found it."

"Well?" Peter said, hoping that one word conveyed his desire for more information.

"Well," the orderly said, "the device is implanted in his arm. It's deep but I think it might be operable. But, that's up to the doctor." He replaced the scanning device to its appropriate tray and picked up a hand-held phone. "Nurse... yes, this is operating room three... please let the doctor know we're ready."

A minute later a tall man in a white lab coat entered into the room. His hair was graying and thin on the top and he walked with a slight limp. "What's your report, Airman Mallory?"

"Sir," the orderly said, "the device is implanted in his right arm. I believe it is sub-muscular and it might be attached to the bone."

"Bring me the delta scanner," the doctor ordered.

The orderly moved what looked to be a computer monitor attached to a wheel-mounted tripod, with all manner of wires and buttons available for the doctor to utilize. He removed a glass-eyed scanning device from its mount on the side of the monitor and handed it to the doctor.

After pressing several buttons, the screen came alive with a swirling rainbow of colors. The doctor pressed the glass eye of the scanner against David's arm and slid the device up and down until a distorted image manifested on the screen. It looked like an oblong cylinder that pulsated with a faint orange light.

"What's that?" Peter asked.

"That is the tracking device," the doctor said. "And," he added, "it cannot be removed."

"What!" David and Peter belted out their exclamation in unison.

"Mallory was right when he said it's attached to the bone. In fact, it is grown over with bone. In order to remove it, I would need to cut away too much material and leave your arm nearly crippled."

"Is there an alternative?" Randal said, surprising everyone as he walked into the room.

"Oh, captain," the orderly snapped to attention, "I didn't know you were here."

"At ease, airman," Randal ordered. The captain turned his attention back to the doctor. "Is there the possibility of disabling the device without removing it?"

"It would take a massive electrical pulse to cripple the device, and the pain would be excruciating." The doctor looked troubled by the prospect.

"There's little choice, doctor," Randal said. "The snowstorm is lifting and the incursion has begun. There are troops heading this way. We need to get Sheridan and the others off the base before we're overrun."

"Do what you need to," David winced.

The doctor took a deep breath and brought out a defibrillator box. "Do you know what this is?" he asked David.

David nodded with his eyes wide.

"This is the only thing that I have that can deliver enough voltage to disable it. I will place these paddles on either side of your arm and discharge 5000 volts through the tracking device." The doctor pulled out the paddles and began charging up the unit. "I'll need you to remove your shirt."

David complied, and Peter gasped when he noticed the scars that crisscrossed his chest and back. He looked like a man who had been beaten regularly and whipped repeatedly. Even the captain let out an audible groan when he observed David's condition.

"Who... how... What happened to you?" Peter stammered.

"This is the price you pay for failure," David said.

"Can I have everyone stand back," the doctor said. "Now, David, when I apply this electrical charge to your arm, you will feel it. You may find that your arm is useless for a while, but that will be just nerve shock. You will regain its use in due time."

"Just get it over with, please," David said.

The doctor nodded and pressed the paddles to either side of David's arm. Instinctively he shouted, "Clear!" then pressed the button on the discharge paddle.

A snap, a flash and David's arm stiffened. He yelled out a scream as the rush of electricity pulsed through his arm. But in a second it was over and his arm hung limp at his side, tears streaming from his eyes.

The orderly quickly scanned David's arm. "I don't read any signal," he shouted. "It worked!"

"Thank God!" David exclaimed. "I doubt that I would ever try it a second time."

"Now that it's over, I need to get you to your aircraft," Randal ordered. "We have had crews clearing the runway and the weather has cleared enough for you to take off. George and Crystal are waiting for you." David retrieved his shirt and the doctor placed his arm in a sling.

336

Randal exited the building with Peter and David on his heels. They passed through the barrier of evergreens and noticed a dark blue, four-door truck waiting for them. A young soldier sat at the wheel with the engine running. Randal stepped quickly and it was all Peter could do to keep up.

The captain jumped into the passenger seat in the front while Peter and David sat in the back. Peter noticed a look of panic on the young soldiers face as he revved the engine and pulled away from the hospital. He drove as quickly as the slick conditions allowed, and made for the hangar where their plane waited.

Randal picked up the handset for the two-way radio, "Sergeant, report."

"Captain," a static voice replied, "we've lost the perimeter and they're pressing their way to the secondary defenses. We've slowed them down, but they'll be on base in less than an hour." The sound of gunfire cracked over the speaker. "Captain!" then the voice went silent.

"Hurry up, airman," Randal ordered. "Get to that plane right now!"

The driver pushed the pedal and the truck skidded along, fishtailing as they went. Peter was amazed at the driver's skill to keep the vehicle on the road. Snow kicked up from the tires like a wake from a boat and a swirling mass of white powder flew off the hood. Through the haze, Peter watched the hangar grow. He silently prayed and hoped that they were not too late. They slid to the front of the hangar and the plane sat with chalks under the tires and the propeller spinning.

Randal turned around and reached over the seat with his hand outstretched. "Sheridan, it is a pleasure to serve with you."

Peter reached out and grasped the captain's hand in his. "Thank you, Captain. I only hope it's worth it."

"Young man," Randal said, "if our country learns the truth and finds freedom again, it is well worth it." He glanced at the aircraft. "Now, the both of you get going. Our forces cannot hold back the attack forever and I'm needed with my men."

Peter and David nodded and rushed out of the vehicle. The truck sped off and they ran to the airplane. George sat at the controls and Crystal stood at the door waiving for them to hurry.

In a mad dash, they jumped into the plane. David entered first, and then Peter who helped Crystal as she closed the door. They aircraft rumbled to life and lurched forward, exiting the hangar. Snow swirled in the prop-wash as they sped down the runway, faster and faster, until the tires lifted off the ground. Once again, they soared through the skies.

Peter sat back as the aircraft climbed into the clouds. The howling wind drowned out all sounds but the engine as the whirring prop pulled them through the atmosphere. He glanced out the window to watch the snow-laden clouds rush past in a flurry. The world outside was shrouded in grey, with an eerie, iridescent glow that grew brighter as they neared the upper reaches of the storm. His heart raced as fast as the snow flew by.

The plane shuddered as it plowed through the turbulence. Peter looked toward the cockpit and watched George grip the yoke with white-knuckled hands, glancing back and forth from the instrument panel to the window and back again. Peter gazed back out the window. In a flash of blue, the clouds fell beneath them. He looked down at the top of the storm, and it seemed no more threatening than a blanket of cotton.

"George," Peter called.

The aged man looked back from the cockpit. "Yes... what is it? I'm trying to fly here you know."

"Were heading to Colorado Springs," Peter said. "How far is it?"

"Several hundred miles," George shouted to be heard over the noise of the aircraft. "It'll be a couple hours before we drop below the storm again."

"Do you need me up there?"

George nodded toward the other two. David had reclined in his seat, his eyes closed, and Crystal was already lost to unknown dreams as she nestled against Peter's arm. "It looks like you're stuck back there. Why don't you follow their example and get some rest. I suspect you'll need it."

Peter returned the smile and sighed then nestled down a little deeper into the chair. As the world rushed beneath them, exhaustion washed over Peter like a wave and he began to slowly drift into sleep. He fluttered his eyes momentarily, concerned that George alone had to keep alert. But his weariness sank him and he faded into silent slumber.

* * * *

"Pete!" A distant voice seemed to echo within his vacant dream as Peter turned his face away from the window.

"Peter, get up!" the voice demanded again.

Peter stirred and looked at the face of Crystal who hovered over him with eyes wide in terror. Having forgotten for a moment where he was, he jumped up, cracked his head on the top of the aircraft and immediately fell back into the chair.

"Peter, get up here!" George bellowed from the cockpit.

Fully roused and thoroughly anxious, Peter hopped over the center panel and fell into the co-pilot's seat. He donned the headgear and positioned the microphone to his mouth. "What?" he asked. "What's going on?"

Before George could answer, Peter heard the engine sputter. He cast his gaze out the front windshield and watched the propeller shudder and then rev back to life. His eyes were wide as he came to grips with the situation — the engine was failing.

"Peter," George's voice crackled in his ears. "We have a major problem! Something's wrong with the fuel system. I'm afraid the lines might be freezing up."

Again the engine stuttered.

"What does that mean... are we going to crash?" Peter did not try to disguise the desperation in his wavering voice.

"Well... let me put it this way... we're landing whether we want to or not. If the lines completely freeze the engine dies!"

Peter looked out the window and realized that they were near the cloud layer. Ahead, like a monolith in the sky, a massive mountain peak jutted up from the blanket, with several more in the distance.

George didn't wait for Peter to ask. "I had to lower our altitude. We're near eleven thousand feet and dropping. Some of the peaks around here are over fourteen thousand feet." The engine sputtered again and their elevation dropped.

"What are we going to do?" Peter asked.

"Strap in," George demanded. "I'm gonna try and get below the cloud layer and land this thing before we fall out of the sky like a stone."

Peter turned to look at Crystal and David. "Strap in! We're going to land."

Frantic, the two quickly fastened their seatbelts around their waist and waited. David mouthed something but was drowned out by the noise of the aircraft. George pushed the yoke forward and the plane began to descend rapidly into the clouds.

Immediately the world was engulfed in grey. The instrument panel flashed warning lights and the engine revved as they dropped through the storm. It reminded Peter of the sounds he heard when he watched movies of World War Two fighter aircraft when they started their attacks. Peter looked back again and saw Crystal with her head bowed and hands folded beneath. David looked up at him with wide-eyed desperation, clinging to the arm rest of his seat as if he might be flung away without warning.

Then they broke through the clouds.

The world rushed up at them and George pulled upon the yoke to level the aircraft. The plane seemed reluctant to obey his commands and shook violently. The earth beneath them rushed past in a blur and flakes of snow pelted the outer skin of the airplane.

"The wings are freezing up!" George cracked through the headset.

"Of course they are!" Peter yelled back as he rolled his eyes in frustration. *What else could happen*, he thought. "Do you know where we are?"

"We're a bit off course," George said. "We're south of an old ski village called Breckenridge." He weaved his way through the valleys as he fought against the turbulence.

Then the engine died.

An eerie silence filled the cabin as the propeller sputtered and stopped. For a moment they glided through the air and Peter wondered if angels held up their aircraft when George shouted, "Brace for impact!"

Instinctively he held his breath and prayed. The right wing clipped a tree and sent them into a dizzying spin. End over end, they tumbled out of the sky. With a crack, they struck the ground. The left wing snapped off like kindling and, upside-down, the plane plowed through the snow. The windshield shattered and Peter struck his head against the console. Then all went dark.

CHAPTER TWENTY-THREE

"Although the Lord gives you the bread of adversity and the water of affliction, your teachers will be hidden no more; with your own eyes you will see them." ~ Isaiah 30:20

Disoriented, Peter tried to look around. His vision was blurred, but the warm air he felt upon his skin told him he was not in the wreckage. His head throbbed with every heartbeat, keeping a steady rhythm of renewed agony. Peter tried to sit up, and suddenly realized he was under a heavy blanket on a soft, plush bed. He squinted and tried to see through his hazy eyesight and determined he was in a dark room.

"Well, I guess I'm not dead," Peter stammered, his voice hoarse and strained.

"No, you're not dead," a quiet, deep voice said from the darkness beyond his bed.

Startled, Peter tried to move but every joint screamed in agonizing protest. He fell back into the bed, grateful for the soft conditions. "Where am I?"

"In a small village in Colorado," the voice said.

"What about the others?" Peter's voice trembled, fearful of what the answer might be.

"You just get some rest. You were injured in the crash and need time to recover."

Peter felt weak and didn't have the strength to argue. He sighed. "How long have I been here?"

"Three days," the stranger said. A door swung open, letting in a stream of light and then it closed with a quiet click.

Peter closed his eyes and drifted back to unconsciousness.

Dreams plagued his sleep as his mind raced with the memory of the crash. He looked behind him and saw Crystal. She was out of reach and her body broken upon the rocks of the mountains. He tried to scream but found his voice was silent and his mouth filled with snow. He gagged and coughed and let out a cry for help. As he fought against his fear he thought he heard Crystal's faint voice.

"Peter..."

He stirred and his eyes fluttered as he tried to wake up from the dream.

"Peter, wake up!" Crystal stood by his side and shook him.

Peter bolted upright in his bed, a cold sweat hung upon his body and he trembled from the terror of his dream. He cast his wide-eyed gaze upon Crystal and gasped, "You're alive!"

She smiled at him, but her face bore the lines of sorrow. "Of course I'm alive and I'm pretty sure that this ain't heaven."

Peter heard in her half-hearted laugh an underlying sadness. He relaxed and sighed as he swung his legs over the edge of the bed. His body ached as if he had run a marathon. His balance was shaky and he held his head in his hands as he regained his equilibrium. He glanced up at Crystal who stood over him with her eyes cast to the ground. "What is it, Crystal?"

She sighed with regret, "You need to come downstairs." Tears welled up in her eyes and she reached out for Peter's hand.

"Tell me... what's going on?" Peter's words were gentle but firm.

"It's George... he... he didn't make it." Crystal paused as she tried to gather her emotions and regain her composure. "It's been five days since we crashed and there is a funeral service planned for him. I came up to see if you were strong enough to attend."

Peter sat stunned. He looked up at Crystal who had tears streaming down her cheeks as she trembled with grief. He motioned for her to sit beside him and she nearly collapsed onto the bed. She leaned against his arm and he held her as she sobbed. "Tell me," his voice cracked as he tried to speak through his own emotions. "David... is he alright?"

"Yes," she said. "David and I walked away with little more than a scratch. You and George took the full force of the crash. We thought..." she took a deep breath to regain her voice. "David and I feared that you were gone to. I couldn't wake you." She threw her arms around him and cried. "I tried to wake you and you were hardly breathing." Her words rushed forth from her as if a dam had burst. "I thought I lost you and I just couldn't bear it. Peter... I love you!"

Peter put his arms around her and held her close. With those three words it seemed as if every pain he felt vanished in the warmth of her embrace. "I love you too," he whispered in her ear. She held him a little tighter and he could feel her body relax in their embrace.

She pulled back and wiped tears from her eyes. "Talk about coming a long way from where we started," she said with a teary-eyed chuckle.

"To let you in on a little secret," Peter said, "I was certain I loved you from the day you crashed through the woods on the island." He gently wiped a tear from off her cheek.

"I never *crash* through the woods," she said in mock annoyance. "And remember, you're still just a newbie." She wiped her eyes dry and stood up.

Peter tried to get on his feet, but the world suddenly spun out of control and he nearly collapsed back on the bed. Crystal snatched him up under his arm and put his arm around her shoulder. "I didn't think I'd be so weak," he said.

"That's from lying around for five days," she quipped. "C'mon, let's get you downstairs."

He stood and noticed that his left ankle was wrapped. The toes stuck out from the bandages and they were mottled blue, bruised and swollen. His arms and chest were covered in welts from various scratches and his shoulder ached from the old gunshot wound. Gauze wrapped most of his right arm and both hands were cut and bruised.

He leaned heavily upon Crystal. As they turned to leave the room he caught his reflection in the mirror. He could tell that he had been cared for. His hair was combed and beard shaved. However, his face looked as if he had been in a boxing match. His eyes were swollen and bruised and a large gash crossed his forehead. Both cheeks were welted with scratches and some gauze was taped on the back of his neck. The condition that alarmed him more was the strands of grey running through his hair.

"Surprised?" Crystal asked.

"Yeah," he replied as he ran his fingers through his hair. He felt several lacerations on his scalp that stung with each touch. "I'm surprised and very thankful to still be alive."

They walked out of the room and carefully navigated down a wide flight of stairs. The building they were in was warm and comfortable with soft, burgundy carpet and rustic wood paneling. With his right arm slung around Crystal's shoulders, Peter gripped the banister with his left hand. He had to take brief steps, but made his way to the ground floor and found several men sitting near a stone fireplace that glowed with a crackling fire. David sat among them and quickly moved to help Peter. Crystal released her hold on him and stepped around the corner.

The other men departed and Peter sat upon a soft, cushioned chair near the fire. His body ached and every joint felt stiff, but he thought that the pain was manageable. With a quick glance at David, Peter saw the concern in his friend's eyes. "I'm going to be alright," Peter said to answer David's unspoken question.

"That is good to know," David said with a quiet sigh.

"Where are we?" Peter asked.

"This is a little town called Fairplay. We are nearly a hundred miles from our goal. I do not know how we will get there for these people do not have any means of adequate transportation." David raised his hands in frustration.

Peter nodded. "I think we have other things to tend to right now."

"You are right, of course," David agreed. "The funeral is set for this afternoon at a place called the Baptist church."

A tall man strode up to where they sat. Peter glanced up at the grey-haired stranger and thought he almost recognized him. The newcomer pulled up a cushioned chair and sat down opposite the other two.

"Have we met?" Peter asked.

"Briefly, but you were a bit under the weather." the man spoke with a rich, baritone voice.

"You were in my room!" Peter exclaimed.

David looked at Peter, "He has been in your room since we were brought here from the crash. It was Pastor Martin and some from his church that came and carried you and George back here."

"*Pastor* Martin?" Peter asked.

"Yes, my name is John Martin and I am the pastor of the local church." His voice resonated with calm assurance.

"I must say that I'm a bit surprised." Peter felt a sense of uncertainty as he looked at the man who sat across from him. "How is it that you openly say such things?"

John smiled, "I'll tell you about it at dinner tonight – if you're not too tired. Right now I need to prepare for your friend's service." He stood and nodded his farewell and strode out of the main exit.

Just then Crystal returned, carrying a tray laden with several cups and a steaming carafe. "I thought you might like a hot cup of coffee," she said as she sat in the chair that John vacated. She offered cups to Peter and David and then poured the beverage for them.

The three friends sat silently as they sipped at their drinks. Peter cherished the moment of peace. Yet, there hung in the air between them a lingering sorrow. They glanced up at each other and shared their quiet grief.

Minutes passed and Peter broke the silence. "What happened after?"

"After what?" David asked.

"After the crash," Peter said. "The last thing I remember is that we hit a tree and flipped upside down."

David nodded. "You are right; we did tumble down the mountainside. The plane crashed through rocks and trees and the windshield shattered when it hit a fallen log. That's when we finally came to a stop. Crystal and I hung from our seats, still strapped in until I was able to maneuver myself free. We both climbed out of the aircraft and then pulled you and George from the wreckage."

Crystal nodded. "We thought that both of you were gone. You're breathing was so shallow and you had so much blood covering your face." She was visibly shaken as she spoke. After a deep breath, she continued, though tears streamed from her eyes. "It was obvious that George was killed. You were unconscious

348

and David and I were in the middle of a wilderness that neither one of us were familiar with."

"That is when we were taken by surprise," David continued.

"By surprise?" Peter asked.

"Yes, they came up on us without warning. The pastor and several others were snowshoeing in the hills near the crash sight and happened upon us not more than thirty minutes after we escaped the wreck." David stood and warmed his hands by the fire. "It is fortunate they were there right then. If they did not come when they did, I fear we would be having a funeral for you as well."

Peter nodded his understanding. "How did I get down here, though?"

"Pastor Martin made a sled from tree branches and put you on it," Crystal said. "He pulled you all the way to this building and with the help of another man, carried you up to your room."

A young man, no more than sixteen, with short blonde hair, entered through the main door and let a blast of cold air rush through the hall. "Are you Peter?" he asked as he stepped near the fire.

"Yes," Peter said.

"I was instructed to bring you and your friends to the church. The funeral will begin shortly." He motioned toward the door.

Crystal stood beside Peter and helped him up. David came to his other side and they all three walked toward the exit. His joints were stiff and yet, he was amazed at how much the pain had subsided. He kept his arm around Crystal's shoulders as David moved to open the door.

The day was bright, clear and crisp. Snow had fallen for several days and covered the entire town in a white, shimmering blanket but now the azure sky showed no signs of snow and no clouds to the edge of the horizon. Shops lined the street and several people moved along the wide road, guiding mules laden with any number of assorted items. In the distance, grand mountains loomed like sentinels that guarded the clandestine town.

Peter grinned when he saw a mule and cart waiting for them, with the blonde teen holding the reins. "I see what you meant, David, about not having adequate transportation."

"It certainly is a far cry from your dad's car," Crystal said. She held Peter around the waist and helped him into the back of the wagon. David hopped on and the young man guided the mule and cart through the wide streets of Fairplay. Several other carts moved through town, as well as an assortment of people.

Peter marveled at the kindness shown by the townspeople. Many greeted them as they passed, and several were walking in the same direction as their cart. They followed the street until it ended at the edge of town and their guide led the mule to a long, narrow building with a pitched roof and what looked to Peter like a small tower at the top.

"We're here," the young man said. "The service will be conducted inside the church."

Crystal hopped off, followed by David, and they helped Peter slide off the cart. A path had been cut through the snow so that they could walk two abreast toward the church. Again, Crystal took Peter around the waist and draped his arm around her shoulder.

He stepped with care, but was grateful to discover that the more he moved around, the better he began to feel. "You know," he said, "I think I might try to walk on my own. My joints aren't so stiff and I feel a bit stronger." He lowered his arm from around Crystal's shoulders and took her by the hand. Together, slowly, they walked into the chapel.

It reminded Peter of the old church he had hidden in when he fled from Darrington. This one, however, was well maintained.

A small, raised platform with a podium in the center faced row upon row of benches. Just in front of the platform was a small table, and upon the table was the casket. It was a plain, wooden pine box that boasted no great décor. They stepped quietly up to it and peered inside.

Peter had half-hoped that it would be empty, that this was some elaborate ruse or a crazed nightmare, but George's body lay in solemn repose, eyes closed. Crystal broke down in tears and David glanced away. Peter gazed upon his fallen companion and time seemed to come to a halt until Crystal tugged on his hand. He looked to her, and reached his hand to wipe a tear from her cheek.

Then John Martin stepped to the dais. "If I could have everyone take their seats, we will begin." His rich voice echoed through the hall and a hush fell upon the room. Then the pastor sat in a small chair behind the podium.

Peter marveled at how many had turned out. Not a seat was empty, and many stood in the aisle and entryway to hear the message of the pastor. Tears and sobs flowed freely, and he began to wonder if the townspeople knew George. A white-haired pianist softly played a stirring, melodious song and many quiet prayers were lifted straight to heaven.

Then the pastor stood. "My friends," he said, "we have gathered in this hall in sadness and mourning. But there is another gathering taking place, a gathering in heaven where this one who has departed from us has been ushered in and is even now celebrating eternal life. For even as the great Apostle Paul had written to his young disciple, Timothy, 'I have fought the good fight, I have finished the race, I have kept the faith.' We can say, as well, that this man has done no less with his life.

"Each of us has a mission, a divine purpose from the Almighty God, and we are tasked to complete it. Let us, as we look upon this life well lived, remember that we too must be willing to risk all, to meet the challenges before us and, by faith, step out of the boat of our doubts and walk upon the sea of life, trusting that it is our Savior who will hold us secure. And we are reminded of those great words: 'For to me, to live is Christ and to die is gain.'"

The service continued with more music and prayers and yet, Peter marveled at the ease with which the people of Fairplay seemed to practice their faith. No one showed a sense of fear. As far as he could tell, the people behaved as if this was quite normal.

The final prayer was said and people began to rise from their seats and move in procession to look upon George one last time. Peter rose but found his legs stiff from sitting, and was glad to have a chance to stretch them out. The words of the pastor rung in his ear: *each of us has a mission.* He took Crystal's hand and they exited the building, as many warm-hearted congregants offered their sympathetic condolences. David followed close behind and they climbed onto the mule cart and went back to the inn.

They entered and sat near the fire as a young girl brought them three steaming cups of hot chocolate. A tear still hung in Peter's eye as he smiled. He raised his mug. "To George," he said. Crystal and David raised theirs as well and joined in the toast to their fallen comrade.

"Now what do we do?" David asked. "I could get used to living in a place like this, but we set out on a task that needs to be completed."

"I don't know," Peter said. "We need to find a way to get to Colorado Springs, but something tells me that we're here for a purpose. I'm not sure what it is yet, but I'm sure that it must have something to do with my father's mission."

David stood and warmed his hands by the fire. "On the way to the funeral, did you see the large transmission towers on the mountain?"

"I did," Crystal nodded.

"If there were some way I could hack into the tower signal, we could accomplish our mission without being detected." David tapped on his mug as he thought.

A chill blast of air turned their attention to the door. Pastor Martin entered and made a direct line toward the three friends. His face was ruddy from the brisk walk and his hair seemed to briefly steam as he approached. The pastor took a seat directly opposite Peter. He could see in the preacher's eyes a thoughtfulness and intensity of purpose.

"Pastor Martin," Peter said.

"I wanted to come and check on how you three were doing," the pastor said. "I know what it's like to lose a friend and want you to know that if you need to talk, I'm here."

"That is very kind," David said. "I think we all understand that George died doing what he knew was right."

"He died doing the Lord's work," Peter added.

Pastor Martin nodded. "Tomorrow's Sunday," he said. "I would be delighted if you would come to services at the church." He gave a quick glance at Crystal who looked down with a slight smile.

"We'd be happy to attend," Crystal said.

Peter glanced at the both of them, perplexed. "Yeah, that'd be fine."

"Good!" The pastor exclaimed. "I'll see you at the church tomorrow at 10:30 a.m." He stood and reached over to shake Peter's hand, then turned and walked out the main door.

Peter's eyes narrowed as he looked at Crystal. "Okay… what was that about?"

"What?" She said with mock surprise.

"That little nod and smile," Peter said.

"You'll see," Crystal smiled as she stood. "It's a surprise. But I think you need to get back upstairs and get some rest. Let me help you."

"Yeah, I think so too." Peter stood carefully. His leg felt stiff and his head throbbed with pain. With David and Crystal's help, he managed the stairs and made his way back to his room. Crystal entered with him and sat in a chair next to the bed. She picked up a book – it was Joshua's Bible. "You saved it!" Peter exclaimed.

"Actually it was Pastor Martin who saved it. He went back to the wreckage and recovered all of our things." She flipped through the pages, careful not to tear the delicate parchment. "Shall I read to you?"

"By all means," Peter said even as his eyes grew heavy. He closed them, shutting out the light to try and diminish the pounding ache that echoed in his head.

Crystal took a deep breath and began reading. "I thank my God every time I remember you…"

Her voice was soothing and Peter relaxed as he began to drift into sleep. Her words dimmed and he heard the chair creak as she stood. He felt her hair brush against his cheek as she kissed him on the forehead and whispered, "I love you."

* * * *

Peter woke with David shaking him. He startled and bolted upright, trembling from a dream. "What!"

"Steady," David said. "It is time that we go to the church building. Crystal has already left and she asked me to make sure you arrive on time."

Groggy, Peter rubbed his eyes. "What time is it?"

"It is ten in the morning," David said. "Now get ready because our mule and cart are waiting for us outside."

"Okay… okay," Peter stammered. He rubbed his leg and looked down at his foot. The swelling had diminished to nothing more than a serious bruise and he tried to support his entire weight on it. He sighed with gratitude when no pain radiated up his leg and he could stand without help. So, with as much haste as he could muster, he dressed and left the room.

Outside, he found David waiting next to a flatbed wagon. The same young man who had taken them to the funeral held the mule steady as Peter and David climbed on. Peter glanced up to see a sky so blue it looked like sapphire. The mountains glistened in the sun like white sentinels guarding the village of Fairplay.

"Those are the fourteens," David said as he pointed to the peaks.

"The what?" Peter asked.

"The fourteens... they are the mountains that rise over 14,000 feet in elevation. Now look up there." David pointed to a distant mountain that boasted a large radio tower with massive satellite disks anchored to it. "That is the main communications tower from where the government controls all broadcasts. Nothing ever gets transmitted unless it goes through that tower."

"What if it breaks down?" Peter asked.

"Oh, there are auxiliary towers and communication points, but if we can tap into that, we can broadcast our message to the entire nation. Radio, internet, television... it all goes through there."

They arrived at the church and dozens of people milled about the front entrance. The white steeple and wooden walkway welcomed the crowd as Pastor Martin shook hands with those who entered. "Peter... David!" the pastor exclaimed. "Welcome. I am so glad that you can worship with us today." Rev. Martin shook Peter's hand with such vigor that he wondered if he might dislocate his elbow.

"I'm glad to come," Peter said. "This is going to be the first actual church service I've ever attended."

"I, as well," David said. "I have not been to a gathering of so many who openly express their faith. It amazes me that there is no fear upon these people."

"Well," the pastor said, "we can discuss that at lunch today. There are many things we can talk about later. For now, come in and join our fellowship."

Peter looked around for Crystal but did not see here anywhere. At the front of the chapel, a large trough filled with water shimmered in the flickering glow of the incandescent light. An elderly woman sat by a piano on the right side of the podium and began to play music that Peter had never heard. The crowd noise dimmed and the pastor walked to the center of the stage.

"My friends, we have a tremendous blessing in store for us. Today, we have the privilege of celebrating with one who, some time ago, believed on the Lord and is now coming to us for baptism." He motioned his hand toward a small door behind the piano.

Peter nearly jumped off the bench when he watched Crystal enter the room. She walked with simple steps, barefoot, and stepped carefully into the water. Adorned in a white robe, she had her hair carefully pinned so that it cascaded down her back. Her eyes sparkled and joy radiated from her smile. Peter might have been less surprised had it been an angel from heaven.

"Crystal," the pastor said, "you have come to the waters of baptism today to express your faith in the Lord Jesus."

"Yes I have," she said with clarity.

"Do you believe that Jesus died for your sins and that by the power of God He was raised from the dead and is alive even today?" Pastor Martin asked.

"I believe that with all my heart," she replied.

"Then, by your confession of faith, I baptize you in the name of the Father, and of the Son and of the Holy Spirit." He lowered her backward into the water and lifted her out again.

Everyone in the church stood to their feet with shouts of "amen" and "hallelujah!" The building began to shake from the joy expressed by the congregation. Hands were raised in the air and numerous people applauded with such gusto that Peter nearly laughed with the overwhelming joy of the church.

Crystal stepped out of the water and threw her arms around the pastor, soaking his coat and tie as he hugged her in return. She departed into the room she had come from as the pianist struck up a lively tune and all the people began to sing.

Soon, Crystal emerged and took her place next to Peter. Her smile was infectious as she looked up at him with her eyes like emeralds. "Surprised?" she asked.

Peter leaned down to her. "Yes, I'm a bit surprised," he said.

Before he could continue, the pastor began his sermon and roused the congregation to new heights of "amens" and "hallelujahs." They spent nearly two hours in the service, singing and praying, listening to testimonies and the message from Pastor Martin.

"Now," the pastor said, "we are going to have a meal together at the rec. center. Let's all gather there and we can enjoy the company of our new friends." He pointed toward Peter and the others.

The crowd mingled and slowly thinned out as several offered their warm greetings and congratulations to Crystal. Eventually, the congregants all departed and only Peter, David, and Crystal remained with Pastor Martin.

"Before we go to the lunch," Pastor Martin said, "I'd like to talk with you a little." The pastor's resonant voice seemed to echo with confidence.

"That's not a bad idea," Peter said.

"I had the chance to find out about your mission from your friends," he motioned toward Crystal and David. "You will never make it into the communications center. It is the most highly guarded facility in Colorado, if not the country."

"How would you know that?" Peter asked.

"I used to work there," John answered. "I was a communications relay control officer with the government—handling information as it came in and processing the data before it was sent to the programmers. I finally got fed up when every bit of information I passed on was "cleaned up" so they say. I challenged my superiors with the lies that were being broadcasted and was summarily discharged from the communications services and ordered to a re-education center.

"To make a long story short, I escaped and found my way through the mountains until I stumbled upon this little town. It was a town that the world forgot—and it was perfect for me. The people here are independent and determined to survive. I needed that."

"But why does the government not come here and shut this community down?" David asked.

"Like I said, it has been forgotten. After the war, whole communities were disconnected from the rest of society. Most failed—but not Fairplay. These people simply went back to their roots and found the will to thrive."

"How did you become the leader of the church?" Peter asked.

"I arrived here about twenty years ago—broken, disillusioned and filled with anger. It was then I met an old pastor—a man named McGahhey. He was a third generation pastor in this town and he began to teach me about the truth, about God, and eventually I did what you did today, Crystal. I was baptized in that very same trough. He passed on ten years ago and I have been the pastor of this church ever since."

"What does that have to do with us?" Crystal asked.

John looked at the three of them with a determined gaze. "When I worked for the communications services, I learned of an old access bunker—a maintenance shed that was used for the communication tower you see on the mountain. The bunker is not more than six miles from here and I know where it is."

"Won't it be guarded?" Peter asked.

"It's unlikely. It has been abandoned for over thirty years and I doubt that anyone even knows how to get there. I stumbled upon it on a hike and I think you can finish what you started right from there." Pastor Martin stood and moved toward the door. "Now, let's go. Lunch is waiting and the women of this town know how to cook! We'll make plans for the ascent to the bunker later."

Peter looked over at David who had begun to weep. "What is it?"

"It was something George said to me, before we left. He said that God would make sure we arrived at the right location. I believe He did." David stood with the rest and all three left the building.

CHAPTER TWENTY-FOUR

"Greater love has no one than this, that he lay down his life for his friends." ~ John 15:13

Several weeks passed and Peter felt his strength increase daily. His leg and foot were healed so that he no longer needed the splint and he walked without a limp. Over his brow, a long thin scar punctuated his adventures and his hair was salted with streaks of grey. He looked at himself in the mirror and began to realize how far away his former life now seemed.

All he had wanted was to escape the education center. Now he and so many others were working toward a goal that somehow fell to him. The only thing that remained, he thought, was to find the abandoned repair bunker, hack into the net and tell the country the truth. "No problem," he said, voicing his sarcasm out loud.

"What is 'no problem'?" David asked as he stepped into the room.

Peter startled for a moment, but smiled at the sight of his friend. They had been working with the locals of Fairplay and the three friends had little time to do much else. David worked to fix every circuit board in sight. Crystal had taken up with several other women in town to help at the food co-op and Peter felt as if he and Pastor Martin were joined at the hip. He went nearly everywhere with the pastor and discovered that John Martin knew everyone by name and could do almost everything from fixing a leaking water pipe to encouraging a distraught family from the brink of despair. And, to everyone the pastor spoke with, he related something from the Bible.

"I was just thinking about our mission," Peter said. "These past weeks have been so good — almost like a normal life. But I cannot forget what my dad wanted me to do."

"No, you should not forget that," David agreed. "We are here and, if you are strong enough, must finally do what has been given us to do."

Peter sighed. "I know, but now that we have found some normalcy, I don't want to give it up." He walked toward the door and looked David in the eye. "But I will."

"That is good," David said, "because Crystal and I are ready any time you are." He smiled at Peter and moved into the hall.

"So, why *are* you here?" Peter asked. "Don't you spend your days working on everyone's electrical equipment?"

"Yes," he said, "but today Pastor Martin met me on the road and asked if we could join him at the church building." They walked down the stairs and Crystal waited for them near the fire.

"Well, sleepy," Crystal teased, "it's about time you woke up!"

"About time?" Peter quipped. "The sun's not even above the horizon." He smiled as he glanced toward the window by the front door. A beautiful day waited upon the sunrise as a thin line of orange and amber light glowed in the east. The sky began to shift from deep black to rich blue and a slender crescent moon hung just above the mountains.

"Well..." Crystal stammered as she rolled her eyes, "the sun gets up later here than in other places."

Peter stepped off the stair and sat near the fire. Three mugs of coffee waited upon a tray and they all took a moment to enjoy the rich flavor of the morning. A few passersby walked past the window and waved at Peter and the others. He delighted in the kindness of the people and their rugged determination. It reminded him of living on Joshua's farm or on the island and he began to clearly see the reality of living independent and free. Left to themselves, the people of Fairplay built a strong and thriving community and yet they cared for each other and worked together. But a nagging concern gripped his thoughts.

"What is it, Peter?" Crystal asked. "You have a far-off look in your eye."

"It's about this town," Peter said.

"What about the town?" David asked.

"I'm worried that if we finish our mission, this town will be exposed." Peter stood and moved toward the fire. He watched the flames dance upon the logs, hoping to coax some insight from them.

Crystal moved to stand beside him. She took him gently by the hand. "Pete?"

He looked down at her. Her green eyes sparkled, moist with tears. "Yes."

"You know that I love you," she said.

"Of course," he said as he let slip a little smile.

"Do you remember why I came with you? Do you remember what I told you?"

"That you wanted to save Jack and the others."

"That hasn't changed, Peter." She took his other hand and stared straight into the windows of his soul. "We can't stop now and let all the people we love wait in vain for us. George, Joshua, Jack, Patrick, Martha and who knows how many others have tried to do this. But it has been given to us."

"I know," he said as he gently brushed a tear from her cheek. "We won't give up now. But I want this town to know what might be coming if we succeed."

"Then let us go and talk with Pastor Martin," David said.

Peter nodded. They all gulped down the dregs of their coffee and exited the inn. Outside, the chill air was invigorating. Peter and the others pulled their coats tighter against their skin and walked through the town to the old chapel. The sun crested the horizon and splashed the world in golden splendor. Icicles glistened like ornaments and the snow sparkled as if they strode across a field of diamonds. Mules pulled carts, people bustled about, and everyone seemed to have entered the day at once.

They found the pastor outside his church building, eagerly shoveling snow from the wooden walkway. The grey-haired minister looked up and waved at them to come. "I'll be with you in a bit," he said, panting with the exertion. "Go on inside and we'll talk."

"Can we help you?" David asked.

"No," John said. "I need my exercise anyway." He offered a less-than genuine smile and motioned for them to go inside.

Peter entered, followed by Crystal and David and they all sat in one of the central benches. The church building began to feel like a second home to Peter as he had come to the services every Sunday since waking up in Fairplay. He devoured Pastor Martin's sermons with passion and found that the minister reminded him of Joshua: bold, direct, but filled with a seemingly inexhaustible well of grace.

Crystal sat beside Peter and held his hand as they waited for John to enter. He relished his growing relationship with Crystal and smiled as he thought of her. Though the strong-willed girl was as fiery and active as ever, Peter recognized a new peace was growing like a rose from within her. David sat in the bench just in front of them and thumbed through the bible he retrieved from the rack. Peter never knew a friendship like the one he had with David. Joshua was a great friend, but was more of a mentor to him. David, however, was a comrade.

A blast of cold air, and John entered the room. "Peter," he began, "Do you think you're well enough to take a hike into the mountains?" His rich voice echoed in the empty hall and steam wafted off his coat and hat.

"There's something I want to talk over with you, first," Peter said. "In fact, I'd like to set up a town meeting to discuss it with whoever wants to come."

"Oh," John's voice resounded with perplexity. "It sounds serious."

"It is," David offered. "We are concerned that if this mission succeeds, then Fairplay will be found out and targeted by the government."

John nodded as he took a bench opposite them. "That is a fair concern… but I don't think that the people will worry over it."

"But why?" Crystal asked. "It might mean that they will suffer because of it."

John grinned with a broad, warm smile. "Think about it," he said. "You're talking about a community that lives at nearly ten thousand feet, rides mules for transportation and has fashioned a life without help from anyone. These people are as tough as granite and twice as durable. A few federal agents aren't going to disrupt them."

Peter sighed. "It won't be a *few* federal agents." He looked at Crystal and David and he wondered if he should share his entire story. After a deep breath, he spoke. "You see, I'm Peter Sheridan."

"Yes… so?" John asked. "You say that as if it might change something."

"It changes everything!" Peter's voice grew louder in frustration. "For the past few months I have been hounded by the government and now I am considered the most wanted man in the country. I am thought of as the defacto leader of the…" Peter paused with trepidation. "...of the Shadow Remnant. My father was Major Patrick Sheridan who worked with the Remnant to bring about a return to freedom. To make a long story short, his mission was given to me."

John stood and moved toward the front of the church. He leaned back on the table that sat before the podium and faced the three friends. "You don't really know what the Shadow Remnant is, do you?"

"Yes," David said. "It is a small band of citizens who hold to a desire to restore the country back to the former political structure."

Peter looked puzzled at the pastor. "What do you know about the Remnant?"

John nodded and grinned. "A lot more than you might suspect," he said. After what seemed like an interminable pause, the pastor continued. "You see, I have been a member of it for the past eighteen years. Most of the townspeople are either connected to it or at least sympathetic to its purpose. But the Shadow Remnant is not a political movement – it's much bigger than that."

"What do you mean?" Crystal asked.

"It began almost a hundred years ago when the government outlawed religion. When it became clear that everyone who openly practiced their faith were hunted down, they went underground—into the shadows. That's what the Remnant is, believers who have taken to the shadows and kept their faith secret. As time progressed, there were others who saw the potential of the Shadow Remnant and began to connect them." John turned to look at Peter. "Your father was one of those men who believed that if the entire population knew about freedom – about the truth – then they would rise up and reclaim their heritage."

"And that is when his plan was put into action?" David asked.

366

"Yes, exactly," the pastor said. "There are many here who knew Patrick Sheridan. He visited Fairplay and talked with this church before the former pastor died." John stood from leaning against the table and moved toward the exit. "I met him once, a fine man." He motioned for Peter and the others to follow. "C'mon, let's go talk with the people."

Peter followed John out the door, with Crystal and David right behind them.

* * * *

An hour passed and Peter, David and Crystal were summoned to the community center. Pastor Martin had organized a town meeting and as they walked in, the large room began to fill up with the residents of Fairplay. At the head of the room, a single podium stood on an elevated platform. Dozens of people were filing in from every available door, taking their seats. A murmur, like a low rumble of thunder, echoed in the hall as John escorted them all to the podium.

Pastor Martin stepped up to the platform. "Let me have your attention," he said as he raised his hands to silence the crowd. Slowly the murmuring died down and he continued. "Peter and the others have decided to finish their task. But..." he paused to get everyone's attention. "But they are concerned for you. So I have invited them to come and speak to you and hear from you. Many of you knew Patrick Sheridan." Several in the crowd nodded and mumbled agreement. "Well," John said, "you may not have guessed, but this is Peter, Patrick's son."

Suddenly the entire gathering sat in silence, with only the gentle whisper of the furnace filling the air. Peter didn't know what to make of the crowd's reaction, but he stepped up to the podium and began. "I'm Peter Sheridan," he said, "and Pastor Martin is right, Patrick is my father. My dad is held captive for his belief in the old truths and it has fallen to me to fulfill his mission."

For several seconds the stillness hung in the air. Then the entire assembly erupted in a stunning and enthusiastic round of applause. Peter turned to look at the pastor who sat in a chair behind him. John Martin grinned from ear to ear. Crystal and David sat beside him with their mouths hung open in surprise. He turned again and raised his hand as slowly the boisterous expression of the people died down.

"If I do this," Peter said, "then it is a sure bet that the government will fall upon this town."

An old man, grey and wrinkled stood from the center of the crowd, shaky as he leaned on his cane. "Let them come, we dealt with 'em before."

Another, a young woman who held two children, stood and spoke. "Peter," her voice trembled but she stood strong. "Peter, it's time my children knew the taste of freedom. If your mission is successful, then the entire nation will know that liberty is our right!"

Others stood and spoke, many voicing similar sentiments, and some even offering to go with Peter. He watched the crowd's enthusiasm grow to a fevered pitch and knew that his time had come. If everyone in this town longed for the taste of real freedom, he hoped that hundreds and thousands of towns across America still ached for it as well.

He was about to step down from the platform when movement from the back of the room caught his attention. A dark-haired man stood and looked up. It was Mark!

"Stop that man!" Peter shouted as he pointed. The crowd, stunned for a moment, turned to look as Mark rushed through the door. At once, a dozen young men took off, chasing Mark through the exit and down the road.

A few minutes later, as the crowd settled down, two men walked in, followed by several others who had Mark firmly in their grip. Blood ran from his nose and his right eye was swollen. The men dragged him up the center aisle and threw him to the floor in front of the podium.

"Well, well," Peter said. "It's *Mark*, isn't it?"

"A handy group of thugs you have here," Mark said, his voice seething with anger.

"What are you doing here?" Peter demanded.

A slight grin crossed Mark's bruised face. "Tracking you," he said.

"Who sent you?"

"You're a bigger idiot than I thought if you don't already know."

"You called the feds, didn't you?" Crystal shouted.

"Yeah... I called the feds. But not just any... I called the man himself."

"Johansen..." Peter said that name and let the rest of his sentiment trail off.

"You're too late," Mark said. "He'll be here with a squadron of agents to finally capture you. I'm going to go down as a hero."

"Some hero," David said under his breath.

"What did they promise you?" Peter asked.

"Power," Mark said. "You should have killed Johansen, but you chickened out! That's when I realized how stupid I was to believe that the Remnant actually sought the power needed to change the system. But I know what power is, and I went after it!" Mark quickly stood to his feet and with a shove, pushed the man away who held him. He punched another man behind him and spun to face Peter—a revolver in his hand. "Now, I'll show you power!"

Peter heard Crystal shout, saw the flash from the barrel and heard the crack of the gun. He fell to the ground—pushed out of the way just in time. Several men tackled Mark to the ground and pummeled him until he gave up the gun.

Peter looked up to see Crystal lying in a pool of blood. His heart screamed as he scrambled up behind the podium. With the gentleness of a feather, Peter cradled Crystal in his arms.

"No... no... no..." Peter stammered. "You can't leave me. Not now..."

Crystal's eyes fluttered as she slowly regained consciousness. "Peter," her voice was a hoarse whisper.

"I'm here."

"Peter... finish..." She spoke through labored breath.

"I can't leave you now... not like this."

"Please help Jack and the others." She gazed at him, her deep green eyes piercing his. "I love... you." She collapsed, unconscious.

He held her close as tears flooded his eyes. "I love you," he sobbed.

"Peter?" Pastor Martin said.

Peter looked up as a commotion of people came barreling into the room.

"Peter, the medics are here and they need to get Crystal to the doctor right away." John touched Peter on the shoulder and pulled him gently from her.

In a flurry of activity, six men rushed to Crystal's side, bound her to a stretcher, gave her an I.V. and rushed her out of the building.

Peter looked at John and David. The crowd had not diminished, but he felt as if only the three of them were in the room. David stood behind the chairs, his eyes still wide and hands trembling. John remained beside Peter with his calm demeanor shaken by the events.

"What will you do?" David asked.

Peter was in shock, stunned and confused. "What?"

"What are we going to do, Peter?" David asked again.

"You will never get another chance to finish this," John said. "It's unlikely you will get any closer than you are right now."

"What about Crystal. I can't just leave her."

John looked Peter in the eye. "I promise you, Crystal is in the best hands in the world. Our doctor is a combat veteran and has dealt with gunshot wounds before. He will be able to take care of her."

Peter nodded as he resigned himself to the situation. He took a deep breath, "I am sure that my dad would finish the mission." He looked at John. "You've even said that it is to God's glory to finish a matter, so let's finish this."

The crowd had thinned and Pastor Martin took David and Peter to a map that hung on the auditorium wall. It was a topical relief map of Fairplay and the legion of mountains that surrounded the town. Several roads meandered like snakes in the assorted canyons and John pointed to one in particular.

"This is road fourteen," John said.

"Road fourteen?" David asked. "Not a very clever name for a road."

"No, but it is practical. We will need to take road fourteen to the abandoned repair shed where we can gain access into the system."

"What are we waiting for?" Peter asked. "The sooner we get there and get this over with, the better."

John continued. "I have taken the liberty to have the necessary provisions ready for the hike. It'll take us a couple of hours to get to where we need to go. It's about six miles from town and we will be walking through deep snow." He looked at David and Peter. "Have either of you ever snow-shoed?"

"Walk in the snow with shoes on?" David asked.

John chuckled. "No. How do I describe it? It's like strapping tennis rackets to your feet and walking on top of the snow. The snowshoes keep you from sinking in the drifts."

"We'll have to learn as we go," Peter said. He stepped through the door, ready to face the final challenge of his father's task.

* * * *

They retrieved their packs, donned their winter gear and left the town heading west. Their feet sunk into deep snowdrifts, so they stopped outside the edge of town to strap on the snowshoes. David struggled with the ties, but with Peter's help he finally secured the oval-shaped equipment so that they didn't fall off.

A quick glance from John and they began what Peter hoped was the final leg of the mission. The mountains loomed before them in the brilliant sunshine as they hiked along the road, through deep snow. John led the expedition and it wasn't long before they left the road and traveled over the rugged terrain beyond the town, moving through the woods.

"I thought you said that we would travel along road fourteen?" David questioned. "How is it that we trudge through these desolate woods with no road in sight?"

John grinned. "I thought it better that we take a less traveled way. I know these hills quite well and I promise we will find our way to the shed."

Peter slogged through the snow in silent thought as he grew increasingly fearful that Crystal lay dying. Ahead of him, Pastor Martin weaved his way through the pine forest but Peter's mind wandered back to the island as he recalled how Crystal would run through the woods. Anger filled his heart and he wanted to rush back and make sure she would survive.

"She will recover," John said.

Peter was taken out of his rumination and looked up to see that the pastor had stopped right in his path. "I hope so," Peter said.

"Look, Peter, you need to have faith." John reached up and placed his hand on Peter's shoulder. "God has purposed this in your life and you need to trust that He is working it out. But you also need to keep your head in the moment and not drift off into speculating on things you can't control."

John's words fell hard upon Peter's heart. "I know... but how?"

"Remember the words of Scripture: *I brought you glory on earth by finishing the work you gave me to do.*" John turned again and continued walking through the woods.

Peter thought through John's words and then remembered what Crystal said—*finish*. A growing determination warmed his heart and he picked up his pace.

Hours passed as they trudged in the snowdrifts that had gathered through the winter. The sun was near the peaks of the Rocky Mountains when they finally stepped onto a road that meandered through the woods. John continued west and followed the road.

"How deep do you think this snow is?" Peter asked.

"About six feet," the pastor said without stopping. "If we didn't have this snow gear we never could have ventured this deep into the wilderness."

"Are you not worried about wild animals?" David asked? His voice trembled as he kept looking around through the trees.

"Oh we might encounter something," John said. "But the bears are hibernating and the wolves are farther north. I doubt that we have anything to worry about."

"I wish I shared your confidence," David mumbled.

They rounded a bend in the road and John led them off the path and back into the woods. When they were out of sight of the road and deep into the forest, he stopped and looked at Peter and David. "The repair cabin is just up ahead. It is partially buried and we will have to dig through some snow to get to it. You have shovels in your pack and, Peter, the document that you brought is with you."

"How will I access the central network?" David asked.

"A computer terminal is in the cabin that links directly to the net. It is used for diagnostics but has full functionality and can transmit as well as receive. But I'm sure my old pass codes have long since become obsolete so you'll have to hack into the system."

"That is what I am here for," David said with a smile.

John turned and continued through the woods for several hundred yards until they happened upon what looked like a small log cabin half-buried with snow. John walked around the structure and threw his pack to the ground, retrieving his small, collapsible shovel and began to dig at the front of the cabin. Peter and David followed suit and the three men quickly excavated several feet of snow until they were able to access the door.

"Wow, look at that!" David exclaimed.

"What?" Peter asked.

"It is an actual padlock... I have never seen one of these. This is old-school security." David looked to the pastor. "Do you have a key?"

"Ah... no," John said. "But let me see what I can do."

David stepped out of the way and John stepped down to the door. He jiggled the lock and looked at the keyhole that boasted the word: *Master*. With a sigh, he backed off and turned. Then, with one swift kick to the center of the door, the entire panel of wood shattered.

"Well, that's one way to pick a lock," Peter said.

"Get inside," John said, "I don't know how much time we have."

"Why?" David asked. "Nobody knows where we are."

"John's right," Peter said. "If Mark made contact with Johansen, we must assume that he'll send reinforcements. In this snow, it won't be hard to pick up our trail."

They quickly entered into the old cottage and found a dusty room, half-covered in cobwebs. It was a single room, with a chair and table, a small cot and mattress and a kitchenette. No other furniture adorned the small space. At the back of the room, a trapdoor pulled up with a single rope and opened to a rod-iron, spiral staircase that descended into darkness.

"You'll find a couple flashlights in your packs. We'll need to go into the basement to gain access to the terminal." John pulled a two-foot long flashlight from his pack that looked more like a small baseball bat than a source of illumination.

Peter recovered a light that looked more like a lantern, but glowed bright in the darkness. David had a smaller light that shone a beam with powerful brilliance. In single file, with Peter leading the way, the three men entered the basement.

The stairs descended nearly a hundred feet into the earth and ended in a long corridor. With patient steps, not knowing what to expect, Peter stepped into the hall, holding his lantern before him. It filled the hall with its light. The passage was made of concrete and had a long row of florescent tubes lining the ceiling. They arrived at a door that was locked, and the hinges rusted.

"Well," Peter said as he looked at John. "Do you want to try your lock-picking skills on this door too?"

"Why don't you give it a try," John said with a grin.

With a quick strike of his foot against the door, Peter smashed the old wood as it splintered and fell into the room beyond.

"Not bad," David said.

Peter felt on the inside wall and found a switch that would turn on the lights. He flipped it and a quick flash burst upon their eyes. Three bulbs burned out while several others slowly grew in brightness until they were able to see the room without the use of their flashlights.

The space held numerous pieces of electronic equipment. Video cameras, audio systems and microphones gathered dust on an old shelf while cables of all shapes and sizes lay like coiled snakes waiting to strike. On the farthest wall, a solitary terminal and keyboard sat upon a desk with a chair in front of it. David's eyes were wide with delight as he began to piece together several items to form a makeshift studio.

"Peter, why don't you go and get that chair from the cabin above us?" John suggested. "I think that David and I can handle this down here and you'll want to be comfortable as you talk to the country."

Peter looked at David who sat busy clicking on the keyboard, working his algorithmic magic on the terminal. "David?" Peter asked.

"I will be fine. Go ahead while I solve some equations." David turned back to his task.

Peter took his lantern and walked back down the dark corridor. He climbed the spiral stairwell, the iron creaking under his weight and he recalled the escape from Marcus' home. He opened the trapdoor and stepped into the cabin as the last vestige of daylight faded in the west. A quick glance around and he spotted the chair—with Kyle Johansen seated on it!

"Well, well," Kyle said, "if it isn't Peter Sheridan."

A quick reflection of light caught Peter's eye, and he noticed that Kyle held a pistol trained right at him. "How did you find me?"

"Oh, it wasn't hard to follow your tracks in the snow. I arrived at your little town, along with ten federal agents, about twenty minutes after you left."

"Where are they?" Peter feared for the town of Fairplay.

"Oh, well, that's a story… it seems that the entire town was waiting for us!" Kyle's voice grew louder. "My agents were all taken captive by those simpletons. I was able to escape in the confusion and, after circling the outskirts of the town a bit, I came upon what I assumed were your tracks and followed them here." He stood from the chair and Peter noticed that the man's face was bruised.

"Why did you lie?" Peter asked. "I saved your life back in Portland. Mark would have killed you."

"Yeah, you're right," Kyle said. "But when I convinced him that he would not be prosecuted if he gave you up, he was more than willing to join forces with me." Kyle waved the gun and motioned for Peter to back away from the trap door. "You see, you already had a reputation and it was simple to pin it to you. But, right now, you're more important to me than you realize."

"Oh?" Peter tried not to show the dread that welled up in his heart.

"Oh, yes," Kyle mocked. "You see, you're going to make that transmission – but you're going to do it my way! You will get on the network and tell everyone how you now know that the only way to live is to submit to the government in all things. Then you will disown this Shadow Remnant as a traitorous group of terrorists."

"Or what?"

"Or I'll kill you and your friends who are underground."

"What friends?"

"Don't play dumb, I know they're there. In fact, why don't we go and meet them now." Kyle motioned with the gun for Peter to climb back downstairs.

Peter stepped onto the iron staircase and made his way to the darkened hall. Far in the distance the light of the room glowed with foreboding as he tried to take slow, loud steps, desperate to warn his friends. Through the shattered remains of the door Peter could see David working on the computer terminal, unaware of their approach. His mind raced with the effort to come up with a way to disarm Johansen.

As he stepped through the door with the barrel of the gun in his back, out of the corner of his eye Peter saw Pastor Martin hiding against the wall, poised with his flashlight over his head.

In a rush of motion, John swung his club and struck Kyle's hand. With a dull thud and the sound of cracking bones, the gun fell from Johansen's grasp as he screamed in pain.

Swiftly, Peter spun around and struck Kyle across the head with his lantern. The frame shattered and the light bulbs flew from the device as the director fell to the ground, blood trickling down his cheek. Kyle struck back, and threw his weight against Peter as they tumbled to the ground. Both men rolled upon the floor and swung wildly as they grappled for dominance. Peter shoved him with his feet, and Kyle hurtled into the wall. Then Peter jumped up and slammed Kyle in the chest with his shoulder and threw him back, deflecting a quick punch.

CRACK!

The sound of the gunshot stopped the fight as they looked over at John who held the pistol. "I think that's quite enough. Peter, you have a task to complete. I'll keep Kyle occupied while you go back and get that chair."

"John, you don't understand!" Kyle protested. "If you do what you're planning, you will send this nation into chaos."

Peter looked at the two men. "Do you know each other?"

John nodded. "Yes, we do. I worked with Johansen for years before I realized that the government was lying to the people."

"Not lying... protecting," Kyle said.

"That is such propaganda, Kyle, and you know it," John said. "Now, Peter, let's get this over with."

Peter nodded and rushed out the door with David's flashlight in hand. He retrieved the chair and brought it back to the room. David had arranged the microphone and camera so that it would pick up Peter's image and voice.

"When I press this button," David said, "you will be broadcasting to every radio channel, internet and television station in the country. If anyone is watching or listening, the only thing they will get is you."

Peter sat down and retrieved the old parchment that George had so long and carefully preserved. His thoughts drifted as he wondered if Crystal could hear him. Would his father be listening as well as Joshua and the others? With steady eyes, he looked up at David.

David wore a set of headphones plugged into a soundboard. He raised his hand and signaled with his fingers: three... two... one... and then pointed at Peter as the camera light came on.

Peter looked directly into the lens and took a deep breath. "People of America... my name is Peter Sheridan. For decades our government has held us in bondage to the cruelty and fear of martial law. They have discarded the ancient ways, the foundation upon which our nation was built and have hidden the truth from you. Those who have stood up for the truth have been locked away or are in hiding. These are the ones who are called the Shadow Remnant. It was through this group of people where I learned the truth.

"This is why I speak to you today. Our country's foundation was built on freedom—a freedom that we have not known for generations. Hundreds of years ago, people died defending this freedom and today we stand with those patriots of the past. Liberty must come back to the light. I hold in my hands a copy of one of the original documents that our nation was built upon. This is the truth of our country and this is what you have been forbidden to know. I come to you tonight to share it with you, for if this truth is lost, liberty dies."

Peter held the document and gently unfolded it. Old and worn, the paper felt and sounded like dried leaves in his hands. A tear welled up and a lump filled his throat as he looked at the words before him. He glanced back up at the camera, and then he began to read:

"We the people..."

Other books by Michael Duncan

Fiction:
Shadows: Book of Aleth, Part One
Revelation: Book of Aleth, Part Two

Non-Fiction:
From Vision to Victory
Starting Out: A Study Guide for New Believers
A Life Worth Living
Becoming a Man of Influence

To purchase these titles or contact the author, simply go to:
http://www.authormichaelduncan.com

55708136R00211

Made in the USA
Charleston, SC
03 May 2016